Graham Travers

Windyhaugh

A Novel

Graham Travers

Windyhaugh
A Novel

ISBN/EAN: 9783337000875

Printed in Europe, USA, Canada, Australia, Japan

Cover: Foto ©Andreas Hilbeck / pixelio.de

More available books at **www.hansebooks.com**

WINDYHAUGH

WINDYHAUGH

A Novel

BY

GRAHAM TRAVERS

(MARGARET G. TODD, M. D.)

Author of Mona Maclean, Medical Student,
Fellow Travellers, Etc.

NEW YORK
D. APPLETON AND COMPANY
1899

CONTENTS.

PART I.

WINDYHAUGH.

PART I.

CHAPTER I.

ON THE SUGAR-BARREL.

THROUGH the narrow doorway of the grocer's shop a great barrel of Jamaica sugar had just been carefully steered, and now seven-year-old Wilhelmina was perched on the top of it, in earnest conversation with the grocer.

A pair of chubby sunburnt legs drummed nervously now and then against the side of the cask, and an ill-used sun-bonnet had been carelessly pushed back, revealing a chubby serious face.

"For you see, Mr. Darsie," the child was saying, "p'raps I'm even—not—one of the elect."

A smile of keen amusement puckered up the grocer's queer old face, concealing for a moment the shrewd grey eyes.

"I'm no' feared o' ye, Miss Mina."

She looked up hopefully, but her face clouded over again before she spoke.

"You can't tell. Nobody can."

The hot little hands tugged at each other strenuously for a second or two, and then the child continued, with the air of one who, at great personal cost, contributes an all-important factor to a discussion—

"I s'pose you know I'm not saved?"

He picked up a fine kidney potato from a creel that stood by the door, surveyed it carefully, and then tossed it back to its brethren.

"And what for no'?"

She shook her head sadly.

"I don't seem able to *believe* somehow. I try an' try, and sometimes I think I've done it. But it's no use; I don't believe a bit. I s'pose *you're* saved, Mr. Darsie?" She paused, and then went on suddenly in a tone of half-envious disappointment—"Oh, of course—I forgot—you're an elder, so you must be saved."

"It's to be hopit so, Missie."

"And did you ever find it difficult to believe?"

How differently the lines in a human face affect us at different times! As a rule those countless folds and pencillings were suggestive mainly of a hard and miserly disposition; but now they seemed with one accord to lend the old man's face a very pleasing air of wisdom and tolerance.

"That did I!" he answered heartily; and he added to himself, with a queer little smile that was not meant for his visitor, "An' no' sae lang syne neither."

He swept up a few stray tea-leaves from the counter with his time-chiselled hands, and carefully deposited them in a great canister near the window.

"Dinna pit yersel' aboot, Missie," he said in a fatherly voice. "If ye werena ane o' the elect, I'm thinking the Lord wadna let ye fash yersel'—a wee bit bairnie like you!"

This was cheering; but, from the standpoint of theology, it struck the well-taught child as flabby.

"Will you please help me down, Mr. Darsie?" she said. "I think I see Nurse coming back for me." Then, as for the moment her lips came on a level with his ear, she whispered, "You won't tell her what we were saying?"

"Na, na, Missie, that's between you and me."

She nodded. "Nurse would only laugh," she said. "She wouldn't understand, and I believe she'd go and tell."

She went to the door, stopped to pull up her socks, and then looked back wistfully.

"I'm—going, Mr. Darsie," she said. "Good-bye."

He chuckled, and, taking from the shelf a large glass jar, slowly extracted from it two sugared almonds. He surveyed them doubtfully for a moment, then dropped

one back into the jar, and held out the other to the
child.

Wilhelmina made a wild search for her pocket, but
wisely relinquished it in time, and a moment later the
young nurse arrived, looking hurried and guilty, to find
an innocent, uncomplaining child awaiting her on the
doorstep.

For a minute or two they walked on in silence.

"Were you wearying?" asked Nurse tentatively at last.

The child shook her head. Her thoughts at the moment were pretty equally divided between the chances
of her own election, and the almond cruelly dissolving
in her hot little hand.

Then she suddenly awoke to the significance of the
situation. "You were a very long time," she said with
gentle emphasis.

The young woman frowned and laughed, and produced a couple of sweet biscuits from a paper bag.

"There!" she said coaxingly. "Don't say a word
to your Grannie!"

Wilhelmina would not have said a word in any case.
She was not on terms of intimacy with her grandmother,
and she was devotedly attached to poor faulty nurse.
Moreover she had no wish to forego her rare visits to
the grocer; but when a *douceur* was to be had so easily
as that, it would be a pity not to secure it.

Five minutes later they were out on the open country road, with a cloudless blue sky overhead, and a faint
breath of air on their heated faces. Wilhelmina was
free now to dance ahead or to lag behind as the impulse
moved her.

Little by little the thought of her soul dropped away,
and she lapsed unreservedly into the healthy animal.
She munched her biscuit, stowed away the grimy sugarplum for future consumption, switched the heads off the
wild flowers as she bounded on her way, and finally
burst into blithe unconscious song—

"I thank the goodness and the grace
That on my birth have smiled,
And made me in these latter days
A happy Christian child."

CHAPTER II.

WINDYHAUGH.*

THE discerning reader scarcely needs to be told that
Wilhelmina lived alone with her grandmother.

And their home was a quaint old place, almost
worthy of a visit for its own sake in these days of artistic villas. The sun and storm of a century or two
had called forth no mellow colouring in the massive
iron-grey walls; but here and there a yellow lichen had
woven its dainty web, and ivy and old-fashioned roses
clambered about at will, concealing as best they could
the cold neutral tints of the stone.

A straggling tangled old shrubbery flanked the house
on the right, and in front the close-mown lawn was sheltered from the road by a little plantation of lime trees.
Very cool and inviting these looked to the dusty way-
farer when the sunlight streamed through the boughs,
and the shadows played on the lawn; but in cloud or
storm their shade amounted to gloom, and a sense of
mystery, of a haunting "beyond," hung over the whole
place.

They never seemed to be at rest, those trees, and the
sweeping sough through their branches was never still;
for the house stood high on a terrace above a great arm
of the sea; and night after night Wilhelmina was lulled
to sleep by the murmur of wind and wave, or startled
into wakefulness by their fury.

Ah, yes, it had its moods, that quaint old homestead
of Windyhaugh. It could look grim enough at times—
grim as the rows of leather-bound divines in the library;
but to-day, when we visit it first, the whole place is
flooded with sunshine, the very shrubbery is robbed of
its spells, and all things, indoors and out, look as bright
and peaceful as the great bowl of old-fashioned roses
in the hall.

You would like, I am sure, to see the home of those

---

* Pronounced *Windyhaw.*

roses; and indeed the high-walled garden tnat lies to
the left of the house is the one part of the whole domain
that can rarely be brought to share the gloomy moods
of the rest. To-day it lies half asleep in a haze of sunshine and hum of bees, breathing out the delicious fragrance of old-world flowers. The crisp brown shoots
and crimson blooms of the roses stand out vividly
against the sunny blue water down below, and the fruit is
ripening almost visibly on the ruddy brick walls. Each
wall is curved to meet the full glow of the sun, and so
the long strip of flowering land is divided into a series
of gardens linked each to each by an archway of nod-
ding roses.

The weeds, to be sure, have made rather more headway than one might wish. Grannie pays the old job-
bing gardener some ten pounds a year, and trusts to his
honour to give the garden a fair equivalent of attention; but she often has reason to complain of her share
of the bargain. The crafty old man is well aware that
he has a monopoly; for what newcomer could possibly
know the capability and constitution of the gardens as
he does? "I'll be round i' the tail o' the week," he says
evasively when his employers waylay him with re-
proaches on the road; and so by degrees he has come to
be known by the name of "Tail-o'-the-week."

Grannie is out in the garden herself to-day, in her
spotless white cap and second best silk gown, gathering
the first luscious coral-pink strawberries in a fresh green
cabbage-leaf, for the delectation of a favoured visitor.

Let us follow her into the house, and watch her pour
the fragrant tea into those dainty shallow cups.

The visitor is no less a person than the parish minister, and Grannie is particularly glad to see him, though
she has maintained all along that the patrons have in-
curred a grave responsibility in electing one so young.
She is not susceptible to the breeziness of thought and
expression which many of the congregation have found
so refreshing. Just as her physical frame is supported
now-a-days by a mere bite and sup, so did her spiritual
nature find food enough and to spare in the lengthy
doctrinal dissertations of the former pastor. However

she cannot deny that the young man's teaching is sound, and to-day she is fain to appeal to him for help and sympathy.

"Of course the Lord knows His own business best," she is saying with troubled face, "and I didn't invite the laddies to please myself; but it does seem an awful pity they should have come just now."

The kindly face beneath the broad brows broke into a smile.

"I wouldn't trouble about that, my good friend. The Lord knows His own business best, as you say, and He doesn't need us to put his saplings into the forcing-house. Wilhelmina is thrown quite enough with grown people. I was delighted to see her romping with her cousins in the hay. What fine little fellows they are!"

"Ay, they are well-set-up callants enough, but they haven't a thought beyond their games and their plays. And I am sure a work of grace had begun in the bairn's heart."

"She is very young," he said almost deprecatingly.

The look of pain on the old lady's face hardened into one of severity. "So I said once myself!" she exclaimed almost bitterly. "'We spend our years as a tale that is told,' and when we look back from the end, as I do now, there is but a sentence—a word— between 'too young' and 'too old.' No, no, Mr. Carmichael, it can never be 'too young.'"

She broke off abruptly, and her voice vibrated with earnestness as she went on slowly—"My tale is all but told. I seem to see the Lord with the pen in His hand. *Finis!* He may begin to write it this very day—*and what chance will there be for Wilhelmina then?*"

A passing cloud went over the sun, and the room became dark and oppressive. The old woman's face gleamed out white and earnest from the dusky shadows behind it. She reminded the minister of an ancient sybil foretelling a doom.

A moment later she broke the spell. "I forgot," she said with a little smile of courteous apology. "You can't know the sorrows of your people as Mr. Johnstone knew them; and no doubt you think me sorely wanting in faith. I have sown the seed in season and out of season, and yet I can scarce believe my eyes when it begins to take root." The speaker seemed unaware of the significance of her own metaphor.

Yes, the spell was broken. For a second or two her earnestness had forced him to thrill in sympathy; but now that the weird prophetess was merged in the conventional parishioner, the manhood in him waxed pitiful for the childhood of Wilhelmina.

He drew down his brows. "When did it begin?"

"It would be about six weeks ago. I had been telling her that she must search her own heart, and make *sure* that she loved the Lord Jesus. Bairns are so apt to take things for granted; they say pretty things, and then, as they grow up, it all slips from them like a garment. Well, ever since then I can see she's had something on her mind. She'll not answer questions—she has an awful will of her own—but at. times she'll ask one—offhand like—about faith or election or justification. She is extraordinarily forward in doctrine for her years."

The minister sighed, but reflected that after all the Lord knew His own business best.

"You have got the start of us all with your strawberries, Mrs. Galbraith," he said, striking off cheerily at a tangent.

But she did not seem to hear him.

"I wish you would speak to the bairn," she said. "You're used to putting the plan of salvation in different ways so as to appeal to all; and she would pay attention to you."

He bowed, drawing down his heavy brows rather grimly.

But the old lady went steadily on round the centre of her thoughts. "If she gets her mind past it this time," she said, "there's no saying how long it may be before the Lord will lay His hand on her again."

. . . .

The children lay stretched full length in the hayfield, like kittens momentarily exhausted with a romp.

For a whole half-minute nobody spoke.

"Let's pretend," said Wilhelmina dreamily at last, "that we are out in the desert." She had had a rather nice reading-lesson that morning, and she almost knew it by heart. "There's nothing but sand to be seen for miles and miles—not a tree, nor a flower, nor—nor anything."

"What's that then?" said literal Hugh, pointing to the row of scraggy sycamores that bounded the field.

"That's a mirage."

"A what?"

"A mirage. There's something about it in my reading-book. It's not real."

"And what's that?" He indicated a haycock.

"That's a castle!" shouted Gavin, lifting an innocent baby face from his arm.

"All right," said Hugh. "I'll be a knight."

Wilhelmina looked at him witheringly. "There are no knights in the desert," she said.

He drew himself up. Criticism was not to be tolerated from a girl younger than himself. "*Silly!*" he ejaculated. "How could there be a castle without knights? What will you be, Gavin?"

Gavin's downy face beamed with the sweetest of smiles. "I'll be a robber!" he piped.

"All right. Wilhelmina, you'll be my wife, and Gavin will run away with you; and then you'll see a fine shindy!"

"I won't!" said Wilhelmina indignantly. "As if Gavin could run away with me! I'll be a Bedouin."

Hugh frowned indignantly. His disgust was not lessened by the fact that he had no idea what a Bedouin was.

"Look here now!" he said. "How can we have a game when everybody chooses? Girls must do what they are told."

There was some sense in the question, if not in the deduction, and Wilhelmina looked doubtful. She was not used to boys' games, but she thought she could organize this one a good deal better than he could. It was the whole question of the rights of women in a nutshell.

She honestly tried to give in, but it must be admitted that the game suffered considerably as a work of art from the presence in it of a strong-minded woman. Hugh might have become accustomed to the new element in time, but at present it proved rather disturbing, and there was a general sense of relief when the minister appeared and challenged Wilhelmina to race with him across the field.

He did not seem to be much of a runner, however, for in a few seconds he cried out for quarter.

"It is nice having your cousins to play with, isn't it ?" he asked.

"Yes."

She had grave doubts on the subject at the moment, but in those days well-brought-up children first answered a question prettily, and then stopped to consider it—if indeed it was worth consideration at all. The questions of grown-up people are seldom worth much, and yet they are so slow to learn that their business is to *answer*, not to *ask!*

"You know, dear," he went on, painfully conscious that his manner was becoming heavy and pastoral, "God loves to see you enjoying yourself like that. Why else does He give us the blue sky and the sunshine, and send the breeze to make those poppies dance? So long as you love Jesus, and try to be kind to everybody, you can't be too gay and happy to please God."

The child did not answer. Her face had assumed an expression of stony indifference.

The minister was scarcely disappointed, and yet he had hoped something from the sheer novelty of his Gospel of Joy to this solemn little hearer. Some men would have pursued the conversation by the simple method of asking questions; but Mr. Carmichael possessed a reverence for the personality of a child that in those days was very rare. He was afraid of meddling with what he did not understand, and Wilhelmina's face was an impenetrable mask. It made him think—irrelevantly enough, perhaps—of Matthew Arnold's Gipsy Child by the Sea-shore.

"Thank you for your escort," he said kindly, holding

out his hand. "Good-bye. Run back and take care of the boys."

But the child walked across the field with steps as heavy as lead. Why had he come to remind her of her troubles? Of course what he said was very pretty— the old minister never talked like that—but the thorn was there just the same, concealed among the flowers— "So long as you love Jesus"!

And what he said was not only pretty, but true. She knew from the stories she had read that some children did find a short and easy way to salvation by "loving Jesus"; Hugh and Gavin, when questioned by her grandmother, were ready with a glib assurance that they loved Him; and, until she began to "search her own heart," had not she taken for granted that she did too?

But now the short and easy way was closed to her. How was it possible to feel sure that one loved, when so much depended on it? When it came to searching one's heart, even believing seemed easier than loving.

.   .   .   .

Hugh was very meditative as the children sat at tea that evening, and when his hunger was appeased, his reflections found voice.

"I don't believe anybody will ever marry Wilhelmina," he said dispassionately.

Nurse's feathers were out in a moment. She often seemed to "favour" the boy visitors, but her heart was in the right place after all.

"Well, I never!" she cried. "And why not, I'd like to know?"

Hugh shrugged his shoulders. He had a number of queer little man-of-the-world airs that at his age were very amusing. "I know *I* won't; and I don't believe any of the fellows would. They like the gentle, clinging sort."

Wilhelmina's rosy face turned almost white. So life had room for one terror more!

But nurse took up the cudgels gallantly, half laughing, half indignant.

"You didn't suppose she was going to cling to *you*,

did you?" she asked—"for all your grand words? Why, she's more of a man than you and Gavin put together! Wait till she meets somebody worth her while!"

Wilhelmina looked up gratefully—but she was only half comforted. Nurse was very kind; but after all Hugh was a *man:* he ought to know.

She looked so unhappy that dear little Gavin laid his peachy face consolingly against hers. "Never mind, Vilma," he chirped, "*I'll* marry you—some day—if nobody else does!"

But it was a very weary downhearted little girl that buried her face in the pillows that night. What between "getting married" and "getting converted," life really was too difficult! And yet so many quite common people were being married and converted every day!

CHAPTER III.

A NEW DIMENSION.

ANOTHER autumn day was drawing to a close, and the glamour of sunset lay upon Windyhaugh. The constant murmur of the leaves was lulled for the time into a fitful breath; and the red-gold rays shot in a level shaft athwart the tree-trunks, casting long straight shadows, and lighting up the interior of the little plantation into the semblance of a cathedral. One almost expected to hear the pealing of the organ at vespers from the arched tracery overhead.

The song of the birds had died away into a sleepy intermittent twitter, but out on the lawn a half-grown kitten leaped at the flitting moths, and Hugh and Gavin chased each other through the shrubbery with peals of excited laughter.

It was long past Gavin's bedtime—under Mrs. Galbraith's old-fashioned *régime;* but the mother of the boys was expected that evening, so he had been allowed to stay up. Wilhelmina was in bed as usual.

2

She lay in her little white chamber, all athrob with expectation. Visitors were rare at Windyhaugh, and to-night was to bring her dead mother's very own sister. Once and again the child sprang up in bed, fancying she heard the distant sound of wheels on the country-road. First, a corn-cart passed, then a brake with belated excursionists; but, as a rule, the sounds she heard existed only in her busy little brain.

And it seemed to the child that hours were passing by.

"Oh, do you *think* she'll come?" she asked, half crying, when the nurse came in to fetch a garment that needed repair.

The young woman looked half contemptuously at the flushed face and trembling lips.

"Come? Of course she'll come. Why wouldn't she come? Lie down and go to sleep, and you'll see her all the sooner."

Ah, *now* there was no mistake! Those wheels must be on the avenue under the limes: that was Gavin's voice raised in a squeal of glee: now Hugh was firing off an ill-timed volley of petty experiences: there was a quiet word or two from Grannie, and then——

Oh, what a beautiful voice!

Hugh's "English accent," as Mrs. Galbraith termed it, had struck Wilhelmina at first as affected and ridiculous; but this voice was quite a different thing. It brought a rosy flush of intense appreciation to the eager listening face. There might almost be fairies after all in a world that could produce a voice like that. Surely just so would the wonderful Godmother have spoken—if—alas!—she had ever appeared to light up the dreary kitchen. Happy Hugh! Happy Gavin!

In truth the voice was soft and musical above the average; but what really came upon the child as a revelation, introducing, as she afterwards said, a new dimension into her life, was the cultured, gracious, flexible manner of speech. It formed a wondrous contrast to the staid and rigid directness with which Grannie went straight to her point.

The house was dark and quiet before Wilhelmina fell

asleep, and she did not wake the next morning till the nurse came in. There were a thousand questions then that she longed to ask; but Jane would only laugh at her eagerness and talk of it to the other servants, so she resolved to wait and judge for herself. She could be troublesome and impatient enough on occasion, and to-day she did not reflect that her aunt would not be visible for hours; but she resigned herself to the varied operations of her toilet with absolute stoicism. Nurse almost thought she had forgotten the new arrival. Luckily for both, nurse was a stolid young woman, quite insensible as a rule to the child's state of mental vibration, and she did not realize that the occasion was too great for words.

When at length the nursery door opened, Wilhelmina walked out very slowly. She scarcely expected the old house to look the same as it had done yesterday.

A great shock awaited her on the threshold. A stranger was coming upstairs with a cup of chocolate on a salver. Could it be——? No, it could not be!

Nurse laughed. She had an irritating power of reading her charge's thoughts when they were in any way laughable or petty or contemptible. It is not an uncommon power among minds of a certain rank.

"Were you thinking that was your aunt?" she said, as the stranger disappeared into the best bedroom. "That is Pearson, her maid."

"I *never* thought she was my aunt!" said Wilhelmina indignantly; but a minute later she heard Jane laughing in the kitchen, and knew that the joke was being duly repeated. It was only by dint of the most cheeseparing economy that the servants at Windyhaugh could get enough food for gossip to keep them in life.

Almost for the first time in her experience, the child had difficulty in disposing of her porridge that morning. Hugh, on the other hand, who had hitherto manifested a hopeless cockney inability to understand how porridge should be eaten, got rid of his with extraordinary dispatch, not even pausing when, from time to time, he kicked Gavin meaningly under the table.

As soon as they had finished, Hugh rose, pulling

Gavin by the sleeve, and asserting that their mother had wished to see them "directly they finished their breakfast."

Wilhelmina looked at him with blazing eyes. "I wouldn't be a *mean!*" she said scornfully. "Do you think I didn't see you kicking Gavin? You *know* you never told your Mother that Grannie likes us all to be at prayers!"

Of course her indignation was augmented by the fact that she would fain have escaped prayers herself. Besides, if Hugh was not there, she was bereft even of the consolation of showing how much better she could tackle the big words than he could.

"Aunt Enid wanted them," she said shortly, when Grannie questioned her as to the absence of the boys. She had lived too much alone to understand the principle of honour among thieves, as most children understand it, but Nurse's unconscious training had made it a matter of second nature "not to tell."

"Fetch the books," said Grannie severely. She was apt to be severe to her grandchild, not—Heaven knows! —from want of affection, but from an ever-increasing sense of responsibility; and now the gracious ease of Enid Dalrymple's manner had the effect of making Mrs. Galbraith, in reality as well as in semblance, more stern and uncompromising than ever.

Wilhelmina took two Bibles, two psalm-books, and a volume of Family Prayers from the shelf, and Grannie solemnly "gave out" a chapter in Ezra. She would much rather have chosen a passage from the New Testament—something bearing more immediately on the subject of her prayers—but it seemed to her that a departure from the ordinary routine would argue a want of faith in one who professed to believe that "all Scripture is given by inspiration of God."

So they read monotonously through the chapter, "verse about"; and, after a metrical psalm had been treated in the same fashion, Grannie opened the mighty prayer-book. It was one of her thorns in the flesh that she had no gift for extempore prayer; and, however far afield Wilhelmina's thoughts might be wandering, she could always tell when the old lady put in a bit of her own by the pathetic quaver in the feeble voice.

The child was looking very thoughtful when they rose from their knees, and the rare, beautiful smile broke over Grannie's face.

"What are you thinking of, bairn?" she asked kindly.

She scarcely expected a reply, but for once Wilhelmina was frank.

"I was wondering," she said, "how Hugh would have per—pernounced Zerubbabel."

Poor Grannie!

Wilhelmina put away the books—very reverently, as Grannie's eye was upon her—and then timidly lifted one of the slats of the Venetian blinds to look out on the glorious sunny morning. The windows of the room looked south and east, so the blinds were kept down in the morning, and the windows themselves were kept shut all day. It was very childish and undisciplined, of course, but just after prayers one did feel an almost irresistible longing to prance out on the lawn, and a race through the shrubbery down to the beach would have been very heaven.

"Now see and fetch your slate and copy-book," said Grannie quietly; and so the eternal treadmill began once more.

By half-past ten slate and copy-book were put away, and Wilhelmina was hemming her handkerchief. We all know that handkerchief!—limp and crumpled and grimy, with its little landmarks of blood all along the track; the original ones very brown and dark, the recent ones vivid and bright with the most glorious colour on earth—so Ruskin tells us—the red of stained-glass windows.

The last landmark was the largest of all, for, just as Wilhelmina got to that point, the door opened, and the Fairy godmother drifted in.

Of course she was not beautiful. In real life beautiful women are so rare! And yet—*how* beautiful she was!—all mellow and gold and full of harmony, like the voice Wilhelmina had listened to the night before.

The good Pearson had spent a full half-hour over that wonderful mass of hair that looked like last year's beech leaves in an April shower, and yet one might have thought that Nature had twisted it just like that. Indeed I don't feel sure that Nature would have blushed even for the gown, so much did it resemble a great dewy bunch of lilac blossom. And the complexion and eyes and teeth made up the wonderful chord that vibrated through poor little puritan Wilhelmina for many a long day.

The child rose to her feet and stood speechless. Her thick brown hair was brushed smoothly down behind her ears, and, in honour of her aunt's arrival, she wore her Sabbath frock, a slate-coloured garment that contained rather than clothed her, a structure built to allow for the expansion of its contents, a thing of excellent material, ill-shaped and beautifully sewed by a conscientious, expensive, provincial dressmaker.

An artist would have failed to recognize the child as the witch of the sugar-barrel; but, in those days, if children were works of art at all, the credit, as a rule, was quite their own, and their unconscious efforts in this direction were not invariably appreciated by their elders.

"So you are Wilhelmina!" said the Fairy godmother, stooping to kiss the upturned face.

She pronounced the name very prettily, taking time to round off the liquids; and she looked at the child as if, just at that moment, there was no one in the world whom she cared so much to see. "Is it Mina for short?"

The child shook her head.

"Grannie doesn't like them to call me Mina; but Gavin is so little—he calls me Vilma."

"Really? That's quite clever of Gavin. Wilhelmina must be rather a mouthful for him, poor little man! Now, do you think you would like to come up to my room, and see what I have got for you in my trunk?"

A great red wave surged into the child's face; the element of surprise was so rare in her little life! But the red died away again before she said shamefacedly—

"Grannie said I was to get to the corner of my hem."

Was there just the least ring of amused contempt in the pleasant laugh?

" Oh! Quite right. I see you are a very good little girl. I hope Hugh and Gavin will take a lesson from you. Do you think Grannie would mind our opening the window?"

Of course Grannie would mind! The window never was opened except at long and stated intervals. Wilhelmina did not dare to commit herself either way in words, nor could she leave the responsibility wholly on the shoulders that were so well able to bear it. She simply looked on at the perpetration of the deed with a face of quiet unhappiness, not attempting to blink the fact that she was an accessory.

But Grannie did not seem to notice the window when she came in a minute later. She greeted her guest with dignified courtesy, and enquired how she had slept.

Mrs. Dalrymple looked as if for once it was a real pleasure to answer that question. " I don't know when I have had such a restful night. After that noisy houseful of people in Perthshire, this seems like a haven of rest. What a situation! and what a view! This little girl "—she passed her hand lightly over Wilhelmina's hair—" is fortunate indeed to grow up in a home like this."

She laughed softly, and went on with a deprecating docility that was pretty to see—

" You must think me shockingly lazy, and as a rule I am such an early riser! But the pleasure of looking out on the blue water over the tree-tops was more than I could resist. If I were a rich woman I should have a country-house just like this."

Wilhelmina's eyes grew very round. Here was poverty in a new form!—poverty in a lovely gown that would soil so easily, and that certainly wouldn't wash.

" Grannie," she said when the conversation came to a pause, " I have got to my corner. May I go with Aunt Enid?"

Mrs. Galbraith looked at the visitor enquiringly.

" I wanted her to come to my room, and then to take

me out to the grounds; but she was very conscientious
about finishing her task first."

Grannie examined the hem with doubtful satisfaction, but decided to be lenient for once. " Run and get
your hat," she said, " and see and don't weary your aunt.
Your nurse will soon be ready to take you for your
walk."

Wilhelmina scarcely recognized the best bedroom.
She had been wont to enter its shrouded, lavender-
scented precincts with awe, and to speak, if she spoke
there at all, in a low hushed voice; but to-day the room
was full of air and sunshine and the song of birds; a
profusion of silver lay about the dressing-table; photo-
graphs in morocco frames stood here and there; a basket
of hothouse fruit had been half rifled by the boys; dainty
wraps, dainty linen, dainty shoes peeped out from this
corner and that; and withal there was such a profusion
of luggage as Wilhelmina could scarcely believe to be
the property of one individual.

The child was completely dazzled and bewildered.
Hitherto life had arranged itself for her in a definite
design, like iron filings round the poles of a magnet.
Right and wrong, good and bad, Heaven and Hell: these,
in her childish way, she understood. But now a new
element had come into view, and it seemed impossible
to find a place for it in the original scheme. Here was
something that was neither right nor wrong, neithed good
nor bad. Make a second chart, and put it in a separate
pigeon-hole? Some of us accumulate a dozen or more
such charts as we go through life, and steer our course
by whichever chances to come to hand. Only the very
wise and the very simple become possessed of a single
chart that will answer all their needs.

Of course Wilhelmina dreamt of a doll. What else
appeals so strongly to the feelings of seven years old?
But dolls are awkward things to pack, and the child
was abundantly content with a great box of chocolates,
encircled as it was with a rich red ribbon. What would
Mr. Darsie say to a box like that?—he whose imagina-

tion was bounded (as Wilhelmina's had been hitherto)
by the tin-clad slabs of butter-scotch, and the faded tar-
tan packets of "mixtures" in his cobwebby window.
Wilhelmina felt a sudden sense of superiority to poor
Mr. Darsie.

She had no power of expression, and circumstances
had not tended to develop in her that "sense of favours
to come" which may lend a gift of utterance even to the
dullest. She said "Thank you" very solemnly, and
gazed at the box with devouring eyes.

Mrs. Dalrymple laughed good-humouredly. "There!
run and show it to nurse," she said, "and ask her to
put your hat on. You know you are going to show me
the garden."

But Wilhelmina did not move.

"May I eat one now?" she whispered gravely, "or
must I ask Grannie first? If I took one from underneath she would never know."

Mrs. Dalrymple laughed again. Assuredly this was
not an attractive child.

CHAPTER IV.

LIFE WIDENS OUT.

'A DAY or two later the sun still shone down royally,
and, as Enid Dalrymple stood by her ivy-framed window, she could see the blue waves break on the shingle
below the fort.

But for once her fair face was clouded.

"A gay place this, Pearson!" she cried, "actually a
military station! A handful of soldiers in charge of a
powder magazine! What time is it? Two o'clock?
Two o'clock, and dinner—*dinner*—is over. Nothing—
save perhaps a call from the minister—can possibly happen for the rest of the day. Does the butcher come this
afternoon, Pearson, or did that great event occur yesterday? *Mon Dieu!* but we are fallen on stirring
times!"

She threw herself into an old-fashioned arm-chair, but rose to her feet again with a petulant sigh. "Don't you think you could arrange the cushions so as to make this chair a little less intolerable? There! Give me the French book I was reading, and bring me a cup of tea when you have finished your dinner. This is Tuesday, and we must hold out till Friday. What in the world made me promise to stay for a week?"

"Would you not care to go for a drive to-morrow, Madam? I saw a very fine turn-out to-day—a landau. Jane said it came from the Cat and Cucumber. You could drive through the Duke of Carsland's grounds, and lunch at Spanforth."

Mrs. Dalrymple looked up sleepily from her book. "That's not a bad idea, Pearson," she said. "The boys must be dull enough, poor little souls. Mrs. Galbraith doesn't understand children, and it won't do to have them put her family prayer-book in the water-butt again."

Pearson left the room, and her mistress was just beginning to take a languid interest in the novel when a timid tap at the door announced the arrival of Wilhelmina.

"This is the new Good Words," she said. "Grannie sent me up to see if you would like to read it."

Mrs. Dalrymple held out her hand with an indulgent smile. "That was very kind. Good—Words. Is that a magazine that Grannie takes in for you?"

The child shook her head. "Grannie says the stories are not for children. She doesn't read them herself, but Jane does, and she tells me bits. They're nice."

"So you like stories, do you?"

Wilhelmina nodded. "I like grown-up stories best."

"That's like Hugh. But I see there are sermons here as well as stories. Does Grannie let you read them?"

"I don't know. I suppose so."

"I am sure a good little girl like you must be very fond of sermons?"

Wilhelmina looked puzzled. The old Adam certainly

did not like them much, but she had an uneasy feeling
that they were essential to the birth of the new Adam,
and therefore highly desirable. As the result of a long
process of reflection she replied briefly:

"I don't know."

"'Don't know—don't know.' What a queer little
girl you are! Suppose you tell me something you do
know. What do you all do with yourselves here at Windyhaugh in winter?"

Another long silence. "It's just the same as summer—only different."

"Come! That was worth waiting for. I always felt
sure your father had a touch of the blarney. The Irish
strain takes another form with you. Don't you get very
dull sometimes?"

"I don't know."

"Or cross? I am very cross to-day, little Vilma."

Wilhelmina stared. A grown-up person who owned
to being *cross* was almost a monstrosity.

"I expect the weather must be at fault. I think I
hear the wind rising. Where does the wind come from
to-day?"

"I don't kn—that is—I think it comes from the
trees."

"Ah! That would account for a great deal! Can
you reach that large wicker bottle on the dressing-table?
Doesn't it smell good? Would you like some too?"

Wilhelmina drew in the fragrance with a long breath,
and the pleasure of it tingled along her susceptible
nerves. "It's nice," she said briefly.

"So I think." Mrs. Dalrymple began to wish that
the child would go, but it was characteristic of her to be
unwilling to say so. Meanwhile innocent Wilhelmina
had seated herself on a low stool, and, face in hand, was
staring with all her might at the Fairy godmother in
her wondrous draperies.

Mrs. Dalrymple tried to go on with her book, but
the mesmerism of those eyes was too much for her.

"Why, child, you make me quite nervous," she cried
at length with an uneasy laugh. "What ever are you
thinking of behind that solemn face?"

"I was thinking——" Wilhelmina began; but her courage failed, and she stopped.

"How pretty you are," were the words on her lips, and what a difference they might have made in her life, had she uttered them!

"Well," said her aunt almost sharply, "what were you thinking?"

"I don't know."

"Of course not. Run away and play, like a good little girl. My head aches."

There had been a time when Windyhaugh took an honourable, if modest, place in the social life of the country, but of late years Mrs. Galbraith had withdrawn more and more from conventional intercourse with her neighbours. One or two families still paid her an occasional duty-call; but the old lady's interests were becoming more and more circumscribed, and her real friends were few. She was said by some to be the victim of religious melancholy; for there is no subject on which people are more ready to dogmatise than on the limits of sanity in the religious life; and yet, when one comes to think of it, the problem is involved and far-reaching enough to be treated with some respect.

Remote and forgotten, however, as Windyhaugh had become, it could not long conceal a woman of Enid Dalrymple's social gifts; and the day before she took her boys to London, a pair of high-stepping horses pranced up the carriage-drive.

"Robinson Crusoe sees a footprint in the sand," she remarked *sotto voce* when the visitors' names were announced. "I had no idea Ryelands was in this part of the world. Tell Pearson to find the children and send them in."

The children, as it chanced, were building castles in the sand, and, when Jane heard the message, she chose to consider that it included her special fledgling.

An odd trio they made as they entered the white and gold drawing-room—Hugh more like a miniature man of the world than ever in his new Eton suit; Gavin, a baby cherub in dark blue velvet and fine old point; Wil-

helmina—— But the reader has already seen Wilhelmina in her Sabbath frock, and can guess the worst.

Of course it was an excellent thing for her to learn
that life contains wider problems than the pronunciation
of Zerubbabel, but the lesson was a bitter one. She
would have seemed dull and unresponsive in any case,
but the sight of Hugh, standing in front of those magnificent ladies calmly twirling his watch-chain, and
remarking that the society of women (to wit, Mrs.
Galbraith, his mother, Wilhelmina, and Jane) palled
after a time, and that he would not be sorry to go
back to school—deprived her completely of the power of
speech.

Gavin did not say much, but he smiled like a baby
angel, and allowed himself to be idolized in a way that
was simply irresistible.

"Who did you say the little girl was?" asked one of
the ladies at length. "Wilhelmina Galbraith?—not
George Galbraith's daughter?"

Mrs. Dalrymple nodded, and a significant smile
passed between her and the visitor. "She is not at all
like her father, is she?"

"Extraordinary! What a fascinating man he is!
We met him at Homburg last month. Poor fellow——"

. "You would like to go back to nurse, wouldn't you,
dear?" said Enid kindly; and thus ended Wilhelmina's
first glimpse of fashionable life.

Though thankful to escape, she felt herself dismissed
in disgrace, and, rushing into the shrubbery, she threw
herself down on a friendly stretch of warm brown
turf.

"They think Hugh so clever, and me so stupid,"
she sobbed, "and it's not right, it's not fair, it's not
true!"

Never in her life before had she felt this tearing pain
at her heart-strings. She did not know that it was common to all mankind, and that centuries ago dear Mother
Church had classified it as one of the seven deadly sins.
She only knew that it hurt—hurt horribly.

Poor little soul! And at your age the true cure for
that pain is so far out of reach—so far that most men

live and die without finding it, so far that he who makes
it his own has risen above happiness and attained to
blessedness.

But if the cure for the disease seems unattainable,
the cure for the symptom is always at hand. In a few
minutes Wilhelmina dried her tears, and began to look
round the tiny circle of her acquaintance in search of
someone who appreciated her, someone who thought her
"clever." Nurse would not do; nurse was rather silly
herself; but Mr. Darsie——! He never said she was
clever, but he thought so. Wilhelmina was perfectly
sure that he thought so.

A great rush of affection for the old man came over
her heart. She wished in her crude childish fashion
that she could give him something, but the only thing
she had to give was her treasured chocolates, and he
would not care for them. She had found out to her
great surprise some time ago that, living, as he did, in
the midst of a limitless store of sweets, he was never
tempted to touch them.

He was fond of books, but books cost a lot of money,
and Wilhelmina had only a penny in the world. He
enjoyed a quiet pipe—was it possible that men enjoyed
tobacco as she enjoyed chocolates?—and if so——

A minute later she was running through the shrubbery in the direction of the high-walled garden. The
gate was kept locked as a rule by Mrs. Galbraith's orders, but Tail-o'-the-week was at work to-day and she
had no difficulty in getting in.

She wandered about for some time among the tall
flowers and hedges before she came upon the old man
laying down fresh hay in a late strawberry bed. He
did not notice her approach, but the sight of his occupation was sufficient to shunt her thoughts for the moment on to a siding.

"I am very fond of strawberries," she said tentatively.

He did not turn his head, nor rise from his stooping
posture.

"Ye'll no' need to be fond o' them the day," he said
grimly.

So, like a wise woman, she returned without delay to the main line.

"Tail-o'-the-week," she began reflectively, unconscious that this appellation was not strictly intended for his ears, "does tobacco cost a great deal of money?"

Now this, as it chanced, was a home-thrust. Tail-o'-the-week and his old woman held widely different views on the subject.

He straightened his bent back as far as the rheumatic muscles would allow, and scratched his bald head. "Weel—no' that muckle," he said apologetically.

"Could I get some for a penny?"

"Weel, Missy, there's a' sorts o' tobaccy an' a' sorts o' prices. The like o' me is no' able to buy the same as what the laird smokes. Wad it be for a freen o' yer ain?"

Here was a poser, but the answer was strictly non-committal.

"It's for—a middling sort of person," said Wilhelmina.

"Noo, Missy," said the old man severely, "ye're no' gaun to gie it to yon bit callant. I've nae doobt ava that he's keen to try; but it's no' the like o' baccy that's gaun to mak' a man o' him."

"Do you mean Hugh?" cried Wilhelmina indignantly. "I never thought of giving it to Hugh. He's only a little boy." Then her face softened into a smile. "Are you coming again to-morrow?"

"Ay."

"Then, dear Tail-o'-the-week, bring me a pennyworth of tobacco!—just a middling sort of tobacco, you know. If there's enough to fill two pipes it'll do."

She pressed a hot penny into his horny hand, and rushed away before he had time to refuse so extraordinary and dangerous a commission.

The whole enterprise had been no small strain on the child's limited stock of courage, and she trembled with excitement as she took her way back towards the nursery.

Unfortunately the visitors had gone, and Jane was already on the war-path. She and her charge met at the garden gate.

"What are you doing here?" cried the angry nurse. "You have been at the fruit."

But at this the child's overstrained nerves gave way. "*It's a lie!*" she shouted.

All through life we have to pay the penalty of these delicious, soul-satisfying cessions to impulse, and Wilhelmina was not surprised when a shower of smart slaps fell about her head and shoulders. Her screams brought Mrs. Galbraith to the spot; and Jane gave her own explanation of the circumstances. For all Wilhelmina could find to say, she might as well have been born dumb.

Jane was reprimanded in private afterwards. For Wilhelmina the day closed in deep disgrace.

"And do you suppose she *had* taken the fruit," asked Mrs. Dalrymple, when Pearson explained to her the cause of the turmoil.

"Well, Madam, if you'll excuse me saying so, I don't think Miss Wilhelmina is a straightforward child. Yesterday evening I met her coming out of your room, and there was a strong scent of eau de Cologne about the place. I looked at the bottle and found it had gone all milky, so I charged her with adding water to it; but she denied that she had touched it. She turned very red. I'm afraid——"

Mrs. Dalrymple laughed. "I don't mind her taking, or even *spilling*, my eau de Cologne; but it is a pity she should spoil what little she leaves for me. But I am sorry you spoke to her, Pearson. Don't on any account say a word to anyone else. We will leave the eau de Cologne to balance a few of the punishments that may have been undeserved. Poor little sinner! This comes of being brought up by a pious grandmother!"

CHAPTER V.

IN THE GROCER'S PARLOUR.

THE shop was shut for the night, and the grocer was comfortably ensconced in his snug little quarters upstairs. The house was a queer old place, with low ceilings and uneven floors; the unwary visitor had always to be warned concerning certain treacherous steps that led unexpectedly from room to room; but, such as it was, the quaint little place realized the old man's idea of a home.

His books, chosen so lovingly one by one through a long period of years, were carefully garnered in odd bookshelves against the walls, and over the mantelpiece hung the portrait of a great man who had lived here once, and in whose aura the grocer lived humbly and contentedly.

A tiny fire burned in the grate, for the night was chilly; a black kettle purred on the hob; and the grocer himself, pipe in mouth, sat in the horsehair arm-chair, with a book before him, and a spirit-stand on the table by his side.

There was a loud knock at the door, and a pleasant young voice called out:

"May I come in, Mr. Darsie?"

"Ay, come in, come in, Mr. Carmichael," cried the creaky old voice. "I'm sure ye're heartily welcome."

There was not many men in the town for whom, at this particular hour of the twenty-four, the grocer would have risen to his feet and placed a chair; but he had a profound respect, if not for the bands, at least for the college gown.

"Have a drop of something hot?" he asked, apologetically.

"No, thanks; but I shall enjoy seeing you have it. How cosy you look!"

And then they both relapsed into silence, as men do who are at ease in each other's society.

.3

"Weel," said the old man at last, "have ye been reading onything new in a theological way since I saw ye?"

The other laughed and shook his head. "Pastoral
visitations, Mr. Darsie," he said. "Nothing but pastoral visitations!"

Now-a-days all our young preachers, and most of
their hearers, are dashed with free-thought, modern science, and German philosophy; but, at the time of which
I write, Essays and Reviews was still a comparatively
recent work. We have gained much since then, no
doubt; but some things at least we have lost. We have
lost the subtle thrill of intense delight with which an
awakening mind scented a kindred mind from afar;
we have lost the exhilarating sensation of being in the
vanguard; our treasured watchword, which seemed to
us eternal, has become an empty shibboleth, and we are
thankful to fall back on that which binds us, not to the
few, but to the many.

We were so young then! We had not guessed—what
the years have since taught us so abundantly!—how
trivial a matter is mere intellectual agreement after all.
What we learned in the watches of the night, with
strong crying and tears and groanings that cannot be
uttered, may be picked up now in the pages of a popular
magazine; and those who are familiar with the formula
cannot guess all it meant to those who felt the fact.

Yet, when all is said, the recollection of the time
"when we felt the days before us" is something with
which we would not lightly part: the sensation once experienced is ours for ever. To us too it was given to
see the sunrise—

> "Bliss was it in that dawn to be alive,
> But to be young was very heaven."

So the reader may imagine the rush of delighted
surprise with which Mr. Carmichael, when he first came
to Queensmains, found on the grocer's bookshelves, not
only the orthodox divines who are a literary staple in
every middle-class Scotch household, but also such writers as Maurice, Robertson of Brighton, Macleod Camp-
bell, and Erskine of Linlathen. I do not mean to imply

that Mr. Carmichael was what, even in those days, would have been termed a heretic, for the effect of his wider reading had been, not to shake his faith, but rather to encircle his creed with a sunny margin of hope and charity. It was the spiritual, rather than the intellectual, fibres in him that had vibrated to the words of the teachers I have named, and it was natural that at first, in his youth and inexperience, he should imagine the bond of union between himself and the grocer to be stronger than it really was.

For Mr. Darsie's was hardly a devotional nature. It may almost be said of him that he collected theological books and theological views as other men collect butterflies or stamps or rare china. Among the green pastures and beside the still waters he wandered as far as he readily could, but his tether was short.

His shrewd grey eyes disappeared now, as they were apt to do when he was amused.

"An' what ails ye at pastoral visitations?" he said.

The young man rose to his feet, and paced up and down the tiny room.

"I think," he said, "it was Dr. Hanna who pointed out how tremendously 'churchy' we Presbyterians are, for people who pride themselves on their Protestant principles. You, with your views, must wonder how anyone can see anything more in me than a crude well-meaning young man, and yet, from the way some people treat me, I might be the priesthood incarnate."

He paused, but his friend only ventured on an appreciative smile.

"What I long to draw the line at is 'speaking to' people. You know the hushed monotone in which the expression is used. Heaven knows I give them of my best—such as it is—in the pulpit! But who am I that I should pursue them into their lairs? Of course there are moments when one must speak: the fire is kindled and it must blaze: the sphere is charged with electricity and the spark must pass. But 'speaking' in cold blood to a fellow-creature who, in overwhelming probability, is listening in even colder blood—upon my soul, Darsie, it is more than any human being has a right to ask."

The old man's face broke into furrows again. "Who have you been speaking to now?"

"You don't expect me to answer that, of course; but of one I may tell you—it is almost absurd—a child of seven whose grandmother is half in despair about her salvation."

"I ken fine who that'll be—little Miss Williamina."

The minister looked greatly taken aback. "Do you know her?"

"I do that. My word, Mr. Carmichael, but that's a golden girl! If your seed came to naught, it wasna the fault o' the soil."

The young man seated himself again, his chin in his hands, his earnest eyes fixed on the queer little figure opposite.

"It is quite obvious," he said, "that the sooner you and I change places the better. The grocery business would suffer, of course; but the other is usually considered more important. If you have been able to get into touch with *that child*——"

The grocer beamed in his placid self-content. She's a great friend o' mine is little Miss Williamina."

"Then perhaps you can tell me whether the old lady is quite sane."

"I'm no' layin' claim to the friendship o' Mistress Galbraith. But she's sane enough when ye consider her point o' view. Her only son—that's Williamina's father —turned out a wastrel, and she hauds hersel' responsible to God for him. She is persuaded her time is at han', and, when she dies, Williamina goes to her father. If a' be true o' him that folks say, it's sma' wonner that she's keen to see the bairn on a sure footin'."

"And is there anything in the child?"

The old man stared. "Onything in her? My word! I niver met the bairn yet wi' the promise o' Williamina."

The minister looked up with the expression of one who schools himself to docility.

"Go on. Talk. Tell me about her."

"Weel," said the grocer, the warmth of his feelings fusing his speech into broader vernacular, "she just beats a'thing. In ae sense, she's no bairn ava. She's a woman grown. She has a grup o' doctrine——"

He paused in search of suitable words, and the young man took advantage of the pause.

"Is that all?" he asked drily. "What interests me, Darsie, is to know how you found it out. I am free to confess that she didn't inflict much of her doctrinal erudition on me. You must have found an inflammable corner somewhere. Where was it? and how did you chance to light upon it?"

"Hoot, I nae ken. I've a sittin' ahint Mistress Galbraith i' the kirk, and it was aye a real divert to see that bairn tackle the sermon. Yon earnest bit facie was a picter. I spoke till her aboot it ae day when her nurse left her here i' the shop—she's an awfu' lassie, yon. I doot we'll hear o' mischief yet. But the bairn took no heed. Then anither day I said, says I, 'It's a peety but what you had been a boy, and you'd ha' gien us a fine sermon yersel' some day.' Then in a meenit oot it cam—'You see, Mr. Darsie, perhaps I'm not even one of the elect.'"

The minister smiled in spite of himself.

"And do you mean to say she has any notion of what it all means?"

"She has that."

"And you think she is unhappy?"

"I've nae doobt ava that she's 'unhappy,' as ye ca' it; but at her age the Lord tempers the wind."

The young man rose to his feet once more. "But, my dear friend, as you have found your way to her confidence, can't you help her? It is awful to think of a baby like that worrying over election. At her age it is so easy to believe that God is Love. It seems to me that a few words from one she trusted would put her right."

It was some minutes before the old man answered. When he did, the rare look of elevation had risen to his worn face.

"At my age, Mr. Carmichael, ye'll no' talk sae glib o' puttin' folk right. I've seen them that were better men when they were seekin' God, than when they were

sure they had found Him. I'm no scholar like you, but
I seem to mind the story o' a King of England—you'll
ken it fine—who was lookin' frae his castle at the battle.
His ain son was sore beset i' the thick o' the fight, and
the nobles were keen to send somebody to his relief.
But 'No,' said the King, 'let the lad win his spurs.'
That's what I say o' Williamina. It's no' a'body that's
worth it; but she is. Let her win her spurs."

He spoke so earnestly that the minister was impressed, but a few minutes later he returned to the
charge.

"Frankly," he said, "I disagree with you from first
to last. I don't admit that it is a question of spiritual
experience at all. At her age we are—mainly—what our
circumstances make us. All her life she has been hearing of justification, sanctification, election, and reproba-
tion, and she talks of these things as a matter of course.
Other children hear about natural history, or steam-
boats, or agriculture, and talk of them. Where is the
difference? If I went in for betting, I should be prepared to bet that Wilhelmina does not know the name
of a bird or a flower that she meets in her walks. She
must occupy her mind with something. One child calls
its doll Beelzebub, and another calls its doll Tweedle-
dee; but the dolls are the same, and, for all I can see,
the children are the same."

The old man shook his head with a quiet smile of
superiority. He did not reflect that the minister's argument would include others besides Wilhelmina; but,
like the rest of us, he had a strong sympathy with a
taste that ran in harness with his own.

"Na, na, sir!" he cried. "Williamina is no' the
first bairn that was brought up in a pious home."

The minister's face fell into lines of deep thought,
and it was some minutes before he spoke again. "I
don't know," he said slowly, "that I am justified in expressing my thoughts in the making—even to you; but
it does seem to me that, even if your view be right, such
a state of things is most abnormal and undesirable.
You know they tell us now-a-days that the development
of the race is repeated in the development of each indi-

vidual, and although of course one may carry such a
parallel too far, I do think that in a sense a child should
begin life as a healthy pagan, taking the world for
granted as God's world, and certainly not analysing
its own beliefs and feelings. If there be any truth in
my half-fledged fancy, your little friend is simply precocious—abnormal—scarcely human.

The old man rose to his feet. "Na, na, Mr. Carmichael!" he said. "I canna sit still an' hear ye say
that, even if ye dinna richtly mean it. Scarcely human!—little Williamina!" He walked slowly over to
the cupboard. "I didna think to show it to onybody,
but I'll show it to you," he said, and he put something
into the minister's hand.

Mr. Carmichael surveyed the treasure solemnly for a
moment.

"It seems to require an explanation," he said at last.
And so it did.

It was a large and perfect sea-shell, adorned with a
rich red ribbon, and packed full of cheap tobacco. To
the ribbon was attached a tiny card, on which were inscribed in an uncertain round hand the words—

"*Mr. Darsie, with Wilhelmina's love.*"

"Ay, ye may say it requires an explanation. A deal
o' thocht an' contrivance went to the old man's present.
Whaur she got the tobacco I canna say, but I ken fine
that she didna ask her Grannie for it. The shell, nae
doobt, she picked up on the beach, an' she tied it up wi' a
bonny bit ribbon frae ane o' her dolls. But that's no' a'.
She's mony a time seen Mistress Galbraith send a present wi' a visiting-card to say wha it cam' frae. She
hasna a visiting-card, puir lamb! and she canna tell her
secret, so she taks a Sabbath School ticket—I hope ye
havena forgot the value o' a Sabbath School ticket, Mr.
Carmichael!—four means a big ane, an' three big anes
a little book—and she writes her message on the back.
She wad hae blotted oot the text, but the text is the
word o' God, an' she daurna. So she draws a shaky bit
pencil-line across it—just to let me see that she wasna
meanin' to preach me a sermon."

As he turned over the "ticket," his voice broke into

a cackling laugh that was half a sob, and the minister read the words—

"*We all do fade as a leaf.*"

"Any reference to the tobacco?" asked the young man flippantly.

Then his face grew grave.

"I admit that I judged the case on insufficient premises," he said. "Your Wilhelmina is certainly human."

CHAPTER VI.

THE PROCESS OF WINNING ONE'S SPURS.

THE sun was obscured by leaden clouds, and a tempest raged over Windyhaugh.

Never had the old homestead been in a more sinister mood than now. Night itself has no darkness so drear as the shade of the limes that day at noon. The rain dashed drearily against the window-panes, and the trees slowly tossed their mighty arms from earth to firmament. The air was full of the sobbing of the wind and wave, and, as the evening came on, every chimney and corridor took up a note of its own, and wailed and shrieked in sympathy. One might have fancied ever and again that armed men were battering against the doors, or forcing their way up the creaky oaken stair.

Mrs. Galbraith's thoughts took an even gloomier turn than usual as she sat by the fire with a great Bible on the table by her side: the servants neglected their work, and conversed in awe-struck whispers. Wilhelmina felt sure that the end of the world had come.

And she was still unsaved.

Every nerve in her body vibrated to the storm, and for terror her tongue well-nigh clave to the roof of her mouth. The sight of the supper that often seemed limited enough was loathsome to her; she would have left it untasted, but that Jane might have seized the occasion to taunt her with being afraid; and she could not

bring herself to speak of her fear, though, in the grop-
ing fashion of childhood, she fancied the others shared it.
This must be why her grandmother looked so stern;
she expected the Son of Man. The impending day of
wrath must be the subject of the servants' whispers.
How relieved the child would have been had she known
that they only talked of ghosts, robbers, murder, and
sudden death!

Surely nothing is more amusing and pathetic than
the want of perspective in a child's knowledge of the
world and of humanity! In one place we find the focus
sharp and clear, and we do not guess that close at hand
is an outline magnified and blurred beyond all recognition. Poor little Wilhelmina! Do you think it would
be thus that your friends would await the coming of the
Judge?

Things nearly came to a climax when Jane left her
charge in bed and went down to the kitchen for company.

"Don't bite your nails," she had said sharply, as she
brushed the silky brown hair. "It's the sign of a bad
conscience."

Bad conscience, indeed! It was the sign of a nervous system strained almost beyond endurance; but Jane
was nervous herself to-night, and well-nigh as self-cen-
tred as Wilhelmina. Of course she knew that her charge
would rather not be left alone; but she did not guess
the measureless dread with which the prospect was regarded. She had not the least idea of the amount of
self-control it took to keep the child from crying out,
"Don't leave me!"

She paused on the threshold, however, and threw a
sop to her own kindlier nature. "Go to sleep, like a
good girl," she said. "I'll bring you one of those penny
dolls to-morrow, when I go to town."

A quiver of relief shot through the child's frame.
A penny doll is not much to set over against the terrors
of eternal doom; but, if Jane could even speak or think
of buying dolls, she must have a fair hope that to-morrow might dawn even as to-day, and all the dear earthly
days behind it, had dawned.

"Don't pull down the blind, please," said the child very quietly in a small shaky voice.

"Are you cold?"

"No—not very."

"Why do you want to look out? You'll never go to sleep if you watch those trees. They're not cannie to-night."

But Wilhelmina carried her point. She did not want to watch the trees at all: it terrified her to see them—now grovelling with head and arms down to earth, and again sweeping themselves up as if in a last despairing appeal to Heaven; but she wanted to watch the sky, to see that night came on steadily and normally, without any of the "signs" that might be supposed to herald the great trump. The season was late, and a crowd of green and yellow leaves went whirling and eddying past the window-panes. "The harvest is past; the summer is ended," they wailed in their fearsome flight—" and *you are not yet saved!*"

How good and reassuring were all the well-known commonplace sounds, as they made themselves heard in the pauses of the storm—the pumping of water into the cistern, the far-off raking of the kitchen fire, the closing of shutters and doors!

Wilhelmina was too young to seek sleep, and, seeking, she might well have failed to find it; but sleep understands the children so well, and she came on this child unawares, and folded her into kind motherly arms. For hours she held the little one close, and then the riotous nerves broke loose, and awoke to a silent house, and a raging storm outside.

Minutes passed before the child knew what oppressed her; then she sprang out of bed and ran to the window. The sky was very dark, and only dimly could she see the dirge-like dance of the trees. There were no "signs" here; but the window looked out to the front, to the plantation of limes. Perhaps Christ was coming behind, through the sky above the sea. The sea was no obstacle to Him. Had He not walked on the water long ago?

Shivering with fear, the little bare feet stole out on

the oilcloth that covered the landing, and two great terrified eyes looked forth on the blackness beyond the
panes. Nothing could be seen—nothing—nothing.
Her ears were baffled, deafened by a multitude of
sounds—was this perchance the great trump?—but sight
she had none.

Suddenly—suddenly—while she stood, such a light
as the child had never seen flashed out over the sky and
sea, and distant hills. It was too much. Poor tortured
self-control gave way, and the little bare feet went pat-
tering—flying—into the nurse's room.

"*Jane!*" cried a choking voice. "*Jane! Wake up!
wake up! Christ is coming, and I am not saved!*"

It was severe treatment for a phlegmatic young woman who had believed in a general way all she had learned
in Sunday School, without ever trying very hard to put it
in practice. Jane fell on her knees, and began to cry—
then realized the situation, and took the child in her arms.

"There, there!" she said soothingly. "You've got
into a state—that's what it is. I told you how it would
be if you watched those trees. There's nothing wrong.
Christ is not coming at all!"

Ah me, but the mills of God grind slowly! If Christ
had come—if Wilhelmina could have seen or guessed
who and what the eternal Christ was—how surprised she
would have been!

But her nurse's pity was really roused now.

"You poor little thing!" she said. "Your teeth
are chattering, and you are just starved with cold.
Come into my bed. There! Put your head on my
shoulder and say your prayers. 'Our Father——'"

"No, no!" sobbed Wilhelmina, half comforted, but
shivering more than ever. "'Our Father' is no use.
There's nothing about salvation in that!"

And nurse, still pitiful, began again.

"'Now I lay me down to sleep——'"

Wilhelmina joined in, breathing hard—

"'Now I lay me down to sleep,
I pray the Lord my soul to keep.
If I should die before I wake,
I pray the Lord my soul to take——'"

"What's the use of praying like that when you don't 'believe'?" cried the traditionary creed. But, with all the force in her being, Wilhelmina closed her ears to its voice. Over and over again she repeated the words—

> "'If I should die before I wake,
> I pray the Lord my soul to take,
> And this I ask for Jesus' sake,'"—

daring God, as it were, to send her to hell with those words on her lips; and so kind sleep overtook her once more, and lulled her to rest.

. . . .

"Neurotic, ill-balanced, overstrung——"
It may be so. I might urge that Wilhelmina simply believed what she was taught—or rather what her baby mind could accept and formulate out of all that she was taught; but, if one is to attempt the defence at all, it is wiser perhaps to take the question on a wider ground, and remind ourselves how *flexible* is the nature of a child.

"Childhood," says Dr. Clouston, "is a condition of healthy physiological mania"; and I think—if I have grasped his teaching aright—he would allow us to extend the remark, and say that children may run safely and sanely through such a gamut of moods and feelings as, in the adult, would almost necessarily imply mental disease. Nature does not restrict the little ones to the upper half of the key-board. The sorrows, as well as the joys, of childhood are keener than those of later life; and we are blind to this fact mainly by the exquisite resiliency with which the nature of the child vibrates to each in turn, and springs without a jerk from one extreme to the other.

If we adults could retain this resiliency, we might safely retain the mobility; perhaps the rare power to retain both is one of the characteristics of genius; for is not the genius god, madman, or child, according to the point of view from which we regard him?—or according to the note he sounds at the moment on the gamut of human life?

"Neurotic, ill-balanced, overstrung——"

It may be so, but who shall describe the rapture of
Wilhelmina's awakening? Who shall describe the exquisite reaction into sanity with which she sprang up in
bed to see the dear old sun blazing down on a world all
fresh and fragrant, and dripping with yesterday's rain?

Are we not apt to overdo our pity for those who at
times are "troubled by an evil spirit from the Lord"?
They are not necessarily of finer calibre than their fellows; but one thing at least is preëminently theirs—the
joy of being sane. It is a mistake to attribute this joy to
the man whose mental and spiritual life resembles a successful jogtrot along the highway. It is possible to be
so sane that one does not know what sanity means.

Jane showed herself amazingly tactful that morning.
She was kind, without being effusively so. There was
nothing in her manner that forcibly reminded Wilhelmina of the unparalleled self-revelation of the night before, and for this the child was tacitly grateful. In
truth Jane's conscience had received a shake. It was a
vulnerable citadel at the best of times, and particularly
so just now. She had vague thoughts that morning of
turning certain traitors out of the garrison; but, before
taking any important step, she decided to make a few
general enquiries about the Second Coming. The old
gardener was reported to have strong views on the subject, and she determined to consult him; then burst into
hysterical laughter as she fancied she heard him reply,
"He'll be round i' the tail o' the week!"

She was shocked at her own profanity, and put up a
mental prayer for forgiveness. Poor Jane! She judged
her own sins and peccadilloes by a curiously arbitrary
standard—a standard that gave the Almighty little
credit for any sense of humour.

But what put the crowning touch to Wilhelmina's
happiness that morning was the fact that Mrs. Galbraith
remained in bed to breakfast. The old lady never allowed herself such an indulgence without serious cause,
so no doubt she was suffering a great deal in mind or
body; but it did not occur to Wilhelmina to look at the
matter from that point of view. The aspect of it that

occupied her mind to the exclusion of every other was
the expectation that the servants would seize the opportunity to send up a crisp rasher of bacon, or a slice of
cold pie, for breakfast, along with the invariable porridge; and that Jane—being in so delectable a frame
of mind—would allow her to run out and play by herself
the moment the choice morsel was disposed of.

How she did run!—with her pinafore flapping in the
wind, and her sun-bonnet blown back from the ruffled
hair! Tail-o'-the-week was at work in a little garden
close by, digging some "seedy" and storm-tost annuals
into the ground. Wilhelmina caught hold of the railing
with sunburnt fists, and looked through with pitiful eyes.

"Will they come up again?" she asked shyly.

The old man chuckled.

"Na, na, Missy," he said. "They'll no' come up
again."

So she frowned and danced away. It jarred on her
mood to see the poor things being buried out of the sunshine this wonderful morning. It was pleasanter to
watch the trees. They seemed so happy as they laughed
and clapped their hands by the wayside.

"It's as if they had been praying for something last
night, and had got it now," thought Wilhelmina. But
this fancy too was speedily cast aside as being too painfully suggestive. Happy though the child was, she was
firmly persuaded that *she* had not got what she had
prayed for.

And now she was down on the beach, singing softly
to herself while the blue waves tossed their white caps
merrily into the air. She enjoyed, without analysing,
the vivid intensity of colour. A stray brown sail glowed
red as fire; a white one gleamed like Lohengrin's mantle.

All the poet in Wilhelmina awoke and struggled for
expression—so she gathered nice flat stones, and, with
shrieks of triumph, sent them skimming over the blue.

Happy Wilhelmina!

Jane went into town that day; but she forgot to buy
the penny doll. No matter: the penny doll had served
its turn.

CHAPTER VII.

AT THE COSMOPOLIS.

A DRIZZLING rain fell softly on deserted London streets; but the bright façade of the Hotel Cosmopolis stretched out inviting arms into the dusk.

The day had been oppressively warm, and Enid Dalrymple was very tired; or, as she would have expressed it, London was sordid, Pearson obtuse, Hugh indescribably exasperating, life a slow meaningless martyrdom. It was cheering, after the dust and tedium of the journey, to see that brightly-lighted vista with its crimson floor-cloths, fine palms, and groups of immaculate waiters.

" Tell them where to put the luggage, Pearson," she said wearily, as they waited for the lift to ascend, " and take the children straight to their room. Order supper for them there, and tell the chambermaid I want a bath in my own room immediately."

Hugh stole a grimy little paw coaxingly into his mother's hand.

" I'm going to dine with you, Mother dear," he said.

She looked at him with an air of sublime impartial justice. After a long day of ineffectual strife and protest her turn had come at last.

" You have not made your society so delightful to me during the day, Hugh," she said quietly, " that I should care to have any more of it."

" I couldn't help it. The train was so beastly hot and shaky. Please, Mother! I do want a glass of champagne."

" Ah! You should have thought of that before."

He scowled. " It's not fair to treat me just as you treat Gavin."

" Not at all fair. Gavin would have behaved like a little gentleman if you had allowed him. If I wanted company, I should take him down to dine with me; but he is too tired, poor little man."

"I'm not tired, Muvvy dear," piped Gavin in that clear, sweet, penetrating voice of his. "I want some champagne too."

"Hush, hush!" They were up on the first floor now, and Enid looked round with an amused, shocked, apologetic smile. She could seldom ignore the existence of a possible audience.

This time the audience consisted of a few chambermaids and one guest, a fine-looking man with one of those inscrutable faces that pique curiosity.

"Champagne!" he said, pinching Gavin's dainty pink ear. "You've begun early, young man. What do you say to a brandy-and-soda with me in the billiard-room?"

"Why, George! It *is* a pleasure to see you," said Mrs. Dalrymple with a restful sigh that was infinitely flattering. "I can't think what has put such an absurd idea into the children's heads. I don't believe they have ever tasted champagne."

"Oh, Mother!" protested Hugh. His brow ran into furrows as he proceeded to formulate his statistics on the subject, but this time his mother's glance was sufficient to silence even him.

Of course the glance did not escape George Galbraith. Few things did. He knew Enid Dalrymple well, and appreciated most of her pretty poses. Naturally he liked her all the better for them. A woman without foibles was to his mind destitute of that atmosphere through which alone she could form a sane opinion as to the proportions of the other sex.

"Are you alone?" he said. "Come, that's right! You'll dine with me, of course. What time shall we say? A quarter past eight? I'll go down and see what they can do for us."

His step was light and he hummed an air as he ran down the broad easy staircase. He had scarcely thought of Enid for months, and now she had come into his life at the very moment he would have chosen. So clever of her! Money chanced to be plentiful, he was hungry, he wanted to be amused; and, behold, Providence dropped down for his delectation a woman beautiful and fascinating, a woman who knew one man from another, and who yet was content to take men as she found them —above all a woman who really, without any pretence, understood that a good dinner does not mean an interminable series of kickshaws and a glass of sweet champagne.

The head waiter thoroughly appreciated the importance of the situation, and the dinner of which he and Mr. Galbraith drew out the sketch between them was quite a little poem in its way.

George Galbraith might or might not enjoy the unqualified respect of his equals, but there could be no doubt whatever as to the estimation in which he was held by the whole class of men-servants. For them he was a real gentleman—a gentleman after their own hearts. Even their practised eyes never detected the cloven foot. He was a man of the world in all things, down to his most trifling possession, his most involuntary habit. Frank and openhanded, he yet was possessed of a reserve unlike the reserve of other men—a certain aloofness which was always present as the shadow side of his gaiety, an aloofness of which he had been unconscious until a sense of its market value had been thrust upon him.

" You think I play the game rather well," he seemed to be saying with mild surprise. " *Au contraire*, I have never exerted myself to play it at all. I am out of the running. But at least I see through *your* game."

" Damned impertinence! " a friend of his youth was wont to say. " You'd think the fellow was Jove himself, and we his puppets. And I'd like to know what he has done to qualify himself for the rôle beyond failing in the work he put his hand to! "

Thus variously was George Galbraith reflected in the eyes of his fellow-men.

Reverently, and with the hand of a master, the waiter uncorked a dusty old bottle, and, as he placed it on the table, he wondered whether it was within the limits of reasonable expectation that the unknown quantity, the lady, could be on a level with the other factors—including, of course, himself—in so exquisite an entertainment.

4

And I think most women would have felt their sex abundantly justified for the moment in Enid, had they seen the effect she produced as she entered the room with a self-consciousness so perfect as to be imperceptible. Her full, sunny-white throat rose vividly above the soft black draperies; her tawny hair, kindling into red gold in the shaded light, was arranged as only an artist can arrange it—in that great loose knot that suggests how readily it would fall in a cloud about the owner's shoulders.

The waiter's bow was less perfect than usual: he was taken aback. The faintest ripple of expression passed over Mr. Galbraith's sensitive face, but he met her eye only for a moment with his courteous, conventional smile. He was too much of an epicure to exhaust his enjoyment in a draught. He could afford to wait.

"It's awfully mean of Mother," Hugh was exclaiming upstairs. "I am sure Uncle George would have liked to have me too."

Pearson laughed. She was much more tired than the others, and she had little sense of humour at the best of times; but Hugh's remark appealed forcibly to such as she had.

He felt he had said something naïve, and he hated to be naïve. That was Gavin's rôle.

"Just wait till to-morrow when Mother is buying me things for school, and wants me to *care*," he said fiercely. "She'll see that somebody else can be horrid too."

"There, there!" said Pearson, at the end of her patience. "It's easily seen that what you want is a good night's sleep."

And, writhing under this final insult, the poor little man of the world betook himself to bed.

Downstairs, conversation did not flow very freely just at first, and they were both too wise to force it. It was sufficient for the moment to relax, to appreciate and to feel oneself appreciated, to smile those little smiles that mean so much and that seem to mean even more.

Life gives us some very good half-hours when youth is past and we have ceased to demand the impossible.

Dessert was on the table before Mr. Galbraith said casually, "I took it for granted that you were in Norway with Fergus."

"Did you? I fancied you knew me better. Before Norway is furbished up to the level of my requirements, I shall be ambling along marine parades in a bath-chair. No, no. Fergus and I are old married folk. We live and let live. Guess where I went after leaving Perthshire."

He shook his head lazily, but his smile was full of subtle flattery. "I can't guess. My faculties are otherwise employed. Be kind and tell me."

"Windyhaugh."

She pronounced the word suddenly, and raised her eyes to watch the effect.

It is impossible to describe the change that came over his face. It was instantaneous, but for that instant Enid almost felt as if she had struck him.

"Did the Highlands prove so exciting, then," he asked, with elaborate carelessness, "that you were forced to go into retreat at once?"

He really wondered very much what had induced her to go; but he knew he was more likely to find out if he did not ask. In point of fact she could scarcely with decency have told him that it had suited her convenience to send the boys there for a time, and that she had thought it only fair to follow up the bitter draught with a sugarplum in the shape of her charming self.

"I went for pleasure, of course," she said, mendaciously. "Windyhaugh is charming—just the sort of place one reads of in books."

"Is it? That is the kind of book I make a point of dodging."

"And your mother is a wonderful old lady, George."

He bowed gravely.

His face was quite impenetrable now as he held his wine-glass against the light, but it was some seconds before he could bring himself to say—

"And Wilhelmina?"

Enid thought her little laugh was perfect, but there was a note of apology in it that spoke volumes.

"Oh, she is the quaintest little woman imaginable—so old-fashioned!"

"Poor little soul!" His accent was pitying, but scarcely fatherly. He was thinking more of his own past than of Wilhelmina's present.

"Oh, I don't know. I think the life suits her. If she were a different sort of child, one might be almost sorry for her. The life is a little—well, it isn't a gay life."

He filled her glass.

"No," he said dispassionately. "When I recall those days, 'gay' is not the adjective that suggests itself."

"Poor boy! I know. I often thought of you. Even Hugh and Gavin——! But it is different for a girl, and Wilhelmina is such a sedate little maiden."

He nodded. "It is a great thing for a girl to be brought up sheltered—in a quiet haven."

"No doubt. Still—perhaps as your daughter she is scarcely getting a fair chance. To tell the truth, I did half mean to speak to you about her. Hugh says she doesn't understand games in the least, and when I took them to lunch one day at Spanforth she was so unlike the others!—counted up what the drag and the lunch would cost!"

"I have no doubt the splendour of the entertainment struck her as barbaric."

"She is afraid of an open window, too. Think of it at her age! Now Hugh is old-fashioned too in a way—quite grown up—his Uncle Ronald makes so much of him—but then he is *chic* and amusing and makes people laugh. Wilhelmina is so deadly serious. She really is just your mother over again."

"A reversion to type. That's lucky."

"I used to *love* to have the child in my room; but when she sat fathoming my soul with those great solemn eyes, I was forced to think of my sins. They were so kind, she and her grannie, and yet one was under fire all round, so to speak. A frivolous person like me began to long for a little close time, like the partridges."

He laughed appreciatively, and his eyes caressed her fair face. "Poor little Enid! Is she having a slice of close time now?"

. "That she is! She is being just as wicked as ever she likes. Isn't it good to be able to let oneself go?"

He nodded.

"I did admire your mother so. She is a saint if ever there was one, and looks the part to distraction. But when one wants good company——"

"One lifts up the light of one's countenance upon the sinners." His face was grave. "Thank you, Enid. I assure you they are not inappreciative. But Wilhelmina is young to be a saint. Has she succeeded in 'getting converted' already?"

Enid was taken aback. Mrs. Galbraith did not choose her confidantes at random. "Oh, in her cradle, I should think," she answered flippantly.

"Then she won't be eternally chivied on that score. She's not pretty, I suppose?" These words betrayed a keener interest than he had shown yet.

If Mrs. Dalrymple prided herself on anything it was on her tact. "She doesn't take after her father," she said, "if that is what you mean. At her age it is impossible to tell."

He sighed, but the sigh was not a very deep one. "Well," he said, "if she is good and happy—that is the main thing; and after all there is a great deal to be said for an old-fashioned education."

"Is there?" she asked quickly. She was sensitive on the subject of her own method—or want of it—with her boys. "Don't you think it tends to make children a little—a little wanting in frankness? Hugh and Gavin are shockingly troublesome, I know; but at least they have no secrets from me."

He smiled. He was used to this pretty little fiction on the part of young mothers.

. "So Wilhelmina is not a model of frankness?" he said indulgently. "Can you wonder? I seem to remember sliding down the water-pipe myself on Sunday afternoon, when I was supposed to be seated in my room, meditating on Pike's Early Piety; and it is not part of

the recollection that I thought it necessary to make public confession at prayer-time."

She laughed. "Ah, that was different. I can understand her not being quite frank with her grandmother.
Don't you want to smoke, George?"

"Thank you. If you are sure you don't mind."

There was silence for a minute or two. "Tell me
how Wilhelmina deceived you, Enid?" he said at last.

"What nonsense, George! How you do misrepresent
one!"

He nodded. "All right," he said. "I quite understand; but you needn't be afraid that I shall interfere.
I am interested in Wilhelmina psychologically—that's
all."

The word impressed her. "Yes," she interposed
eagerly. "It is psychologically that I am interested in
her. Though, of course," she added hastily in response
to his smile, "I am very fond of her too."

"Ah! There I have the advantage of you. I am
not fond of her. I can afford to enjoy the game æsthet-
ically. I made a muddle of it many years ago. It interests me to see what she will make of it."

He paused, smiling, while the metaphor expanded in
his mind.

"When I was a young man," he said, "I took violin
lessons, not so much with a view of playing myself, as
to appreciating the technique of other men. You've no
right to criticise unless you have served in the ranks.
In Wilhelmina's case the stage is small, and the play is
pas grande chose. You suspect me of wishing to take
the part of heavy father? God forbid! I haven't the
smallest intention of crossing the footlights. But it
pleases me to think I am the one man in the auditorium
who is really entitled to form an opinion of the performance. You see there is a certain piquancy in the situation?"

She smiled appreciatively, though she felt sorely perplexed. If she understood his drift at all, he was assuredly right in saying that the play was *pas grande
chose.* She was conscious of a vague feeling of envy.
Surely Wilhelmina was not worth all this. "Do you

know, I believe if you gave your mind to it you would make a splendid father?"

He laughed. One half of him was surprised that she should take the other half seriously.

"*Ah!* But I don't give my mind to it, you see. No, no. Wilhelmina's chance may be small, but it would be a great deal smaller if I took her. Fie, fie, Enid! Is that all a residence at Windyhaugh has done for you? And now we will drop the subject—as soon as you have told me how Wilhelmina deceived you."

"George, dear, for a clever man you are very absurd," she said almost pettishly. "She never deceived me. The child was more than welcome to help herself to my perfume; and if she did fill it up with water when she spilt it—the action was only *gauche*—nothing more. I only thought that Hugh and Gavin——"

"——wouldn't have taken the trouble to fill it up," thought George. But aloud he said—

"So that is what she did. Nasty mean little trick. And yet you know, Enid, the child must be made of good clay." He began to feel almost fatherly. His somewhat jaded emotions were responding to the thoughts of old days—and to the *grand vin* he had chosen with such care. "This particular pitcher"—he tapped his broad chest—"was broken at the wheel or at the furnace; but, if I were to begin life over again, I don't think I should ask for better clay."

"I should think not," she replied a little vaguely, "and I hope you understand, George, that, although you have made me tell you this—this ridiculous little story —I never spoke of it to anyone else. Mrs. Galbraith had no idea of it."

"You didn't speak to the child yourself?——"

She shook her head with a little air of self-congratulation.

He raised his eyebrows. The vintage of that comet year was certainly loosening his tongue.

"——didn't improve the occasion—make a turning-point in her life, and all that sort of thing—speak to her like a mother?"

Mrs. Dalrymple made a charming little *moue*.

"Or like a grandmother?" she said sweetly. "No, George, I did not. I assure you she gets quite enough of that kind of thing as it is."

He did not answer, and she felt she had lost ground, so she assumed an air of deep seriousness.

"What she wants is something very different from that. Could she not have a French *bonne?* I believe her memory is prodigious: Hugh says she knows the Bible by heart; and, with such a gift, it does seem a pity that she shouldn't be learning something—something that would stand her in real stead in her future life, don't you know. What *are* you laughing at, George?"

"Did I laugh?" he asked. "I was only thinking that I could wish few better things for Wilhelmina than that she might come some day to appreciate her Aunt Enid as I do."

CHAPTER VIII.

MADEMOISELLE.

THERE are times when we choose a seed with the greatest care, lay it in friendly soil under favouring skies, tend it day and night, nay, water it with our tears —but our labour is all in vain. Again, almost without our knowledge, a puff of our breath bears a floating seed to some chance scrap of soil where it lies neglected—and behold, a plenteous harvest!

So it was—if I may use to so small an end a metaphor that has long been accustomed to better company— with Enid's suggestion about a *bonne* for Wilhelmina. There was every reason why it should not bear fruit. In the first place, no one greatly cared that it should; in the second place, money at Windyhaugh was at this time a scarce commodity; in the third place, Mrs. Galbraith had been wont to see in every Frenchwoman a possible papist and Jesuit.

And yet the suggestion was carried out.

It happened on this wise.

"Don't put the idea of a bonne quite out of your mind, Enid," George had said on the morning after their conversation. "If you hear of a suitable person, write to—to Wilhelmina's grandmother. Be sure to specify that the woman is an evangelical protestant, and if you can get her to lay claim to a drop or two of Huguenot blood——"

Mrs. Dalrymple laughed and agreed, and forthwith forgot all about it. But some weeks later a friend who was going abroad asked her if she knew of a situation for a French governess with an admirable accent.

Enid shook her head reflectively. "Stay," she said as an afterthought—"would she go to a quiet situation in the country?"

"Well, to tell the truth, she can't afford to be particular. She is not so young as she was, and she is so busy saving that she doesn't manage to dress very well—though of course she knows how to put on the clothes she has. But her accent is something exquisite."

"Is she a protestant?"

"Oh, yes. At least I think so. I must have known at the time I engaged her. I am sure she never goes to mass."

"That's all right. I think perhaps I do know of something that might suit her."

So much for the seed, but of course the most serious part of the difficulty was the soil in which it was to grow.

It so chanced, however, that when Enid's letter arrived, Mrs. Galbraith was deeply interested in an evangelical mission in Paris—a mission worked by English people—and she fancied she saw a "leading" in Mrs. Dalrymple's suggestion. If Wilhelmina really was to be the chosen vessel her grandmother dreamed of night and day, perhaps it was the Lord's will that Paris—that Sodom and Gomorrah of modern times—should be the scene of her labours.

"Bairn," she said pathetically, overcoming for the moment her rigid reserve, "I'm taking an awful responsibility upon myself. I am putting in your hand the key to a world lying in wickedness. Mind, mind, if you enter in, that you go as the messenger of the Lord!"

She took off her spectacles, wiped them slowly, and opened the great Bible.

"We'll not take the usual lesson to-day," she said. "Hearken, bairn." And she read in her quavering voice—

"'Awake, awake; put on thy strength, O Zion, put on thy beautiful garments, O Jerusalem, the holy city; for henceforth there shall no more come into thee the uncircumcised and unclean.

"'Shake thyself from the dust; arise, and sit down, O Jerusalem; loose thyself from the bands of thy neck, O captive daughter of Zion. For thus saith the Lord, Ye have sold yourselves for nought, and ye shall be redeemed without money. . . .

"'How beautiful upon the mountains are the feet of him that bringeth good tidings, that publisheth peace; that bringeth good tidings of good, that publisheth salvation; that saith unto Zion, Thy God reigneth!

"'The watchmen shall lift up the voice; with the voice together shall they sing; for they shall see eye to eye when the Lord shall bring again Zion.

"'Break forth into joy, sing together ye waste places of Jerusalem; for the Lord hath comforted his people, he hath redeemed Jerusalem.'"

Wilhelmina listened mechanically. One lesson was the same to her as another, unless there was a story in it. Such poetry as this was far above the level of her mind, and she could not foresee how in later days it would ring in her ears like battle-music. Ah yes, when all is said, there are many worse training-schools than a home like Windyhaugh. "How beautiful upon the mountains are the feet of him that saith unto Zion, 'Thy God reigneth!'"

Pathos had to be on a lower level if it was to appeal to Wilhelmina at this time, and on a much lower level Jane contrived to supply it in abundance.

"I know how it will be," she said, day after day, "you'll forget all about your poor old nurse when the grand new mademoiselle comes."

"Oh, Jane, you know I won't love Mademoiselle the tiniest bit!"

" So you say, so you say! Before a week's out you'll have told her all our secrets."

Wilhelmina raised her head.

" I wouldn't be a *mean!* " she said indignantly.

" And you and she will have a lot of secrets of your own."

" I won't tell her a thing, not the least thing! And I'm sure I won't listen to her horrid old secrets. Besides, I daresay she'll tell them in French."

" You *used* to tell me things," Jane went on reproachfully.   •

The child's brow furrowed. This subject was threadbare, and she foresaw the retort. " I do tell you things, Jane," she said.

" Then tell me what you did with the red ribbon you were so fond of—that was round your chocolate-box."

Wilhelmina bit her lip. She was afraid of her nurse in this mood. " I can't tell you that,' she said timidly, but in a tone that was perfectly final.

Jane shook her roughly by the shoulder. " Nasty close little thing! " she said crossly. " It won't be a week before Mademoiselle gets it out of you! "

But she was well aware that she was losing her whip hand, and she felt constrained to make terms.

She put her arms caressingly round her charge's waist. These sudden changes of mood were in themselves nothing surprising. " You wouldn't like me to tell her about your chats with Mr. Darsie, would you? " she said—" or about the sweets he gives you? *She'd* soon tell your Grannie."

Wilhelmina raised solemn protesting eyes.

" There, there! You know I wouldn't do such a thing; and you won't tell her about—about the gentleman who meets us sometimes in our walks? "

" Course I won't! " said Wilhelmina. " Nor about the soldiers either."

" Oh, the soldiers! " said Jane contemptuously. " Soldiers speak to everybody. That's a way they have."

Mr. Darsie too had a word to say when he heard of the impending change in the household at Windyhaugh.

He was almost tempted at first to think that Mrs. Galbraith's detractors were right, and that the old lady was going out of her mind.

"Eh, Miss Williamina!" he cried. "That's no a guid hearin' ava. I dinna hold with the Frenchies. They're flighty folk—no' for the like o' you." He strove to think of anything he might add that would put the child on her guard against the wiles of the foreigner; but was forced to content himself with a philosophic reflection on the limitations of human influence.

The reader's sympathies are no doubt abundantly awakened for poor Mademoiselle, and in truth she was a small and harmless mouse to come out of such a mountain of apprehension. She had, it is true, no settled religious convictions; but, as she was not conscious of having lost any, she could scarcely be expected to be aware of their absence. She would have thought it very bad taste to talk to her pupils on such a subject, and, in any case, the "first five years" of Wilhelmina's life had been already appropriated.

It was late in the evening—late for Windyhaugh—when Mademoiselle drove under the limes. At this hour the pupils she had left would just be rising from dinner in their dainty evening dress; and the Frenchwoman's heart sank within her at the sight of the great silent rambling dimly-lighted house. She could not believe at first that this was really the normal aspect of affairs. She thought some sudden calamity in the form of illness or evil tidings had fallen upon the place; and Mrs. Galbraith's manner—hospitable though it was in a reserved Scotch fashion—certainly did not tend to dispel the impression.

In the course of a very brief interview, Mrs. Dalrymple had told Mademoiselle that the household at Windyhaugh was "quiet"; but "quiet" is a relative term, and Enid's surroundings were not such as to suggest that she placed a very rigid interpretation upon the word. In truth she scarcely considered an elderly governess to be of the same flesh and blood as herself.

Teacher and pupil did not meet till next morning,

and then Wilhelmina—feeling Jane's eye upon her—was as stony and unresponsive as even she could be. Children are true conservatives, and something in Mademoiselle struck the child immediately as "queer." She wished the little lady would go away, and leave her in peace with her dear Jane.

When twenty-four hours had passed, and Mademoiselle realised that she had now tasted a fair average sample of the life that lay before her, she was only deterred from immediate flight by the reflection that the railway station was four miles off. So she took refuge for the moment in a long letter to a friend in Paris. Poor Windyhaugh! Seldom' has an innocent, unpretending homestead been confronted with such an indictment. The climate, the situation, the building, the people, the *cuisine*—all in turn supplied her with a text on which to deliver her soul. Her eyes were red with crying when the housemaid knocked at the door.

"The mistress has gone to her room," she said. "She thought you might be tired and prefer your supper here."

Mademoiselle nodded. Her face was so woe-begone that the girl lingered on the threshold.

"I doubt you're homesick," she said in a friendly voice. "Everything'll seem strange at first."

Mademoiselle tried to smile. "It is a little sad—dull—here," she said. "Is it like this always—every day?"

The girl hesitated. She was anxious to offer consolation; but facts were strong.

"Sundays are different," she said deprecatingly at last. "If you know nobody in the place, I doubt you *will* be dull then!"

And so it proved.

When Sunday came the rain poured in torrents. Mademoiselle had not the least intention of going to church; but, so definite was Mrs. Galbraith's assumption to the contrary, that, without a word of protest on her own part, the poor little governess found herself wedged into the hired landau along with the old lady, Wilhelmina, and a maid-servant. The landau was an

expensive luxury, and must be made to serve as a means
of grace for as many as possible. The windows were
kept closed throughout the long drive, so there was nothing to be seen save the channels of rain as they made
their way down the translucent window-panes. Mademoiselle became almost hysterical in the effort to avoid
meeting the eyes of the others.

The old church was dark and chilly, and Mr. Carmichael's manner was less breezy than usual. The strain
of producing two sermons in the week was proving rather
heavy. He had the true pastoral eye, however, and he
did not fail to observe his new "hearer," nor to note the
fact that she seemed unhappy.

His was not the only eye that singled her out. If
Mademoiselle had been less absorbed in her misery, she
must surely have been aware of the trenchant gaze that
transfixed her obliquely from behind. Mr. Darsie was
striving to read her inmost soul; and, not being on
her guard, she certainly gave him every opportunity for
doing so. The one thing that really impressed her was
Wilhelmina's unimpeachable behaviour. The child sat
through the sermon, attentive and motionless as Mrs.
Galbraith herself.

"She does behave very well," said Mademoiselle when
they were seated once more in the stuffy carriage.

Mrs. Galbraith looked annoyed. The remark was not
inacceptable in itself; but it was most unsuited to Wilhelmina's ears.

"Indeed I'd be sorely ashamed of her if she didn't
behave well," she said severely. "I hope at her age she
has sense enough to know how highly she is privileged.
When one thinks of the thousands of children who grow
up in heathen lands——"

It is needless to quote the rest. Mademoiselle drew
as far as possible into her corner of the carriage, and
volunteered no further remarks.

There was an appreciable amount of solid comfort to
be derived from the cold beef and cold fruit-tart that
formed the midday meal. When that was over the old
lady said with the coldness that betokened timidity—

"I always have a little class with Wilhelmina on Sun-

day afternoon, now that I'm not able to go a second time
to church. You are welcome to join us if you like."

But the worm turned.

"Thank you, I will go to my own room," said
Mademoiselle. "I too have some religious books in
my box."

She made her escape at once lest any effort should be
made to detain her; but I need scarcely say that the book
she took from her box was not strictly religious.

Mrs. Galbraith was relieved to see her go. In truth
the invitation had been far more magnanimous than the
Frenchwoman supposed.

The class began with prayer, and then Wilhelmina
"said her ticket." It was the last of four, which were
now duly exchanged for a "big one," as Mr. Darsie had
said. The ticket was followed by the repetition of a
hymn and of several answers from the Shorter Cate-
chism; and thus was ushered in the solemn business of
the afternoon—the reading of a portion of the Bible in
Mrs. Galbraith's monotonous voice, with the running
accompaniment of Matthew Henry's Commentary.

It *was* dull, and yet Wilhelmina was forced to listen
with one ear on account of the questions that were to
follow. One ear was sufficient, however, for the old lady
had not been educated in a modern training-college, and
was apt to word her questions in such a way that, after
a little experience of her method, the answer could
scarcely be missed.

"I'll put the things away, Grannie," said Wilhelmina cheerfully when the long ordeal was over; and, as
soon as Mrs. Galbraith had left the room for her afternoon rest, the child proceeded—like the actors who seek
recreation in each other's theatres—to play at Sunday
School!

Not a moment was lost before the decks were cleared
for action. Bibles, commentary, and hymn-books were
now converted into benches. Small paper booklets, more
or less attractively attired in pink, white, or grey covers,
represented the scholars. A larger booklet was wont to
do duty as teacher, but Wilhelmina could not lay her
hands on this at first. Such trifling hitches were wel-

comed as affording opportunity for a little legitimate by-
play, and the scholars forthwith took advantage of the
interval.   .

"Teacher's late," said one innocently.

"Perhaps she's ill," said another. "Let's go out and
play."

They were on their way to the door when the teacher
appeared, and a certain amount of horse-play ensued.
Wilhelmina was quite artist enough to feel the necessity
of relieving the game with touches of comedy. In this
case, I fear, it degenerated into farce, and some of the
scholars played quite openly to the gallery.

They were called to order, however, and the class proceeded. The opening exercises were reduced to a minimum, and then the "hearing of tickets" began. This
was the *raison d'être* of the whole game, and, to appreciate the point of it, the reader must remember that each
scholar was as distinct an individuality in Wilhelmina's
eyes as are the horses entered for the Derby in the estimation of the turf.

Solemnly closing her eyes to ensure impartiality, she
took a ticket from the box and read it aloud—

"'Blessed are the merciful, for they shall obtain
mercy.'

"'*Blessed.*'" She glanced over the title of the first
book in search of the word; but it did not appear in that,
nor indeed in any of those assembled.

"'*Are.*'" This was more hopeful. It did not occur
in the first nor in the second; but it did occur in the
title of the third, so the third scholar—rejoicing in the
cognomen of "Are you happy?"—claimed the prize.

Thus the game went on. Sometimes every word in
the text was exhausted before the ticket was earned, and
it had to be put back in the box, having served only as
the excuse for a severe reprimand on the part of the
teacher.

"I really will not take the trouble to come and teach
you," she would say, "if you can't learn your texts better
than that. There's nothing to laugh at, Sunshine. Go
and stand in the corner."

"Sunshine and Storm," a torn and unattractive grey

book, accustomed to the rôle of scapegoat, was placed in the corner accordingly.

"And your frock isn't mended yet," pursued the teacher relentlessly. "You are quite incorr—incorr——" The delicious big word that Aunt Enid had applied with such effect to Hugh when she was angry with him, danced tantalizingly just out of reach. "You are a very bad girl, Sunshine."

The game was not highly intellectual, I confess, nor had it any profound spiritual significance; but, when relieved by plentiful touches of comedy, it helped to pass the time amazingly. And the beauty of the whole scheme was that, if anyone came to the door of the room, a sweep of Wilhelmina's strong little arm was sufficient to destroy all traces of her guilt. She could be scolded for nothing worse than for strewing the books over the table. On such occasions the closing exercises had to be murmured in a whisper over the ruins.

These closing exercises were absolutely *de rigueur.* Not having a companion to urge her on and to chase away self-consciousness, Wilhelmina suffered from a recurrent suspicion that this fascinating game was displeasing in the eyes of God. So, before putting away the books, she would close her eyes, drop her chubby chin on her breast, and pray devoutly—

"Forgive us our sins, Lord, for Christ's sake. Amen."

She thought it more prudent not to specify exactly what the sins were to which she referred, and in this respect I fear she resembled her betters. Mother Church shows her wisdom when she compels her children to give a name to their iniquities. Regarded simply as a means of moral progress, confession is surely more helpful to the rank and file of humanity when it says, "I ate too much of that lobster mayonnaise last night," than when it lays claim to the proud but indefinite position of the "chief of sinners."

If conscience was unusually alert, Wilhelmina added a clause to her prayer and said, "Forgive us our sins, Lord, and *make us good,* for Christ's sake. Amen." But when the fascination of the game was upon her, she

5

quite shared St. Augustine's human dread of being
"made good" too quickly. We learn, alas, as we grow
older, that we need not have been at all uneasy on that
score!

So sped the afternoon; but Sunday evening was still
to come—there was no shirking that!—Sunday evening
with its nameless melancholy, its twilight, its distant
church bells, its thoughts of eternity! At this hour Wilhelmina was wont to wander listlessly about the house
in search of distraction, landing as a rule in the old-
fashioned kitchen, where she listened to conversation of
which she understood little, and might with advantage
have understood even less.

The governess would gladly have taken shelter in the
kitchen, too, before the evening was over, but that of
course was out of the question.

"Did ye see the new mademoiselle in the kirk the
day?" said Mr. Darsie to his minister. "It's a queer
like thing for Mistress Galbraith to have done. I doubt
she'll no' have a vera guid influence on little Miss Williamina."

"Why?"

"Eh, they're flighty folk, thae Frenchwomen, ta'en
up wi' their dress an' their folderols an' the like."

"I am sure this one was quiet enough—almost
dowdy."

"Na," put in the old man quickly and decisively.
"I thocht sae mysel' at the first; but when I cam' to
tak' a guid look, there was a perkiness about the set o'
her bonnet that I didna approve o'. She may be a well-
meaning woman eneugh, but it was easy to see frae the
ways o' her during the service that she hasna muckle o'
the spirit."

Poor Mademoiselle!

Let us hope there is no Mr. Darsie in the pew behind
you and me.

CHAPTER IX.

A NEW REGIME.

Few things could be worse for the nervous system of a child than was the emotional strain to which Wilhelmina was subjected during the next few weeks.

" See and learn your lessons nicely," the kind-hearted housemaid had said. " It's lonesome here for Mademoiselle, and the time may come when you're a stranger in a strange land yourself."

Wilhelmina did not reply. Hitherto her loyalty to Jane had prompted her to pay little attention to Mademoiselle's instructions, but the temptation to show how clever she could be was great, and she was glad to have an excuse for yielding to it. Her memory was not, as Enid had described it, " prodigious," but it was excellent; and her receptivity was quite above the average. Moreover her ear was true, and she had few interests in life to distract her attention from her French lessons. So she threw herself into the work—and Jane made her suffer accordingly.

But from that day the tide of Mademoiselle's misery turned, at least for a time. She would have told you quite frankly that she taught for her daily bread, and in order to make provision for her old age; but although she never acknowledged it, she felt a subtle thrill of joy in a responsive pupil that linked her to the born teachers in all ages. She loved her language as some men love their religion, and, although she could teach it on no modern nor logical system, she taught it well, insisting with infinite care on a pure production of the vowel-sounds.

" *Mieux,*" she said.

" Mioo," said Wilhelmina.

Mademoiselle closed the book.

" Now, let us understand one another, little one. *Eu* is not *oo*. It is as different from it as light is from darkness. No, you come no nearer it when you close up

your lips and say *u.* You must listen to me often, often;
then take plenty of time, and open your mouth wide.
I have not met ten—no, not five—English people, outside my own pupils, who could say *eu.*"

Her ambition thus fired, Wilhelmina determined that
she would add one to the choice little circle on which
Mademoiselle had been pleased to set her *cachet,* and,
long after she went to bed at night, her efforts could
be heard.

"Mew, mew, mew!" said Jane irritably. "I never
heard the like. If that's all Mademoiselle came to teach
you, it seems to me the cat would have done as well!"

To which Mademoiselle would have replied that Tabby certainly came nearer the *articulation* of "mieux"
than did most English people, inasmuch as she at least
took the trouble to open her mouth.

But Jane really was unbearable in those days. She
constantly took her charge to task for a lack of affection; she seized every excuse for bouncing into the
schoolroom to make sure that no endearments were taking place between governess and pupil; and she practised
an irritating supervision of Mademoiselle's habits and
customs in the hope of discovering something that would
discredit the new arrival in the eyes of Mrs. Galbraith,
and of the household.

Mademoiselle, on her part, was of course not devoid
of blame. She had treated Jane from the first as a
mere servant, ignoring the privileges due a person
whose father had been coachman in the family as long
as it was in a position to keep a coachman at all.

Christmas was drawing near when the strain was unexpectedly relaxed. Jane was summoned to the sickbed
of her mother; and, although Wilhelmina shed many
genuine tears, I think at the bottom of her heart she
was thankful to be free. She spent most of her time
now with Mademoiselle, drinking in French as, in her
babyhood, she had drunk in her mother tongue. Mademoiselle, on her part, made Wilhelmina's progress the
main object of her life: but for that, she wrote to her
friends, Windyhaugh would have driven her crazy. "I
little thought that at my time of life I should enter a

convent; but so it is, and I assure you the step—if advisable at all—should be taken in early life."

"Run on into the warden," she said to the child one day when it was time for their walk. "I will join you in a moment."

But great was her surprise when a few minutes later she found Wilhelmina swinging on the gate in earnest conversation with a soldier.

"*Mais, mon Dieu!*" cried the governess, forgetting in her excitement how much Wilhelmina had been shocked by the expression on a previous occasion, "how had he the effrontery to stop and speak to you? This is Jane's doing!"

"No, no, Mademoiselle!" exclaimed the child too eagerly. "It was only a soldier," she added a moment later. "Soldiers speak to every one, you know. It's a way they have."

Mademoiselle looked appalled.

"*Mon Dieu!*" she cried again, heedless now whether her pupil was shocked or not. "It is not Mrs. Galbraith whom you have heard say that!"

Wilhelmina seemed to be painfully aware that it was not.

"It is possible you do not know that soldiers are just the worst of all?"

Any aspersion on her intelligence cut the child to the quick. "No," she said. "I thought the other kind was worst."

"What other kind?" Mademoiselle's keen perceptions scented mischief.

But Wilhelmina saw she had gone too far.

"*Any* other kind," she answered doggedly.

"My child, are you not aware that it is not *comme il faut* to speak to *any* man whom you do not know? And soldiers! Of course if it is an officer who has been introduced to you by your family—that is another thing; but these soldiers here, they are—*canaille!*"

This sounded terrible in its incomprehensibility, and Wilhelmina began to fear that the story would find its way to Mrs. Galbraith's ears.

"Mademoiselle," she said coaxingly, raising a chubby

pathetic face, "I don't believe he is a *real* soldier! I asked him once about his battles, and he said he had never been in one!"

But Mademoiselle did not seem to find this evidence particularly conclusive.

She would certainly have spoken to Mrs. Galbraith, but she and the old lady had never taken to each other, and she reflected that no farther harm could be done while Jane was away. In the meantime Mademoiselle resolved to keep a strict look-out.

A few days later, when governess and pupil were walking on the outskirts of Queensmains, they met a showily-dressed man, belonging apparently to the shop-keeping class, who looked at Wilhelmina as if he would fain have spoken. The child did not meet his eye; but her face flushed so red that Mademoiselle's suspicions were aroused.

"Do you know that person?" she asked seductively.

"No," said Wilhelmina stoutly.

"He seems to know you."

"No." But the child sighed. Here was another lie, and, although there was no real use in being good till one was converted, every lie did make it seem so much less likely that she could possibly belong to the elect. She did not recover her spirits till Mademoiselle unexpectedly turned in to the shop next door to the grocer's.

"I've got a penny to spend," pleaded the child. "May I run in and buy some sweets so as not to keep you waiting?"

"No, no. There's a much nicer sweet-shop than that."

Wilhelmina's lip quivered. "He's got the partic'lar kind of butter-scotch I like."

"*Eh bien! Dépêche-toi.*"

Wilhelmina turned like a dog at the magic words, "Paid for!"

And her welcome was worth going to meet. Mr. Darsie's old face beamed, and he made short work of the customer he was serving.

"Eh, Missy, but ye're a sicht for sair e'en," he cried.

"If I hadna seen ye i' the kirk on Sabbaths, I'd ha' thocht ye was awa' wi' your nurse."

Wilhelmina shook her head. "It's Mademoiselle," she said apologetically. "She's so dreadfully partic'lar about the—the gentlemen I speak to."

"Weel, weel, I've nae doubt she's richt."

"I'm not sure that she'd even let me smile to *you* in the street without asking a lot of questions; but, if we meet you, you'll know I'm smiling *inside*."

"I will that. It's ower late to prevent you an' me frae bein' freens, but, if she speirs, you only need to tell her I'm an auld body that sits ahint ye in the kirk. Mr. Carmichael tells me she's gey wiselike. Nae doubt she's making a gran' scholar o' ye?"

Wilhelmina nodded. "I like French," she said.

"My word! Ou ay, Mademoiselle's a better companion for ye than yon nurse o' yours."

"No, no!" cried Wilhelmina. "I *love* Jane!"

He smiled and stroked her hair timidly with his worn old hand. "Puir lassie! puir bit thing!" he said gently. "Weel, an' what did ye think o' the sermon on Sabbath?"

She did not reply; but he guessed from the quickness of her breathing that something serious was coming.

"Mr. Darsie," she said at last, "you must have met a lot of the elect in your time?"

Here was a poser! Perhaps the theologian and the man-of-the-world suggested widely different answers, and while he weighed one against the other, the old man had much ado to keep his face straight.

"Weel"—he said slowly—"ye'd wonder! Maybe no sae mony as ye'd think, Miss Mina."

"Far more than I have?"

"Oh, nae doubt!"

She poked her umbrella into a chink in the floor. "And were they—were most of them good sort of people —in a common way, you know—before they were converted?"

He looked perplexed.

"I mean," said the child desperately, "of course till they were converted you couldn't tell whether they were elect or not. But afterwards—when you came to think about it—had most of them been good?—sort of good, you know?"

His face was grave. "Eh, Missy, I'd be loath to answer 'yes' or 'no' to that; but I'm fain to think God's ain elect had aye gude stuff in them!"

This was hopeful so far. She thought he would say, if asked, that she too had good stuff in her.

"On the one hand there's the story o' Cornelius," he went on reflectively, taking refuge on the sure ground of history; "on the other hand there's John Bunyan. Ye'll have heard o' his Grace Abounding to the Chief of Sinners—that was himsel', ye ken."

A minute later Wilhelmina went bounding back to the draper's where she had left Mademoiselle. It was annoying to find that she might have stayed a little longer; the governess was still absorbed in her purchases.

"Well," she said absently, "did you get the partic'-lar kind of butter-scotch?"

The child's face fell. She had forgotten all about it!

But she did not forget to rout out Grace Abounding from the library shelves, and she fell asleep that night with the musty old book in her arms.

CHAPTER X.

FOG.

WHEN Mademoiselle had spent a couple of months at Windyhaugh, she assumed—somewhat rashly—that at least she knew the worst of the old place. It was dull beyond conception, of course; but the very extremity of its dulness provided food for those piquant letters on which she not unjustly prided herself; and, when things seemed intolerable, she often laughed to think how she would entertain her friends when she was free to reveal by word of mouth the secrets of her prison-house.

Her pupil's progress, too, continued to be a matter of
real interest; and, by dint of making the most of every
scrap of gossip—not to say scandal—that came within
reach, the governess hoped to be able to endure her surroundings till midsummer. She no longer had any scruples about joining the servants in the fine old kitchen
when the day's work was done; and, although they
showed a laudable freemasonry in their information
about the absent Jane, they said enough to convince
Mademoiselle that the girl had mistaken her vocation.
For the first time now she heard, too, the mysterious tales
about Wilhelmina's father with which the neighbourhood
was rife, and he began to loom in her imagination
as an injured hero of romance. "He is certainly a
roué," she wrote—"though of *such* a superior kind!—
and who can wonder? I shall be ripe for a round of the
music-halls myself when I leave Windyhaugh, and, if
there is a *risqué* item in the programme, I am sure *I*
shan't be the one to protest. You can't imagine how de-
moralising the religious life is!"

So, what with one thing and another, she bore up
wonderfully till Christmas came. She had expected
little from the festival, but, beyond a few greetings from
absent friends, it brought her absolutely nothing. The
day was simply ignored. "And we call ourselves a
Christian household!"

To be sure, it was to the Lord that the day was not
regarded; but, in spite of the religious books—in her
box—Mademoiselle could scarcely be expected to appreciate the distinction.

When evening came, she shed actual tears in the
kitchen over Wilhelmina's hard fate, and made the
mouths of the servants water as she related tales of the
kind of Christmas she had been wont to spend in the
South.

But in truth Wilhelmina considered herself a very
lucky little girl. In addition to Mademoiselle's Christmas greetings, the postman had actually brought a book-
packet that morning addressed to her very self! She
had not been able to believe her eyes at first, and,
when at length she was convinced, she had opened it

with the most reverent care. "Wilhelmina, with love from Hugh and Gavin," was the inscription on the fly-leaf.

"Not from Aunt Enid herself?" asked the child wist-fully.

"But yes, to be sure," answered Mademoiselle quick-ly. "It is really from her, though she has put the boys' names in it."

Wilhelmina clasped the gaily bound volume to her breast. "*Dear* Aunt Enid!" she murmured.

The book was the bound volume of a children's paper —rather below the intellectual level of this particular child. Presumably Mrs. Dalrymple had forgotten the "prodigious memory" of which she had spoken to Mr. Galbraith; and indeed, when one reflects on the endless round of shopping—in her comfortable brougham, of course—that Christmas meant for her—the only wonder is that she remembered Wilhelmina at all.

But the child was far too happy to be critical. She pored over the sparsely-printed pages of the book, and weeks went by before she would even allow herself to admit that "there wasn't much reading in it."

New Year's day passed as Christmas had done. "After the pudding had left the table," wrote Made-moiselle, "it flashed upon me that there may have been an extra plum in it; but at that stage of affairs it was of course too late to institute inquiries." True, Mrs. Galbraith celebrated the day by the donation of flannels and coal to Mrs. Tail-o'-the-week, and other folk of the kind; but so careful was she to keep her left hand un-aware of the doings of her right, that her household failed to wring the least drop of seasonable excitement from her charities.

Then the weather turned against them, and that was the most unkindest cut of all. Rain and wind there had been in plenty, but now a thick fog came up from the sea, and hung over the homestead like a cloud of doom. At first it was amusing, but, by the third day, it was becoming almost terrible. Mrs. Galbraith's great idea was to "keep it out of the house," so no windows were opened, and the air became stifling. Mademoiselle's spirits failed completely, and Wilhelmina began to look as if she had committed a crime. Most of us have a weak point that is the first to suffer under a strain. Mademoiselle's weak point was her head; Wilhelmina's was her conscience. She could keep it at bay during daylight, though she was not allowed to leave the house; but she began to dread the nights unspeakably.

Fortunately, on the fourth day an event occurred that broke the dreaded monotony. The fog did not clear away. No, but the cat kittened. "And I assure you," wrote Mademoiselle, "no long-delayed birth of an heir to a noble house was ever hailed with warmer acclamations than was the arrival of those three morsels of felinity. I fear the moral effect on Tabby will be disastrous, but we are all too glad of the distraction to think of her character and welfare."

At the end of a week the fog was dispersed by a gale; but the gale brought snow which rendered the roads impassable, and, before the resulting slush was gone, the fog returned.

"No," said Mademoiselle. "'The life is more than meat and the body raiment.' I must go."

She was leaning against the garden gate, and her long wavering had just ended in this conclusion, when a cheerful face broke through the fog.

"Ah, Monsieur," she cried, "so there really are some men still out there in the world?"

Mr. Carmichael laughed. "There are," he said—"a few that one could dispense with even. Had you begun to doubt it?"

She nodded, and, to her great disgust, her eyes filled with tears. Really her nerves were going to pieces in this terrible place.

He took note of her tears in his own fashion.

"You are well met," he said cordially. "I was hoping to see you by yourself for a few minutes. I wanted to ask your advice. A friend has asked me to recommend a few modern French books—fiction that steers a middle course between the Scylla of goodiness and the Charybdis——"

She nodded again with ready comprehension, and for

some time they paced up and down the avenue discussing literature. When that subject flagged, he fell back on Paris. He had spent a week in the gay metropolis during his student days, and the amount of capital he had made out of that week in his conversations with Mademoiselle was not a little to his credit.

"I fear it is dull here in this trying weather," he said at last, when she was obviously herself again.

"Oh, Monsieur, dull? No! Leave that mild little word for the prisons and reformatories!"

He laughed. "Is it so bad as that?"

"I can't tell you what it is. No *fête de Noël!* no *jour de l'an.* I assure you I have wept for the *pauvre petite.*"

She was a tactful woman, Mademoiselle. She had taken his measure carefully, and was now giving him just as much of her native language as was likely to flatter without overwhelming him.

"No one could wish for a better pupil," she continued, "but it is no use. I cannot stand it. I grow ill and unnerved. Just as you came I have made up my mind that I must go."

"Ah!" he said. "That will be a great loss to the child."

Mademoiselle sighed. "I too have many regrets in leaving her, especially as her nurse is not a person to be trusted."

Mr. Carmichael remembered vaguely that Mr. Darsie had remarked the same thing.

"That is serious," he said.

"I assure you it is very serious. I wish you would counsel me, Monsieur. The young woman is away just now, and, as I mean to leave myself—— One is unwilling to do an injury to a girl who must earn her bread."

He drew down his brows, as his habit was. "Have you definite facts?"

"But yes, yes."

"Then surely your path is clear. Speak to the young woman herself. If she has done anything wrong, persuade her to own up to her mistress. At the worst she

will do it to prevent your doing it, and you are bound
to give her that much moral chance."

Mademoiselle laughed—one of those light little
laughs that float like bubbles on the well of worldly
wisdom.

" Ah, Monsieur ! " she cried.

But he continued to look at her gravely, and she was
forced to go on.

She could turn the facts into nothing, if she had the
relating of them. Mrs. Galbraith believes in her, and
she has never quite believed that a Frenchwoman may
be honest. I suppose I had better let things alone. I
shall only burn my fingers if I interfere."

" Then burn your fingers in God's name," he said
gravely, " if there is any question of injury to the child.
But, if I were you, I should speak to the young woman
herself first. Do you think Mrs. Galbraith will be able
to see me this afternoon ? "

They had come in sight of the house, and of poor
captive Wilhelmina, whose woe-begone, conscience-rid-
den face was pressed against the window-pane. Her
expression changed in a moment when she saw she was
observed.

" You have never walked from Queensmains through
such roads," said Mrs. Galbraith as she greeted the minister.

" No; my landlady is ill, and I am spending a few
days with her brother, Mr. Dalgleish, at the farm here.
He has offered me his gig for the afternoon, and, now
that the sun is trying to break through, I want you to
lend me Wilhelmina. She looks as if a drive would do
her good, and it is time she and I made friends. I will
bring her back quite safely before dark."

So Wilhelmina was smothered in wraps, and perched
up on the high seat beside her pastor. The sun fairly
broke through the clouds, and the colour came to her
cheeks as they trotted swiftly along. She was dreadfully shy at first, but she soon began to look as if a
mountain of apprehension had been lifted from her
mind, and she chatted gaily, as a child should, about
the people and things they passed on the way.

At the grocer's door, Mr. Carmichael drew up, and took her in his arms.

"A visitor, Mr. Darsie!" he cried. "I will leave her here for half-an-hour in case she should catch cold, while I make a few brief visitations."

"My word!" cried the old man delightedly. He left the boy to mind the shop, and took his little lady upstairs to the snug sitting-room, where he contrived to find a slice of cake. She still felt the exhilaration of the drive, and prattled away light-heartedly; but when the time drew near for her to go, she became suddenly pale and silent, and began to tug at her damp little hands.

"Mr. Darsie," she said at last in a hurried undertone, taking the fence at a run, "I get so frightened at nights now. I can't help saying things against the Holy Ghost—in my mind, you know, not loud out—and I pray for the awfullest things. Last night I couldn't help praying God to make me blind before morning!"

Her face quivered painfully, and she looked as the prisoner might who awaits the appearance of the black cap.

The old man laughed quite tenderly as, for the first time, he lifted her on his knee.

"But He didna do it, did He, Miss Mina? Na, na! I wouldna wonner but He was better employed. The Lord's no' in sic a hurry to answer our prayers when they're wiselike that He should pay ony attention to foolishness like yon. Put your mind past it a'thegither; an' if the thochts will come, just think o' something bonny—your books, or your dolls for the matter o' that. It's a peety to pay ower muckle attention to the wiles o' the devil."

Wilhelmina could not speak; but she clasped the old hand in both of hers, and the blood rushed back into her face with such force that it almost blinded her.

It is not the cassock that makes the priest—and, whatever his own spiritual experiences may have been, old Mr. Darsie had not studied the lives of the saints for nothing.

CHAPTER XI.

A BOLT FROM THE BLUE.

"Flighty she may be," said Mrs. Galbraith, "and I know she is quick in the temper; but she has grown up in an honest family under my own eye, and I have every reason to believe she is a Christian woman."

"Oh, no doubt she is that!" said Mademoiselle flippantly. She had grown sick of the word "Christian" at Windyhaugh, and she thought the sarcasm would escape Mrs. Galbraith.

But the old lady was not quite a fool. "I am sorry you have not been happy with us," she said with dignity. "I know it is very quiet here. I am too old to care for worldly gaiety, and I am anxious that the child should grow up independent of it. Besides, in the country here it is not easy to provide entertainment for our—for those who sojourn with us."

"One would think I had asked for a Punch and Judy show on the lawn!" thought Mademoiselle indignantly, and the tears gathered in her eyes. She had meant to take this opportunity of striking a blow for Wilhelmina; but, behold, the fortress was quite impregnable!

"It grieves my heart to part with the child," she said. "I never had a better pupil. Already she can read a little French story with charming accent. I am sure her father would be proud of it." Poor Mademoiselle! How she had longed for some accident that might bring Mr. Galbraith to pass a skilled opinion on her work.

The old lady winced. She quite appreciated the slight stress on the word "father."

"I hope you will get some one to take my place," continued Mademoiselle. "It is a thousand pities that the lessons should be interrupted."

Mrs. Galbraith smiled quietly. "I have no doubt you have done your duty well," she said; "but—I fear our country life is not adapted to your countrywomen."

This was too hard.

"But, Madame," cried the little governess, you are unjust! I have met many, many of *your* countrywomen, and I find them no less frivolous than my own. I too have been—ah, so happy!—in the country; but here—here——!"

It was useless. She had not an arrow in her quiver that was worth trying against a citadel like that.

Mrs. Galbraith rose to her feet with a sigh. She was not feeling well to-day, and this interview had excited and tired her.

"I hope the maids have done all they could for you," she said courteously. "I will tell cook to prepare your sandwiches."

The word "cook" always irritated Mademoiselle. She had never, she declared, seen anything at Windyhaugh that justified the name of cookery, and poor old Ann figured in her letters under the soubriquet of the *cordon bleu.* In truth Ann's position approached as nearly that of confidential servant as was possible where Mrs. Galbraith was the mistress. She was the one person in the house—perhaps the one in the world—for whom the old lady was really a human being, to be loved and cared for as well as respected and feared.

"Ann," said her mistress now, "you will see that Mademoiselle has some sandwiches; and as soon as Jane comes, send her up to speak to me."

The woman saw that something was wrong.

"Yes, ma'am," she said. "Can I bring you a cup of soup, ma'am? You made a very poor dinner."

"No, no. I want nothing now. Send Jane up as soon as she comes."

Meanwhile Mademoiselle was seeking her pupil in the garden.

"Ah, *petite,*" she said, "I wish I could say anything to convince you *how* important it is that you should not forget what I have taught you. You will have a battle to fight with life some day, and I have put one weapon in your hand—a better weapon than you know. Don't throw it away! You can think of nothing now but your dear Jane "—Wilhelmina's eyes were scanning the highroad—" but promise me one thing. Promise that every day you will read aloud one of the little French stories you have read with me—carefully, carefully, saying to yourself, 'Is that how Mademoiselle would like to hear it?'"

"Why, of course I will, Mademoiselle," said Wilhelmina readily, "and I am so sorry you are going;" but her eyes still scanned the highroad.

Mademoiselle drove off in a hired trap, and ten minutes later Jane arrived on the baker's cart. She looked flustered and unlike herself, but she clasped Wilhelmina in her arms with all the old fondness. "1 didn't forget you," she whispered. "I've got a doll in my box—not very grand, but the nicest I could get."

"The mistress wants to see you at once," said Ann quietly, and, with a vague sense that something serious was impending, she ushered the girl into the old lady's room.

"Well, Jane," said Mrs. Galbraith, "I hope your mother is really better."

Jane seemed sorely nervous and upset. "Yes, ma'am, thank you," she stammered; "but she can't do without me as well as she once could. I think—that is, I'm afraid—I shall have to go back to her in a month or so."

"I hope the doctor doesn't think there is anything serious?"

"No, ma'am, no. But I think—she thinks—I had better go home."

Her manner was so distraught that Mrs. Galbraith looked at her sharply. "She could turn the facts into nothing," Mademoiselle had said, "if she had the relating of them;" but there are facts that cannot be turned, facts that need no relating.

Mrs. Galbraith rose to her feet, pale with righteous indignation.

"Jane," she said, "is it possible?—you that I have known from a bairn?—is it possible you have deceived me?"

The girl dropped down on her knees.

"Oh, ma'am," she cried, "I am engaged to him, I am indeed! He had promised to marry me by now."

G

" Is he here ? "

" At Queensmains."

" So that is what brought you back—for a month," said Mrs. Galbraith drily. " No, Jane, it won't do. You must go home to-morrow. And to think that I trusted you with the child! Go downstairs—go, go. I cannot speak to you now. I will see you before you leave. Tell Ann to send Wilhelmina to me."

Tell Ann to send Wilhelmina! It was more than Jane could bear. " Oh, my darling, my darling!" she cried, waylaying the child on the stair. " They'll teach you to look on me as the dirt under your feet; but I aye loved you, I did indeed!"

" See an' not anger your Grannie," said Ann severely. " She's no' hersel' the day."

All this was quite sufficient to shake Wilhelmina's nerve for the interview, and the sight of her grandmother looking flushed and disturbed did not tend to reassure her.

" Wilhelmina," began the old lady; and then she stopped. Her heart was so full of love and fear for the child that she had not reflected how difficult it would be to express her feelings in words.

So there was a painful silence.

" Wilhelmina," she began again, " I fear your nurse is not as good a woman as I thought her."

" I think she's good," said Wilhelmina quickly. She had long suspected that Jane was not converted. Had Grannie only now discovered the fact?

" I trusted you to her, and I doubt she's deceived me. I hear she has made you acquainted with—people—that weren't fitting company for the like of you."

" No, she didn't," said Wilhelmina stoutly. " I only saw them now and then. Oh, dear! I hope she won't think I told."

" What do you mean, child? You only saw them now and then?"

" She left me behind."

" Where did she leave you?"

" In a shop."

" What shop?"

Wilhelmina hesitated, but she had been told not to anger her grannie. " Mr. Darsie's."

One would have thought this likely to be reassuring enough; but Mr. Darsie, with all the respectability conferred on him by his proud position as an elder of the kirk, had a reputation for being a trifle " unsoond," and to Mrs. Galbraith " unsoondness " was almost worse than immorality.

" Mr. Darsie! " she said, " and what did you and he find to talk about? "

Wilhelmina hesitated again.

" Sermons and things," she said at last. So long as Grannie did not find out about the sweets, surely no great harm was done.

Mrs. Galbraith wrung her hands.

" Bairn," she said, " Jane's not a good woman. She's going away. I don't say a word against Mr. Darsie. He's an elder of the kirk; but he's not a fitting companion for you. You'll smile to him when you meet him, of course; but you must promise that you won't go into his shop any more, or speak to him more than you can help! "

This was too much. Wilhelmina forgot all about Ann's warning.

" *I won't* " she cried. " I love Jane! I love Mr. Darsie! They are my two partic'lar friends. I *must* see them! "

She was prepared for almost anything in return for so unprecedented an outburst; but what happened was precisely the thing she did not expect. The old lady did not speak. She was looking so queer. She made a little movement with one of her hands, and then, to Wilhelmina's horror, she began to slip heavily over sideways in her high-backed chair.

The child rushed to support her, but had only strength enough to break the inevitable fall.

" Grannie, Grannie! " she said.

There was no reply. She was not dead. No, her face was still red, and she was breathing so loud. It was terrible to have her so near, and yet so far away.

Wilhelmina lay the poor grey head on the floor.

" *Grannie!* " she cried again.

Then with a bound she reached the door.

"Jane! Jane! *Ann!*" she shrieked. " Grannie's tumbled down. Come quick! *Come quick!* "

CHAPTER XII.

TEA AT RUMPELMAYER'S.

SUNSHINE without a cloud, and the blue water breaking with a delicious splash on the shingle of the beach.

The band was playing a waltz by Strauss in the pavilion among the palm-trees, and Enid sat just within hearing of it as she sipped her afternoon tea from Rumpelmayer's dainty china.

. She looked like the very spirit of the Riviera in a wonderful toilette that flashed subtly into blues and greens; and not a few curious glances were directed towards the chair she had reserved.

Yet the man who took it eventually did not seem to be overwhelmed by a sense of his privileges. He was a great, bluff, tweeded, well-groomed Englishman, and at the present moment he was in a very surly humour.

"Bad luck, I see," said Enid laconically in the well-modulated voice that is so seldom heard in places where the nations congregate. "Have some tea?"

He nodded to the attendant who offered it.

"Deuced bad luck," he said under his breath. "I shan't go near the confounded place again."

"Oh, you are going to take me one day next week— unless Ronald comes out. *I* never have bad luck." And she sighed. She did so hate to see money thrown away!

He shook himself like a great St. Bernard, and changed the subject. "I met Gavin out there on his donkey. What a capital seat the little fellow has already!"

She nodded. "I had a letter from Hugh this morning."

"Oh? I suppose he is delighted at the prospect of joining us at Easter."

"I think so. He always expresses himself philosophically, that young man. He wants to bring a ferret with him."

"Good Lord!"

"Is anxious to know if he will have to pay duty on it."

"I should think there is no precedent. Tell him they will retain the ferret at Calais while they bring the question before the ministry."

"Are they vicious things?"

"Custom house officers?"

"No. I know all about *them*. Ferrets aren't as bad as that, are they?"

"Much the same, I fancy; and, as Hugh is certain to starve the little brute sooner or later, it will have abundant excuse for making a meal off anyone who comes handy."

Enid sighed. "I do hate to disappoint him." She always found that absence endeared her son to her, and she gave it abundant opportunity of doing so.

"Don't disappoint him. Tell him to stay at home with the ferret."

"Poor boy!" She drew the letter from her pocket. "Oh, I see, there is a postscript over the page—'P.S. The ferret isn't born yet.'"

Mr. Dalrymple threw back his head, and laughed as only an Englishman can. "Let us hope there has been some little miscalculation as to dates. I have known it happen. Have you finished your tea? Come out. I want to talk to you."

It was a considerable time, however, before he said—

"Who do you think I saw at Monte Carlo?—enjoying a jolly run of luck too!"

"Not Ronald?"

"No. George Galbraith."

"Indeed! Well, I am glad of it, poor fellow. Did you speak to him?"

Mr. Dalrymple nodded. "He says he met you at the Cosmopolis in the autumn."

" Yes. Didn't I mention it ? "

" No."

" Really ? George Galbraith's little dinners deserve more notice than that, I assure you."

" Dinners! Did you dine with him ? "

" At the hotel. We met by chance."

Mr. Dalrymple seemed to find some difficulty in going on.

" I'll tell you what it is, Enid," he said at last: " you mustn't see more of that fellow than you can help. You may have to drop him any day, and you needn't make the business more difficult than necessary."

" I haven't the least intention of dropping him. My own brother-in-law ? "

" Worse luck ! "

" What *do* you mean, Fergus ? You always took his part. You always said the worst thing he did was to give in to circumstances when they were overwhelming."

" I know I said so. But, upon my soul, I don't feel quite sure. If everything was above board then, why has he been going downhill ever since ? "

" I assure you he didn't at all give the impression of going downhill when I met him in London."

" No. Every now and then he has a run of the devil's own luck at the tables, and then he holds his head as high as ever; but between times—he has sense enough not to show between times, but I hear all sorts of rumours. He *is shady*, Enid, and that makes me wonder whether there was no more in the old story than we thought."

" You are very unjust. What can you expect ? Give a dog a bad name——! I admit he was a fool to resign his position in the embassy. He should have stouted it out. But he is far too sensitive for a man of the world."

Fergus frowned. " I wish I knew positively that he didn't get a strong hint to resign. Of course if there had only been the affair with Lady Ellingford, he would simply have been moved on to another diplomatic centre. There was nothing in that to make him lose caste with men. If he had only been content to lie low for a bit!

But to have that phenomenal success at baccarat just when the *scandale* was at its height——!"

"The success would have done him no harm if that young idiot hadn't gone and shot himself. That was what did the mischief. Why can't people see that, however regardless a suicide may be of the happiness of others, he at least rates his own life at its true value."

"I know. It *was* hard lines, and I made up my mind I'd stick to him. But I didn't allow for his going forthwith to the bow-wows."

"I do wish you would be explicit. I never mistook George for a saint; but which of the commandments are you referring to now?"

Fergus shrugged his shoulders. "No need to drag the commandments into it. I will tell you something that will appeal to you. They say your 'brother-in-law' is paying attention to a woman who keeps a boarding-house in Harley Street."

Enid turned her head away.

"*Really*, Fergus!" she said. "I did think you had more sense than to listen to rubbish like that."

"I didn't listen the first time; but yesterday I heard the story again with all sorts of circumstantial details. Wait a bit. Hear me out. She is by way of being a a gentlewoman and showing the world how the thing should be done—trails of smilax up and down the dinner-table and all the rest of it. She really has some good people in the house."

Enid's lip curled. "I hope she has something more substantial than trails of smilax to offer them."

"Oh, yes—as it chances; but it is a pure fluke. She has an excellent cook: but she isn't aware of her good fortune in the matter, and hasn't the sense to grovel to the woman when they have a difference of opinion. The cook is the lynch-pin of the whole establishment, I am told. When she gives warning——"

"Let us hope," said Enid with burning sarcasm, "she will give warning in time to save George from his doom. *Really*, Fergus! George may have gone downhill, as you say; but at least—if he chose to marry again —he could have a nice girl with money."

" Could he? I am not so sure. I should advise the
nice girl's father to make enquiries. The tables are an
uncertain source, of income. You have no notion what
low water he has been in sometimes. On the other hand,
here is a well-appointed house where he is received with
open arms, where a good dinner awaits him any day, with
society not so *very* good but what he can star round in
that interesting pose of his. He always had a weakness
for playing the part of Cæsar in a village. Of course I
don't suppose he has any intentions of matrimony *now;*
but you know how that sort of thing is likely to end—
though of course this run of luck at Monte Carlo may
postpone matters——"

" Till the cook gives warning?" Enid fell into a
reverie. " Old Mrs. Galbraith can't live for ever," she
said at last. " She has only a liferent of the property."

" I should think she might outlive George from what
you tell me. Besides, he must have been a tremendous
drain on her resources. Didn't you tell me she had
given up her carriage and everything? I expect he converted his expectations into hard cash some time ago.
I doubt if the money that actually comes to him will
be enough to pay his debts."

" And what about his daughter?"

" Poor child!" he said. " Poor Rhoda! And what
a brilliant marriage it seemed at the time! From the
day his father sent him to Rugby, George Galbraith had
the ball at his feet. How I used to envy that easy
graceful way of his! And now—he is glad to hang up
his hat in the hall of a boarding-house! You might
have done worse, Enid, after all, than marry the clumsy
old fellow."

But she was not in a mood to respond.

" Well," she said, " if that is how things stand, I can
only wish Mrs. Galbraith long life for Wilhelmina's
sake."

" When she dies, we must see what we can do for the
little puritan."

" Oh, my dear Fergus, you don't know the child as I
do! Rhoda was always the serious member of our family; but I wish you saw Wilhelmina! For sheer stodgi-

ness, she surpasses your wildest conception. As her father's child, she is a pure freak."

"She may be none the worse for that in the long-run. By the way, you didn't gather that Mrs. Galbraith suspected George in the matter of the baccarat?"

"She never referred to him in the most distant way. Oh, no; I shouldn't think so. Gambling is so heinous a crime in her eyes that the mere formality of adhering to the rules of the game is neither here nor there."

"Well, take my advice. Let him down gently. He will be over to see you one of these days. And, by the way, Enid, when Ronald comes, I will not have him take Hugh to Monte Carlo. Of course they are not supposed to admit minors in the rooms; but I won't have Hugh go near the place at all. Ronald will be the ruin of the boy if we don't take care."

Enid feared the loss must be rather serious which entailed such moralizings as these; but she had sufficient self-restraint to keep the reflection to herself.

Two days later George Galbraith came over to Mentone. He found Enid ensconced in a great basket-chair among the palms and orange trees of the garden.

"Ah!" she said pleasantly. "Am I to feel myself flattered? I was wondering when you would be able to tear yourself away from the tricksy goddess. I was glad to hear from Fergus of a run of luck."

He smiled. "The wheel was at that particular stage, was it, when I met Dalrymple? Ah, well! I did not come to talk about that." He paused. "I want your advice, Enid," he said simply.

A vivid picture of trails of smilax flashed upon her mental vision. "*Mon Dieu!*" she thought. "Has it got so far already?" But his next words reassured her.

"I have had a letter from—my Mother's—man of business."

"No bad news, I hope."

"She is ill—has had a stroke of apoplexy."

"I am so sorry," said Enid conventionally. "Then I suppose you are leaving immediately?"

"No. Her directions in case of such an emergency

were perfectly explicit. No one to be sent for: the domestic routine to be undisturbed; she is to be nursed by
her maid, Ann." His manner was quite formal and
colourless: it pronounced no judgment on his mother's
wishes. "They know where I am to be found if—if I
am wanted."

"Poor old lady! She was looking so well when I
saw her. I shouldn't wonder if she pulled through
yet."

He bowed gravely. "I believe the doctors say that
at her age it is only a matter of time. The question is
—What am I to do with Wilhelmina?"

She did not answer immediately, and he laughed softly; then became suddenly conscious that the laugh had
been rather an uneasy one.

"This is how I like the Mediterranean best," he said,
"seen through a tracery of foliage. Has anyone sketched
you in this corner? Do you know, Enid, I have never
felt so much afraid of anyone in my life as I do of that
little girl?"

"Poor George!" she said sympathetically. She knew
that what he said was not true—knew that he feared
Wilhelmina simply because she was the pale reflection of
his mother. It had been his fate all along to suffer
from the superiority of his womankind. He would have
been a better man if they had not been so good. First
there was his mother; then dear Rhoda, who had been
"superior" in quite a different way; and now Wilhelmina. It really was too hard that she should not have
inherited from him the flexible disposition that would
adapt itself to his habits and moods.

"Poor George!" she repeated reflectively.

"I understand now how a man may be tempted to
marry a second time."

Visions of smilax again, and a sudden rush of loyalty
towards her dead sister.

"Nonsense!" she said lightly. "Wilhelmina is eight
years old, and she has been overmothered till now. What
she wants is a good school. In the natural course of
events, you would scarcely see her for the next ten years.
Marry by all means if you meet a nice girl whom you—

care for, and who—would be a credit to you; but don't talk of marrying on Wilhelmina's account."

He did not speak at once. With half-closed eyes he was watching the smoke as it rose against a background of brilliant blue from the choice cigar in his hand.

" First-rate schools," he said quietly, " are an expensive luxury for a poor man's daughter, and anything short of first-rate does not seem to me worth while. What is the use of paying a couple of hundred a year to have a girl made commonplace? And, from what you tell me, Wilhelmina is not likely to prove a great success on conventional lines. Who cares what a girl *knows?*— or whether she knows anything, for the matter of that? What signifies a rag or tag of ' accomplishment ' more or less? I confess I should like her to marry young, and to marry reasonably well. The question is—What is the best means to that end? "

He paused, but she did not help him out.

" Two things have occurred to me," he said, forced to go on, " either of which might answer, though neither would be cheap. First, a convent education—that always gives a woman a certain *cachet;*—or, second, a school where they pay special attention to physical development—golf and rowing and all that sort of thing." He mechanically extended his arm, and then contracted his biceps sharply; there had been a time when George Galbraith was an athlete, and even now he kept himself in very fair condition by an occasional round with the gloves or with the foils.

A low laugh of intense amusement was Enid's first reply to the suggestion. She was thinking that if George Galbraith wished to see the last of his mother when she was laid in the grave, he had better not talk of sending Wilhelmina to a convent; but this remark she was obliged to reserve for her husband's benefit.

" You suggest the title of an up-to-date novel," she said, " Saint or Amazon? Frankly, I don't fancy Wilhelmina in either rôle. Why not send her in the first instance to a quiet little school in France or in the south of England? By and bye, when there is a question of her coming out, I shall be glad to do what I can."

She paused, wondering vaguely whether ten years
hence the Galbraiths would be in a social position in
which " coming out " was possible. Then she raised her
eyes to the clear-cut, cynical, cultured face beside her,
and banished the smilax from her mind as a meaningless
nightmare.

" George," she said in a tone of which the candour
and cordiality were unmistakable, " I do wish I could
offer to take your daughter into my own home. If she
took after our family—or after her father—nothing
would give me greater pleasure. She is a dear child,
and I love her; but I am not *en rapport* with her. I am
ill at ease when she is in the room. She always seems
to be saying, 'You are weighed in the balances—with
my grandmother in the other scale—and are found wanting!' Do you see? Then she succeeds in putting
Hugh's back up somehow. But I do advise you to send
her to a good school, and later on I will do what I can."

" It would be the making of her," he said with real
feeling, " if you would give her a hand. She couldn't
but catch something of your sympathy and tolerance.
She must learn from you in spite of herself that nothing
is so unbecoming to a woman as the disposition to sit
in judgment on the world. It will be a thousand pities,
Enid, if you have not daughters of your own."

She laughed, turning on him now a glance as warm
as that in which he had sunned himself at the Cosmopolis.

" You must introduce me to that blarney stone," she
said, " when I come over to Monte Carlo. I didn't know
they kept one there. Heigho! With all your knowledge of women, have you yet to learn that they do not
look on women as men do? You would have to teach
your daughter to see me with your eyes! "

Ah, Enid, Enid! How dull you were with all your
cleverness. Would you have known yourself, I wonder,
had you seen the halo of romance that enshrined you in
little Wilhelmina's mind?

CHAPTER XIII.

THE LORD WRITES FINIS.

IT was growing dark. Wilhelmina sat in the high kitchen window-seat, with her feet drawn up, and her chin resting on her knees. She spent much of her time in the kitchen now-a-days, and—although the servants were constantly checking the conversation on her account—she heard enough to make her feel that the great mysteries of birth and death were drawing very near.

Life for the moment was one great puzzle, and of course nobody would help her out. Nobody would answer her eager questions, or explain why Jane was more to blame than all the other women to whom God had sent the privilege of motherhood. Ann had been sorely distressed because Wilhelmina, on meeting her old nurse accidentally in Queensmains, had rushed impulsively into her arms; and the extraordinary thing was that even Jane, though more affectionate than ever, had looked ill at ease, and had cut the interview as short as possible.

" If God sent a baby to me," said Wilhelmina afterwards, " I couldn't help it, could I ? " ·

Ann begged the question by assuring her that the event was not at all likely to happen—at present.

" But how can you tell ? "

As it chanced, however, the child had the run of her teeth in the library at this time, and a perusal of Christopher North's Lights and Shadows convinced her of the undesirability of asking questions any more. Now that the inherent curiosity of childhood was passing by, her mind shewed itself receptive rather than enquiring. When, in the course of her future life, she came near the bottom of a subject—as we, with all our limitations, reckon nearness—the process was one of intellectual gravitation rather than of boring and blasting. So now, although the subject of birth came so near, it remained for years a gloomy and depressing mystery—gloomy and depressing because the servants spoke of it as a vulgar unmentionable commonplace.

Death too! Death so near that the household had become used to its shadow, and lived as if this transient state would never end.

Wilhelmina had suffered acutely for a time on account of her share in causing her grandmother's illness. Fortunately this was a sorrow at which those around her could guess, and neither doctors nor servants had been slow to administer rough and ready consolation. But still, when night came on, and her mind began to work on lower planes, the anguish returned, shutting out even her fears about her own salvation.

Mrs. Galbraith's wishes in the event of her illness had been carried out almost to the letter. Indeed, Ann's loyalty to her unconscious mistress was a beautiful thing to see. "She says I'm to leave the morn," Jane had wailed when she went down to the kitchen after that painful interview; and leave she did, Ann standing by the door the while with a face as impartial and inexorable as that of the angel with the flaming sword.

At first the nursing had proved exceedingly hard work, and Mrs. Tail-o'-the-week had come in occasionally to help; but by degrees a routine was established, and no extra hands were needed. Ann seldom left the sick-room without calling either Betsy or Wilhelmina to take her place, and on these rare occasions a bell was fastened to the patient's unparalyzed hand, so that the slightest movement might summon her attendants.

The evening had closed in wet, and the wind was rising every moment. Already its breath went sobbing through the trees, and the queer old house began to moan in sympathy.

Suddenly Wilhelmina remembered that she had not read her French story for the day, so she sprang from the window-seat to fetch the book. True, she knew the stories by heart now; but she had promised Mademoiselle that she would *read* it, and it did not occur to her to fulfil her promise in the spirit only.

She had just finished her task when Ann entered the room, looking worn and worried.

"Betsy not back?" she said. "I'll no' let her go to her mother again, if she bides so late. The farm folk will be in their beds before she goes to fetch the milk; and I can't see your Grannie wanting it! I'll just run along and get it myself. I'll no' be long. Put the chain up after me, and sit with your Grannie till I come back. I doubt I must have dropped asleep, for I see the fire's gone out; but the day's been warm, and Betsy'll light it when she comes in."

The fire in the kitchen was burning brightly enough, but a ripple of physical cold ran over Wilhelmina's body.

"Can't I fetch the milk?" she said eagerly.

"No, no. I'd be feared to have you on the road so late, and a storm coming on too! Take your book in your hand, and I'll be back before you know it."

Futile consolation! Time passes slowly when we count it by heart-throbs!

Wilhelmina put up the chain with trembling hands and crept upstairs. The curtains were drawn for the night, and the sick-room was lighted by a single candle. With noiseless feet she approached the bed. She never entered the room without making sure that Grannie was still alive.

There was no doubt about it now. The patient's breathing was audible and laboured; so the child sat down on a low stool beside the candle, and essayed to read.

She could hear her own heart ticking like a clock, and she shook so that she was afraid of disturbing the patient. Every moment the wind seemed louder, more *unlike wind*. The house, the night, the world, were one great loneliness and terror.

The child drew her hand across her forehead.

"God!" she moaned. "Put good stuff in me! Make me one of Thine own elect! And leave Grannie here till Ann comes back, please! For Christ's sake, Amen."

There seemed to be all sorts of noises in the house now, that she could not understand. It was absurd to suppose that she and the patient were the only people in it. Every moment she expected the door to open, and admit—*whom?*—*what?* She had never seen death. She did not know what it meant.

"Don't take Grannie yet, God!" she gasped—"not quite yet. Wait till Ann comes back!"

Still those awful noises in the house, and worse far! —a noise that seemed to be in the room: a noise that did not come from the bed, a noise that was close to her, and that was unlike anything she had ever heard in her life. Was it the messengers of God?—or was it the struggling of the soul to be free?

Presently it ceased; and Grannie was breathing still. Thank God for that!

But a moment later it began again.

Wilhelmina sprang to her feet. The impulse to fly was almost irresistible; but what might not meet her on the threshold?

Her nerves were strained now to such a point that a fall of dust and soot in the chimney sounded like an avalanche; and all the time that noise went on—the movement of something unseen.

She was praying still in snatches; but her voice was inarticulate, and the sweat stood in great cold drops on her brow. .

Then came the crowning terror of all. The noise deepened into a mighty rushing that must end in something, and a queer shapeless thing flew wildly from the fireplace through the room. It swept over the bed, leaving a trail of black across the snowy sheets: even as it did so, it lengthened out—parted in two, and—the mystery was solved.

Only two birds that had taken refuge in the chimney, and—after suffering an anguish perhaps which might almost be compared to Wilhelmina's own—had made their way down into the room!

Relief and terror struggled for the mastery in the child's breast. Birds were less awful than messengers of God; but even they were uncanny enough as they fluttered and circled about the dimly-lighted room. Their terror was infectious, and then—were they only birds? If the Holy Ghost had taken the form of a dove, might not——? But that train of thought was too appalling to be pursued.

Summoning all her courage, Wilhelmina went to the door and opened it. A moment later the birds were out in the hall.

" Well, did the time seem long? " said Ann's friendly human voice a few minutes later.

" Rather long."

" What in the world have you done to the bed? "

" It wasn't me. It was two birds. They came down the chimney."

Ann looked uneasy. " Were you feared? "

" It was queer. At first I didn't know what they were."

And that was all the reference Wilhelmina made to the terrors she had undergone.

But next morning they took her in to see her grand-mother lying so straight and stiff on such a smooth, cold bed!

Were they only birds after all?

CHAPTER XIV.

MEETING AND PARTING.

AM I to write now of deeper depths than all? Not so. The next three or four days were crowded with interest and excitement.

A few minutes of genuine emotion Wilhelmina experienced as she stood by that straight, still couch. From the moment she left the darkened room she felt herself a celebrity.

With Mrs. Galbraith's death, Windyhaugh rose again for a brief space into the social position it had enjoyed years before. Carriages stopped at the gate to leave cards; four telegrams came in before dinner-time, straining the ready-money resources of the household with the

7

porterage due; and a number of people of the baser sort, who would not have dreamt of disturbing "the family," called to pick up what gossip they could from the servants. How had it happened in the end? Was Mr. Galbraith expected? And what was to be done with Wilhelmina?

After a first chance experience, Wilhelmina usually contrived to be in the hall when Betsy answered the door. It was nice to feel herself surrounded with such a halo of interest. Even the dressmaker, who came to arrange for the household mourning, had much to say about the important people whose gowns must "stand over" till Wilhelmina and the servants were supplied.

Everybody looked at the child with so much interest that she took the occasion for the first time in her life to arrange herself before the mirror in order to see just what impression she made. The glass suggested an improvement on her natural attitude and expression, and she adopted it accordingly.

Poor Mrs. Galbraith, whose last hope had been that her death might accomplish what all the efforts of her life had failed to achieve.

By the time Mr. Galbraith arrived, Wilhelmina was looking almost sanctimonious. She stood at the top of the stair looking down through the banisters while the driver carried in the solid travel-worn valise and dressing-bag that would so have delighted Mademoiselle's heart, had she been there to see them.

Everybody in the neighbourhood was wondering how George Galbraith would face his home-coming; but in truth his simple gravity and absence of pose were very disarming.

He held out his hand to Ann with the air of a comrade in sorrow, when she opened the door.

"I was expecting you last night, sir," she said severely.

A look of almost boyish appeal broke through the gloom of his face. Just so had she seen him long years before, when he had got into some scrape of which his mother must not know.

"I could not face it, Ann," he said wearily, with a

wan little smile. "The place is too full of ghosts for
me."

And Ann, who had been hardening her heart against
him for years, forgave him straightway his many sins
against her dear dead mistress. She felt a lump in her
throat as she thought of the promise of his youth. After
all, there was no one—no one—like Master George.

As for Betsy, she was simply bowled over at once.
Never in her life had she seen so handsome a gentleman.
"You may indeed, Miss, be proud of your pa!"

Wilhelmina considered it beneath the dignity of her
present position to show excitement about anything; but
I know not whether she or her father dreaded the meeting more.

In a nightmare of inspiration the dressmaker had
conceived for her a roomy black silk gown, heavy with
crape; and Ann had brushed her hair into preternatural
smoothness.

Mr. Galbraith could not bring himself to kiss her,
but he stroked her cheek caressingly with his hand.

"Well, little girl?" he said kindly; and then he
turned to Ann. "She is her grandmother's own child,
is she not?"

"She is that, sir."

He looked at his daughter again, and smiled.

"Poor little Enid!" he murmured under his breath.

Wilhelmina did not catch the words; but she smiled
back in reply.

The funeral was largely attended. There is nothing
like a death for bridging over the chasm of years, and
some men came a long distance to offer this last tribute
to the memory of a good woman.

Wilhelmina was keenly disappointed that she was not
allowed to go. She had listened to every word the servants said on the subject, and would gladly have given
all her handful of toys to see the ceremony; but she was
not even allowed to peep out from under the window-
blind at the plumes and the carriages. "It's a real
grand funeral!" said Betsy in a delighted whisper.

Half an hour after the procession had started, old

Mr. Darsie came ambling down the road. He found Betsy still standing at the end of the avenue, gazing in the direction the funeral had taken.

"It's an awfu' loss this for little Miss Wilhelmina," he said.

"It is that; but it's proud she may be to have a faither like yon!"

He held up his hand. "Eh, you women! Ye're a' fitted wi' the ae last. A handsome face an' a fair word, an' there ye are! Can I see the wee lassie?"

"She's awa' doun to the beach; but she'll no' be that far."

He continued his walk, and before long came upon Wilhelmina—so absorbed in what she was doing that she did not notice his approach.

She had mapped out a square of sand with stones, and had planted it here and there with weeds and flowers. Beside her lay a little box with some short pieces of white wool, and she was busily engaged in digging a deep square hole. This completed, she broke some dry twigs into uneven lengths, and planted them round about. Obviously they were meant to do duty as mourners.

She opened the box, and took a fond look at the broken doll inside it; then closed it again and proceeded to adjust the ends of wool. With considerable "previousness" she had already erected the headstone—a slab of slate on which she had laboriously printed the words—

ALL FLES
H IS
GRASS.

It reminded Mr. Darsie of some very old inscriptions in the churchyard, and he remembered Mr. Carmichael's remark about the childhood of the race being repeated in that of the individual.

An involuntary movement on his part startled the child. She sprang to her feet, blushing furiously, and, with one movement of her foot, obliterated the whole scene.

"I—I didn't mean it!" she stammered, "I—I——"

"Puir lassie! Puir bit thing!" he said kindly. "Come an' sit doun on the rocks, an' tell me aboot it."

Of course she had little to tell. She had scarcely seen her father, and had no idea what his plans might be concerning her. Moreover there was a subtle barrier now between her and her old friend. She had become an important person since she last saw Mr. Darsie.

"I doubt they'll tak' ye awa," he said, "an' ye'll forget the auld man. But maybe the day'll come when ye'll tak' thocht o' him again; an' then I'd like ye to mind that his heart was fu' the day, though he couldna find words."

Wilhelmina nodded. She was tracing a pattern in the sand with the toe of her little shoe.

He laughed awkwardly. "It's no' likely that ye'd be wantin' to write to me; but ye ken fine how proud I'd be to get a letter—if ye was in ony trouble like. I'm no' a rich man, Miss Mina; but if—but if——"

Wilhelmina blushed painfully. The sight of her father and the events of the last few days had raised her social standard, and she began to wish she had never accepted Mr. Darsie's sweets. She noticed for the first time how green and shiny his coat was.

"I suppose you haven't seen my father, Mr. Darsie," she said shyly. "He's a grand gentleman."

"Ay, ay," he said, "I ken fine. That's just what he is—a grand gentleman." He paused and looked at her with a pawky smile. "I hope you're going to be something better than a grand lady."

Wilhelmina reflected.

"I'd like to be clever," she said.

"Cliver you'll be, nae doubt, whether you like it or no'." He sighed. "I'm tempted whiles to think that ony fule can be cliver."

Any fool can be clever! Was the old man dreaming? He looked so wise, though, as he said it, that Wilhelmina laid the remark on the shelves of her mind for future consideration.

"Queer folk you'll meet, an' queer things you'll see,"

he continued meditatively; " but I think you'll no' give up the search for God."

She did not respond, and indeed he seemed scarcely aware that he had spoken aloud. The intellectual or spiritual growth of this child was one of his main interests in life, and it was a real grief to him that she must go. His theological museum contained many skeletons, fossils, mummies, microscopic sections, and the like; but his live specimens were few, and there was not one on which he set so high a value as he did on Wilhelmina. He longed to say some brief word that would influence her whole future life; but the fewness of her years seemed to throw her out of reach of his voice. One remark after another he discarded as a mere platitude— no more worth saying than a thousand other things.

At last he rose to his feet with a sigh.

" It's getting late," he said sadly. " We'd best be on the road."

CHAPTER XV.

TRAILS OF SMILAX.

THE drawing-room certainly was a very attractive place. Had you seen it that evening, you might have been tempted to question Mr. Dalrymple's assertion that the cook was the one lynch-pin of the whole establishment.

The evening was cold for the time of year, and the fire—instead of sulking and shivering in a black corner, as boarding-house fires are apt to do—stretched out inviting arms across the friendly tiles. The decoration of the room was on broad and simple lines, and, although the hostess was not responsible for this, having taken the house as it stood, she at least had the sense not to counteract the restful effect by crowding walls and tables with interesting trifles which her guests must strain their eyes and crane their necks to see.

It was somewhat past the usual dinner-hour, but the

ladies gathered in the room were in high good-humour.
Mr. Galbraith was expected that evening, and Mr. Galbraith was a guest worth waiting for. True, there were
other men in the house—an old general, a Polish count,
a widowed city magnate, an unattached clergyman, and
one or two more; but none of these gave the fillip to
social intercourse that was the invariable result of a
visit from George Galbraith. He did not even need to
talk; indeed he never talked much, though on occasion
he talked well. The very presence of his grave observant face at the dinner-table raised people above their
ordinary level. He was worth exerting oneself for. He
might seem absorbed in thought, yet women and men
felt instinctively that when he was there no dainty gown,
no bright *bon mot*, was ever thrown away.

To-night a greater interest than usual attached to
his coming, for he was bringing with him his little
daughter from Scotland.

"Imagine George Galbraith with a daughter!"
laughed old Lady Molyneux. "I should as soon have
pictured him with a perambulator. Poor Lothario! It
is too bad. I wonder what she is like?"

"Oh, an uncompromising little puritan, I believe,"
said the hostess sweetly. She leant forward to poke the
fire—from the top—and the lace fell back from a pretty
white arm as she did so. "Her father has had nothing
to do with her," she added apologetically. "She comes
from the wilds of the country."

The note of apology was a mistake. Lady Molyneux
was always irritated when Mrs. Raleigh assumed an air
of proprietorship in Mr. Galbraith. "First catch your
hare!" she would say, with a cynical smile on her handsome old face when her hostess's back was turned.

At present she had to content herself with a meaning
glance across to Miss Evelyn—a beautiful girl of fairly
good family who had made a sudden success on the
stage.

"The train must be late," said Mrs. Raleigh anxiously, looking at her jewelled watch. "Shall I ring?—or
do you mind giving them five minutes more?"

"Oh, give them five minutes by all means—the 'British Matron' dines out to-night, I think?—if your cook won't mind."

"I am very angry with cook," said the hostess irrelevantly. "You remember the trouble I took some time ago to get her daughter into Whiteley's? Well, I find cook has been smuggling this young person's washing in along with mine every week. I only found it out because to-day they omitted to sift out a white petticoat much more pretentiously beflounced than my own. I thought the laundry people had made a mistake till I saw the girl's name on it."

"The salmi last night was a work of art," said the old lady significantly.

But Mrs. Raleigh ignored this. "Of course, with all the house-linen used, the week's bill is enormous, and I have always left it to the servants to check it. I hate supervising every detail. I like to do things in a liberal spirit, and it is disgusting to find oneself deceived."

"Disgusting," said the actress with a yawn.

"By the way, Miss Evelyn, I hope it doesn't inconvenience you to have dinner a few minutes late?"

"Not a bit, thanks. I am understudying Mrs. Carrington. If I get in for the third act to-night it will do. She really is superb in the third act. Do you care to have a stall, Lady Molyneux?"

"One of these days, thank you, if the piece is not too deadly sentimental."

"Oh, no. Parts of it I think you would like. I should love to have you come, for I know you will pick holes, and give me a chance to score when my turn comes. I have had heaps of tips from you." She lifted eyes full of girlish flattery. Lady Molyneux was a friend worth having.

The Boarding-House as a Social Bridge—or as a Jacob's Ladder?—What a fascinating topic! What a pity the Autocrat had raised the whole theme out of reach for ever!

A loud knock and ring at the street door put a stop to the conversation.

"There they are!" cried the hostess gaily. "I must go and welcome the little girl."

"Humph!" ejaculated Lady Molyneux when she was gone. "The 'little girl' takes the trick, I fear. What a fool he is to give that woman so good a card! If George Galbraith had been the man I thought him, he would have suppressed the—'little girl'!"

"I lay two to one on him still," said the actress languidly. "She really is too great a fool. How she bores one with her eternal talk of the servants, and the money she spends on the establishment!"

"You may rest assured that she doesn't talk to him like that. One catches a pregnant glance now and then. Softness, worship, coddling—that's her cue. It's apt to pall after matrimony, as George Galbraith must be aware. But he has had a stormy life, poor man, and there is no saying what may happen."

"I think she is too good for him," said a voice from the window recess.

"Why, Mrs. Carlton, I had quite forgotten you were there. How odd that we didn't feel the leavening influence of your presence! But I thought you liked Mr. Galbraith?"

"I do. I can't help it. But I try not to let my tastes influence my judgment."

"Now that must be so difficult! But you are always admirable."

"She is a good, kind woman, if she is a fool."

"Oh, come! I am glad you have admitted she is a fool. That was handsome of you. We are all in the same boat now—more or less. No doubt, with your habit of observation, you have noticed how extraordinarily successful a fool can be?"

"If the fool chances to be a woman!" threw in the actress.

Mrs. Carlton smiled.

"I am afraid before we go farther we should have to agree upon a definition of success," she said, with the little air of unconscious superiority that annoyed Lady Molyneux.

At this moment Mrs. Raleigh returned, leading by the hand a quaint, solemn child in a funereal frock. Truly father and daughter were an oddly assorted pair! Now

that he saw her in surroundings so different from those
at Windyhaugh, George Galbraith wondered that he
could have allowed that frock to pass; but it was too
late to regret his carelessness.

He was becomingly grave, but his manner was as
fascinating as ever. His momentary glance reminded
Lady Molyneux how refreshing it must be for a man of
the world to meet a really clever woman; it left the
actress blushing with renewed pleasure in her Bond
Street gown.

Of course everyone was oppressively kind to Wilhelmina—even the tall footman, who made her feel as if
she were in church. Old Lady Molyneux in her usual
high-handed fashion insisted that the child should sit
by her at table. She could not have endured, she told
the actress afterwards, to see " that woman purring over
the poor innocent." Everyone wanted to know how the
little Scotswoman had enjoyed the journey, and what
were her first impressions of London. Wilhelmina said
" Yes," or " No," as the case might be, blushing for the
baldness of the response, but feeling herself utterly unable to improve upon it.

" We tire you out with our questions, don't we? "
said Mrs. Raleigh tactfully at last. " We will leave you
now to eat your dinner in peace."

The conversation ran on lightly enough till the table
was cleared for dessert.

" Any fresh laurels? " said Mr. Galbraith then to the
actress.

She shook her head. " Nothing to speak of. I begin
to wonder whether it is worth all the fag."

" You are hard to please."

" Perhaps I am. Of course as a girl one dreams
of the supreme moment, the crowd, the ovation. Is
anything short of that worth the years of drudg-
ery? "

" Even that may come." Of course he did not in
the least expect that it ever would.

" Nonsense! " said Lady Molyneux sharply. " One
can do good work, I suppose, and amuse folks, without
being a Siddons or a Ristori. I'll wager it isn't the

greatest actors and actresses who have been the happiest."

"Happiest!" repeated the girl contemptuously. "Who cares for happiness? If one could be a Siddons, one would be content to trample on one's own broken heart—not to speak of other people's!"

She glanced at Mr. Galbraith as she spoke; but Mrs. Raleigh shook her head with benign warning.

"'Be good, sweet maid, and let who will be clever,'"

she quoted sententiously.

This was unendurable. The actress had always been considered a stupid girl at school, and the surprise of her sudden success had gone to her head.

'She leaned forward. There was a saucy light in her beautiful eyes.

"So they say!" she cried, with a light little laugh; "but then you see, Mrs. Raleigh, it is so much *easier* to be good than to be clever!"

There was a moment's pause of appreciation. George Galbraith nodded across to the charming face, and Mrs. Raleigh shook her head again indulgently.

But the words had found an answering chord in Wilhelmina, and she had been left so long to herself that her crippling self-consciousness had taken flight.

"But I've been told," she said, meditatively, "that any fool can be clever."

A moment later she could not have believed in her own audacity, had it not been for the extraordinary effect it produced. It was as if a bomb had fallen in the midst of the company, and now every eye was fixed upon her as the thrower of it. Even Mr. Galbraith gave his daughter a quick glance that escaped everyone save Mrs. Raleigh.

Then a ripple of intense amusement ran down the table. The actress was forced to join in it; but she looked as if someone had hissed in the theatre. Lady Molyneux laughed till the tears came.

"But, *petite*, you are adorable!" she cried. "Mrs. Carlton and I were feeling after that epigram an hour ago. You shall come to my room by and bye, and have some chocolates."

Oddly enough, Wilhelmina was destined to surpass herself again before dinner was over.

Lady Molyneux was relating some episodes of her Parisian life. One or two of these were a trifle *risqué*, and, with a fine sense of literary fitness, she discussed them—so to speak—in their native tongue. She was always glad of an excuse for doing this, as it excluded the less eligible members of the party from the conversation.

Wilhelmina was on the alert at once. She felt as if Mademoiselle was with her again, and, leaning forward in her eagerness, she came in contact with my lady's gesticulating hand.

"*Pardon, Madame!*" she cried involuntarily, in the pretty deprecating fashion her governess had taught her.

Lady Molyneux turned and looked through her formidable lorgnette at the small black thing beside her. "*Eh bien! Tu as bien écouté mes petites histoires?*"

"*Oui, Madame,*" said Wilhelmina, simply, "*mais je n'ai pas tout compris.*"

This too, of course, was a remark that she had often had occasion to make to Mademoiselle, but it fell so trippingly from her tongue that another peal of delighted laughter rose from the table. Thanks to Mademoiselle's habit of careful drilling and of arousing the dramatic instincts of her pupils, there was a charm, a flexibility, about Wilhelmina's manner of speaking French—limited though her knowledge of it was—that was entirely wanting in her treatment of her mother tongue. This time George Galbraith did not even lift his eyes. His *savoir-vivre* did not admit of his showing any pride or surprise; but if that clever little woman, Mademoiselle, had seen his impassive face just then, I think she would have felt herself repaid for all she had undergone.

Lady Molyneux shook her finger at him. "Nice person you are to be the custodian of a young girl's morals. Why didn't you tell me she could speak French?"

He shrugged his shoulders. "I don't consider her accent bad for a little English girl—do you?"

Wilhelmina could not understand why they all made such a fuss about her. This was her first experience of the fact that some of the greatest successes of our lives are due to what Fergus Dalrymple would have called a " fluke."

And the worst of such successes is that it is uncommonly difficult to live up to them!

" I assure you, my friend, she is charming—she is positively *chic!* " said Mrs. Raleigh, when Mr. Galbraith had found his way from the smoking-room to her boudoir. " How clever of her grandmother to have the child taught to speak French! "

" That was scarcely her grandmother's doing," said George quietly.

" Ah, I was sure you had been a better father than you led one to suppose! "

" In any case I am most grateful to you for giving the poor little soul a home while I look about me. Her aunt happens to be abroad again, and a homeless man is sorely at a loss with a child on his hands. Of course she must go to school at once."

" No hurry at all. It is a real pleasure to me to have her. Let her see something of this great London after her quiet country life."

" Do you think you could arrange about getting her two simple little frocks? Just give those shapeless sacks to one of your pensioners."

" I will, with pleasure. She would look sweet in white for the evening—with a black sash, of course."

" You will have to convince her that by wearing white she is showing no disrespect to her grandmother's memory."

" But her grandmother is in heaven! "

" True," he said gravely, with the air of one who has overlooked an important detail. " If you remind her of that fact, I have no doubt it will be all right."

The white frock proved an unqualified success, and a few days later, when for the first time Miss Evelyn took Mrs. Carrington's part, she persuaded Mr. Galbraith to take Wilhelmina to the theatre.

"Do, do!" she entreated. "Every child I meet is *born* in the stalls, if not in the green-room. I shall never have such another opportunity of working on an absolutely virgin soil."

So they went, and the effect on Wilhelmina was overwhelming. "I fear it was a great waste," she said long afterwards to Miss Evelyn. "So much less would have been enough to fill my tiny cup. But how that night stands out in my memory!"

She sat still as a mouse, with all her soul in her eyes, till her "friend" came on the stage; then she sprang to her feet with outstretched arms.

"*Oh, Miss Evelyn!*" she cried in tones of burning admiration.

A murmur of amusement ran through the stalls. The young actress hesitated, smiled, forgot her part for the fraction of a second; then bowed and recovered herself in response to a burst of applause.

Mr. Galbraith had no special wish under the circumstances to be *affiché* in this fashion; but, apart from that, he was quite man of the world enough to appreciate the situation. Indeed he and Wilhelmina were really drawn to each other more nearly that night than they had been hitherto. In the interval between the first and second acts he ordered an ice for her delectation, and later he took her to visit Miss Evelyn in her room.

"Isn't he perfectly distracting?" said a young girl who was regarding them through her opera-glass from the front of the dress-circle. "Do you suppose he is her father?"

Her companion shrugged a pair of pretty white shoulders. "Of course," she said with a sigh. "I wonder if the child *in the least* appreciates her good fortune?"

"How should she? No doubt she thinks that fathers like that are to be gathered on every blackberry bush."

"To do her justice she does look happy."

And in truth Wilhelmina was transfigured with excitement—lifted far out of sight of Windyhaugh and the past; but before they left the house the reaction came. In the hansom her father could feel her trembling like a leaf.

"Anything wrong?" he asked surprised.

"No," said the child, and for a quarter of an hour they drove on in silence.

Then she laid her hand on his arm.

"Father!" she said in a tortured voice. "*What would Grannie say?*"

Just at that moment the hansom drove up to the house. Mr. Galbraith lifted his daughter out, paid—overpaid—the man, and opened the door with his latch-key.

By some misunderstanding the lamp in the hall had been extinguished, and long years afterwards Wilhelmina remembered the expression on her father's face as she saw it by the light, first of a match, and then of two flickering candles.

"Your question, little girl," he said slowly, "involves a problem of which you will have to work out the solution for yourself—as your father had to do before you."

PART II.

CHAPTER XVI.

THE OLD PROBLEM.

"Wilhelmina," said a gentle querulous voice, "this is Sarah's night out. Just go down to the kitchen and see that cook has got Mrs. Carlton's tea all right. Ask her to carry it up, and you take it in. Where is that bunch of violets I bought in the Grove? Don't forget to lay that on the tray."

"All right, Mütterchen." The answer came in a dreamy voice from the recesses of the shabby old arm-chair.

Mrs. Galbraith knew well what that tone meant.

"Do go, child," she repeated irritably. "You worry me."

Wilhelmina uncurled herself, and threw down her book with a touch of pettishness. What did it matter whether tea was carried up two minutes earlier or later? She tossed back her splendid mane, and stretched her lanky arms with a yawn.

"Smooth your hair before you go in. How you do stoop, Mina!"

Mrs. Galbraith's voice broke into a note of utter despondency. It seemed hopeless to try to contend against all the minor difficulties of life. Her appearance had changed even more than her voice since we saw her some five or six years ago as Mrs. Raleigh in Harley Street. She looked flabby and elderly now, and at the present moment lay stretched on the couch, attired in a shabby dressing-gown.

106

"Don't fret, Mütterchen," said Wilhelmina cheerfully. She knew by experience how infectious was this mood of her stepmother's, and how fatal the first yielding to its influence. "I'll hold myself like a grenadier, and as soon as I have taken Mrs. Carlton her tea, I'll see about our own."

"You know Captain Stott and his wife are coming to-morrow. You promised to see that their rooms were nice."

"I know;" but Wilhelmina sighed. She too was suffering from physiological inertia, though she thought it was only bad temper.

"Don't forget the violets!" called Mrs. Galbraith as she left the room.

Wilhelmina made her way to the untidy kitchen. The tea-tray was laid, and she surveyed it critically with her head on one side.

"The tray-cloth isn't very clean, is it?" she asked deprecatingly. She was dreadfully afraid of hurting cook's feelings. One has to walk warily with a servant whose wages are in arrears.

"I am sure it ought to be," was the indignant response. "She's only had it a week."

"Well, I daresay it will do for to-night. Perhaps with the violets there she won't notice."

Alas! What would Windyhaugh have said to that?

Wilhelmina adjusted the penny nosegay—pathetic descendant of the trails of smilax!—and led the way upstairs.

Mrs. Carlton had been a good friend to the Galbraiths: she could scarcely have told why, save that as a social study they interested her. She had not been at all surprised when the Harley Street experiment ended in disaster, and of course she had been the only one of the boarders there who had cared to follow Mrs. Galbraith to a Bayswater lodging-house. Mrs. Carlton was fortunately very indifferent as to what she ate, so she agreed to pay a round sum weekly, and left the *menu* to her landlady's tender mercies, which, if not cruel, were at least highly erratic. When funds were plentiful, the lodger's table was furnished forth with game

8

or early strawberries: when funds were low, cold meat hung on with dreary persistence, or she was constrained to share a rabbit with Mrs. Galbraith and Wilhelmina. Much of her time now was spent abroad; but, when she was in London, the Galbraiths' house was her home.

"Don't hurry away," she said to Wilhelmina kindly. "What charming violets! Why, how flushed you are, child! What have you been doing?"

"Reading."

"Reading what?"

"Oh, just a book from the library."

"A nice one?"

"Awfully nice."

Farther enquiries led to some wholesome advice; but, as the books came from the library primarily for the benefit of Wilhelmina's stepmother, who apparently had read all the classic novels at some unspecified period in the past, Mrs. Carlton had not much hope that the advice would be followed.

"Have you heard from your father lately?" she said.

Wilhelmina shook her head. "I don't know. I forget when the last letter was," she corrected herself, blushing.

"You know you don't get out half enough," said Mrs. Carlton irrelevantly. "Put on your hat now, and go for a smart trot. Promise!"

"Very well," said Wilhelmina rather ungraciously; but it was growing dark before she took the latchkey and started off.

When they first came to Bayswater, Mrs. Galbraith had been very particular not to let the child go out alone; but they had so often been left for a day or two without servants, and necessary commodities in their *ménage* were so apt to be found wanting at the eleventh hour, that by degrees they had come to ignore social conventions, and the supposed dangers of the streets. Indeed Wilhelmina never dreamt of fear or harm in this respect, and, consequently perhaps, was well able to take care of herself. A chance accost roused in her, not terror, but simple natural indignation.

She strolled through Westbourne Grove, gazing into

the shop-windows, and thinking of all the beautiful
things she would buy if she had money to spend. One
article of dress she chose after another, till in imagination she saw herself a very different being from the
shabby overgrown scrimply-dressed child whose eyes were
fixed so longingly on Whiteley's resplendent windows.
But she could not be happy alone; and fancy had long
since limned a wonderful Fairy godmother, who rambled
with her through the land of dreams. What exquisite
cakes they bought! what chocolate! what fruit! Perhaps the fruit suggested that pumpkin of old, for now
they must drive away, away—whither?—to the mountains of the moon?—or only to the Prince's ball? In her
anxiety to decide on a fitting chariot, Wilhelmina laid
herself open to repeated offers of "Cab, Miss?" "Hansom, lydy?"

Dreaming thus, she wandered on among tall uniform
houses with scraps of garden in front. She no longer
needed even the stimulus of the shop-windows to fire her
imagination. Rising above mere earthly joys, it proceeded to paint the lineaments, the mind, the soul, of
the wonderful friend, till at last she stood there complete, just the height of the dreamer's ideal. It was a
curious form of protestant—or pagan—Madonna-wor-
ship, perched on a mossy ledge half-way up the bleak crag
of Wilhelmina's Calvinism.

Suddenly the dream came to an end.

From the open door of a chapel a glow of light was
thrown upon the street. Large placards stood about, an-
nouncing a series of evangelistic meetings, which all
were cordially invited to attend.

Wilhelmina stood still.

Her religious life had fallen into abeyance of late.
She went to church regularly on Sunday, and at intervals the old anxiety returned, and she strained every
nerve to achieve conversion. In this she was no longer
actuated merely by the dread of judgment to come, but
also by a real desire for the Personal Communion of
which others spoke in such glowing terms. And yet
she was beginning to despair. She had striven so long,
and she *could not* believe. It seemed to her untrained

mind that she was asked to believe a thing which had
not fully happened until she did believe it; and, although she never doubted for a moment that the fault
lay in herself, the difficulty hitherto had proved an in-
superable one.

"Coming in?" said a boy's pleasant voice. The
speaker had run up behind her.

Wilhelmina shook her head.

"I think you had better. I found the Saviour here
last night."

"*Did* you?" Wilhelmina looked at him with hungry
interest.

"Yes. Have you found Him?"

She shook her head.

"Then come in!"

"I can't. My—people are expecting me."

"But won't they think you worth waiting for if you
go back to them a Christian girl?"

She could not honestly say that this would make
much difference to "them"; but she was well aware
that it would make a great difference to herself. Her
face showed her indecision.

"Come in, come in!" he said again. "We're very
late;" and, with all the zeal of the new convert, he
dragged her, half yielding, into the chapel.

"*Come, ye who have sought Him twenty years!*"
cried the preacher's thrilling voice.

"That's me!" thought Wilhelmina, and she sank
into a seat.

The preacher was a man of wide reputation, and the
place was crowded; but the people had made room in a
moment. They were worked up to the state in which a
sacrifice of physical comfort was almost a relief.

The atmosphere was hot and oppressive. Self-consciousness was dying fast. One or two women had removed their hats, and were pushing back dank hair from
their moist foreheads. "Come in, Lord Jesus!" cried
a man near the door. Obviously the preacher had "the
root of the matter" in him.

Ah, yes, had he not indeed the root of the matter in
him? He worked on the terrors of his audience, no

doubt; he lent overwhelming importance to his own formula, his own shibboleth; but was there not in his teaching that note of true *detachment* that has characterized all real religions from the beginning of time?

> "Which has not taught weak wills how much they can?
> Which has not fall'n on the dry heart like rain?
> Which has not cried to sunk, self-weary man:
> *Thou must be born again!*"

Wilhelmina sat quivering like a reed in response to the passionate appeal, to the mesmerism of this man's personality. It seemed but a few minutes before he resumed his seat.

A number of clergymen were on the platform. One of these spoke a few words, but Wilhelmina scarcely heard what he said. The moment the service was over, she rose to go.

"You'll come down to the Inquiry Room," said the boy who had brought her in.

"No, no," she cried terrified.

But fate was too strong for her. The preacher was making his way down the chapel. His perceptions were extraordinarily keen. He ignored the people who looked at him with adoring eyes, the people who would fain shake hands; but he did not pass small, shrinking, insignificant Wilhelmina.

"You a Christian?" he said cheerily, sending a queer thrill through her body as his hand fell heavily on her shoulder. "No? Mr. Jenkins!"

In a moment she was handed over to a satellite and ushered down below.

Some time later, when Wilhelmina read Romola, she knew what it meant to the stately heroine to be handed over by Savonarola to another confessor. *She* was delivered to a formal, rather fussy, grey-haired man.

Inquirers were so many that night that the large band of satellites was overworked, and Wilhelmina was classed with a stout elderly woman from the country, though an outsider might have been tempted to think that the spiritual conditions of two people so different could not have much in common.

The old man gave her a Testament, expressing surprise that she had not brought one with her, and requested them both to read over a very long verse in the Acts of the Apostles: in after years Wilhelmina could not even remember which it was. "If you believe that," he said, "you are saved."

He read it over himself, dwelling on this point and that. Wilhelmina was so confused and exhausted that, familiar though she was with Holy Writ, she could not even take in what the text meant; and the feeling that this important gentleman was waiting there till she "believed," was quite sufficient to reduce her to the last stage of imbecility.

No, not the last. That was still to come.

"I see it all!" cried the elderly woman suddenly. "Praise God! Praise God! *I'm saved!*"

And then indeed Wilhelmina reached the "last stage."

The old man now directed his attention to her exclusively.

"I like to keep people to one verse," he said, with an air of resigning himself to unmerited failure; "but we'll try a text from St. John."

Here at least Wilhelmina might have hoped to find herself at home; but no. The familiar quotation rang in her ears like a melody of which one strives in vain to remember the words. Her mind was an absolute blank. Would she have to sit there all night?

"Don't you believe *now?*" asked the old man, and to her his voice sounded weary and reproachful.

Wilhelmina was desperate.

"I don't know. I—I think so," she said doubtfully. "I'd like to go home and think about it."

The night was growing late and other inquirers were waiting, so he gave her a little blue book and allowed her to go.

Then indeed a text of Scripture rose with full force and abounding significance to her mind—

"Our soul is escaped as a bird out of the snare of the fowlers; the snare is broken and we are escaped."

But the relief was only for the moment. She could

not sleep that night. Throughout the long hours she lay tossing from side to side, hopelessly praying, and wondering what she had done that the light should be denied to her—only to her!

CHAPTER XVII.

MR. CARMICHAEL.

"WHAT in the world made you so late last night?" said Mrs. Galbraith at breakfast next morning. "I had a headache and went to bed early."

"I went to a meeting," Wilhelmina answered in a lifeless voice. "Did you want me?"

"I was dreadfully low-spirited and nervous. I really don't know how we are to face the winter with its taxes and its bills. Mrs. Carlton goes to Algiers very soon. We shall have the Stotts of course, but what they pay won't much more than meet current expenses, and there are some heavy bills standing. I do wish we could hear from your father."

Wilhelmina rested her chin on the palms of her two hands, and looked across at her stepmother.

"Mütterchen," she said—it was Mr. Galbraith who had chosen the name by which she should call her new mother—"Mütterchen, if we are to know any peace in life, we must trust to ourselves. We don't know when we may hear from him."

A great tear rolled down Mrs. Galbraith's poor flabby face. "Yet last time, just when we were in despair, he came and stayed with us, and left fifty pounds behind him. It was such a help!"

Wilhelmina looked doubtful. She remembered how extravagantly the lodgers had fared on that occasion—how smart a bonnet Mrs. Galbraith had purchased in Regent Street, and she wondered whether the fifty pounds had been so great a help in the end.

Mrs. Galbraith was crying quietly.

"And last night," she said in a quavering voice, "cook was positively insolent to me—positively insolent!"

Wilhelmina turned white. This was serious. With all her faults, cook could not be easily replaced.

"We must pay her wages," she said.

"And where is the money to come from?—unless your father sends it. There are far more pressing things than cook's wages."

A great wave of crimson rushed over the young girl's face. She was having a hard struggle with herself.

"There is my money," she said ungraciously. "It will be coming in very soon now."

Mrs. Galbraith smiled through her tears.

"You poor child!" she said, "and you need a new frock so badly! But that you shall have in any case. You do grow so fast!—And then there were those music lessons you were to have."

Wilhelmina laughed rather bitterly. She was beginning to look upon "those music lessons" as a Will o' the Wisp. "Oh, they can wait another three months!" she said. "I ought to be paying you for my board."

"Nonsense! You are my right hand. What should I do without my dear daughter?"

Wilhelmina looked perplexed. She was her stepmother's right hand without doubt; but was there any use in being right hand to so muddled a head? She longed at times really to take the reins of the establishment herself; but it was so encumbered with debts, with the incompetence of servants, and with Mrs. Galbraith's fitful extravagance, that the task would have been a hopeless one. She would have grudged her quarterly pittance less if it had made any real difference in the sea of their embarrassments.

"If only we could keep the house full!" continued Mrs. Galbraith. "There is Mrs. Brown over the way—quite a common woman, and never decently dressed! I don't believe she spends half as much on her housekeeping as I do, and she has none of the nice little etceteras that count for so much; yet she always has plenty of lodgers. I wish we knew what she charges for her rooms. No doubt, with just one little slavey, she can do the thing more cheaply."

"She does the cooking herself."

"Well, I am sure we ought to have good cooking for the wages I give; and think of my beautiful linen and dinner ware!"

"If we could afford it, I would take cooking-lessons. They would be much more useful than music."

"You poor child! As if I should allow such a thing at your age! Here is a note from Mrs. Stott, telling me what things to get in. You will go along to the Grove presently and order them, won't you?"

At this moment the housemaid opened the door. "If you please, ma'am," she said sulkily, "there has been a great fall of soot in Mrs. Carlton's sitting-room. It'll take me the best part of the morning to clean it up."

"Oh, dear! and I meant to have had the chimney-sweeps this very day!"

Wilhelmina rose from the table. "Mrs. Carlton must sit in the Stott's room," she said. "They won't be here till afternoon. I will go and see if I can find a sweep who will come at once."

Ten minutes later, when Mrs. Carlton was deep in her Daily Telegraph, a visitor was ushered unannounced into the room. He wore clerical dress, and his face would have been sufficient introduction to any woman.

"Mrs. Galbraith?" he said doubtfully.

"No. Mrs. Carlton. I lodge here. Did you want to see Mrs. Galbraith?"

"*Miss* Galbraith. My name is Carmichael. They told me she would be in soon, so I said I would wait. I have called outrageously early; but a Scotch minister in London is fain to map out every minute of his time."

"Are you a friend of Wilhelmina's?"

"A friend of her childhood."

"Then," said Mrs. Carlton in her deliberate impulsive fashion, "I am glad she is out. You will forgive my saying that I have wondered sometimes what the friends of her childhood are about."

He drew down his brows in the old characteristic

way. " To tell the truth, we have scarcely heard a word
about her. Her father's world never came much in contact with her grandmother's world."

Mrs. Carlton laughed. " Her father's world does not
come much in contact with her stepmother's world," she
said caustically. " You heard, of course, that he had
married a lady who kept a boarding-house? "

" Yes. We were much surprised."

" You would not have been surprised if you had seen
the steps by which it came about. She was very amiable, and worshipped him without criticism. I don't
think he ever quite meant to marry her, but her pretty
house was always there with its welcome. He was going
downhill, and, although no doubt there were lots of good
houses where he would still have received a welcome,
he was morbidly sensitive about laying himself open to
a snub. At Harley Street no one was responsible, and
we all received him gladly."

She paused, but Mr. Carmichael did not speak. He
looked the thing he was—an admirable listener.

Mrs. Carlton sighed. " As for her, there is no denying that she belongs to the class of women who are the
despair of those who try to help their sex. She was at
the mercy of her servants, and, if she had only realized
the fact, all might have been well. But she wouldn't
realize it. Those of us who know life, and who can't
afford the services of a *chef*, understand that we must
choose between two alternatives—good cooking on the
one hand, sobriety or good temper, or both, on the other.
Personally I prefer the second alternative; I think good
cooking may be bought too dear: boarders—who don't
come into personal contact with the cook—are apt to
prefer the first. Mrs. Galbraith was a born optimist
who persistently believed in the possibility of combining
the two—and so the establishment came to grief."

Mr. Carmichael smiled.

" You can imagine the rest. It is only by slow degrees that we have sunk to our present level."

He smiled again—deprecatingly this time—as he
looked out on the sunny street with its tall cream-col-
oured houses.

"Pardon me," he said. "You forget that I am only a country cousin."

"Or that we are on different sides of the footlights? You must take my word for it then, Mr. Carmichael," she continued hurriedly, as if realizing for the first time how much she had to say, "that many people in the slums suffer less from the *evils* of poverty than do the tenants of this pleasant house. Wilhelmina is going to waste. She is a dear good girl, and it is often she who keeps the house together; but the supervision she is under—if supervision it can be called—is of the most undisciplined kind, and in all her spare moments she is reading arrant rubbish from a circulating library in the Grove. She has had no education; and, although she often works hard—it is such frightfully misdirected energy! It all just tends to keep things shuffling along. She isn't learning to do any one thing *well*."

Here Mr. Carmichael interposed his first question, an irrelevant one as it chanced.

"May I ask what keeps you here?"

She shrugged her shoulders. "Oh, I am all right," she said lightly. "Mrs. Galbraith is generous as a land-lady. Besides——" she flushed slightly—"in the old days in Harley Street I was in temporary difficulties of a very painful kind, and she rose to the occasion as only a gentlewoman would have done. I take care that people don't suffer for that kind of thing, and, as it happens, I like Mrs. Galbraith. She certainly has the *qualités de ses défauts*."

"She is kind to Wilhelmina then?"

"As she would be to her own daughter."

"Do I understand you to say that the child doesn't go to school?"

Mrs. Carlton's lip curled. "For a year or two after her grandmother's death she went to some ridiculous school down in the country; but even that farce soon came to an end. Since then she has had a stray term here and a stray term there; but it has all amounted to nothing. She has a great idea of being clever and methodical. Periodically she maps out her time, and begins to work at her old lesson-books; but she is too heavily handicapped. Energy is not unlimited at her age, and what she has is already overtaxed."

"But what is Mr. Galbraith about? Any court would compel him to support his wife."

"If she was the sort of woman to appeal to any court. He does send her money occasionally, and indeed I have even seen him here once or twice, but of course we can't expect much of his society. Have you met him?"

"No. I was away from home at the time of his mother's funeral."

She leaned forward. "You see, Mr. Carmichael, George Galbraith is a picturesque figure, and his sense of fitness is such that he must have a harmonious background. To do him justice, he can make most backgrounds appear harmonious; but a Bayswater lodging-house is one of the few that are, on the face of it, impossible. I can't fancy him at fault in an imperial court, in the wilds of Arabia, or indeed in a lunatic asylum; but Bayswater——! It won't do. We all recognize the fact."

"But what does he live on himself?"

"The gaming-tables, some say. I believe his first wife left a little money; and I suspect him of writing occasional man-of-the-world articles for the smart papers. I don't know, but I fancy sometimes I have recognized his hand." She sighed. "I suppose Wilhelmina is quite dependent on her stepmother."

"Practically, but not quite. Her grandmother had only a life-rent of the family property; but, with the exception of a small legacy to an old servant, all her savings went to Wilhelmina. She has an annuity of about forty pounds a year."

"Paid through her father?"

"No. Old Mrs. Galbraith took care of that. It is paid straight to herself by the family man of business."

Mrs. Carlton rose to her feet. She saw Wilhelmina coming down the street.

"Then in Heaven's name, Mr. Carmichael," she said, "arrange that the child be taken right out of this life. Forty pounds wouldn't do it; but sixty would with care. Surely her relatives will raise the other twenty for a few years. She is worth it. When I think how that quaint sturdy Scotch thing came in upon our frivolous scandal-mongering boarding-house life—— It was like a mental vision of breezy moorland through the fumes of a music-hall!"

After hearing all this, Mr. Carmichael was agreeably disappointed when, himself unseen, he watched Wilhelmina come bounding up the steps, casting a glance over her shoulder at two very black chimney-sweeps in her rear. She was enjoying a rebound of vitality after the sorrows of the night. A touch of frost in the sunny morning air had brought a glow of colour to her cheeks, and the scrimpness of her dress adapted itself rather pleasantly to her rapid movements, for there was not yet a suspicion of coming womanhood in her lanky boyish figure. Moreover—and few things lend a more becoming light to the human countenance than this—she felt herself at the moment an exceedingly competent young person. Had she not convinced the grocer that he was twopence out in his reckoning? And could any one else have produced the chimney-sweeps with so little loss of time?

"They happened to come into the shop while I was there," the minister heard her say, laughing, "and I thought I had better just take them in tow at once."

It was fortunate that Mr. Carmichael got this pleasant little glimpse of her, for in his presence she was painfully shy and embarrassed. Her social life for years had been almost a negligible quantity: it had consisted of more or less unpleasant relations with servants, lodgers, and shopkeepers. Mrs. Galbraith had been constrained for a time to keep aloof from her own immediate circle, having already borrowed money from all who could be induced to lend it; and, although in the Harley Street days she had been extremely generous, keeping open house even for some who had little claim on her hospitality, they had shown no desire to follow her down into the valley of poverty and disappointment.

The minister was hampered too in the interview by the thought of all the questions Mr. Darsie would have to ask when he got back to Queensmains.

There was no doubt, however, about Wilhelmina's pleasure at the sight of him.

"You have not forgotten Windyhaugh, I see."

Forgotten Windyhaugh!

"And I assure you Windyhaugh and its surroundings have not forgotten you. Do you know, I never see Mr. Darsie but he talks about you?"

"I hope he is quite well."

This was frigid enough certainly; but it sounded so like what other people would have said under the circumstances that Wilhelmina was quite proud of it.

Mr. Carmichael smiled. "Oh, yes, he is quite well; but he doesn't grow any younger, and he is very lonely. It would be a real kindness if you would write him a nice chatty letter sometimes."

Wilhelmina looked distressed. "I am afraid there is nothing to write about," she said shyly.

"Nothing to write about! Why, tell him about the books you read, and the places you see—Westminster Abbey, the Tower, St. Paul's. You have no idea how interesting all that is to us country-folks."

But she shook her head. "I haven't seen any of those places," she said.

Mr. Carmichael looked incredulous. This was a hard saying to the provincial mind. He was learning now for the first time, what most men know so well, that Windyhaugh itself is not farther from London than are some of the suburbs thereof.

"In any case," he said cheerfully, "there remain the books; and that would please him most of all."

Wilhelmina did not answer. Had she lived with grown people of average intellectual interests, or with children of her own age, she would have long since learned to give a glib opinion of a book. As it was, the suggestion that she should do so seemed to her positively terrifying. She knew when she disliked a book— a rare occurrence—and when it was "awfully nice," but, with the best will in the world, one can't make a letter out of that.

She looked so unhappy that Mr. Carmichael hastened to change the subject.

"And how are the lessons getting on?"

But this was going from bad to worse. She coloured painfully. "I haven't been going to school—just lately," she added, loyally.

"That seems a pity. Wouldn't you like to?"

Like to? Like to be clever? What a question!

"I—I don't think my stepmother could spare me," she faltered; "and—and I'm going to have music lessons—next term."

Next term! As she had once said to Mr. Darsie, she felt herself "smiling inside" as she uttered the words, and the smile was not a very sunny one.

Mr. Carmichael drew a note-book from his pocket, and proceeded to modify his complicated programme.

"Suppose you come with me to Westminster Abbey this afternoon?" he said. "I should enjoy having a companion."

Her face lighted up, but she shook her head.

"There are some new people coming," she said; "I must be here."

"But everything is ready, isn't it?"

She nodded, with the first gleam of humour she had shown. "So you would think; but they always want something that we just haven't got."

Mr. Carmichael felt oppressed by a sense of his own incompetence as he ran down the steps. He was aware that he had not said a single word that could be of use to the child. We are all so apt to forget that it is not mainly the spoken word that counts.

A few minutes later he passed the door of the chapel where the evangelistic services were being held, and he made a note of the place, as he meant to be present that evening. The revivalist was said to be a man of great power.

"I wonder whether I should have advised Wilhelmina to go," he mused. On the whole he decided that he had done better to refrain. His breezy nature shrank instinctively from morbid emotionalism in religion.

But the fascination of the preacher was on Wilhelmina, and evening found her once more in the chapel. This time she went early to secure a back seat. Noth-

ing would have induced her to face the Inquiry Room
again.

Two young men beside her had much to say of their
gratitude to the preacher. "I have found him even more
helpful since I was converted," said one. "He gives one
so many straight tips for the higher life."

Wilhelmina was shocked at the irreverence of the
remark; but the preacher, had he heard it, would have
felt differently. Indeed he might not improbably have
made use of the words as the title of a discourse or
pamphlet. Nature does sometimes confer even on the
truly devout a taste for racy expression.

At last the door opened and the revivalist entered,
accompanied by a party of ministers of all denomina-
tions. Wilhelmina's heart leaped to see Mr. Carmichael
among the number. In truth he had not meant to take
so prominent a place; but he had arrived to find the
hall overcrowded, and the doorkeeper had directed him
to the platform.

The address was full of mesmeric power. It was
mainly adapted perhaps to the stony ground, but even
the good and receptive soil showed a marvellous willing-
ness to let itself be harrowed.

When the speaker resumed his seat, an opportunity
was given for others to say a few words. There was a
pause, and then Mr. Carmichael rose. The self-restraint
of his manner was in striking contrast to the methods
of the evangelist.

"I am sure," he said, "we have all listened with the
deepest interest to our brother's powerful and most moving address. One is diffident about adding a word to
such an appeal, and yet, as I have sat here, looking
round upon so many anxious faces, I have wondered
whether some were not distressing themselves unnecessarily.

"It is not so much what a man *believes* that saves
him: it is his *faith*. Are not some of you torturing yourselves about your inability to go through an intellectual
process, your inability to grasp an intellectual proposi-
tion? If so, you are mistaking the gate. It is strait, I
know; but the straitness is not for the intellect; it is

for the soul: the narrowness is not for the mind; but for the heart and conduct. He who would walk with Christ must simply want to be good more than he wants to be rich or famous or popular or clever. Think no more of your mind: let your mind have a rest: does your *heart* run to meet the Lord Jesus?

> " ' Who fathoms the eternal thought?
> Who talks of scheme and plan ?
> The Lord is God ! He needeth not
> The poor device of man.'

" Can you honestly say, ' Lord, I am a sinner and a very stupid sinner; I don't know much about doctrine, but I do honestly want to throw in my lot with Thee. *I want to be good!* I know I shall sin again, and yet again; but, with Thy help, *I will not be beaten by my sins?* '

" If you can say all that, don't try to say any more; the more will come. You have wasted time enough. Gird up your loins, and ask what you can be about.

" If you can say all that—not only in the heat and excitement and fear of the moment, but as the deliberate aspiration of your saner hours—I hold out to you the right hand of fellowship in the name of Christ! "

Who shall reckon the force of the unconventional word—the word that dispels the vapours and glooms, not because it is learned or clever—not even because of its inherent truth, but just because it rises molten hot from a human heart?

Mr. Carmichael had got into touch with Wilhelmina at last.

CHAPTER XVIII.

ROUNDS BY WHICH WE MAY ASCEND.

On any theory of the religious life—nay, on any theory of the physical life—on the sheer frigid doctrine that pleasure is the absence of pain—I feel that I ought to write of raptures for Wilhelmina now.

9

But the simple truth is that no raptures occurred.

> "The spirit bloweth and is still,
> In mystery our soul abides."

And apparently in her case the time for rapture was not yet. Almost in spite of her own will, something within her perceived the reasonableness of Mr. Carmichael's test, and that was all. Relief she experienced certainly, and an ability to sleep at night, even when she was tired or excited, without the haunting fear of waking up in hell; but of all the wondrous joys she had expected, she tasted almost none.

In spite of her relief she could not shake off a vague feeling that she had been defrauded. Through all the disappointments and hardships of her life she had looked forward to her conversion as some young men look forward to the time when they shall be really in love; and now apparently the long-dreamt-of moment had come and gone without even giving her a chance to cry, " Stay, thou art fair! " She felt—though of course she did not so express the feeling—that, from an artistic point of view, her conversion had fallen flat, that it had come about with an ease—I might almost say a cheapness— that was out of all proportion to the agonies of the preceding years.

She was as one who, after knocking vainly at a door, has turned his back, and, leaning against the gate-post, has gazed long and dreamily at the prospect before his eyes. At length he turns again to the door, and behold it stands open wide! When did it open?—and why, if not in answer to his knocks? Is it possible that he might have entered long ago?

Moreover, now that the door is open, it reveals no celestial vision—only the first few steps of an uphill path.

Wilhelmina did not shirk the deduction. She was saved—if indeed she *was* saved?—and she must now begin to work out her own salvation. There was a little —just a little—inspiration in this thought, to atone for all the joys she had missed.

And having received spiritual sustenance in a somewhat indefinite form, she must needs make haste to cast it into an evangelical mould. A subtle form of temptation is that—"*Im Ganzen—haltet euch an Worte!*" She attended more of the services, and adapted her feelings as far as she could to what she ought to have felt. When she dreamt of saving other souls—as some told her she must strive to do at once—she adopted, not Mr. Carmichael's words, but those of the evangelist.

There was much truth in the words of him who said, Give me the first five years of a child's life, and I will give you the rest.

It may be that the increasing worries of her daily life had something to do with her lack of the spiritual joy to which she felt herself entitled. Hardship and deprivation have often proved "rounds by which we may ascend," but carking care, recurrent dread of importunate creditors, of summonses and the like—it is not at the beginning of the spiritual life that one can rise by these!

"Wilhelmina," said her stepmother one morning, "just go up, will you, and listen to Mrs. Stott's views on the subject of lunch and dinner? Tell her I am not well."

Wilhelmina glanced rather enviously out of the window at a crossing-sweeper over the way. What a luxury it must be to have nothing more complicated to do than to sweep and gather pennies, buy a twopenny pie when funds allowed, and tumble into one's own quiet little corner at night!

She went upstairs with slow unwilling feet, but there was just a touch of graceful dignity in her manner as she said, "Mrs. Galbraith is not well. She asked me to come instead of her."

"Well, you look a purposelike young person," said the lodger brusquely, and she entered somewhat lengthily into her "views" for the day. "We are going out this afternoon, so we shan't want dinner till half-past seven; and say to cook that the fried potatoes were greasy last time. Tell her Captain Stott can't *touch* them unless they are perfectly dry and crisp!"

"Perhaps she'd like to come down and fry them herself," was cook's rejoinder to an euphuistic paraphrase of this message. "Half-past seven! I'd like to know when the washing-up will be done. You can tell your ma that she had better be looking out for somebody else to cook for these here Stotts!"

The familiarity of the last sentence cut Wilhelmina to the quick; but she could not afford to show her feelings.

"I'll come and help you with the washing-up," she said gently.

But it was not in her power to make things go smoothly that evening. The Stotts did not come in till after eight, and the dinner cook sent up then was even less inviting than it need have been. Moreover, bad as it was, it failed to give the woman's ill temper sufficient vent, and Wilhelmina had much to bear and still more to ignore during the process of washing-up.

"My little helper!" said Mrs. Galbraith kindly when she returned to the sitting-room. "Are you going to make the toast again to-morrow?"

"Yes."

"Nobody makes such delicious toast as you. And, while you are downstairs, I wish you would give an eye to Sarah as she fills the coal-scuttles for the sitting-rooms. Make her put some small stuff into each, and see that she doesn't fill them too full. She just wants to save herself the trouble of going up for them again. She never thinks of my poor purse."

It was a good deal to ask of so sensitive a child, and many a heartfelt prayer went up over the filling of those coal-scuttles; but assuredly the answer to those prayers had no immediate bearing on the matter in hand. Wilhelmina never acquired the gift—I had almost said the *knack*—of gaining by prayer the petty temporal things she longed for.

"Mrs. Stott says they must make a change," said Mrs. Galbraith a few days later.

Wilhelmina's heart sank. Mrs. Carlton had just started for Algiers.

"What is wrong?" she asked.

"Oh, everything; meals unpunctual, cooking unreliable, coal-scuttles not full enough. I told her I always impressed upon the servants that they must fill the scuttles *well;* but that they found them easier to carry when they were not too full."

" But *had* you told the servants that ? "

" Well, no; I don't suppose I had; but one must say something. I don't think you in the least realize how difficult it is to make ends meet—or rather to keep them from gaping quite too wide! I said I would speak seriously to cook, and Mrs. Stott has promised to try us a little longer. She is not a gentlewoman. It is dreadful to be at the beck and call of these people with their bourgeois notions of comfort."

Wilhelmina felt an odd sense of physical *chill.* She had often heard her stepmother lie before now; but she had never heard her recount a lie with such absolute *sangfroid* and self-complacency. At Windyhaugh the child had been taught that affliction was the forcing-house for the Christian virtues; but assuredly her stepmother was growing more hardened and callous about many things. Was it possible that they were going downhill together?

" My money comes to-morrow," she said. " Cook will do better when she gets her wages paid. I don't want a new dress, Mütterchen. Let us pay them both up to date, and start fresh. It will put them in such a good humour."

The money duly arrived, and by the same post came a ten-pound note from an uncle of Mrs. Galbraith's. Enclosed with this was a letter intimating that no more need be expected from the same source; but Mrs. Galbraith declined to be depressed by the warning. " I knew the tide would turn!" she cried delightedly; and it was all Wilhelmina could do to prevent her plunging into divers small extravagances to celebrate the turning.

The servants seemed pleasantly surprised when they received their wages, and for the rest of the day everything went as smoothly as possible.

Next morning Wilhelmina was awakened by the violent ringing of bells, and a minute later Mrs. Galbraith came into her room.

" Just run down, dear, and see what the servants are
about," she said. " It is eight o'clock, and no one is
astir. Mrs. Stott is ringing for her hot water."

Wilhelmina's teeth chattered as she slipped on the
roomy dressing-gown that had formerly been the property of her stepmother. The dim light of the winter
morning revealed the hopeless confusion of the kitchen,
the dreary lifeless ashes of the fire.

" Cook ? " said Wilhelmina in a startled voice.

There was no answer, and she made her way to their
room.

The beds had been slept in, and the bed-clothes were
all in confusion, but not a scrap of the servants' property remained—save indeed two poor little coloured religious cards which Wilhelmina had given them, out of
her poverty, on Christmas day. These lay trampled un-
derfoot on the dirty floor.

For a few seconds the child gave way to the feeling
of heart-sickness that rushed over her. Then she opened
the window, and the raw morning air seemed to give
her fresh life.

With a bound she was back in the kitchen, raking
the lifeless embers from the grate. She could not stop
to do it thoroughly: in a minute she had seized paper
and sticks with a reckless hand, and had set them alight.
A few little bits of coal completed the pyre, and then
she ran upstairs.

" Well," said Mrs. Galbraith, " I hope they are
ashamed of themselves."

" I hope so," said Wilhelmina dryly. " They're gone."

She could not resist this bit of dramatic effect, cruel
though it was.

It was a full minute before Mrs. Galbraith found
voice. Her face was very white, and for the first time
Wilhelmina saw her look positively vindictive.

" *This*," she said at last in tones of suppressed fury,
" comes of paying their wages ! "

Wilhelmina nodded. She was hurrying on her clothes
with all the speed she could muster. " I know," she
said stoically; " but there is no use fretting, Mütterchen. I have lighted the fire. I'll tell Mrs. Stott she

shall have her hot water in a few minutes, and then I'll get breakfast as fast as ever I can. I won't tell her what has happened till afterwards."

" I don't see that we need take her into our confidence."

" I thought of that," said Wilhelmina sadly, as she drew the comb through her rebellious hair, " but she is bound to know sooner or later."

" But, child, I can't believe it. There must surely be some mistake."

" So I thought. But I don't know where the mistake can be."

Now that Wilhelmina had merged her feelings in action, she was as happy as a child need be—happier certainly than she had been for a long time. She knew she could surprise the whole household by her competency, and it really was much easier to do the necessary work for the moment herself than to be the central point of a triangle composed of mistress, lodgers, and servants. She flew around like a bird; and, although the servants had levied an extortionate toll on the cold bacon, she contrived to send up a creditable breakfast in a very short space of time. It was quite true, as Mrs. Carlton had said, that she had learned to do nothing well; but in a great emergency people are not hypercritical, and she seemed to do things superlatively well.

For the first time her heart was in a glow of religious feeling, and, childlike, she fancied that the glow would last for ever. The spirit in which she washed the dishes used by the servants for their last hurried meal was surely just that in which the saints of old had tended the sores of the afflicted, and washed the feet of beggars. Natural disgust was *burned out* of her like alloy from gold in the furnace. Surely she had hit the focus of the divine rays at last.

It was well perhaps that this mood should be sharply tested at once, for the test never tarries long.

" How bright you look!" said Mrs. Galbraith enviously as they sat at breakfast. " I can't tell you how this kind of thing upsets me. Look how my hand shakes."

" Poor little Mütterchen!" Wilhelmina thought of

course that religion steadied her own nerves, but fortunately she had grace given her not to say so. Youth
cannot be expected to realize the difference that sheer
youth makes. Even in a sad childhood there is a certain amount of freshness, of originality, about the blows
and rebuffs of life. Each one gives us a new chance
of earning *kudos*, of developing our moral thews and
sinews; but, when we grow old, hardship and suffering
wear a familiar face. We have passed that way so often
before!

"I do feel so poorly," continued Mrs. Galbraith. "I
don't see how I can go out in the rain to the registry
office. Do you think you could go for once? You are
growing to be such a comfort to me!"

Wilhelmina looked down at her short shabby frock.
"You *look* so different from me, Mütterchen," she said,
with a pitiful little shake in her voice. "When you wear
your best things you look like a duchess still. I am
afraid they won't pay any attention to poor me."

"Nonsense! Mrs. Stott has just been saying what
a capable person you are."

"Very well; I'll go," said Wilhelmina; and she may
be pardoned if she had a mental picture of herself laying
a costly sacrifice "on the altar."

"Get them to come to-day if possible. Say I will
write for their characters later. Mind you don't say anything about its being a lodging-house; and if the woman
at the corner has cheap chrysanthemums, bring in a few.
I will send them up to Mrs. Stott."

Wilhelmina did not think chrysanthemums would
have much effect on Mrs. Stott, but she had another
battle to fight at present.

"Mütterchen," she said, "I *must* say we keep lodgers. We don't want the new servants to leave the day
they arrive, as Matilda did."

"Matilda was a goose."

"And if they begin by despising us——"

Mrs. Galbraith drew herself up. "Despising us!"
she said. "You forget yourself, Wilhelmina. If you
tell them this is a lodging-house, they will think of a
common place like Mrs. Brown's over the way. Whereas

if they come and see for themselves that it is a *lady's* house, and that things are done properly—the chances are that they will be only too glad to stay."

Wilhelmina did not answer. Indeed there was nothing more to be said. She no longer had a mental picture of a sacrifice laid on the altar; but she set her teeth and determined to "worry through."

The rain poured in torrents as she trudged along, wondering how she was to satisfy both her stepmother and her own conscience. Fortunately—as is so often the case when we distress ourselves most—the difficulty existed in prospect only. "You keep lodgers, don't you?" said the manager briskly, when Wilhelmina stated her requirements, and no one could find fault with her for replying, "One or two."

But she suffered many humiliations in the course of the morning. She was no match for shrewd London servants, and she felt their contempt even when it was not expressed. Only one was rude enough to say, "But *you* are not the young lydy, are you?" Yet even that was better than the patronizing kindness with which most of them treated her. At last she got hold of a substantial "general" who promised to come the next day, and then she was fain to run home in humble triumph.

"Only a general!" said Mrs. Galbraith resignedly. "Well, she will at least tide us over till we can look round."

But this was hoping too much.

Late in the evening a dirty blotted postcard was handed in—

"on thinking it over I don't see my way to take in hand with your situation."

Wilhelmina looked at the card fixedly for some time.

"I wonder," she said at last, "why she took the trouble to write."

CHAPTER XIX.

THE INGLE NEUK.

THE grocer looked at the clock.

It was near closing time, and the shop was full of people. " Hurry up, Jim," he whispered uneasily. " I want to get through."

The grocer was a famous gossip. I am not sure that the word does full justice to the human and philosophic interest he took in his fellow-creatures; but I know that if you wanted local information, you bethought yourself forthwith of the co-existing want of soap or sugar, and, if you had a valuable secret to dispose of, you were in no doubt at all as to your market.

Nor was the dusty little shop a meeting-ground for the lower classes exclusively. The days had not yet come when the gentry ordered down a box from the stores. " Darsie's mixture "—at four shillings a pound —was equal in quality to any tea you could get in Edinburgh: Darsie's whisky was simply first-rate: and he even had a brand of tobacco that would pass muster in an emergency.

So my lady's carriage stopped at his door just often enough to keep him in touch with high life; and the neighbouring lairds, when they found themselves in Queensmains with a little odd time on their hands, were well aware that they might spend it worse than in a chat with the grocer. His range of subjects was wonderful. With the one important exception of horse-flesh—on which, by the way, he rather fancied himself— there were few topics on which he was not an authority. He was well read in politics, conscientiously squeezing the last drop of nourishment out of his daily paper; he could tell you who was who with a nicety that was beyond praise; and an Oxford undergraduate, who chanced to be in those parts, had been heard to say that his knowledge of books fairly took one's breath away.

Poor Mr. Darsie! What it was to him to get hold of a college man! It is pathetic to think that he should not have had his fill of their society, for after all, they are so common! But I fear they voted him rather a bore with his eager questions. When you had come straight from a jolly sociable athletic life—a life just sprinkled over perhaps with a little Latin or Mathematics—it was rather disconcerting to be asked, What influence in your opinion was being exercised on the thought of the English Universities by the works of the late Mr. Robertson of Brighton? The chances were that you had never heard of the man, and your surprise was great when you accidentally discovered next term that his "works" really were in the University library, and that some of the fellows had read them!

Heigho! One hopes there is a big English University in heaven for all the good folks who ought to have been in one on earth.

But, failing the college man, some interest or amusement might be derived from everybody. Even the poor old washerwoman who came in on Saturday night for her pinch of tea and tobacco was something more than a mere supernumerary on the stage where history was daily being made—for the benefit of the queer little grocer.

To-night, however, his puppets did not interest him, and he made haste to "put them past," as he would have expressed it, in their drawer. "Up wi' the shutters, noo, Jim!" he said briskly, "and I'll lock the door ahint ye."

He hastened upstairs, changed his greasy old coat for one of tolerable respectability, stirred the fire, set the spirit-stand within reach, and composed himself to wait. The book he had on hand at this time was Martineau's Types of Ethical Theory; but he could not fix his mind on that now.

He had not waited long when Mr. Carmichael's characteristic knock was heard at the door.

"Come in, sir, come in! I'm sure ye're heartily welcome."

The minister laughed. "No need to tell me that to-night, Mr. Darsie," he said. "'How beautiful upon the mountains——'!"

The old man looked at him anxiously. "You'll ha' seen her?"

"Oh, yes, I have seen her."

Mr. Darsie's face brightened. "And how did you find the mighty city?"

Mr. Carmichael laughed again. "Oh, we'll take Wilhelmina first," he said. "I think she is looking well —in fact she attracts me much more than she did as a child. She is well grown;" and he drew a bright picture of the young girl as he had seen her first, "like a freshly painted tug with a couple of coal barges in tow."

The grocer nodded repeatedly like a mandarin.

"Ay, ay," he said. "I was sure she'd be tall. They're fine folk to look at on both sides o' the house. She'll promise to be bonny?"

"I think so: she is thin and lanky, but her features are good."

"An' she'll be making gran' progress at the schule? I mind o' your telling me what a fine scholar yon Mademoiselle found her."

Down came the heavy brows.

"Mr. Darsie," said the minister, "till this moment I meant to answer your questions with discrimination, but now I think I will tell you everything exactly as it happened, and we'll talk it over together. Wilhelmina was out when I called, and I had the advantage of a chat with a lodger of theirs—an extraordinarily sensible and competent woman—so sensible, indeed, that one was distinctively on one's guard against what she said."

He related the whole story very simply.

"Did you see Mistress Galbraith?" asked the grocer.

"She came in for a few minutes before I left—told me Wilhelmina was a great comfort to her."

The grocer sat gazing into the fire for a time; then he raised his eyes and looked full into the minister's face.

"*Damn him!*" he said deliberately.

"Mr. Galbraith? Is he worth all that? I confess I am at a loss where to place him in the animal kingdom. It is a sheer abuse of language to call him a mammalian.

And yet I suppose he might be worse. He is evidently
one of life's failures, but at least he doesn't sponge on
his wife as some men do. If he can't help, perhaps he
is better out of the way."

"An' what right has he to be ane o' life's failures, as
you ca' it? He's cliver eneugh for ten. What w'y
would he sponge on his wife? He had money frae his
faither, an' a tocher wi' the first ane. If the world used
him ill—an' I aye thocht he got nae mair nor his deserts
—it at least gi'ed him a guid education. He was bound
i' the eyes o' God to hand it on to his bairn."

"But, good friend, is the loss so great? What is a
girl's education worth as a rule?"

"I ken. Ay, I ken a' that; but Wilhelmina was no'
a common bairn. She'd ha' made a scholar."

"She may make something better."

"I ken that too. My quarrel's no' wi' the Lord. It's
wi' George Galbraith."

"I would like to give him a piece of my mind, I confess. The lady I mentioned, Mrs. Carlton, says Macintyre pays Wilhelmina's money direct to herself. I
will call on Macintyre to-morrow, and see if he can be
induced to write to Mr. Galbraith. Failing that, is
there any other relative he could apply to?"

"There's yon Mistress Dalrymple. Her man's rich
eneugh. The Dalrymple's mines maun be worth a duke's
ransom the noo."

"All right. I'll see what can be done." The minister stretched himself. "Well-a-day! It seems ages
since I last had a chat here with you."

"I mak' nae doobt. A week in London—my word!
It maun hae been a michty experience."

Mr. Carmichael laughed and blushed. "It was, in
some ways. I have got into such hot water!"

The old eyes twinkled sympathetically through the
gold-rimmed spectacles. "No' of a domestic nature, I
hope?"

"No—thank Heaven! And yet I am not sure that
it isn't worse. It is theological. Think of my letting
myself in for a heresy hunt!"

The old man drew himself up. "An' what w'y would

ye no' let yersel' in for a heresy hunt? It has whiles
been the lot o' your betters."

"No doubt. But why should I? The creed of my
fathers is good enough for me."

"Yet there are gey queer things i' the creed o' your
fathers."

"Perhaps. No, no! Don't confront me with chapter and verse. It is barren work tinkering at a creed.
So long as the confession permits me to believe that God
is bigger than any creed, I'll undertake to find room."

A shade of disappointment crossed the old man's face.
"Weel, maybe ye're richt," he said resignedly. "I'm
free to confess that some o' our heretics have no' been
precisely an edifying spectacle. They read twa-three
new books, then 'Verily we are the men,' they cry, 'and
the presbytery's nought but a wheen doited loons!' But
the presbytery ups and on wi' its war-paint, and lo, my
knight is unmasked and doun on his knees—an impident
college lad!"

The minister laughed. "You are crushing," he said.

"Na, na. I'm only speaking o' the ae sort. I think
if you were minded to play the reformer you'd hae the
spunk to carry it through. Ye mind o' Carlyle—'If any
man hold, or is convinced that he holds, any truth, in
God's name let him utter his truth or conviction, and
leave the consequences with the God who gave it him'?
That would be the w'y o't wi' you, nae doubt?"

Mr. Carmichael looked ashamed of himself. "It was
—in a humble fashion," he said simply.

"Were you preaching in London?"

"No. You have read no doubt of Freeland's great
revival mission. I went to hear him, and the place was
so crammed that I had to sit on the platform."

"Ay?" The old man's face was aglow with interest.
This was his very own ground.

"It was magnificent. It really was. His power of
rousing the hardened must be extraordinary; and yet
all the time he was speaking in that hot reeking atmosphere I had a mental picture of the Man of Sorrows
standing in the sweet morning air on the open hillside,
preaching a sermon that no one ever has contracted into

a creed. I am not sure that the revivalist did not reach some souls the Master would have missed; but his hearers were not *all* hardened, and his ways seemed to me so much too brutal and sensational for some. His sieve retained the large stones, but the small ones seemed to be slipping through his meshes. I felt that many there should be seeking God in action, not in sensation, so when an opportunity was given to the rest of us to speak——"

"Well done!" cried Mr. Darsie.

"Wait a bit! Wait a bit! It was very forward and rash, for many of those on the platform were my seniors —and betters to boot. But somehow it was just borne in on me that faith for many of us—thank God!—simply means a turning to the light, so I rose to my feet."

"And said——"

"Oh, bless me! I don't know what I said. I know what *they* said, and what they made me *feel*. Of course there wasn't a word that they could exactly object to on doctrinal grounds, but they said I had turned from its course a swift and well-thrown dart. Perhaps they were right. I lay awake half the night thinking what a fool I was. One often recalls that fine expression, ' the *foolishness* of preaching.' Who shall define faith to him who has not felt it? We strive and strive to *generate faith*, and all the time—the wind bloweth where it will!"

Mr. Darsie was gazing fixedly into the fire. The minister had wandered a bit beyond that limited spiritual tether of his. "It's a pity," said the old man at last, "but what Williamina had been there!"

CHAPTER XX.

A RESCUE.

MR. CARMICHAEL interviewed the lawyer next day, and obtained his promise to write to Mr. Galbraith.

"He is not a rich man," said Mr. Macintyre gravely,

"and I was under the impression that he already contributed a considerable sum to his wife's support."

"He had money with his first wife, I understand?"

"Very little. She would have been a rich woman had she lived; but the money that would have come to her is not likely to come to Mr. Galbraith. I suppose it will all go to Mrs. Dalrymple now."

"In any case you see how undesirable it is that a clever child like that should be growing up without any education."

"Oh, quite—quite. But the stepmother must be to blame. I don't believe he realizes the situation in the least."

"At any rate you will admit that it is his business to realize the situation?"

The lawyer raised his hand. "It is not my business to sit in judgment on him, sir," he said. "He is a man on whom life has been hard. But I will write to him, and if nothing comes of that, I'll write to Mrs. Dalrymple. I am very sorry to hear such an account of little Miss Galbraith."

Mr. Carmichael was glad to have a disagreeable business behind him. "It seems to me," he said to himself as he ran down the steps, "that what George Galbraith wants is a good kicking."

It was a fine cloudless afternoon in January. The minister was in a mood for a good walk across country, so he resolved to look up a few humble parishioners in the outlying hamlet of Windyhaugh. "It seems an age," he said, "since I saw the old place."

He strode along the crisp roads at a good swinging pace. Windyhaugh had been let for a few years, but now it stood empty, save for the presence of old Ann who acted as caretaker. The shrubbery was tangled and overgrown, and the whole place had an air of neglect. "I will look up Ann on my way back," thought the minister. "No doubt she will give me a cup of tea."

At the outskirts of the village he was waylaid by an old woman. "Will you please gang doun to the shore, sir?" she said. "There's been an awfu' accident. Twa

gentlemen were crossing ower frae Silverton, an' the
boat capsized close to the shore here."

"They got to land, I hope?"

"Ou ay, sir. Ane o' them is a' richt, but they're no'
sure o' the tither. I was no' to tell folk, for they're no'
wantin' a crood; but they sent my Jack for the doctor."

"The *doctor!*" said the minister aghast. "It may
be midnight before they find him!"

He took to his heels at once, and ran in the direction
of the beach. Some months before, he had come across
a paper on the treatment of the apparently drowned,
and had resolved to impress the directions on his memory in case of such an emergency as the present. Unfortunately he had omitted to carry out his laudable intention, and now he strove in vain to recall the directions prescribed.

"One ought to be able to think out the *rationale* of
the thing," he said to himself indignantly as he ran; but
his knowledge of physiology was even more elementary
than he supposed, and he had come in sight of the little
group on the beach before he had decided on any plan of
action.

He remembered afterwards how striking was the
scene that met his anxious eyes. The sun was setting
over the sea, and a few weird wisps of black cloud stood
out in strong relief against a ruddy background. The
whole group was in silhouette save for the figure of a
young man who lay stretched on the rocks, with his
shoulders propped on a bundle. At his head knelt an
older man—also dripping wet—in his shirt sleeves. He
had taken a grip of the lad's arms above the elbow, and,
with a deliberate rhythmical movement, was pressing
them against the patient's sides and then raising them
above his head. His whole attention was fixed on the
supine figure; but the calmness of his manner was such
as to suggest preoccupation in a game of skill rather
than in a hand-to-hand tussle with death.

"Thank Heaven!" said the minister, relieved to find
his own incompetence merged in the competence of another.

For a short time he watched the slow masterly move-

10

ment with admiration, and then he threw off his coat.
" I think I see now how you do it," he said. " You must
be tired. Let me relieve you."

The stranger looked up without disturbing the
rhythm of the movement. His grave eyes took the
measure of the speaker, so there was a tacit compliment
in the movement of the head with which he motioned
to the minister to take a place beside him. Mr. Carmichael felt a sudden desire, not only to save a life, but
to gain the approbation of this man.

The work was much harder than he had anticipated,
but he did his best, as indeed most men would have done
with those critical eyes upon them.

"*Surtout point de zêle*," said the stranger gently.
" I think he will be all right, but his gratitude might be
tempered if he woke to a dislocated shoulder."

The minister smiled.

" Slowly! Steady! Press his elbows well into his
ribs. Now you have got the knack." For the first time
the speaker took his eyes from the patient.

" Well," he said quietly, turning to the little group
of lads who were looking on, " have you got the shutter
and the blankets? That's right."

He threw a blanket over the prostrate figure, and
showed two of the lads how to chafe the cold limbs.

" I think we might get a little brandy down now," he
said, producing a flask, and he succeeded in administering a few drops with excellent effect. The young man
swallowed them, then opened his eyes and looked around
him. A fine face his, blurred and dreamy though the
eyes were—the face of a young idealist.

The minister was growing very tired with the unaccustomed exertion, but he was determined not to cry
for quarter. His breath came fast, and the sweat stood
on his brow before the stranger interfered.

" Now then, *padre*," he said. " I think he is all
right. You take one arm, and I'll take the other for a
few minutes, just to make sure."

This was easy, involving as it did a change of position and of muscular strain. It was pleasant too to work
with such a man—to watch how smoothly his muscles

moved in obedience to his bidding. A line or two of poetry ran persistently—with what he himself deemed irrelevant profanity—in the minister's mind—

> " Here, work enough to watch
> The Master work, and catch
> Hints of the proper craft, tricks of the tool's true play."

A few minutes later they lifted the patient on to the shutter, and gave it to two strong young fellows to carry.

" Take him up to Windyhaugh," said the stranger. " Steady! We'll follow in case you grow tired."

" I am afraid that won't do," said the minister. " Windyhaugh is shut up."

The stranger gave him a curious glance. " I think I can gain entrance to it," he said.

Just as they were leaving the rocks he laid his hand on the minister's arm and turned towards the sunset. The colour of the sky had deepened to an angry red, and the clouds had assumed an aspect more weird and grotesque than ever. " Strange," he said, " an hour ago the sky was pale blue, with golden white clouds like a flight of angels—far more like angels than Doré's picture. And now, look! It is a regular Brocken dance."

" It is very remarkable," said the minister.

He was ashamed of the stiff conventional response, and indeed his feeling for this strange man was anything but stiff and conventional. He keenly appreciated that friendly touch on the arm, that casual little remark. Moreover, had he not read Martin's translation of Faust? —and did he not come straight from Doré's picture?

" I suppose you are a doctor? " he said as they made their way up to the house.

The stranger laughed. " Oh, no; but I have found that kind of thing useful before now. I have done a deal of yachting in my time."

" Can I be of any farther use? "

" I think not, thank you. He is all right for the moment, and the doctor will be here before night."

" May I call to-morrow to enquire? "

" I am sure the young fellow will be delighted to

have an opportunity of expressing his gratitude. I fear
I must leave the place to-night."

"There is no question of gratitude to me," said the
minister impulsively. "Your friend owes his life to
you."

The stranger looked up. "I think you are under a
misapprehension," he said. "I don't know the young
fellow. I chanced to see the accident from the terrace.
Oh!"—he glanced at his dripping clothes—"I did lend
a hand to pull them out of the water. The other was
all right, save for a rap on the head, so I sent him
straight up to my house. My name is George Galbraith."

CHAPTER XXI.

THE FAIRY GODMOTHER.

THE grey light of a February dawn was breaking over
London.

The month was one of the coldest on record, and
most of the pipes in the neighbourhood were frozen.
Wilhelmina was out in the garden, armed with a shovel
and a huge kitchen kettle, fetching in snow to melt for
household use.

A number of servants had come and gone since the
"general's" fine feeling had prompted her to send that
post-card. The difficulty was to get two at a time, and
hitherto the single one had always declined to stay, for
in truth the housework was falling into arrears sufficiently alarming even to a competent person. Moreover the servants next door were ready now with a
mysterious whisper that Mrs. Galbraith's was a "bad
place," and there was no fighting against a rumour like
that, though beef and beer were plentiful in the kitchen,
when Mrs. Galbraith was living mainly on bread and tea.

The departure of the Stotts had come almost as a relief at last, especially as their rooms were quickly taken
by two quiet elderly ladies who were fairly easy to

please; and indeed the absence of servants was almost a relief too in its way, now that there were so many enforced petty economies to make mother and daughter ridiculous in vulgar eyes.

Still, when one first woke up on a bitter winter's day, one would have been thankful for the veriest cockney slut just to bring in the snow, and light the kitchen fire.

Mrs. Galbraith's health was really giving way under the strain and privation. About the end of January she had been made very happy by a letter from her husband—a letter enclosing a twenty-pound note, and expressing the hope that Wilhelmina was " getting on with her lessons; " but of course the twenty pounds slipped at once through the sieve of their requirements, and left them to all practical purposes where they had been before.

Wilhelmina had to work much harder than was strictly desirable at her age, but many a girl has had to do that before her. Fortunately her appetite was good, and she justified a traditional belief in the virtues of oatmeal porridge; but this did not prevent her suffering acutely when she and her stepmother were preparing the lodgers' simple midday dinner, and night after night she dreamed of sweetmeats and cakes with a persistence that seemed pitiably carnal in a child of light. Her great prayer at this time was to be delivered from temptations of the flesh.

" I have had such a happy idea," said Mrs. Galbraith one afternoon. " You must write to your Aunt Enid. I can't imagine why we didn't think of it before. She couldn't refuse to help us."

Wilhelmina shook her head. " No, Mütterchen," she said, " that's impossible. I can't write to her."

" Then all I can say is that you are very proud and selfish. I have written to all my relations, and this is the first time I have asked you to write to anybody."

" Mütterchen," pleaded Wilhelmina, " do let us go and live in some tiny cottage."

" On forty pounds a year? And what about the lease of this house? If we could only let all the rooms and get a couple of capable servants, we should be all right."

"*If!*" thought Wilhelmina.

"Even supposing your aunt refused to lend us money, which is impossible, think how easy it would be for her to send us lodgers now and then."

Wilhelmina sighed. Her life had taught her some sharp lessons in worldly wisdom, but she could not bring herself to point out to her stepmother how impossible it would be for Mrs. Dalrymple to own to her friends that she had relatives who kept a lodging-house in Bayswater. "Of course we wouldn't say she was my aunt," thought Wilhelmina, "but I can't *tell* her that we wouldn't."

"In the meantime," continued Mrs. Galbraith, "think what a difference a few pounds would make to us! And there is your aunt living in boundless luxury."

"It's no use," said Wilhelmina. "I cannot write to her. I would rather sweep a crossing."

"Oh, that is cheaply said. You are not likely to be asked to sweep a crossing. It is easy for you with your healthy appetite. Think what it would be to me to have even a little nourishing food."

"You would like tea now, wouldn't you, Mütterchen?" said Wilhelmina, glad to strike off at a tangent. "I will get it before I get the Miss Prynnes'."

She laid out the tray as attractively as might be. On the larder shelf stood a small roast turkey which had been sent to Miss Prynne a few days before. "It will take them weeks to nibble through all that," thought Wilhelmina. "They will never miss a tiny morsel." The smell of the turkey seemed to penetrate to the child's very finger-tips. It was more than she could bear. With hasty trembling hands she carved a few ragged slices, and ran upstairs.

"There, Mütterchen!" she said defiantly. "I have helped myself from Miss Prynne's shelf in the larder. They'll never miss it."

"Well, I am sure they pay little enough for all the trouble they give!" said Mrs. Galbraith. (Was it possible that this was not the first occasion on which the lodger's supplies had been forced to render tribute?)

" I quite expected they would ask us to share that turkey."

She partook of the luxury with something more like appetite than she had shown for many a day, and insisted that Wilhelmina should eat what remained. The child refused at first, but she had tact enough to see that her stepmother might well resent such self-denial on her part, and besides—she was so hungry!

But retribution was destined to come with swift and sure foot. " I think," said Miss Prynne, severely, that evening, " we will keep our provisions in the cupboard here for the future. I do prefer to have them in the larder downstairs where it is cool, but—but I think on the whole you had better leave the turkey here."

Wilhelmina had deserved far less merciful treatment, but her face burned like fire. Never in all her life had she known such humiliation as this. Only the constant habit of self-restraint in petty things enabled her to go on with her work, and to leave the room without some kind of hysterical outburst. The reproof was cutting— and well merited—and she was a Christian, a child of light! A nice one she to mourn over her stepmother's defections from the standard of rigid rectitude! " Oh, God! " she cried in her sore distress, " how easy it would be to be good if one had no temptations! " She laughed at herself in later days when she recalled the words of the prayer; but after all it is one that has gone up from human hearts—I don't talk of lips—more often perhaps than any other.

The evening was Sunday, and Wilhelmina was going to chapel. In truth chapel-going was the one recreation of her life at this time, for, acting on a suggestion of the revivalist, she had ceased to read any but purely religious books.

As so often happens, the text seemed to fall in surprisingly with her train of thought—

" *Who shall ascend into the hill of the Lord, or who shall stand in his holy place?*

" *He that hath clean hands and a pure heart.*"

She never knew how much of the sermon that followed was the preacher's, and how much was evolved in

her own busy heart and brain; but she made a few reso-
lutions that evening of the imminent kind that bring
sweat to one's brow. All innocent of modern criticism,
she put her own construction on a later verse of the
psalm—

*"Lift up your heads, O ye gates; and be ye lift
up, ye everlasting doors; and the King of glory shall
come in."*

An alienist would have said that the child was in a
bad way, that she wanted cheerful society, good food,
and a few pretty frocks. Of course the alienist would
have been right, but at least the patient's will-power had
suffered no diminution.

"Miss Prynne," she said next day with flaming face,
"would you like your things to go back to the larder?
I did take some of your turkey, but it won't happen
again."

Miss Prynne looked startled, as most of us do when
a human soul throws off its wrappings before our eyes.
Who was she that St. Peter's keys should be thus suddenly thrust into her hand? Fortunately for Wilhelmina she elected to loose and not to bind.

"Thank you, my dear," she said kindly. "I shall be
glad if you will take the things downstairs."

She reproached herself afterwards for not having
farther improved the occasion. We are so slow to realize
that our inborn shyness is a far more precious gift than
most of our talents.

Wilhelmina almost staggered from the room. The
feeling of humiliation oppressed her still, but she was
very thankful too. True, she had only ascended one
rung of the ladder she had set before her; but what a
step that had been!

Mrs. Galbraith was very poorly that morning, and
as the next day and the next brought no improvement,
Wilhelmina begged to be allowed to fetch a doctor.

"Nonsense," said her stepmother sharply. "It is
weakness, that is all. He would only give me a tonic
that would make me long for the food I can't get."

"But the pain in your side?"

"Well! He would recommend a cutlet and a glass

of Burgundy for lunch. Why pay for a piece of advice that I have been giving myself for weeks."

Wilhelmina expected a renewal of the suggestion about applying to Mrs. Dalrymple, and she steeled her heart. It was not only "pride and selfishness" that made her hold out: she had learned by bitter experience that any help her aunt could give her would only postpone the evil day. Their affairs were involved beyond hope. She had just found out that Mrs. Galbraith was still paying interest on debts contracted in Harley Street.

But, to her surprise, her stepmother did not renew the attack. "I'll tell you what, dear," she said—"we must let that pearl bracelet go. I could not bear to part with it—as—as we have parted with other things; but I quite hope to be able to redeem it next week. Will you take it this afternoon?"

Wilhelmina nodded, wondering by what means her stepmother proposed to redeem it. At one time a visit to the pawnbroker had meant torture to the child, but the disgrace of it seemed small now in comparison with that of an appeal to her aunt, and, moreover, there is nothing like hunger for blunting one's delicate sensibilities. Wilhelmina would have faced a good deal to obtain *that cutlet.*

It was afternoon when she set out. She put the jewel-case into her pocket, and inserted a great safety-pin above it to keep it in place. She would not go to any shop in the neighbourhood. A 'bus from the Royal Oak took her to Oxford Street, and thence she proceeded on foot. She knew a number of pawnshops, and meant to get offers from several before closing with one. "I will be as hard as nails," she said to herself stoutly. "I mean to get out of this bracelet just as many cutlets and glasses of Burgundy as ever I can."

The first two offers were distinctly disappointing, and, somewhat crestfallen, she bent her steps farther into the city. She was in the region of the theatres now, in the thick of the rush and roar; and already the carriages were assembling for the close of the morning performances. At one door a crowd had gathered, and Wil-

helmina heard a murmur of "the Princess." She wondered whether she too should stop and peep, but decided
that her errand would not admit of any delay. As she
came to this decision, she instinctively put her hand for
the fiftieth time in the direction of her pocket.

The familiar lump was gone!

Her heart gave a leap that nearly choked her, and
she made several frantic clutches about her dress. Then,
with unconscious frankness, she lifted the scrimp, short
skirt to look. Someone, alas! had done that before her.
The safety-pin remained as she had placed it, but pocket
and jewel-case had been removed with a sharp, jagged
cut.

Wilhelmina scarcely believed her eyes. She did not
see how the theft *could* have been done. She had never
ceased thinking of the jewel-case for a minute, and how
was it possible that her pocket had been cut away without her knowing it? She had fancied herself a match
for this big, clever, wicked London—alas! alas!

If she had in the least realized the danger of faint-
ing, she would certainly have fainted then, for she was
weak for want of nourishing food; but fortunately such
an idea never occurred to her, and the thought of her
terrible loss prevented her paying attention to the queer
lightness of her head. The people were pouring out of
the theatre now, and instinctively she moved aside to
let them pass.

"Are you ill, little girl?" said a pleasant voice, and
Wilhelmina looked up to see a beautiful lady resplendent
in silks and furs.

"*Miss Evelyn!*" she cried.

The actress would certainly not have recognized
her face, but something in the eager cry recalled the
night long ago when she first took Mrs. Carrington's
part.

"Why, it is Wilhelmina Galbraith!" she said, shocked
at the child's obvious poverty. "Have a sniff at my
vinaigrette. Hansom!"

Two minutes later Wilhelmina's head was pillowed
on the delicious soft sealskin, and they were trotting
away westwards as fast as the crowded state of the streets

would permit. It almost seemed as if the dream of the
Fairy Godmother had come true.

"And I am *dining* to-night, as it chances," said Miss
Evelyn hospitably. "As a rule I have a horrid nondescript meal at four; but I went to see Burleigh Debrett
at the Agamemnon to-day, and ordered dinner for six
o'clock. We'll have a bottle of fizz, and drink old times."

Her pretty sitting-room was gay with flowers. "I
had rather a success last evening," she said half apologetically—"quite a shower of bouquets."

She established Wilhelmina on the luxurious lounge
by the fire, and moving quietly to the mantelpiece, turned
the face of a photograph to the wall. She was talking
gaily all the time, and Wilhelmina did not notice the
action; indeed, she was quite sufficiently interested in
watching the preparations for dinner.

What a royal feast it seemed to the half-starved child
—soup, a brace of pheasants, a dainty cream, and hothouse grapes! The first whiff of the savoury soup
brought the tears to her eyes, and, try as she would, she
could not keep them back. Miss Evelyn only half filled
her visitor's glass with champagne, but of course even
that was too much, and as soon as dinner was over, the
child sobbed out her tale of woe. For years she had confided in no one, and now, topsy turvy, out came the
whole story with a rush.

"There, there! Poor child! Poor little one!" said
Miss Evelyn kindly. "I suppose some brute of a lounger
about the pawnshop saw you putting your hand to your
pocket and followed you. He could manage that little
feat quite easily in the crowd. Mrs. Galbraith ought to
do such errands herself."

"She is not well."

The actress nodded unsympathetically. She had never
considered Mrs. Galbraith's life worth while.

"See," she said, "I am going to pack a basket for
you to take home. Nonsense! Fortune's wheel is always spinning. You'll do me a good turn some day;
or, if I don't want it, you'll do it to someone else. That
is very fair claret. It will do your stepmother good;
and you will answer, won't you, for the pheasant and

grapes? I am in funds just now, so you shall take two gold pennies, and pay me back when you are a rich woman."

"Oh, Miss Evelyn!" said the child, "how can I?"

The actress pinched her ear. "You are a great deal too proud—that is what you are. Do you know, half the pretty things in this room are presents?—and I assure you I made no bones about accepting them. Now I know you are longing to be off. I am sorry I can't go with you, but I am due at the theatre very soon. My maid shall take you home in a hansom, and hurry back to me."

She watched the hansom drive away, and, returning to the sitting-room, she buried her face in a choice little bouquet of orchids. A card attached to it bore, in a pencil scrawl, the initials G. G.

Then she restored the slighted photograph to its original position, and looked with calm criticism at the fine features it portrayed.

"It's a mad world, my masters," she said with a philosophic shrug of her shoulders; "but I don't see why I should be the one to apply the strait-jacket. It's a mad, mad world!"

CHAPTER XXII.

TWO WORLDS MEET.

"I WILL have tea in the boudoir this afternoon, Pearson," said Enid. "Tell them to say I am not at home, unless it is someone special."

"Yes, madam."

"I think I must have that gown at Lucile's, after all, Pearson, though I don't in the least know how I am to afford it. It's a lovely thing."

"And might have been designed for you, madam. It will be thrown away on a short squat figure and colourless hair."

"Oh, depend upon it some bald dwarf like Lady Fan-

shawe went in to-day after we left, and snapped it up.
I never resist the devil without regretting it afterwards.
Well, go and give the order about the tea."

As she spoke, Enid disposed herself comfortably in
her favourite easy-chair. The day was cold, and the glow
of the wood fire fell on the ermine bands of her tea-
gown like sunlight on foam. The gown was one of her
own happy ideas, an unusual combination of myrtle
green velvet and turquoise blue. She took up a piece
of embroidery, but her work had made little progress
when a "special" visitor was ushered in—Mr. Ronald
Dalrymple.

Ronald Dalrymple bore a considerable resemblance to
Fergus; but, although the tailor had turned him out
more expensively than his brother, nature had econo-
mized in various ways, producing, indeed, a cheaper
article altogether. The reduction of a few inches in
stature makes comparatively little difference, but when
the same process is applied to the forehead, the chin,
the lower jaw—the effect is out of all proportion to the
saving of material. Enid and Ronald had always been
good friends, and, since George Galbraith had rendered
himself impossible, she had found her husband's young
brother particularly useful.

"Well," she said, smiling, "did you bring Hugh?"

"Oh, yes; they made no special difficulty. He is to
go back early on Monday. Rollins indicated that they
do not exactly regard him as a burning and shining
light."

"Poor boy! No; books are not in his line. I do
detest this system of competitive examination for the
army. It is most unfitting for the sons of gentlemen."

"Oh, I've no doubt he'll scrape through. He has
plenty of time yet to come and go upon. I have promised to take him to the Alhambra to-night. I say, Enid,
do you know you look perfectly magnificent?"

She smiled without surprise. "I am so glad. This
thing feels deliciously cosy, but I was afraid it looked
cold."

"*Cold?* With the firelight, and the gold of the room,
and *your hair!*"

Ronald was certainly improving—so much so that Enid thought it worth while to pursue the subject.

"I always envy brunettes," she said, "who can wear amber and yellow and scarlet—make themselves the very incarnation of warmth and colour."

"Oh, I say!"

This was feeble. George Galbraith would have told her that she need not seek to do for herself what Nature had done for her so abundantly; but one must not expect Ronald to rise to George Galbraith's level.

He made no attempt to amplify his remark. For the first time it struck Enid that he was looking extraordinarily ill at ease.

"By the way," he stammered awkwardly at last, "could you conveniently let me have the loan of fifty pounds for a week or two?"

"*You*, Ronald! Why, I always comforted myself with the reflection that, as a last resource, I might make that request to you."

"I should be delighted, I'm sure."

"I look upon you as the monied man of the family."

"Oh, come now!"

"Of course I do. With your Uncle Ronald's money you are to all intents and purposes far richer than we are."

"Well, I do contrive to rub along. This is only a momentary difficulty. The fact is," he added, ashamed of himself for volunteering the information, "Galbraith has kept me longer than usual out of a couple of hundred I lent him."

"Why don't you break with George Galbraith?" she cried petulantly.

"Why? Because he is a rattling good fellow. He'll stump up right enough, never fear. There is nobody like him. I flatter myself that I know my world fairly well, but Galbraith is always putting me up to fresh wrinkles."

"He certainly did so when he married that smilax woman!"

"He drew a blank that time, I confess. It was a case of social suicide during temporary insanity."

" You don't go near the Bayswater house, I hope ? "

" Oh, Lord, no ! " Ronald chuckled. " I shouldn't be likely to find him there. You forget that I really want to see him."

" Will you believe that the woman had the impertinence to write and ask me for money the other day ? "

" No ! That was average cool."

" A woman I never saw, and of whom I should never have heard if she hadn't entrapped that poor fellow into marrying her. I put the note in the fire. If she writes again she shall hear a piece of my mind. Apart from its being a begging letter, just think of her effrontery in assuming that I am aware of her existence ! "

" There is a child, isn't there ? "

A slight shadow drifted over Enid's face. " Rhoda's child, yes. I had meant to do so much for her, but of course this marriage made it impossible."

" Of course."

" Couldn't you ask Fergus for the money, Ronald ? "

He shook his head. " Fergus ! I would rather go back to those Jew beasts, and I had made up my mind not to do that."

" No; don't do that. I wish I could help you; but, to tell the truth, I am rather hard up myself. Lucile is turning restive."

" Oh, nonsense ! You don't know how other women treat her. Besides, it would be worth Lucile's while to dress you for nothing. Order a new gown, and she'll be all right."

" Well," said Enid reflectively, " I might do even that to oblige you. But I can't do without the money long, or Fergus will find out that I have lent it."

" Next week or the week after," he said gratefully. " You are a regular brick, Enid. Upon my soul, I believe you are the only generous woman I ever met."

She smiled and nodded.

" And now I am sure you would like me to make myself scarce. Hugh is dying to see you."

And in truth Hugh greeted his mother with an affection that was pretty to see. Now that he was, as he considered, a man, he had ceased to take her beauty as a matter of course. He had learned that a little beauty in a mother goes a long way, that it is one of the things men are proud of, and that Enid required no indulgence at all.

"If you only saw the frumps some of the fellows have to show!" he confided exultantly to Ronald. "The *mater* never turns up without taking the trick."

"I should think not indeed."

It is a pity Hugh had no sisters. He would have been good to them if they had been pretty and smart; and it is difficult to imagine that a daughter of Enid's could have proved otherwise—unless, like Wilhelmina, she had been a "throw-back." Hugh was a well-grown young fellow, but his face resembled his Uncle Ronald's more than it did his father's. Nature had repeated that unfortunate piece of economy in the material of the chin.

"Well," said his mother, "were you glad to come and see me?"

"Wasn't I just? You've no notion how sick one gets of swot-swot-swotting in that beastly den."

"Poor boy! Plucky old fellow!"

"You'll tip me a fiver, won't you, *Mater*, when I go back?"

Her face clouded. "I don't see how I can, Hugh. I have so many claims upon me just now. And indeed I don't see why I should. Your Uncle Ronald gives you far too many tips as it is."

"Oh, does he? Ronald hasn't been so overly flush himself of late. He wants me to drop the 'uncle' now that I am grown up."

"You grown up, indeed! Ronald evidently means to put Fergus and me on the shelf."

"Couldn't be done, *Mater*. The fellows all declare you must be my sister. I'll pass you off for my daughter before I've done with you."

"You sauce-box!"

"And about that fiver?"

"You know you ought to be above asking for tips when your father gives you so good an allowance."

Hugh shrugged his shoulders. "Oh, that's *comme ça!* I have known fellows that had more."

" Well, we'll see. If I give it to you, you must work very hard when you go back."

He heaved a long sigh. " I do work hard, *Mater*— you've no notion; but it's such beastly grind; and some of the fellows positively enjoy it ! "

" I know. Never mind. Beat them on their own ground, Hugh."

She might as well have told him to be Czar of all the Russias, but there was no use trying to explain that to the feminine mind.

" I do hope I shall meet Uncle George somewhere this time," he said, willing to change the subject.

" Indeed, I hope you will do nothing of the kind."

" That's your little mistake, *Mater*—excuse me. I met a fellow the other day—an awfully clever chap— who thinks Uncle George a regular hero."

" Oh, no doubt. I should think there are lots of young men to whom your uncle acts the part of hero."

" But this one isn't that kind. He's a scholar; not a sad dog like Ronald and me."

Enid suppressed a smile. " I am interested to hear how the sad dog met the scholar."

" Oh, on his own ground. Old Rollins took me to hear a lecture at the Royal Institution. Rigby was there. You remember Rigby at Eton ? He said he had a friend with him who would be glad to make the acquaintance of Mr. Galbraith's nephew. Brentwood was the friend's name—Harley Brentwood. He's got a ripping sister—classic style. As soon as I set eyes on her, I told Rigby I should be glad to make the acquaintance of her brother."

" You think a great deal too much about women, Hugh."

" No, I don't, Mother; but I can't help seeing the points of one when she chances to come my way."

" And how did young Brentwood meet your uncle ? "

" Oh, in the most sensational fashion. It seems the Brentwoods have taken a little place opposite Windy- haugh, and Rigby and Brentwood undertook to row across. They got into a current or something, and cap- sized. Enter Uncle George. Limelight. Rescue."

11

"So that is why he is a hero. I suppose I should call him one too if he had saved my life."

"It isn't only that. Brentwood thinks Uncle George no end plucky and cool; but he says he is a man of such culture too, and so kind. Ronald says it is all perfectly true—there is nobody like Uncle George; and I think it is a great swindle that, when I have got an uncle like that, I should scarcely know him by sight."

"I don't wish you to know him, Hugh. And now it is quite time we were dressing for dinner."

Mr. Dalrymple entered the room as his son left it. Unlike his wife, he had aged considerably in the last six years. "I should like to have a word with you, Enid," he said.

She looked at him coldly. "Shall I ring for fresh tea?"

"No, thank you. I have just got Arrowsmith's bill. It is a little startling. The fact is, Enid, we shall have to pull up. I don't choose to live on the brink of my income, and there is no reason why we should. We must draw in a little all round."

She shrugged her shoulders. "How can I draw in when everybody tries to sponge on me?" she cried impulsively.

He looked up quickly. "Who has been trying to sponge on you?—not Ronald?"

"*Ronald!*" she cried contemptuously. "Is it likely? That disgusting smilax woman is trying to get money out of me; and yesterday I had a letter from a man at Queensmains—Mackintosh or Macintyre or something—who wants money for Wilhelmina. It seems she is getting no education at all."

"Did you refer him to her father?"

"Of course I took no notice; but he said he had received no reply to a letter written weeks ago to her father."

Fergus took a turn up and down the room.

"Of course you will let Mrs. Galbraith alone," he said; "but I confess I feel a little unhappy about Wilhelmina. We are in no way bound to do anything for her; still for poor Rhoda's sake——"

"It is no use, Fergus. She is the smilax woman's child now. I should have treated her almost as my own daughter, if that woman had not inveigled poor George. It is a wretched sordid business, and I wash my hands of the whole thing. And now I must go and dress for dinner."

She congratulated herself on having at least postponed an interview that promised to be unpleasant.

On her dressing table lay an unopened letter addressed in a round unformed hand. "I think you overlooked that this morning, madam," said Pearson quietly.

Enid opened it. "Well!" she said. "So this is the next move, is it? Listen, Pearson—

"'DEAR AUNT ENID: I want very much to see you alone please for a few minutes. I will call to-morrow evening about half-past seven. I won't give my name to the servant. Your affectionate niece,
"'WILHELMINA GALBRAITH.'

"So the smilax creature employs a tool this time—thinks I can't decently refuse money to my own flesh and blood. What do you think of that?"

The confidential maid was too discreet to commit herself.

"It is almost half-past seven now," she said.

"Rather cool to fix her own time for a begging interview. I have a great mind not to see her. You won't go, of course, Pearson. She takes her chance of finding me engaged."

A few minutes later Wilhelmina was ushered in. Enid realized for the first time on seeing her that the child had at least shown some tact in not giving her name.

"Well, Wilhelmina," she said with a little nod; "you have called very near dinner-time, but Pearson is nobody, is she? You don't mind her doing my hair while you talk?"

Wilhelmina was trembling visibly, and her voice shook like a reed. "It is right that Pearson should be here," she said.

Then there fell a painful silence. Mrs. Dalrymple was determined not to help her niece out.

, "I hope you are quite well, Aunt Enid?"

"Yes, thank you," was the dry response; "but I don't think you called to ask me that."

"No. Aunt Enid, do you remember your visit to Windyhaugh?"

"I have not forgotten it."

Was she going to be asked at this distance of time to pay for a week's board? But the next words took her breath away. She little guessed the morbid anguish of which they were the outcome.

"You gave me some eau de Cologne on my handkerchief one day. I liked it very much, and afterwards I went to your room and took some more. The bottle slipped out of my hand, and I was afraid to tell you, so I filled it up with water. Pearson gave me a chance to confess, but I told a lie."

Mrs. Dalrymple did not speak, and the child rose to her feet. "That's all," she said. "I wanted to tell you."

Enid raised her hand to put Pearson aside, and turned to look at her niece. If this was a bid for money, it was a very curious and original one. Or was the child out of her senses?

"What I want to know," she said almost sharply, "is what has induced you to come and tell me this?"

Wilhelmina tugged at her hands in the old fashion of her childhood. Her mind was strung to confession, and she was far too preoccupied to remember that it is scarcely permissible for a young girl to produce a social discord by intruding on her elders a phrase in quite a different key from that of their own mood. She did not realize that, if her aunt chose to ask questions, she was only bound to answer them conventionally. Her one concern was to find a reply that was true without being too painfully personal, and this meant a moral effort almost greater than that involved in the original confession.

"I have been thinking about these things," she said awkwardly. "I must keep my hands clean. I don't want the lowness of the gates to keep out the King of Glory."

Enid started. A conventional expression of religion would have disgusted her. This quaint half comprehensible trope struck her as weird and uncanny. She did not half believe in the child even now; but, if money would bring her down—or up—to the plane of common humanity, she was quite prepared to offer it.

While she was musing, Wilhelmina made a movement towards the door. She did not want her aunt's forgiveness; she quite realized that the old injury was too trivial for that; she only wanted to clear her own soul.

"May I go now?" she said shyly.

Why not put her to the test? "Certainly," said Enid quietly, "if you have nothing more to say. . . . *Vilma!*" she called a moment later; but the child did not or would not hear. Like a hunted hare she had flown down the brilliant staircase, and out into the darkness of the streets.

There was silence in the room after she had gone.

"*Well*, Pearson!" said Mrs. Dalrymple at length.

Pearson, too, was looking rather white. She had always thought of the eau de Cologne episode in connection with Wilhelmina, and the *dénouement* impressed her.

"I hope there is nothing wrong with the child," said Enid uneasily. "What was that she said about the gates and the King of Glory?"

"I think we had something like it in the Psalms on Sunday, madam. Let me see; it would be the 5th day of the month. I can easily find it."

Enid shivered. "No, no," she said. "It is nearly dinner-time. Make haste and finish my hair. I will speak to Mr. Dalrymple about the child. We had arranged to do something for her in any case."

CHAPTER XXIII.

REQUIESCAT.

WHEN Fergus Dalrymple called at the Bayswater house next day, he was rather taken aback to find an ambulance van at the door. A nurse on the steps was administering a last word of comfort to a pathetic-looking girl.

"Now don't you take on," she said kindly. "We'll be very good to her, and when you come to see her to-morrow afternoon, you'll wish you were there yourself."

Mr. Dalrymple waited till the van drove off, and then ascended the steps. "I called to see Miss Galbraith," he said.

"I am Wilhelmina," said the child wondering. "Will you come in?" She decided that this must be one of her father's grand friends.

Her sorrow lent her a little air of dignity, but her eyes were red with crying, and her hands were red with honest hard work. She belonged to a class of women that lay quite outside Fergus Dalrymple's somewhat extensive range.

"I am afraid you have had illness in the house," he said kindly.

She bit her lip, but failed to keep back a fresh cloud of tears. "My stepmother," she replied. "She wouldn't let me fetch a doctor till this morning. He said there was no use in our trying to nurse her here. She has had pleurisy for some time, and her heart is very weak."

"I am sure she is very wise to go to hospital," he said cheerily. "They manage these places so well now-a-days. If I was ill, I should like to go to hospital myself."

Illness, as it chanced, for Mr. Dalrymple, was a thing far off and only dimly apprehended.

"And now," he proceeded, relieved to find his task rendered so easy, "your Aunt Enid and I want you to

go right away from here to school. You would like
that, wouldn't you?"

"You are——?"

He hesitated. "Your Uncle Fergus, my dear."

An unconscious smile of real interest played over her
face as she regarded him frankly. She had often wondered what her Uncle Fergus was like. Then a sudden
fear that he had come to talk of the painful episode of
last night turned her heart sick.

"Thank you very much," she said; "but of course I
can't go. We have got this house on our hands, and we
have two lodgers upstairs."

He looked aghast. "But you are a great deal too
young to have the management of servants."

"Yes," she said simply with a faint blush. "We
have no servants just now."

He was far too kindly a gentleman to look at her
hands, but for a few moments he saw nothing else.
Poor Rhoda! Poor, poor Rhoda!

"Surely," he said, "under the circumstances, these
—these people will have the decency to leave at once."

"Oh, I hope not!" she cried in genuine distress.

"My dear child," he said kindly, "why should you
take the world on your shoulders? You must not be
morbid. You must remember that Mrs.—Mrs. Galbraith
is not your mother."

Wilhelmina's face hardened. "My father married
her," she said quietly. "I couldn't leave her. Besides
—she is all I've got."

She looked so near tears again that he took alarm.

"Is there anything you would like me to do for
you?" he said, rising as he spoke.

She blushed deeply. "I don't think so, unless—
unless you could find my father. He ought to know."

"Of course he ought! And, if he is to be found—
I'll undertake to find him."

Thankful to have a definite course of action before
him, he hastened out of the house, and his hansom was
bowling along the Edgware Road before he remembered
that he had meant to give Wilhelmina a five pound note.

"No matter," he said to himself. "There is no use

tinkering at that God-forsaken establishment. We will
send her to school in spite of herself."

A few weeks after her admission to hospital, Mrs.
Galbraith died. Both medicine and surgery did much
to relieve her symptoms; but at this stage they could
not give her the stamina to fight disease. Mercifully,
she was one of those to whom death on the whole comes
easy. She considered that she had always been a good
woman, as women go; and she readily accepted the
teaching of the clergyman, and attuned her mind to the
prospect of eternal peace and joy. She recognized that
life had given her much that was good, if it had given
her evil also; and her last days were brightened by frequent visits from her husband. She almost ignored Wilhelmina in her joy at seeing him again. He made no
reference to her approaching death, but she found both
comfort and fellowship in his quiet suggestion of "You
to-day, I to-morrow;" and he listened with grave respect when she urged him to "follow her." He had a
curious feeling that he had expected all this from the
moment he first met her seven years before.

And so she slipped quietly away.

Truly Enid had well named her the smilax woman!
Was she not born to look fragile and charming—while
she clung to a firm support in the sunshine? *Requiescat*.

CHAPTER XXIV.

A NEW DEVELOPMENT.

"I CALL it simple spite," said the leading girl. "If
it had been small-pox, or a broken leg, or ery—ery—
what you may call—but mumps! It is too ridiculous."

They were out on the croquet lawn, and the colonial
brunette seated herself on one of the battered posts with
her arms on her knees. Her dark hair fell in a cloud
about her shoulders. "It will be a wonder if it doesn't

go the round of the school now," she observed pessimistically.

"Do not be *silly!* What are we to *do?*"

The dark head waved despondently from side to side. "We'll never get anyone like Miss Smith. Her cheek was sublime——"

A peal of laughter greeted this unconscious sally.

"*Is,* you mean," said some one, inflating her own cheeks to indicate the predominant symptom of the complaint from which the invalid was suffering.

But the brunette went on undisturbed. "——and her rosy face and snub nose were worth a fortune."

"Miss Smith is pretty," said a quiet-looking girl, nicknamed "the quakeress."

The brunette rose from her post, drew herself up, and knocked a ball idly across the lawn with her mallet. "Did I say she wasn't?" Then she turned to the elegant person who had opened the conversation. "What about Miss Galbraith?"

"Miss Galbraith? She is too lean and lanky."

"She is not half so lean and lanky as she was."

"And stupid."

"You say that because she had never heard of Peter the Hermit. You home folks need a year in the colony to teach you what stupidity means. *I* say Miss Galbraith has spunk. Besides nobody else has memory enough to learn the part in the time. She knows six hundred dates by heart already."

"Monsieur says her French accent is the best in the school," said the quakeress. Unlike that of the brunette, her championship lost a good deal of its value by being exercised universally and on principle.

"What is the use of an accent when you don't know your verbs?" enquired the leading girl. She seated herself on the bank that enclosed the lawn. "Fetch Miss Galbraith," she said.

Of course some one ran to do her bidding. A girls' school is the place *par excellence* where human beings are taken at their own valuation.

Wilhelmina was soon discovered poring over her books in the shade of an old lime tree. If even a school-

fellow had noted the change in her, an observant eye
would have been struck by it still more. The drawn
look of anxiety had left her face, and one could see at a
glance that a stream of fresh sweet blood was coursing
through her veins. The effect from a physical point of
view was as when a light is held behind an alabaster col-
umn. Oh, the sheer beauty of life, sheer youth, sheer
health!

"Miss Galbraith," said the leading girl serenely, "we
want you to take Miss Smith's part in the play."

Something of the old look returned to Wilhelmina's
face. "Oh, I can't!" she cried terrified.

The leading girl turned to the brunette. "I thought
you said she had spunk."

The brunette was swaying herself and her mallet to
and fro. At the present stage of affairs she declined to
commit herself either way.

"You see I have never done anything of the kind before——" said Wilhelmina. She did not reckon the dramatic Sunday schools and funerals as something of the
kind.

"Then you should be very grateful for the chance of
beginning now."

"——and I know I should fail."

"Fail then. If you are word perfect, and walk
through the part, the rest of us will undertake to make
it go." The speaker naturally considered her own rendering of the principal rôle sufficient of itself to ensure
the success of the piece.

Wilhelmina looked very unhappy. To tell the honest
truth, there were several parts in the play which she had
often imagined herself taking with great effect; but the
one in question was—or so she fancied—utterly anti-
pathetic—a sort of saucy soubrette part in which the actress must be content to forego her dignity wholly.

"It is a sacrifice, isn't it?" said the quakeress sympathetically.

"It is."

"But you see you must sacrifice either yourself or
the others. You know nobody else could learn it in
time."

Wilhelmina coloured. Her religious life was by no means in flood tide just now, but this was a remark that could not fail to have effect.

The leading girl rose. " Give her the book, somebody," she said. " Rehearsal to-morrow, Miss Galbraith; " and, taking the arm of the brunette, she strolled away.

Wilhelmina had been very ill after her stepmother's death. There was no organic disease—only the severe anæmia which so often befalls girls of her age; and it must be admitted that she had more excuse for it than most. The doctor had ordered her to the seaside, and, as Windyhaugh was again let, Mr. Galbraith had sent her in Ann's charge to quiet lodgings in an unknown place on the coast. Here she read many religious books of a sentimental kind, and toyed with the idea of early death. At this particular period of her life, " the shadow feared by man " had few terrors for her, but the reasons for this were mainly physiological.

Her father came to see her one day, and found her reading a large Bible, flanked by a substantial pile of sermons, tracts, and booklets. A curious little smile flitted across his face as he turned over the pages of one of these. Was he thinking of a time when he too had passed that way?

" Is this to be the end, little Vilma? " he said reflectively.

She thought he was referring to her death, but he had something very different in mind. He had little affection for her, and yet he was disappointed that a daughter of his should be turning out so poor and bloodless a thing. " At least I left her a free hand," he used to say, " and I only wish my parents had done as much for me." He forgot that when he married the " smilax woman," he was scarcely leaving his daughter a free hand. He was quite catholic enough to appreciate religion, but not when it gave the impression of being simply one of a train of physical symptoms.

At the end of a few months Wilhelmina showed so little improvement that the doctor changed his tactics, and sent her to a school, recommended by Mrs. Carlton, on the Yorkshire moors. It was not a first-class establishment at all; but, partly for that reason, it just chanced to suit the patient. The headmistress was a woman of no exceptional culture; but she was kind and sensible, and her main object was to make her girls healthy and happy. None of the pupils belonged to really smart families, and many were the daughters of· Anglo-Indians of moderate means.

When Wilhelmina first arrived, she marvelled, with the tolerant superiority of a child of light, at the importance the others attached to their meals. Before she had been at the school a month, she was munching her bread and butter with the best, and rejoicing as much as anyone at the appearance of a popular pudding.

Regaining thus her grip of life, she began to feel that earthly ideals and ambitions are not such utter dross as she had supposed. What had been shadow took on substance: what had been substance faded—alas?—to shadow. She felt keenly her own want of education, and worked hard to supply her deficiencies. These indeed were not so glaring as might have been supposed. In an average girls' school of those days it was not easy to be remarkable for mere ignorance.

When the hour of the rehearsal arrived, she was almost sick with nervousness; and yet she would have been sorry to withdraw. She was only asked to be word-perfect—to "walk through the part." She would do something more: she would surpass even Miss Smith. The ambition that had kept her awake in the old days, repeating French vowel sounds that she might astonish Mademoiselle by her proficiency, was fairly fired now; and she meant to astonish them all.

Of course she began badly. Indeed she found it as much as she could do to repeat like a lesson the words that fell to her share. Presently she saw a meaning glance pass between the leading girl and the brunette, and she felt that she hated them both. Stung to desperation, she flashed back a pert retort with a vivacity that surprised herself.

"*Brava!*" cried the English master who had come

unnoticed into the room to see how his pupils were getting on.

The "*Brava!*" did it. "Behold how great a flame a little fire kindleth." From that moment Wilhelmina had her cue. If audacity was what they wanted, audacity they should have. She felt that she had struck a new and unsuspected vein of ore in her own character and disposition.

On the evening of the performance several of her school-fellows told her she was looking pretty, and that put the crowning touch to her new-found self-confidence. Why after all should she not be like other girls, and beat them, if she could, on their own ground?

All day the pupils had been busy decorating the large schoolroom with flowers and bracken, and evening brought quite a gay assemblage of local people to see the play.

It was a very simple one, and, thanks to the wholesome outdoor life that hardened the nerve of the players, it was acted with more effect than might have been the case in a more pretentious school. Wilhelmina's part was an attractive one in its way, and she certainly made the most of it. For the first time in her life she really let herself *go*, tossing back her fine hair—which the dresser had transformed into a magnificent aureole—and dropping mock curtseys with an *abandon* that surprised herself, and a kitten-like grace that surprised everyone else. The dancing-master had appreciated her possibilities from the first, and was proud to see his expectations fulfilled.

When in due course she was called before the curtain, she received as hearty an ovation as the leading girl herself, and a bouquet was thrown at her feet. For a moment she seemed uncertain what to do; then she picked it up, curtseyed, smiled a shy childlike smile that was very fascinating—and made her escape.

Poor little Wilhelmina! She had such long arrears to make up. It is no wonder if this draught of trumpery success intoxicated her. As on the occasion of her grandmother's death, and of her own arrival in Harley Street, so now once more she really was a personage.

The play was followed by a dance, and for an hour or two she received as much attention as she could wish. "They say she never acted before." "Quite a remarkable gift!" "And such an attractive face too," she heard people say. Then a series of black-coated youths must needs be introduced, and, although this was an honour that was more terrifying than pleasant, Wilhelmina was too conscious of its importance not to make the most of it. Hitherto young men had existed for her only in the conversation of the leading girl and the brunette, who were older than herself; and, now that masculine homage was offered so unexpectedly, she had no idea how to take it. Almost without her own will, she found herself still acting the part she had taken in the play, and acting it with such effect that she began to wonder whether this were not after all her true character.

But the crowning triumph was still to come.

"Miss Galbraith," said the leading girl affectionately, "my father would like to make your acquaintance. He says he hopes you will spend a week with us during the holidays as you are not going home."

The grey dormitory struck chill on all this glowing life. Wilhelmina slipped her arm into that of the quakeress. "Well," she said, athirst for more admiration. "You told me to do it. Did I do it well?"

But the quakeress was scared. A few months before, Wilhelmina's genuine devotion had been at once an inspiration and a reproach to her, and now——

"What *are* you, Wilhelmina?" she said.

CHAPTER XXV.

LOOKING FORWARD.

THE second year of Wilhelmina's school life was drawing to a close.

It was evening, and she was swaying idly to and fro as she leaned against the bough of an old apple tree in the orchard. An untrimmed garden hat framed her face like an aureole, and her whole attitude and expression suggested a picture of springtime.

The quakeress had had much cause to mourn over her friend in the months that had come and gone since the eventful night of the play. Wilhelmina still read her Bible, and did not refuse to talk of religion when the subject was introduced; but she declined to let the conversation take a personal turn, and there was no denying the fact that the old fervour, the genuine ring, was gone. In truth she was a wonder to herself at this time. She did not blink the fact that she was a backslider, and she was well aware that a day of reckoning lay somewhere in the future. In church on Sunday evening, when the mellow shafts of light made their level way between the columns, and the notes of the organ rose and fell in plaintive harmony, the tears would rush to her eyes, and an impulsive prayer for "reconciliation" would well up in her heart. She did really not expect an answer to this. She had long since proved the truth of Mr. Darsie's remark that " the Lord's no' in sic a hurry to answer our prayers even when they're wiselike," and she looked for no royal road back from the arbour of ease. She felt that she must be willing to exercise violence, to wrestle all night, if she would repossess the Kingdom, rediscover the Name, and as yet she did not feel equal to the sacrifice this involved. Of a religion devoid of morbidity she had no conception at all. The eternal choice was painted for her in the most uncompromising colours. On the one side, sunshine, expansion, dalliance, admiration: on the other, self-sacrifice, narrowness—*God*. She dared not face the last word: it was so irresistible, so conclusive: she felt that sooner or later she must yield to its unswerving force: and yet——

Poor Wilhelmina! It is little wonder if she availed herself of her new-found health and strength to postpone the day of decision—to throw the whole subject into the background of her mind.

Meanwhile her physical nature flourished and bloomed under the pagan reaction. There was in her aspect that look of dewy freshness, of morning brightness, that is

the greatest beauty a girl of her age can possess. The
clear limpid eyes seemed to be looking out with wistful
surprise on a world that was proving itself unexpectedly
gracious and kind.

She had taken part in many plays since that eventful
evening. She belonged now to what can best be described
as the society clique in the school—to the little circle of
girls who had friends and acquaintances in the pretty
hillside town, who were invited to picnics and croquet
parties for their own sake, and not merely out of kindness. This too, unfortunately, was the circle of which
the leading members were busy weaving "pasts" for
themselves, making conquests, suffering disappointments, passing through phases, emotions, episodes of
divers kinds, on a stage so small as to be invisible to the
eye of the ordinary observer. A pleasant accost in the
church porch; a little special attention at an evening
party; the gift of a rose, a song, a book; the arrival
perhaps of a valentine or love lyric by post—these were
the slender pegs on which many a romance was hung.
Of course this whole cult of the sentimental was silly,
and not very high-class; but, as regarded Wilhelmina
and a number of the others, it was quite harmless. It
was simply a game, like any other, and involved no ex-
penditure of emotion peculiar to itself. If one was
handicapped by a meagre wardrobe and scant pin-money,
it was amusing to succeed now and then in a competition
where elegance and smartness were important qualifications. That was all.

The schoolmistress was strolling through the garden
now that the day's work was done, and herself unnoticed,
she paused to admire the swaying aureoled figure, with
its canopy of apple-blossom and background of tender
green. Presently she went forward and took the rounded chin in her hand.

" It is a very different face from the one that came to
me two years ago," she said kindly.

" Oh, Mrs. Summers, it can't be half so different as
the person behind it is! When I look back on the time
before I came here, it seems like a hideous dream. How

surprised I should have been in those days if someone
had told me I should live to be young and happy like
other girls!"

"Poor little one!"

The lady seated herself in the fork of a gnarled old
tree, and looked at her pupil frankly. She had never
heard in any detail the story of the Bayswater days.
Wilhelmina would have regretted her reticence on the
subject if she had known that for a time the traditional
unkind stepmother was made to explain much. It is
perhaps to the credit of Mrs. Summers' insight that she
finally rejected this theory from internal evidence alone.
She came to see that Wilhelmina's sadness and collapse
were the sadness and collapse of one who had been forced
to act, and had not merely been called upon to suffer.

"What are you going to do when you leave us?"
asked the schoolmistress.

Wilhelmina's face became a shade graver. "My father says he is making Windyhaugh his headquarters,
and he wants me to keep house for him."

"I suppose you are devoted to your father?"

This was a kindly and well-meant feeler. Mrs. Summers was quite aware of the fact that she could count
on the fingers of one hand the letters that had passed
between father and daughter during Wilhelmina's residence at school.

The young girl hesitated. "I don't know him very
well. I often think of some of the things he has said
to me." She smiled. "I can't fancy him at Windyhaugh at all."

"Is it a pretty place?"

"I think so. I haven't seen it since I was a child.
It was full of mysterious bogies for me then. I think,"
she continued with another smile, "I can face them
now."

"You look as if you could face most things, my dear,
and you mustn't be surprised if the old self has to be
faced occasionally. It is a queer creature—takes itself
off so definitely that we forget its very existence, and
then reappears as naturally as if it had been there all
the time. I wish you had a mother to take care of you,

12

child. You must be very sensible—live a great deal in the open air and keep strong. I want you to make the best of yourself."

" I mean to." Wilhelmina was in a glow of self-complacency. She could see that her schoolmistress considered her a very attractive girl. She might well have been content for this, for Mrs. Summers was not a demonstrative woman; but the old whisper of the fiends was in Wilhelmina's ear—" *Im Ganzen—haltet euch an Worte*," and she must needs strive to get the feeling precipitated in words.

" Miss Burnet "—she referred to the girl known as the quakeress—" thinks I have degenerated sadly."

Mrs. Summers did not reply at once; in fact, she seemed uncertain whether to reply at all. Wilhelmina blushed scarlet, thinking her mistress saw through her little ruse; but the lady was too well accustomed to little ruses to pay any attention to them as such.

" I think," she said meditatively, " you must make up your mind what you really mean to aim at. Your popularity—your little bit of social success—seems delightful to you because you fancied it lay out of reach; but is it so valuable in itself? Is it the best thing? Is it not a thing that countless women attain who are wanting in something you have got? "

The arrow, well-winged with its word of generous appreciation, made straight for its mark. Wilhelmina had asked for a stone, and had received bread.

It was a long time before she spoke.

" Why didn't you say that to me before? " she asked timidly at last.

The mistress rose to her feet with a smile. " You should rather ask why I have said it now,

> " ''Tis an awkward thing to play with souls,
> And matter enough to save one's own.'

Good-night, little girl, good-night! "

The weeks flew by as happy weeks will, and Wilhelmina's last night at school came round.

A few months before she had been promoted to a

room of her own—a tiny place at the top of the house—
and she was seated there now. The light of a candle
supplemented the faint golden afterglow, and revealed
the undried tears on her cheeks. She was to start very
early next morning on her complicated cross-country
journey, and in the course of the day one after another
of her school-fellows had shyly seized the opportunity
to thrust some pathetic keepsake into her hand. The
quakeress had shown great self-restraint in the choice
of hers. It was simply a blank leather-covered book, on
the fly-leaf of which was inscribed, " W. G. from J. B."
with the date. The giver had hesitated long whether to
add a text, but had decided in the negative. Her own
diary was a powerful instrument of self-examination,
and, if only Wilhelmina would write in this, she had no
doubt that it would prove the same for her.

Wilhelmina stroked the leather cover lovingly now,
then opened the book, dipped her pen in the ink, and
began.

" Well, they are over—these two happy, careless, selfish, irreligious years!

" I don't say I regret them. Why should not I too
know what the joys of this life mean? How kind everyone has been to me! If they could only know how I
bless them in my heart!

" And now I am Wilhelmina Galbraith again—Wilhelmina Galbraith of Windyhaugh. I must gird up my
loins, and 'make up my mind what I really mean to
aim at.'"

Here she paused, and pressed a sodden handkerchief
to her swollen eyes. It was some time before she took
up her pen again.

" 1. *To put my hand once more to the plough.*"

This was underlined as a tribute to its deep spiritual
significance.

" 2. To make Windyhaugh a cheerful home for my
father; to enter (as far as I conscientiously can) into
his pursuits; and to read the kind of books he will like
to talk about."

(Oh, poor lamb!)

" 3. To find out Jane, and do what I can to help her.

How I have neglected her all these years! *'Neither do I condemn thee.'*

"4. To be nice to old Mr. Darsie.

"5. To continue my education, and first of all to finish Sartor Resartus: to take an interest in politics."

She tried to think of a sixth resolution just to round the numbers; but her eyelids were growing very heavy, so she wrote at the end—

"God helping me. Amen;" and so betook herself to bed.

CHAPTER XXVI.

A TRANSFORMATION.

WILHELMINA did not read during the journey next day, and experience had not yet taught her to economize her emotions by forgetting the things that are behind. The things that were before, however, received their due share of attention. She saw Windyhaugh—big, mysterious, and imposing, as it lingered in the memory of the child; she felt the gloom of the shrubbery, and of the old divines indoors; and she pictured her father, languid, cultured, melancholy, vainly striving to lounge in her grandmother's high-backed chair.

To this scene enter Wilhelmina, fresh and buoyant, with a fair knowledge of cooking—had she not learned the trite saying concerning the way to men's hearts?—and some skill in the arrangement of flowers.

At this point in her vision the dreamer broke off to recall the precise recipe for a cheese *soufflé*, and, having impressed it on her mind, she returned with a glad rebound to the reign of romance.

How long, how mournful, were the summer evenings at Windyhaugh! How they played on one's heartstrings like the wailing note of a violin! In winter she could picture the curtains drawn, and herself curled up by a bright wood fire, reading Carlyle or Ruskin to her father; but how should she exercise the weird spirits of a summer evening? She saw herself approach the old spinet, and charm a minuet from its quavering keys with such dignity and pathos that her father paused, cigar in hand, at the ivied window to listen; but this was passing beyond the bounds of legitimate romance. She was well aware that her piano had little in common with David's harp. Fortunately she did at least read aloud well. The accomplishment was a poor one, no doubt, but everyone said it was hers.

She was horrified to feel some slight return of her old shyness and gaucherie now that the meeting with her father was so near. Whatever happened she must not give in to that. Better be saucy, forward, even audacious, than shy. In a dozen different ways she pictured the meeting. Would he be kind and make things easy for her?—or would he be gloomy, mysterious, far-off? "In any case my business is to make him happy," said Wilhelmina. She never doubted that he would come to Queensmains to meet her. Time must hang very heavy on his hands at Windyhaugh.

It was a golden summer evening. The station was rather an attractive one, with brilliant hanging flower-baskets and banks trimly laid out in a simple carpet design. A number of country folk, a few representatives of the country, and a groom in top-boots stood on the platform. George Galbraith's unmistakable figure would have towered above them all—had it been there.

Wilhelmina lifted her small luggage out of the carriage, and walked to the door of the station to see whether her father had sent a fly.

A number of vehicles were waiting there, the best place having been secured by a lady who was driving a smart high dog-cart. Wilhelmina did not even look at this till the lady's whip fell on her arm with a soft flick that might have been accidental.

Then she gazed in amazement.

"Miss Evelyn!" she said.

"I thought it must be Wilhelmina. How you have improved! I sent Charles in to fetch your small things. What a fool he is!"

"Charles?" said Wilhelmina bewildered.

"The groom, yes. Didn't you see a creature in top-boots? Just tell him, will you, to look alive."

The modest luggage was placed behind, and the high-spirited horse was curveting down the hill before Wilhelmina ventured another question.

"Are you staying—here?"

"At Windyhaugh—yes. Didn't you know? Your father has quite a houseful of visitors just now. Colonel and Mrs. Brydon, my aunt and myself, Mr. Ronald Dalrymple and your cousin Hugh."

Wilhelmina framed and rejected a dozen questions before she said quietly—

"I can't think what you all find to do."

"Oh, you know your father added a billiard-room when he rebuilt the stables; and none of us happen to be *difficile*. Mr. Galbraith has an extraordinary gift for bringing the right people together."

There was no reply. Wilhelmina did not ask the actress where her father had got the money for all this. Obviously she must wait and let the information come by degrees.

"It was very kind of you to come and meet me," she said.

"Oh, I love bowling along these level roads, and Oxford is a dear. Just look at him!"

It was not a little to Miss Evelyn's credit that, although she had now been on the stage for the best part of a decade, there was nothing about her that proclaimed, or even strongly suggested, the actress. The sailor hat and well-cut gown might have been worn by any lady whose purse was deep enough to admit of such effective simplicity.

The smiling country looked its best in the mellow evening light. This was the hour when the level rays of the sun single out each blade of grass with a shaft of light and a trailing shadow.

And so Wilhelmina came back to Windyhaugh.

Her heart beat hard as they drove under the lime trees. The plantation was in its vesper mood, and yet she was surprised to see it so overgrown.

"Is Tail-o'-the-week still alive?" she asked.

" *Who?* "

Miss Evelyn was preoccupied with the endeavour to draw up in an impressive fashion before the door, so Wilhelmina did not repeat the question. But think of a Windyhaugh that knew not Tail-o'-the-week.

A smart parlour maid opened the door before the groom had time to ring. Wilhelmina fancied she had seen the face before, and a moment later she said in amazement, " Jane? "

" Yes, miss, Jane," was the self-complacent reply, " and delighted to welcome you back."

There was a note of familiarity in the greeting that chilled the young girl. " Neither do I condemn thee," indeed!

" The gentlemen are round at the stables," continued the maid. " They'll be here in a minute."

Already their voices were heard approaching, but Miss Evelyn looked kindly at the travel-worn figure. She knew how that dusty face would affect George Galbraith.

" Don't wait," she said in an undertone. " Dinner will be ready in half an hour."

Wilhelmina was thankful to turn and fly. She found an elderly woman preparing a bath in the one-time nursery.

" *Ann!* " cried Wilhelmina; and she flung her arms round the old friend's neck.

" Now, missy, *don't cry*," said Ann severely, untwining the arms, and setting her own face hard to restrain the quiver of its muscles. " You've got the whole night before you for that. You're no' wantin' to go doun to dinner red-eyed, an' a' the folk there? "

Wilhelmina nodded gratefully and gulped down the tears. " You'll come and sit with me, won't you," she said, " when I come up to bed? "

" I will that."

When Wilhelmina's bath was over Miss Evelyn came in.

" What are you going to wear? " she asked. " Oh, yes, that white frock will do very well."

" Why, that is the very best thing I've got."

"Never mind. Wear it. We'll soon run you up
something new. At your age dress costs nothing."

She adjusted the soft white sash, and pinned an exquisite spray of wild roses on the child's shoulder.

"There!" she said. "Bear in mind that you are
looking pretty—really pretty."

"You *are* good, Miss Evelyn," said Wilhelmina
humbly.

"Now run down to the drawing-room. Quick. It is
best to be there first."

The room was empty save for Mr. Galbraith, as Miss
Evelyn had meant that it should be. He was sitting at
ease in an arm-chair—not Mrs. Galbraith's high-backed
one!—becomingly dressed in a velvet coat. His back
was to the light, and Wilhelmina could not see the expression of his face; but he held out his left hand without a word, and she went up to him. Her heart was
beating as if it would choke her. A moment later he
had drawn her close, and his arm was round her. Then
he leaned his head on the back of his chair to get a better
view of her fresh young face, and the light from the
window accentuated his iron-grey hair, his fine forehead
and well-cut nose. "Glad to come to me?" he asked
simply; and, such was the magnetism of his presence,
that she answered truthfully, "Yes."

Father and daughter formed a charming picture
when the guests assembled in the drawing-room; and
Mr. Galbraith was by no means insusceptible to the
well-disguised surprise with which Ronald and Hugh regarded the new arrival.

The dinner, though simple, was perfectly cooked and
served. One advantage of Mr. Galbraith's roving life
was that he could usually put his hand on the thing he
wanted, and now he had picked up a youth of unusual
promise, whose health had broken down while he was
working under a well-known *chef*, but who was abundantly equal to a light situation in the country.

The conversation turned mainly on horses; and when
Wilhelmina's first anguish of shyness was over, she gathered that her father and Mr. Dalrymple each kept a racer
in the stable. What would Grannie say? The question

was constantly in her mind, but fortunately she had sense enough now to keep it there.

The afterglow lingered long that night, and the ladies were still on the terrace in their soft fluffy wraps when the gentlemen came out from dinner. The air was fragrant with coffee, and Miss Evelyn was smoking a dainty cigarette. As was not unusual, Ronald had taken a little more wine than was good for him, and now he went straight up to Wilhelmina.

"Doosid pretty girl!" he said, putting his hand caressingly under her chin.

It was the first time any man save her father had touched her face, and she released herself with a scarlet blush, and a spirited toss of her well-poised head.

"Quite right!" said her father playfully, but with an intonation that not even Ronald could mistake. "Hands off! This young lady happens to be my property."

He stretched himself on a rug at her feet, and looked up in her face with a very pleasant smile.

And so it came about that Wilhelmina did not cry herself to sleep—nor did she blister the pages of her new diary with her tears. She was dazzled, bewildered, charmed—by her own father.

CHAPTER XXVII.

GLAMOUR AND ISOLDE.

NEXT morning she was up and out betimes, eager to see the old place, and to pass its changes in review, before curious eyes were about to see how it all affected her.

How small everything looked!—her bedroom, the staircase, and the hall! The shrubbery that had dwelt in her mind as a forest was but a steep bank clothed with undergrowth and trees. Even the great tidal river looked less like the ocean than of old.

Except for the addition of the billiard-room, the

house was almost unchanged. Those of the ornaments that had offended Mr. Galbraith's fastidious taste had been removed, and a few comfortable arm-chairs had been introduced; but the old furniture remained, the wall-papers were shabby, and the woodwork and fittings were in actual want of repair. The garden too was neglected. Tail-o'-the-week was dead, and, although his successor looked in at stated intervals, everything seemed tangled and overgrown. It was obvious that the main interest of the house centred in the stables. The new buildings were not really remarkable, but to Wilhelmina's untrained eyes the roomy, well-ventilated, loose boxes were magnificent, and the coach-house and harness-room, well lighted and lined with varnished wood, seemed quite palatial. She would have spent a long time examining every detail, but the sight of the men filled her with terror. She had never seen people look so knowing, so sure of themselves and their world. Charles was not quite so alarming, but the impish jockey and important stud-groom made her feel herself a shy little guest at Windyhaugh.

There was no lock now on the garden gate, and, once within the high enclosure, she well-nigh forgot the changes that had taken place. Once more the fruit was ripening on the ruddy brick walls: once more the crisp brown shoots and crimson blooms of the roses stood out against the opalescent water away down below. At the far end of the garden stood the old arbour, approached by a flight of steps, and commanding a fine view of the estuary. Wilhelmina seated herself on the wooden bench with a long sigh.

She had scarcely had time to collect her thoughts when Hugh appeared. At this period of his life he cherished a hopeless passion for Miss Evelyn; but as that lady would not be downstairs for hours, he was willing to talk to his cousin.

"It's awfully nice to see you again, Vilma," he said, seating himself on the worm-eaten step at her feet. "May I smoke?"

"Yes," she said doubtfully, "if you want to."

"Do you remember," he went on, as if searching in

the dimmest recesses of his memory, " a visit we paid to you here, ages and ages ago? "

Wilhelmina laughed gleefully. " Oh, yes. I remember it very well."

" Windyhaugh has rather changed since those days."

" It has indeed."

" Mean to say you like the old style better? "

She smiled. " I don't quite know yet what the new style is."

" You'll soon get rid of us, you know. We're all booked somewhere or other for the twelfth."

" Oh, Hugh! I am so glad to see you. I want to hear all about you and Aunt Enid and Gavin. Are you really going to be a soldier? "

His brow clouded. " I hope so. I have been ploughed twice, but I think I'm pretty safe for the next time. If I miss Woolwich, I can still have a try at Sandhurst, but of course the army is no fun unless one's commission is in the Royal Artillery."

" Oh? That is rather hard on all the other regiments."

He laughed at her literal spirit, and then he sighed. " In the meantime, if I can only scrape through this infernal exam.——! "

" Shall you be all right after that? "

" Oh, rather! It is *man's* work then—Military Topography, you know, and Fortification and Tactics and that kind of thing."

Her eyes grew large. " That sounds pretty bad."

" No doubt a girl would find it so, not a man. They say wild horses wouldn't prevent a fellow passing *out*." He paused and added reflectively, " Water on the brain might."

" And how are Aunt Enid and Gavin? Is Gavin still as lovely as he was? I always used to think of him when we read that poem of Wordsworth's at school—

" ' Heaven lies about us in our infancy,'

you know—and then—

" ' Trailing clouds of glory do we come
From God who is our home.' "

Hugh choked on his cigarette smoke. "He doesn't trail clouds of glory—*much*—now," he said. "But he is far too pretty for a boy. I always tell him he ought to have been a girl."

"And Aunt Enid?—is she as pretty as ever?"

"Oh, the *Mater* will never grow old, bless her! She is a regular trump."

"She's beautiful. I often think of that first night when I lay in bed, and listened to her voice."

"You've an awfully nice voice of your own, now," he said, "and you contribute your share to the family good looks."

He watched the rosy colour creep over her face at his words, and wished he could write and tell his mother how pretty she was; but, although Enid knew her son was in Scotland with Ronald, the Windyhaugh part of the programme had been suppressed.

"I? Oh, Hugh!" said Wilhelmina. "Don't you think we should go in to breakfast?"

"I do; but I think you might let me have a kiss first."

She looked unhappy, not wishing to seem ungracious.

"I don't care for kissing," she said hesitatingly at last. "Do you?"

"It is an overrated pastime as a rule, I admit; but in this case—— We are cousins, you know. We were children together."

"Of course—but we never kissed when we were children."

"What a memory you have! and what a fool I must have been! I remember you were a regular martinet— kept me in no end of good order. I can believe that you wouldn't let me kiss you."

She laughed out light-heartedly. "I wish I could feel sure that the objection was entirely on my side in those days!"

"I know I feel very sure whose side the objection is on now. Don't be stiff, Vilma;

"'We twa hae paidl'd in the burn,'

you know, and all that sort of thing."

Wilhelmina's eyes bubbled over in glee.

"True!" she said—

> "'And there's a hand, my trusty fiere!
> And gie's a hand o' thine.'"

She suited the action to the word, carefully keeping
the hands referred to at arm's length.

"You *are* clever after all, Vilma," he said regretfully; "I knew you would be."

"Oh, Hugh, I wish I were!" she cried wistfully. "I
was too happy at school to be clever; but I mean to begin
now, and read very hard."

"*Don't!*" he said earnestly. "Take my advice. I
have met no end of clever women in London, and it is
my deliberate conviction that the game is not worth the
candle."

As he spoke they came in sight of Mr. Galbraith, sun-
ning himself on the doorstep. His worn face brightened when he caught sight of his daughter in her fresh
blue cotton frock, and he drew her to him affectionately,
as he had done the day before.

"Well, little one?" he said.

Most of us lunch and dine in the same conventional
fashion now-a-days. It is in the breakfast-room that
the true character and temperament of a family come
out; and Windyhaugh at this time was certainly a fine
example of the good old barbarous English school. Fish
fresh from the river, fruit from the garden, oatmeal porridge and scones, backed by more substantial dainties,
made a goodly show, while the old world flowers in the
garden vied with each other as to who should send in
the most fragrant greeting on the fresh sunladen air.
One feature these breakfasts had, too, that was not English—delicious coffee from freshly-roasted berries. Mr.
Galbraith did not belong to the great majority of Englishmen, who in this respect are content to grumble and
endure. If Mademoiselle could have but seen the day!

Ann, Jane, the *chef*, and a scullery-maid constituted
the domestic staff, so Wilhelmina escaped as soon as possible to help with the lighter housework. She was terribly shy of Jane, and this feeling was not lessened by

the fact that it did not seem to be in any way recip-
rocated.

"It's no' the richt thing ava that she should be here,"
Ann said mournfully, "the mistress having sent her
awa' an' that; but your father took a fancy to her. He
wanted somebody, too, that would keep a short tongue
in her heid, an'—I'll undertake that Jane'll do that!"

Ann laid a pillow in place with a gesture that seemed
to say, "You presume to move at your peril!" Her
whole life at Windyhaugh was a protest in these days—a
protest that dared not find expression in words, and that
took refuge in a dour manner, and an uncompromising
vernacular.

Wilhelmina's face grew very red. "Is she married?"

Ann did not reply immediately. "She's no' married," she said doggedly at last. "It's no' richt that you
should be under the same roof wi' her—an' a play-actress
i' the hoose an' a'."

"Ann," said Wilhelmina solemnly, "you must never
say a word against Miss Evelyn. I can't tell you how
kind she has been to me. I think once I should have
died if it hadn't been for her."

"An' what would your Grannie say?"

Wilhelmina adjusted the perfumed night-dress case,
and sat down on a low chair with her head on her
hands.

"Ann," she said slowly, with sublime *naïveté*, "Grannie didn't know how difficult life gets. It isn't as if we
planned it all for ourselves. Things happen, and other
things grow out of that, and then we've got to live in
the middle of it all. If a little tree in the shrubbery
finds a big branch above its head, it *can't* grow straight
on. It has *got* to pass either on the one side or the
other."

Ann stared, more than half mystified. If Wilhelmina had wanted an appreciative audience, she should
have made that remark to her father.

"Well, Miss Wilhelmina, I hope you'll no' set your
heart on a' thae braw things. Wha kens how long it'll
last?"

They had gone into another room, and Wilhelmina carefully closed the door. "Ann," she said in a tremulous voice, "whose money is doing it all? Not Mr. Dalrymple's?"

"Na, na. I'll no' say but what Mr. Dalrymple took a share i' the new buildings, an' nae doubt he pays for the keep o' his ain beast; but it's your father's money richt eneugh." And Ann sighed as if that fact were small consolation.

"Vilma! Vilma!" cried Hugh's voice. "Uncle George wants you to come and see the mares. We are going to try their paces in the field."

"Do you hear?" said Wilhelmina with beaming face, "I can't stop. *Father* wants me;" and, seizing her hat, she took the steps almost at a bound.

In after years when she was present at a real race, with its royal enclosure, its grand stand, its smart drags, its elegant costumes, and its undercurrent of sin and squalor, she thought with hungry longing of that first sunny morning.

Only a quiet level green field surrounded by trees; a bright sun catching the fresh morning gowns of the ladies, and the white and tan coats of the dogs; only two beautiful silky thoroughbreds laying back their sensitive ears and throwing out their long shapely limbs as if for the very joy of existence—surely this and not the other was the very ideal of a race!

The animals were back at the starting-point, muffled up, patted and caressed before Wilhelmina took her eyes off them for a moment. Then she turned to her father, and, to her surprise, met his eye.

"How quick they go!" she said breathlessly.

Hugh laughed. "That's not an unusual feature in racers," he said.

"For the future *blasé* people under twenty are requested to pay a guinea at the gate," said Mr. Galbraith quietly.

"And yet," continued Wilhelmina unheeding, "they don't *seem* to be going fast at all. It's like—it's like the sleep of a spinning-top."

At this moment Jane made her appearance with a

card in her hand. "A gentleman to see you, sir," she said to her master.

Mr. Galbraith looked at the card with furrowed brows.

"Harley Brentwood," he said slowly. "Who in the world is Harley Brentwood?"

"I know," cried Hugh, unabashed by his recent snub. "He's a fellow who got upset in the river near here, and you fished him out."

Mr. Galbraith looked at his nephew with expressionless eyes. "May I ask where you picked up that—that cock-and-bull story?"

Hugh knocked the ash off the end of his cigarette. "He told me himself. I met him—let me see—I think it was at the Royal Institution. He has got a sister—an awfully swagger girl."

Mr. Galbraith turned to the maid who was waiting. "Tell Mr. Brentwood we are out here with the horses. Perhaps he would like to join us."

"Now I think of it, Rigby was talking about Brentwood in London the other day," continued Hugh. "I think he said Mrs. Brentwood was dead, and Brentwood had chucked the Church and gone in for literature. Honest doubt business."

Mr. Galbraith's lip curled. "Quite the regulation proceeding," he said. "This little pose of atheism on the part of our young men is becoming a trifle hackneyed."

Ronald yawned. "I can't think what anybody wants to be an atheist for now that Canon Somebody says there is no hell. I have often wondered whether Heaven couldn't be improved upon; but, upon my soul, it never occurred to me to tinker at the other place."

Wilhelmina looked appalled.

"Don't listen to him, little one," said her father. "It is only his nonsense."

"Oh, is it just?" cried shrewd obtuse Hugh. Then he turned to his cousin. "Are you particularly gone on the doctrine of eternal punishment?" he asked.

Wilhelmina drew herself up. "I don't think I understand you," she said with dignity.

Mr. Galbraith looked at her admiringly. " I wish we could manage a season for her in town next year," he thought.

The appearance of the visitor put a stop to an un-edifying conversation. Mr. Galbraith went towards the gate and took the young man's hand with a genial smile.

" Well," he said, " it is pleasant to find you have not forgotten us at Windyhaugh."

" Indeed, I feel like one of the nine. I should have made an effort to find you long ago, but latterly we have spent much of our time abroad, with—my mother."

Mr. Galbraith's face grew grave in an instant. " Ah! I was sorry to hear of your loss."

The young man seemed pleased that he had heard of it. " Yes," he said quietly. " My sister and I are alone now."

" From what I hear she is a sister any man would be proud of."

Mr. Brentwood's face lighted up. " She is much more than that," he said, with a smile that was obviously meant for the absent sister. " By the way she told me to say that she hopes some day to have an opportunity of thanking you——"

" For what? Oh ! " Mr. Galbraith laughed lightly. " I am sure I will glady make the most of any chance service that gives me some claim on her regard."

As he spoke they joined the little group on the slop-ing bank of the field. Brief though her father's absence had been, Wilhelmina greeted him with a quick smile of welcome; and then, quite involuntarily, she extended the smile to Mr. Brentwood. A moment before she had felt a sudden rush of loneliness, a sudden dread of the company she was in. The men had looked so fast, so horsey, and that innocent little cigarette seemed to place even Miss Evelyn at terrible distance. Mr. Galbraith's stately presence brought relief and reassurance at once, and so, strangely enough, did Mr. Brentwood's grave ascetic face and semi-clerical grey tweed.

" Yours is the casting vote, Mr. Brentwood," Hugh called out gaily, when the beautiful creatures had shown their paces once more. " At present the betting is even.

13

We two back Glamour. Uncle George and Colonel Brydon backed Isolde. Glamour won the Maiden Plate, but Isolde has been putting on form tremendously since."

The visitor smiled. "You help me out of a difficulty," he said, "by forcing me to betray the density of my ignorance at once. Like Sidney Smith I don't know a horse from a cow. *As a picture*," he glanced round the field before his eye rested on the ladies—"the whole thing is delightful. If you ask me to bet, I have just wisdom enough to throw in my lot with Mr. Galbraith."

Wilhelmina beamed on the speaker. Hs was young enough to be very appreciative of his own well-turned remark; but only Mr. Galbraith was quick enough to note the self-conscious little blush that accompanied it. He held up his hand with a gesture of protest that was not wholly playful. "Don't! Don't" he said lightly. "My bad luck is proverbial. Glamour is better bred, but Isolde has a heart of gold."

"His bad luck proverbial!" chuckled Hugh in an undertone. "Pretty well that for a man who won three thousand pounds in a day at Monte Carlo!"

Wilhelmina just caught the words. And so the great mystery was solved.

Mr. Galbraith laid his hand on young Brentwood's shoulder, and led him away from the others. "Come to my den," he said, "and have a chat. You will stay to lunch of course."

"Thank you, I shall be very glad. I should like in the afternoon to look up that clergyman who was so good to me, if he is still here."

"Mr. Carmichael? A thorough good fellow. Somebody shall drive you over in the dog-cart after lunch."

"Thanks very much; but I think I would rather walk. My doctor is strong on physical exercise for me just now."

For the first time Mr. Galbraith looked at the lean eager face with an almost professional eye. "You have been none the worse, I hope, for that unlucky ducking?"

Brentwood laughed. "Don't call it unlucky," he said with real feeling, "since it gave me the privilege of knowing you. Æsculapius says I may consider myself lucky to have escaped organic mischief in the lungs. I am all right; but periodically I get the most prostrating headaches. It is a stupid womanish complaint; one would almost rather have something organic; but he says it is a neurosis that I shall probably outgrow."

He was surprised to find himself talking so frankly of a physical frailty; but George Galbraith's face at the moment was that of a born father confessor.

"I think there is little doubt that you will live it down," he said with grave kindness; "but that sort of thing is very trying while it lasts."

"Horribly. And yet—as literature is probably going to be my—my trade, it matters less than if—than it might have done."

An hour or two later Brentwood started on his way to Queensmains. Miss Evelyn and Mr. Galbraith went with him to the gate, and after bidding him farewell, strolled on along the coast. For the first half mile the young man walked with his grave eyes on the ground; then suddenly he stopped; a boyish smile broke up the thought-furrows on his face, and he switched the head off a particularly audacious knap-weed.

"Well, I'm blessed," he exclaimed aloud, "if that isn't the rummiest household I ever came across!"

He seated himself on a low dyke, as if to give his undivided energies to the consideration of the subject.

He passed it all in review—the shabby house, the fine stables; the neglected garden, the cook in his spotless cap and apron. But all this was only the background of the picture. It was the characters who were really interesting. There was Mr. Galbraith, whom for two years Brentwood had regarded with a feeling akin to hero-worship; there was Miss Evelyn, whom, under another name, he had admired repeatedly on the stage; there was that "he-minx, Hugh Dalrymple," of whom he had seen just enough to know that he belonged to a fast set in London; and, in the midst of all, there was the little girl in the cotton frock, "for all the world like a blue-bell that has lost its way in an orchid-house."

Brentwood had belonged to a studious set at Cambridge, and his knowledge of life was not yet very profound, though his insight was keen. He possessed that freedom from prejudice which characterizes most young men now-a-days, but in his case it was balanced by a faculty of reverence that is as rare as the other is common. He did not admire George Galbraith the more because he seemed to live a Bohemian life; but, on the other hand, he declined to admire him the less on that account. Here evidently was a *character*, to be studied and appreciated as such. "I shall certainly avail myself of his invitation to go back," said Brentwood as he resumed his walk. "In the meantime, as a mere matter of curiosity, I should like to know what the country says to it all!"

He had not walked far before a turn in the road brought him in sight of the "blue-bell," and he made haste to overtake her. Her shy involuntary smile of surprise was very flattering.

"Are you walking to Queensmains?" he asked.

"Yes."

"That is lucky for me."

She did not respond, and he added playfully, "—unless I am interrupting an interesting train of thought."

She sighed. "One is glad to stop thinking sometimes."

He nearly laughed outright, but she was evidently very serious.

"In that case I must not even offer a penny for your thoughts."

"Oh, they were nothing particular. I was thinking —how difficult life is!"

"Life at beautiful Windyhaugh?—with its kind people, and those nice horses and dogs to play with?"

He was talking down to her now. Did he know how old she was? She drew herself up, and old Mrs. Galbraith herself could scarcely have looked more uncompromising as she said—

"We were not sent into the world just to play."

"Don't you think some of us were?"

She shook her head. She had not thus learnt the lesson of old Windyhaugh.

" Then shouldn't we look around, and decide what to do, and simply set to work to do it ? "

" It is easy to decide, but suppose the work is taken right out of our hands ? "

" Then we probably made a mistake; but the chances are that our real work is lying close at hand all the time."

She shook her head. This suggestion did not meet the exigencies of the case in hand.

" And at any rate," he continued, willing to be helpful, " don't you think we ought to be glad now and then of a little time in which to lay by wisdom and strength ? The chances are that life will drive us on hard enough by and bye."

" That's true," she said suddenly, becoming unwittingly personal, " and I do mean to read serious books. I am half way through Sartor Resartus now."

Again his eyes bubbled over with laughter. He was quite used to the society of women who read Carlyle; but Sartor Resartus and Windyhaugh—as he knew Windyhaugh—were an irresistibly funny combination. Did the orchid-house grow edelweiss as well as blue-bells ? " And do you understand it ? " he said.

" Yes," she answered a little doubtfully. In truth the atmosphere and imagery of the book delighted her. Poring over it, sentence by sentence, she surely understood it; and yet—somehow she had her doubts.

They walked on for a minute or two in silence.

" I did come to a bit to-day," she said conscientiously at last, " that I didn't quite understand. It was about the Where and the When, and it ended with—' Think well, thou too wilt find there is no Space nor Time. We are—we know not what—light-sparkles floating in the æther of Deity ! ' Perhaps I haven't thought well enough yet. I only read it after lunch to-day, but—but——"

This time he laughed outright. " But Space and Time have an odd air of reality still. I know. It is a way they have."

She seemed so sensitive to his laughter that he grew grave at once.

"Of course you can't make much of a passage that you pick up between your finger and thumb like that——"

"Of course not," she said hurriedly, abashed.

"And yet—hasn't even that fragment a pleasant and restful meaning? When one is irked by the conditions one is in, the time one is in, and the place one is in— isn't it a comfort to shake it all off—to say, ' It's not real '; and simply to throw oneself like—an unattached sea-weed, into the ocean of—God?"

His metaphor was scarcely an improvement on Carlyle's, but it made all the difference to Wilhelmina. Philosophy in the wedding-garment of religion found easy access to her mind. Very slowly she raised awe-struck admiring eyes. And they had dared to talk of atheism in connection with this man!

"I am going to call on the minister," he said a moment later, rather ashamed of the turn his sentence had taken.

"I am going to see a friend too."

"Then if I may, I will take you to your destination first. I have plenty of time on my hands. I was much interested to meet Miss Evelyn in private life. You won't tell her if you think she would be displeased; but of course I couldn't help recognizing her. I suppose you have often seen her act?"

"Only once—oh, a long time ago! I haven't been to the theatre since I was quite a little girl."

"No doubt she is a great friend of yours."

"She is a great friend of my father's," said Wilhelmina simply. "She has been very kind to me."

"He is a wonderful man, your father. I have an immense admiration for him."

She smiled brightly as if that were a matter of course.

A minute later they reached the grimy little grocer's shop—so much smaller, so much grimier, than of old!

"Good-bye," said Wilhelmina; "this is my destination."

"Oh? I thought you said you were going to see a friend."

She blushed. She was neither young enough nor old enough to " see life whole," and she had not been two years at a girls' school without acquiring a veneer of feeble snobbishness; but she was not going to deny the friend of her childhood for that.

" I am," she said bravely. " My friend lives here."

And so the blue-bell disappeared into the dust and cavernous darkness of the shop.

CHAPTER XXVIII.

WILHELMINA FINDS A KINGDOM.

THERE were several people in the shop, and Wilhelmina's eyes were too much dazzled by the glare outside to see just at first that Mr. Darsie was not there.

Of course no one knew her, and indeed the gossips were too much enthralled by the subject under discussion to notice her entrance at 'all.

" What I'd fain ken," an old woman was saying severely, " is what call a play-actress has to be yonder. Card-playing and horse-racing's bad eneugh, but a *play-actress—!* " She brought a horny hand forcibly down on the counter. " It's a disgrace to the memory of a righteous God-fearing woman! "

A murmur of approval greeted this creditable sentiment.

" They do say this ane's respectable," put in a young man feebly.

" Respectable? Hoot awa! Dinna tell me! I never met the play-actress yet that was respectable."

As the speaker had probably never met one of any kind, this statement was not surprising.

" An' if the hussy's pleased to ca' hersel' *respectable,*" she continued with biting sarcasm, " wha' is it she'll be after?—Mr. Galbraith or Mr. Dalrymple? "

The young man grinned. " I'm told she's sweet on

Mr. Galbraith, but weel aware that Mr. Dalrymple has the siller."

"An' there they baith stan'—dancing attendance, an' waiting for my leddy to pick an' choose? Hoots man, ye're doited!"

"Na, na. Mr. Galbraith's no' likely to pit his heid i' the noose a third time; but they say she's bound to catch Mr. Dalrymple."

"Weel, it's a sin an' a shame—when ye mind o' auld Mistress Galbraith—to think that noo nae decent woman wad cross the threshold o' Windyhaugh!"

Up to this moment Wilhelmina had been wondering how she could escape unobserved. Now she accepted the risk, and darted out into the sunshine.

Panting and breathless she walked up and down till she had recovered her presence of mind; then she turned up the steep little lane that led to the rooms above the shop. With her hand on the knocker she paused. What a relief it would be to hurry home, and postpone her visit till to-morrow!

"*Coward!*" she said. "Will you act as if you believed their hateful slanders?" And there was no doubt or indecision about her cheerful rat-tat.

The old man was busy preparing his bachelor tea. The woman who "did" for him usually went home after cooking his mid-day dinner. Wilhelmina had thought him very old when she was a child, but now he seemed much older. His gait was beginning to suggest "the pursuit of his own centre of gravity," and he seemed unable to control the facial muscles that quivered with joy at the sight of her.

He had a thousand questions to ask about herself and her "eddication," but he would not have been human if he had not been curious to hear something of Windyhaugh too; and it must be admitted that on this subject she gave him scant encouragement. Indeed she veered away from it so gaily and persistently that she succeeded in making him think the state of affairs a great deal more serious than it actually was. On the whole, however, the interview was as successful as first interviews after a long separation are wont to be.

Wilhelmina reached home just in time to dress for dinner, and appeared downstairs with a bright red flush on each cheek.

"And where has the missis been all the afternoon?" said her father playfully—"deserting her household without warning."

She looked pleased that he should have missed her.

"I walked over to Queensmains," she said. "Did anybody call?"

She succeeded in asking the momentous question with a casual little woman-of-the-world air that made them all laugh. Ronald grinned across meaningly at Mr. Galbraith, but the latter did not meet his eye.

"Calling, little girl," he said carelessly, "is a frivolous occupation that has been systematically discouraged at Windyhaugh for over a quarter of a century. If it is ever to be reintroduced, the missis will have to assume her full responsibilities."

When Wilhelmina went up to her room that night the brightness of the moon tempted her to draw up her blind and look out. The drive in front of the house was bathed in light, and, away to the left, she could see two figures in the shrubbery. While she stood they emerged into the open, and turned back into the shadow of the trees again. It was her father and Miss Evelyn.

Wilhelmina felt a queer little pang of jealousy as she drew down the blind and lighted her candle.

"I wish I could find God again," she said drearily. "I am so lonely."

She prayed more earnestly than she had done for a long time—prayed that she might "throw herself like an unattached sea-weed into the ocean of God"; but her voice went out into vacancy. There was no response.

At last she rose from her knees, and, unlocking a box, took from it the leather-covered book. Of course the tears filled her eyes as she read the entry of two nights before, but she did not give in for a moment. Her careful handwriting had just a dash of defiance in it as she wrote—

"We are not going to be fools, you and I, old book;

and weep and moan because we can't build the world to our liking. Let us look the situation fairly in the face."

She became a little less coherent after that. She had hoped to be her father's friend and helper; that place was already filled, and only the post of playfellow was vacant. Well, let her be content with the post of playfellow, and "be glad of a little time in which to lay by wisdom and strength." But, because the post of friend was filled by an actress, the world—poor little Wilhelmina, "the world" in Mr. Darsie's shop!—said "horrid things"; and, loving her father as she did, this was very hard to bear.

The page was not blotted with tears. On the contrary, it was almost as immaculate as a leaf from a prize copy-book; but every word in it was alive with genuine feeling. Having thus delivered her innocent soul, she locked up the diary and betook herself to bed.

On opening the book again next day, she accidentally let a penful of ink fall on the written page. She was just at the age when such an accident is intolerable, and, rather than leave a blotted record of her feelings, she carefully extracted the page altogether. She tore it across, and ran downstairs to burn it in the kitchen fire.

In the hall she met her father.

"Hallo, little one!" he said. "I was just looking for you. I want you to come to the billiard-room, and have your first lesson. Make haste, and we'll give them all the slip."

His tone was confidential, and she followed him with delight. For the next hour father and daughter saw each other to the best advantage; and it was not till Wilhelmina was up in her room once more that she bethought herself of those miserable scraps of paper.

Vainly she searched in her pocket: they were not there. Her face turned white, and then the sweat rose to her brow for terror. Stealing along like a thief, she made her way back to the billiard-room in the hope of finding it deserted; but a peal of laughter from Ronald and Hugh forbade her to enter.

Had they found the bits of paper and pieced them together? Were they laughing over *that?* Sick with anxiety she leaned against the lintel—actually listening at the door like any common eavesdropper. No, they were not talking of her. They seemed to be discussing Jane. With a momentary sense of relief, she stole back to her room.

She left the door ajar, resolving to remain awake till she heard them go to their rooms; but they wore out her physical powers, and she fell asleep with her clothes on. About two in the morning she woke, feeling stiff and chill. The house was dark and quiet enough now, save for the glimmer of her candle and the thumping of her heart, but she searched for the paper in vain. It was nowhere to be found.

From that time her sleep was a succession of wild dreams. Now her father had found the scraps, now the jockey; anon she discovered the fateful leaf in her diary, safe and immaculate as when it was first written. The waking from that dream was the sorest experience of all.

Mrs. Summers might well tell her not to be surprised if the old self reappeared. The old self was on her with a vengeance now. For days she struggled to be bright and cheerful, fancying all the while that this one and that was regarding her with a meaning glance.

On the third day after dinner she escaped to the old arbour at the foot of the garden. No one was likely to follow her there; but the river and hills in the sunset light brought no rest or peace to her unquiet mind.

" God," she groaned, " don't let anybody have found those papers, don't, *don't!* "

The absurdity of the prayer—not only in the wording, but in its whole conception of man's relation to God, struck her even as she spoke.

" Some people have the right to go to God with every trifle," she thought, " but not I. The privilege is for those who have given themselves up to Him, body and soul."

Quick as light on the heels of this thought came another. " And what does my whole heart long for more than to give itself up to Him? Is there *anything* I wish to keep back?"

In a moment she had forgotten all about her trouble; she thought of no article of faith; her very will seemed fallen asleep; but the yearning for God went through her like a rushing mighty wind. Her whole being was laid on the altar.

And then the experience took place that in after years she could never forget, never doubt, never quite explain away. Out of the vacancy—*an answer came back!* She saw no face, she heard no voice; but a spark passed between her and the Invisible. She felt herself in actual touch with God.

It all took place in a moment, in the twinkling of an eye; but that moment lifted her as completely above earthly cares as if she had passed through the gloomy river. Her whole aspect, her whole attitude towards life and death, towards time and eternity, were as different as if she had been born again after lying asleep for a thousand years.

She heard no more of the scraps of paper, and she thought of them no more. "I went out to seek my father's asses," said Wilhelmina, "and I found a kingdom."

CHAPTER XXIX.

ON THE SEA-SHORE.

I CAN touch but lightly on the inner life of the weeks and months that followed. Has not the story been told once and again by those who are abler far to deal with it than I? "'He that followeth Me shall not walk in darkness,' saith the Lord." Wilhelmina had stepped out into the light.

Spiritual experiences she had known before, but never anything like this. It was this moment she always fell back upon in after years, when

"—like a man in wrath, the heart
Stood up and answered, 'I have felt!'"

So vivid, so unforeseen, was the flash, that for a
time creed and moral law had no existence for her. Sermons and books were like crutches to the man whose
limbs are sound. She went about the household in a
spirit of radiant gladness; but her greatest joy was to
slip out of sight, to fall behind the others in the course
of a walk, that she might give herself up unreservedly
to this new communion—"throw herself like an unattached sea-weed into the ocean of God."

She was very grateful to young Brentwood for those
unpremeditated words, and they made her feel how deep
his spiritual experiences must have been; but in truth
the phrase meant much more for her than it did for
him. It had risen to his lips in the exigency of talking
to this child as Faust talked to Gretchen about God,
and, having served its turn, had been forgotten.

Step by step Wilhelmina had to follow those who
had trod the same path before her. She had to learn
that, although the light came at first without measure or
stint, the lamp must be carefully watched and trimmed
if its brightness was to last. However much leisure she
might have during the day, nothing would ever make
up for the hour overslept in the silence of the morning.

Once when she reached the arbour as usual before
the household was astir, she was dismayed to find Hugh
already in possession.

"Oh, I say, Vilma," he cried, "I am awfully glad to
see you. Just hear me run over these beastly irregular
verbs, will you? . . . You don't mind," he added, catching sight of her fallen face.

"Why, of course I am glad to help you, Hugh," she
answered cheerfully, resigning herself as she spoke to a
day of spiritual gloom.

He kept her hard at work till breakfast time, and
then—what was her surprise to find her lamp burning
more brightly than if she had spent the hour in prayer.

As the freshness of the new experience wore off, she
began to read more. Sartor Resartus was finished under
protest, because she had said she would finish it; and
then she plunged "soulforward headlong" into books
with which, by a curious spiritual instinct, she felt her

affinity beforehand. The Devout Life, The Imitation
of Christ, The Life of M'Cheyne, and others of varying
literary merit, but all alight with the divine spark.

She began to go to church twice on Sunday too, and
to attend week-day meetings as often as possible. In
this way she made the acquaintance of those who were
and of those who appeared to be, like-minded with herself; and she learned, first, the delight, and then the
danger, of the "communion of saints" on earth. It
was selfish not to tell of the great things one had seen
and felt, and yet—unless one's motives were pure as
gold thrice tried—how apt was the vision to vanish in
the telling of it! She was appalled to find that unless
one was continually on guard, earthly vanities and rival-
ries and meannesses were ready to crop up like weeds
on the very steps of the Throne.

She had pleasant chats with Mr. Darsie at this time
—chats in which she kept well on the outskirts of her
religious life. He had a great belief in her intellectual
powers, and looked forward with interest to the day
when these would join issue with her religious faith.
Often when she was hovering over his bookshelves like a
bee in a flower garden, he was tempted to lay his hand
on Kingsley, Maurice, or Robertson, but something restrained him. "It's bound to come," he said to himself
with a little sigh, "but I'll no' be the man to bring it.
She's ower far ben."

Wilhelmina had promised to write to the quakeress,
and the latter now received an epistle that took her
breath away. She answered it at once in a fervour of
appreciation, and thus was initiated a correspondence
that lasted for some time. The leading girl and the
colonial brunette also wrote just often enough to keep
Wilhelmina in touch with the vanities of life. Their
letters seemed to her like echoes out of a previous incarnation.

Meanwhile outward events were moving on busily
enough. The twelfth of August found her alone with
the servants at Windyhaugh. A couple of months later
the horses were removed, and the servants—all save Ann
—dismissed. Mr. Galbraith was in the trough of the

wave once more. Wilhelmina had become deeply attached to Glamour and Isolde, and even Oxford had a firm place in her regard. There were not a dozen beings in the world whom she loved more dearly than she did those two beautiful racers, and her only consolation in parting with them was the fact that the men went too. Hugh told her when he left that he believed Miss Evelyn was engaged to Ronald Dalrymple, but she could not believe it. She allowed herself now none of those delightful day-dreams that had so brightened the gloom in days gone by—was not every thought a possible link with God?—but even in her schooldays she had been one of those girls whose views on the subject of marriage are a curious mixture of humility and pride. The thought of any actual known man in the relation of husband (as girls understand the relation of husband) is impossible, and yet—" is the ideal fairy prince likely to ride out of the everywhere just for poor little me? " Short of the fairy prince, however, humanity could surely afford many finer types than Ronald Dalrymple!

After all, those were happy days that Wilhelmina spent alone with old Ann at Windyhaugh. She did not realize how completely the difficulties and temptations of life were reduced to a minimum. " Nothing can ever go wrong again," she used to cry exultingly in her heart. " Come sorrow, come sickness, come blindness, come death! What can it matter to me? This side the veil or that—should I even know the difference? Is not the whole of the universe my home? "

Mr. Galbraith came and went, but he was moody and *distrait*, and Wilhelmina found it very difficult to get into touch with him. They had some happy hours together in the billiard-room, however, and she took pains to keep herself in practice while he was away.

One mild afternoon in December Mr. Brentwood called.

" Mr. Galbraith's not at home," said Ann; " and Miss Galbraith is down on the shore. If you'll step in, I'll go and fetch her."

" No, no," he replied. " I will join her there." He was disappointed not to see Mr. Galbraith, and yet he

was surprised to feel a little wave of pleasurable excitement at the prospect of meeting his blue-bell
alone.

She was seated on a jutting reef of rock, with the
green water tumbling about her. He had to speak before she became aware of his presence, but, although she
was taken by surprise, her smile of welcome was more
self-possessed than formerly.

"And don't you find it dull alone here at Windyhaugh?" he said when they had exchanged a few conventional remarks.

A rosy blush mantled her face. She could not tell
him how very far she was from being "alone."

"*Oh, no!*" she said with unconscious reverence.

He looked surprised, and it was a minute before he
proceeded—"So life has ceased to be difficult?"

She smiled. "Yes. Life is easy."

"You have found the key then?"

She nodded.

"And where was it?"

"I don't know. Just *there*. I suppose my eyes were
holden."

He sighed. How easy it was for a flowerlike nature
like hers to find peace and light! She did not seem to
expect conventional conversation from him, so he looked
out over the grey-green sea, moodily recalling that poem
of Heine's—

> "Am Meer, am wüsten, nächtlichen Meer
> Steht ein Jüngling-Mann,
> Die Brust voll Wehmuth, das Haupt voll Zweifel,
> Und mit düstern Lippen fragt er die Wogen:

> "'O löst mir das Räthsel des Lebens,
> Das qualvoll uralte Räthsel,
> Worüber schon manche Haupter gegrübelt,
> Häupter in Hieroglyphenmützen,
> Häupter in Turban und schwarzem Barett,
> Perückenhäupter und tausend andere
> Arme, schwitzende Menschenhäupter—
> Sagt mir, was bedeutet der Mensch?
> Woher ist er kommen? Wo geht er hin?
> Wer wohnt dort oben auf goldenen Sternen?'

" Es murmeln die Wogen ihr ew'ges Gemurmel,
Es wehet der Wind, es fliehen die Wolken,
Es blinken die Sterne gleichgültig und kalt,
Und ein Narr wartet auf Antwort."

He repeated the last line aloud, rashly assuming that
she would not understand.

But the assumption was correct.

" What does that mean ? " she asked smiling.

" Oh, it is only a nonsense rhyme. I beg your pardon for thinking aloud."

A deeper blush than before crept over her face.
" You said something very beautiful about the sea once,"
she said shyly. " I think of it so often when I am sitting here or lying awake at night listening to the waves."

" What did I say ? "

Her voice sank almost to a whisper. " It was about
throwing oneself like an unattached sea-weed into the
ocean of God."

It was his turn now to blush, though fortunately his
tanned complexion did not show the warm blood as
hers did.

The pendulum was rather at the opposite end of its
swing that time," he said to himself with a grim inward
smile.

He noticed for the first time that she was not daintily
dressed as before, and yet she was full of charm. He
was just a little piqued by her obvious independence of
him and his society. A young girl's religion was a
matter of course, and yet there was something here that
tempted him to probe a little deeper.

" You are very happy," he said as he rose to go.

She smiled radiantly.

" Tell me your secret, Miss Galbraith."

No one who held the views she did could refuse such
an appeal; and besides—had he not ears to hear?—did
he not know better than she what the inner life meant?
She had risen to her feet, and now she clasped her
hands behind her head, as if the change of attitude
would aid her in the search for words. Her face was
very pale, and her well-poised figure swayed almost imperceptibly in the soft sea-breeze.

14

"'For I am persuaded,'" she said in a low throbbing voice, "'that neither death, nor life, nor angels, nor principalities, nor powers, nor things present, nor things to come, nor height, nor depth, nor any other creature, shall be able to separate us from the love of God, which is in Christ Jesus our Lord.'"

And that was the mental picture he carried away the second time.

Alas, that Wilhelmina was forced to be the child of her century after all!

CHAPTER XXX.

A LOST OPPORTUNITY.

As the evenings grew long, Mr. Carmichael began to deliver a course of week-day lectures on the Minor Prophets. The first two lectures were well attended, but on the evening of the third the rain fell in torrents, and a mere handful of people assembled in the hall.

Wilhelmina started in good time, but the wind was against her, and when she arrived, the minister was already in his place. For a moment she stood hesitating at the door, dazzled by the gaslight, and conscious for the first time of her wind-tossed hair and mud-splashed boots. A roaring fire reflected on the well-scoured planks like the sun in a pool.

"Come well forward, please, Miss Galbraith," said Mr. Carmichael's pleasant voice. "We are so few tonight that we must rally our forces."

Of course she obeyed at once—though he had no idea of the effort the obedience cost her—and so brought her eager responsive face within range of his pastoral eye. Only the man who knows what it is to address in all earnestness a small and phlegmatic audience realizes how much that responsive face means, even if it be a young girl's.

Mr. Carmichael had not been blind to the fervour of

his young parishioner, but experience had made him wise, and he was in no hurry to fan the flame. " The human soul can never be so safely left to itself," he had said once to Mr. Darsie, " as when it first catches sight of God. Who am I that I should thrust my blundering personality all out of focus into the beatific vision? By and bye when the mists begin to rise, as rise they surely will, one may be able to do a little—a very little."

But, although he had certainly given her no reason to guess the fact, he had seldom felt so deep an interest in a young girl as he now did in Wilhelmina. The whole circumstances of her life appealed strongly to his fancy—her irresistible inexplicable father, her anomalous social position, the genuineness of her religion, her lonely life in the sea-bound homestead—she seemed to him to carry about with her always the sough of the waves and trees at Windyhaugh.

Wilhelmina had not proceeded far on her homeward way that night when the minister overtook her.

" Alone, Miss Galbraith? " he said.

She started. " I usually have Ann's company. To-day it was too wet for her."

" Then you must let me take Ann's place for a mile or two."

" Oh, please don't! " she cried in genuine disappointment and distress. " I know every step of the way. What harm could befall me here? "

What harm indeed? How often had she passed over that road scarcely feeling the ground under her feet for very rapture!

" Nevertheless," he said quietly, " I would like to come a little way. I want to talk to you. Don't you think it is time you were taking a class in Sunday-school? "

" Oh, no! "

He did not reply, and as they walked on in the darkness, she wondered whether she had offended him.

" It is not that I mean to be always saying ' No,' " she said shyly; " but of that one thing I must be the best judge, must I not? "

" I don't know." He spoke judicially, divided be-

tween his desirè to set her to work, and his fear of making her vain. "The Lord's best work is sometimes done
with faulty instruments."

"I know—oh, I do know that. My music-master
used often to tell us how a street fiddle in the hands of
a master is a finer thing than a Stradivarius in the
hands of—one of us. I often think of that. I don't
mind being only a street fiddle if—if—oh, Mr. Carmichael, one can't talk of these things; but don't you
think I should be only too glad if I could say that the
strings of me only responded to the touch of the Master?"

She had begun to speak in all singleness of heart.
Before she had finished she was struck by the fineness
of the sentiment she was expressing, and she was disappointed that he did not reply.

In truth three different answers had chased each
other through his mind, but he had allowed none of them
to find voice. "How many of our teachers do you suppose attain that level?" was the first; but that only
lingered long enough to invoke the second—"'Beware,
oh Teufelsdröckh, of spiritual pride!'" And then he
sighed. "Alas, child," he thought, "do you think you
will ever *reach* the goal you have set before you?"

He felt that he was not in a pastoral mood that night
—the weather and the thinness of his audience had depressed him in spite of himself; so, like a wise man, he
shook off the parson altogether, and allowed himself to
be recreated by the society of his young companion.
Wilhelmina was very ready to follow his lead to a friendly human level.

"My mother is coming to-morrow to visit me," he
said at parting, "and I mean to avail myself of her
presence to return in a quiet way a little of the hospitality the friends here have shown me. Do you think
you could come to the manse some evening? It is a
long way, I know, and we old folks are not very enter-
taining, but I should like you to meet my mother."

Her eyes danced at the prospect of the "ploy." In
spite of all her efforts, human nature died hard, and
months had passed since she had taken part in any social

gaiety. Surely there could be no harm in going to a party at the *manse*. " I should love to come," she said warmly.

She began at once to wonder what she would wear on the great occasion. Miss Evelyn had been as good as her word, and her maid, with the help of a seamstress, had run up two charming muslin gowns for Wilhelmina in dainty shades of pink and blue.

" I will wear the blue," she thought. " It is quieter."

Quieter. Yes, she ought to dress quietly. Was she not a child of light? Then, with a rush of shame, she realized how worldly her thoughts had been. " Vanity, vanity, vanity!" she cried. " What a graceless wretch I am!"

She remembered then how the minister had failed to respond to her sentiment about the violins. " He thought I was posing," she thought humiliated; and a moment later she added, truly humbled, " and he was right: I *was* posing. Oh, God, I have attained nothing. Help me to begin all over again, here at Thy feet!"

By way of a first step she resolved to go to the party in her everyday wincey frock; but, on hearing this, Ann was really roused.

" Sma' respect ye'd be showing to your hostess," she cried indignantly—" let alone the minister himsel'! An' what do ye think the folks'll say? Ye think maybe they'll talk o' the ornaments o' a meek and quiet spirit? Hoot awa! They'll be for saying that Mr. Galbraith canna gie his bairn a decent gown to her back. Puir lamb! Puir lamb! He surely has eneugh to answer for, forbye that."

Ann's apron went to her eyes, and the blue frock was worn accordingly. Moreover it exercised its due effect on the wearer's estimate of herself, and throughout the evening she was gay and talkative, winning the admiration, and in some cases even the hearts, of the other guests. Perhaps she talked a little more than in those days was considered becoming to her years, for the strong tea and the unaccustomed excitement went to her head like wine; but at worst it was simple bright girlish talk, and her voice was a pleasant one at all times.

It sounds like an exaggeration, but her feelings when she awoke next morning enabled her in after life to appreciate the sufferings of a young man of good impulses on the day after a debauch. The people who had envied the child her lightheartedness the night before would have been surprised if they could have seen her now in deep remorse and sorrow fervently repeating the fifty-first Psalm. She had meant to let her light shine before men, and behold, when the moment came, she had forgotten all about it!

"I see I must give up the world *altogether*," she said. "Other people may be able to dally unharmed with its temptations; but it is full of pit-falls for me."

Next morning, to her great surprise, she received a letter from Mrs. Dalrymple.

"DEAR LITTLE VILMA: What an age it seems since I saw you! When I reflect on the depressing subject of dates, I suppose you must be quite grown up; and a little bird whispers in my ear (though of course I should not tell you this) that you are pretty.

"I wonder what you do with yourself at queer old Windyhaugh? Are you becoming very wise and learned?—or are you, like Mr. Micawber, 'falling back for a spring of no ordinary magnitude'? I expect to be in Edinburgh soon. Would you like to come and lunch with me somewhere? If there happens to be anything good in the theatres, we might drop in for an hour or two in the afternoon. I want to talk to you too about your future. I don't believe in 'blushing unseen,' and, if I am in town next season, you must come to me for a month or two, and have a good time. We will manage the frocks somehow.—In great haste,

"Yours affectionately,
"ENID DALRYMPLE."

"How kind she is!" said Wilhelmina, and then her eyes shone. "God is putting me to the test very soon."

It was natural that she should think the renunciation greater than it really was. In point of fact the letter found her in the exalted mood that lies out of reach of such sacrifices. She was sorry to seem ungracious, but, for the moment, that was all.

She attached enormous importance to her answer. In the hands of Omnipotence, what might it not achieve? When finally transcribed in a neat hand on cheap notepaper, it was the outcome—the disappointing outcome I admit—of many fervent prayers.

"DEAR AUNT ENID: I can't give you the least idea how delighted I was to get your letter. I am very happy at 'queer old Windyhaugh,' and yet it did me good to think you had not forgotten me.

"It would be a great treat to meet you in Edinburgh, but I must not go to the theatre, and I must not come to you in London for the season. I don't mean to say that such amusements are wrong, but I don't seem able to join in them without losing something that I value more.

"'God fulfils Himself in many ways,' and it may be that He means me to walk in the twilight—save for the light of His presence.

"Again thanking you a hundred times, I am,
    "Your affectionate niece,
        "WILHELMINA GALBRAITH."

Ronald Dalrymple was alone with Enid when she received this missive.

"Ugh!" she exclaimed, turning away her head in dainty disgust.

"What's wrong?—patchouli?"

"Not patchouli; but it is reeking, simply reeking—with spiritual pride. Read it."

His face was a study as he laid it down; but he did not speak at once.

"I hope you will meet her in Edinburgh," he said at last. "She'll take you to a Salvation Army conventicle."

Enid's lip curled. "I don't fancy I shall trouble her this time. How I hate that word 'niece'!"

"You think it just misses being nice," he observed flippantly.

"For shame, Ronald! Leave that to Hugh."

"Well, I suppose your fair—relative's—letter suits your book very well in spite of its—aroma?"

She shrugged her shoulders. "I confess I should like to know what George Galbraith will say when he hears of it. The child can't have consulted him. He has been gracefully fishing for that invitation since Wilhelmina was a baby."

Ronald laughed. "I thought you wouldn't be able to hold out if you met him again. What a relief that woman's death must have been!"

"I certainly should have held out if you hadn't assured me that Wilhelmina was pretty and—and simplehearted."

"Well, by Jove, I thought she was, but there is no being up to the tricks of a filly. It is uncommonly rough on Galbraith I must say. He is frightfully down on his luck just now, and I thought I had heard of something that would suit him down to the ground. A young fellow I met in the States, whose father made a pile over pepsin or soap or something, wants to make the grand tour, and get put up to all the things that money can't reach. I told him Galbraith was his man, and hinted gracefully that no ordinary honorarium would tempt him. Galbraith had only to sell Windyhaugh and marry Wilhelmina, and the trick was done —for this time."

Enid's smile was not encouraging. "Marry Wilhelmina to the American millionaire, I suppose?"

"Oh, Lord, no! The boy isn't half bad. If Galbraith trots him out, he'll end by marrying a peeress in her own right."

Enid might well wish that she could hear what Wilhelmina's father would say when he heard of her decision. She would have appreciated, though not quite at its true value, the interview that took place a few days after the momentous letter was written.

Mr. Galbraith had expected to be at Windyhaugh when the invitation came, but he had been detained in town for a few days, and he arrived now unexpectedly, late in the evening. As a rule Wilhelmina seemed to know by a sort of instinct when he was near; but to-night no one ran to meet him at the door, and as he hung up his hat in the hall, he heard, for the first time since his boyhood, the quavering notes of his mother's old spinet. The drawing-room door stood open, and Wilhelmina was softly striking the notes of a weird monotonous chant. Presently her girlish voice joined in—

"'My soul is not at rest. There comes a strange and secret whisper to my spirit, like a dream of night, that tells me I am on enchanted ground. The vows of God are on me and I may not stop to play with shadows or pluck earthly flowers. The voice of my departed Lord —" Go, teach all nations," comes on the night air, and awakes mine ear.

"'And I must go. Henceforth it matters not if storm or sunshine be my earthly lot—bitter or sweet my cup. I only pray "God make me holy, and my spirit nerve for the stern hour of strife!" And when I come to stretch me at the last in unattended agony beneath the cocoa's shade, it will be sweet to know that I have toiled for other worlds than this.'"

The spinet was old, the words crude, the voice un-trained, but the passionate thrill of religious fervour was not lost on George Galbraith. When the last faint chord died away, he was surprised to find his hand still raised in the act of hanging up his hat.

He passed unobserved to his room, and rang for hot water. He did not wish his daughter to know that he had heard her song.

"My word, sir, but ye're a sicht for sair een!" cried Ann. "Does Miss Wilhelmina know that ye're here?"

"Tell her I am dressing, and shall be down to sup-per presently."

The old woman's face fell. "If I had but kent you was coming!"

He looked at her with that pleasant weary smile of his. "I am quite content with pot-luck, Ann," he said gently. "Porridge and milk, or bread and cheese, is food for a king."

He poured out the hot water, and then stood meditating.

"Very pretty," he said at last; "extremely pretty and taking; but just at this stage—*it won't do.*"

Ann's supper, as it chanced, really was food for a king—fresh salmon trout, and a bottle of old sherry from the cellar.

Mr. Galbraith's mood was so quiet and yet so genial that Wilhelmina's affection for him rose in full tide, and when supper was over she seated herself confidingly on the arm of his great chair.

He drew her down on his knee.

"Is it still my little girl?" he said kindly.

She nodded, smiling. "Still."

"But she is growing such a big girl! And they tell me that she is going ' to London to see the Queen.' Then I shall have a grand lady to be proud of, instead of a kitten to play with."

Wilhelmina's heart seemed to rise with a great throb into her throat. Not till this moment had it occurred to her that her father knew of Mrs. Dalrymple's letter. "No, no, I am not going to London," she said quickly.

He drew down his brows as if in amused perplexity.

"*Not going to London?* Hasn't your aunt written to you?"

"Yes. Such a kind letter. But I must not go."

He laughed good-humouredly. "Silly child! So she is shy, is she?"

"No; it is not that. I am not shy; at least—I think the shyness would soon wear off, and I should enjoy it. But that is just why I must not go."

He leaned forward to stir the fire, and then met her eyes with a smile.

"Then she must go to please her old father."

Wilhelmina's face burned. "Oh, Father," she cried, "I can't! I have written to Aunt Enid to tell her so."

It was a full minute before he spoke.

"Have you posted the letter?"

"Yes, two days ago."

Another long silence. Then he released her from the clasp of his arm, and rose to his feet with a half-suppressed yawn. Wilhelmina had never seen his face so devoid of expression.

"It is later than I thought," he said indifferently. "Good-night."

And thus she was destined to learn that spiritual victories are not to be won so cheaply after all!

She had expected him to propose a game of billiards as usual, but now, with a heart of lead, she responded to his Good-night, and left the room. This was the first time any cloud had come between her and her father, and she felt it acutely. "Am I wrong? Am I wrong?" she asked herself over and over again. For hours she remained on her knees without getting any fresh light.

"The friendship of the world is enmity against God," said an inward voice.

"Honour thy father and thy mother," said another.

All through the night, sleeping and waking, Wilhelmina swung from one extreme to the other. Now she was writing a humble letter of apology to Enid: now she was standing heroically to her principles. When at length she rose, weary and unrefreshed, she had come to no definite decision.

She had scarcely finished dressing when Ann knocked at the door.

"The Master would like to see you, miss," she said. "He is leaving by the early train."

"Isn't he going to have breakfast?"

"He breakfasted in his room an hour ago. . . . Don't cross him, Miss Wilhelmina; he has had so much against him all his life!"

Pale and heavy-eyed, Wilhelmina hurried downstairs. Her father was writing a letter—his back was turned to the light."

"Sit down, Wilhelmina," he said quietly. "I have not much time to spare, but I should like you—if possible—to understand my position in this matter before we drop the subject finally. Of course I am rather surprised that you should have settled so important a question in this impulsive fashion, but——"

" Oh, Father!——" she cried.

He held up his hand.

" I am quite aware that you have a dozen excellent motives for what you have done. I have no doubt you could give chapter and verse for any statement you have made in your letter to your aunt. As time is short, I must ask you to believe that I fully understand your point of view. The experience you are passing through is not, as you imagine, unique; it is common to a very large proportion of the human race."

" I hope so," she said in all seriousness, yet stung by his tone.

He looked at her with a strange little smile. " On the other hand, I give you credit for fully average intelligence, and you must try to realize that in what you are pleased to call ' the world ' there are women quite as good as you can ever hope to be."

" Oh, Father, I know that."

" Pardon me, you do not know it. You may *believe* it—with a mental reservation concerning a special calling on your part—but that is a very different thing. *Believe* me then when I tell you that there are good and gracious and high-minded women whose very existence is an inspiration to the men who rule the world. Place you with such men, and what would they see in you? A little school-girl—ignorant, awkward, *gauche*. Attractive, no doubt. In a young girl one overlooks— nay, one admires—a thousand little lovable *gaucheries;* but you can't remain a girl for ever, and *gaucherie* in a woman is a very different thing. You are all but a woman now in years, and yet everything you do claims the indulgence one concedes to a very young girl.

" You are utterly ignorant of life, and you should learn to see it, not through the eyes of a provincial *bourgeoise,* but through those of a wide-minded cultured woman of the world. You wish to do great things, and yet you decline to serve your apprenticeship. You are not stupid. If you had formed a just estimate of yourself and your capabilities, surely you would have been glad humbly to learn of the good and wise, before placing yourself on a pedestal in this fashion. Are you afraid of being too refined, too well-tempered, a weapon for the armoury of the Lord? Must He make the best of a clumsy ill-shaped tool? No doubt you find much that is edifying in the society of your sisters in the Lord; but I do not observe that they have taught you that which will make your teaching acceptable in the eyes of the sinners you wish to reach. You have become careless of your dress, careless of your hair, careless how you rise up and how you sit down. There is a button wanting on your gown. If I am not mistaken the same button was wanting when I was here a month ago. Of course all this may be a recommendation in the eyes of some people, but so few of us can rise to that level! An earthen vessel may hold the water of life, and yet one would rather drink from a silver cup."

"Father," said Wilhelmina in a stifled voice, "I will write to Aunt Enid, and tell her I was—foolish and—and ignorant. She will ask me again."

He had sealed his letter, and now he rose to his feet.

"Spare me that last humiliation, Wilhelmina," he said. "That is one of the things people *do not do*. You have made your choice. At least have the pluck to abide by it. Good-bye."

He touched her forehead with his lips and left the house.

CHAPTER XXXI.

BROTHER AND SISTER.

"Awake, Hal?"

"Ye-es," said a drowsy voice.

"Better?"

"Ever so. I'd sell my soul for a cup of tea."

"Dear heart! That is easily got."

Miss Brentwood left the room, and presently returned with a tea-tray daintily arranged for two. "Shall I draw up the blind?"

"Do. I love to see our tame pine-wood."

It was little wonder that Hugh Dalrymple had been impressed by Brentwood's sister. She was one of those statuesque women who transcend the changing dictates of fashion. When others were intent on frizzling, frills, and rampant furbelows, she never discarded her braids and folds and drooping plumes; and yet the most frivolous did not call her out of date. She never seemed to be in a hurry; and in all she did there was a fine breadth of movement that was very restful to irritable nerves.

She sipped her tea in silence, waiting till her brother chose to speak. His face was pale and haggard.

"The sheer bliss," he said, "of just being out of pain!"

"Poor old boy! You have been doing too much. I wish you would remember that our bread is given and our water sure."

"That doesn't alter the fact that my article will be unseasonable after September—or October at the latest. No, I haven't done too much. Railway travelling always knocks me up now-a-days; but I am all right now."

"Well, you must not get up till dinner-time. Shall I read to you?"

"Presently, if you will? How did you get on with Aunt Marian?"

"Famously. She wishes you would marry, and leave me to bear her company for good."

"I like that! And you are to remain celibate for her sake? I hope you told her I am not in the least likely to marry."

Honor laughed mischievously—

> "'I really must contrive to be
> Less pleasant,—if I can;
> And Kate must tell her candidly,
> I'm not a marrying man.'

"Don't brag, Hal. Heaven knows I don't grudge

you a good wife; and you needn't be afraid that I shall
play the jealous sister when you find her."

"I wish you had been with me, Honor."

"You enjoyed it then on the whole?"

"Oh, I enjoyed it immensely—especially the tramp
through Kent. It was a first-rate idea of yours that
'In the Hop Country.' For a wonder I rather fancy
the article myself, and I have got some stunning nega-
tives to illustrate it."

"How delightful! I will start the printing to-morrow."

"Yes, you will have to hurry up." He paused. A
smile of recollection broke over his face.

"I'll tell you an awfully pretty thing that happened;
and yet I shall only spoil it in the telling. When I was
first setting out from Charing Cross, who should I meet
on the platform but Mr. Galbraith—you remember?"

Her smile was a very pleasant one to see. "I should
think I do remember," she said quietly.

"I was travelling third-class, and he came into the
same carriage. We were alone in it except for a young
woman—by way of being a lady.

"At Cannon Street some hoppers joined the train, and
one got into our carriage who simply made me shudder.
A girl of seventeen or so—heavy bang down to her eyes,
greasy clothes adorned with feathers and jewellery, snub
nose, open mouth—! I assure you, Honor, it took
greater 'love and strength' than mine to 're-write the
obliterated charter.' She had all her luggage with her
—an amorphous bundle done up in sacking, just hotch-
ing with microbes. I glanced commiseratingly at Mr.
Galbraith—but I might have known he wouldn't meet my
eye. He was looking through an illustrated paper, and
presently he handed it to the hop-girl with a gesture just
as courtly, just as simple, as if she had been a duchess."

Honor bit her lip. "And she?"

"Upon my soul, she rose—she did indeed. She held
out her poor grimy paw with a bow, and poked her little
red nose into the pictures. When she had finished, she
handed it back. 'Thank you,' he said pleasantly, 'I
have quite done with it.' I should have hurt the girl's

feelings if I had refused it; but not he. It really is a liberal education to know that man."

He paused before continuing with a scornful little laugh—"So the young lady in the carriage thought apparently, for, by way of following a good example, she assailed the hopper with well-meant patronizing questions. I did long to say, 'My dear young woman, the thing has been *done* for to-day. Take a hint for next time, if you like, and start a canvas of your own, but don't attempt to fill in the sketch of a master.'"

"I should like to meet Mr. Galbraith."

"Upon my soul, Honor, I don't dare to introduce him. There must be a screw loose somewhere. If he were all that he seems, he would have the world at his feet. He asked me to spend a few days with him when he returns to Windyhaugh, and I will try to get to the bottom of him."

"He has a daughter, has he not?"

"Yes, a dear little thing, a regular *dévote*. It is a picturesque combination. And now let us have a chapter of the story."

She took up the library volume they had been reading. "We left John in St. Peter's, do you remember?"

She read on till she came to the interview with the Spanish monk.

"'It may be that in some other place God would have found for you other work; you have failed in attaining that place; serve Him where you are. If you fall still lower or imagine that you fall lower, still serve Him in the lowest room of all. Wherever you may find yourself, in Courts or pleasure-houses or gardens of delight, still serve Him, and you will bid defiance to imaginations and powers of evil, that strive to work upon a sensitive and excited nature, and urge it to despair!'

"Oh, Hal," she said, "isn't that fine!"

"Ay."

"It makes me think of Longfellow—

> "'Whene'er a noble deed is wrought,
> Whene'er is spoken a noble thought,
> Our hearts, in glad surprise,
> To higher levels rise.'"

She had scarcely finished the chapter when the maid knocked at the door with a letter for Mr. Brentwood.

"Well!" said Harley, his face flushing with pleasure. "Talk of angels!"

He threw the letter across to his sister and looked on while she read—

"My dear Brentwood: I find I shall be at Windy-haugh sooner than I anticipated. Could you come for a few days next week, and cheer an old fogey's loneliness? I am afraid you will find it dull; but at least I can offer you unlimited boating (*absit omen!*) and billiards. My daughter plays a very fair game.—I am,

"Yours truly,
"George Galbraith."

"Is he old?" said Honor.

"Rather not. That is his little pose."

Harley smiled. A vivid picture rose before him of the "little *dévote*" as she stood on the lonely rocks with the green sea rolling about her feet.

"Cold-blooded little puss!" he said to himself.

CHAPTER XXXII.

A SUNNY DAY.

For nearly a year Wilhelmina's inward life had resembled the drifting of a boat through a sunny lagoon. Ripples had stirred the surface of the water, wisps of cloud had passed across the sun, but in the main her course had been a bright and peaceful one. Now, all in a moment, a puff of wind had carried her near the extremity of the protecting reef, and she felt the swell of the waves outside. Would she turn back into still waters again, or pass out into the open sea?

Moreover the sunlight no longer fell in a golden shield, nor broke in a thousand spangles. A cloud had

15

spread over the sky and all was grey. She still adhered
to the manifold simple observances of her religious life,
and she still knew an occasional hour of happiness, but
on the whole the next few weeks were a time of deep
depression.

"Was I wrong?" she kept saying to herself. "Was
I wrong?" Of course it would have been wiser to have
left the question alone; but she felt that she had taken
a wrong turn somewhere, and she longed to know exactly where and how the error had occurred, that she
might correct her course for the future.

She was suffering keenly too, of course, from sheer
wounded vanity. Hitherto her father had always
seemed to admire her, to be pleased with her, and now
his calm cold words had been far more crushing even
than he had intended. Wilhelmina did not realize that
he was a thing of moods as well as she. Yet after the
first few wretched hours she bore him no grudge. "He
was quite right," she said resolutely to herself; "I am
not going to quarrel with the kernel because the shell
is hard;" and, fetching her workbox, she proceeded
through blinding tears to sew on the defaulting button.

Like all sensitive people, Wilhelmina saw her outward self mainly through the eyes of others. In a medium of genial appreciation she floated out like a sea-
weed in water: on the dry rocks of criticism she shriv-
elled up with unnecessary and exaggerated humility.

It was a real distress to her too that she had displeased her father. Through all the preoccupation of
her religious life, she had never forgotten that "her
business was to make him happy."

So the clouds gathered close.

Never since her childhood had she felt the dulness of
Windyhaugh as she did now. The silence of the house,
the constant murmur of the wind and waves, oppressed
her like a physical weight. She expected a letter from
the quakeress, and each day awaited the arrival of the
postman with a feverish anxiety that was almost intolerable; but the letter did not come. Finally—though
this was opposed to all precedent—she wrote again herself—one of those impulsive, affectionate, heart-hungry

letters that in later years one learns not to write; they are so difficult to live up to when the sun shines again! She counted the hours till an answer by return might be expected, but before that time came, the light broke. She could not honestly call it light from heaven, but— it served.

She had waylaid the postman at the gate as usual, and now she sped to the house like the wind.

"Ann!" she cried, "Ann! *Father's* coming to-night. What shall we have for supper?"

Then she read his kindly note again.

"Thank God!" she whispered. "Thank God! . . . What a comfort Pullar has sent back my white silk frock!"

Mr. Galbraith arrived in royal good humour. "And how is my little white swan?" he said as he kissed his daughter affectionately. "Isn't it a lovely evening? Shall we take a turn in the rose garden before we go in?" He rested his fine sinewy hand on her shoulder as they strolled round in the soft sunset sunlight. "We must see if we can find a rose for her in this waste old wilderness."

Roses there were by hundreds, but he was not easy to please. One and another he looked at and discarded, but at length he chose a few mossy buds, and fastened them in her gown with the easy touch of one who is not unpractised in such arts.

"That reminds me," he said, "that I have brought a *cadeau* for her. Shall we go and see it?"

He opened a box, and from a mass of silver paper, produced a large white hat—very graceful, very girlish.

"Oh, Father!" she cried, blushing with pleasure. "That is far too pretty for me."

He placed it on her head, and, laying his hands on her shoulders, turned her gently to the old-fashioned mirror.

"What does the looking-glass say?" he said gaily. "Too pretty, eh?"

Finding that he meant to treat her like a little queen, Wilhelmina rose to the full height of her privileges. A physical reaction from the depression of the past weeks was overdue, and it came. She grew saucy, piquant, playful, pretending to keep him in order while she humoured his every whim.

"By the way," he said suddenly, "Mr. Brentwood is coming to spend a few days with us. Do you remember him? He seems to have a very pleasant recollection of you."

"I remember him very well." Wilhelmina blushed. She liked Mr. Brentwood, but what pleased her most in the prospect of his visit was the chance of showing her father that she was not so hopelessly *gauche* as he imagined.

She meant to receive her visitor with great dignity, but he defeated her plan by arriving unexpectedly and on foot.

Mr. Galbraith was walking in the garden with a new book in his hand when Wilhelmina joined him.

"What are you reading, Father?" she asked idly, slipping her hand through his arm with her new-found confidence.

He smiled. "Little girls must not be curious."

"I am not curious. I only want to know."

He raised the book just above the level of her eyes, but she saw the expression of his face, and made a spring, like a kitten, in search of the desired information. Thereupon he raised the book higher still—and the pretty contest was at its height when Brentwood appeared.

Wilhelmina's kitten-like curves vanished, and she blushed charmingly.

"Very pleased to see you," she said sedately. Then she turned to her father. "I am glad you will have someone to talk to instead of being reduced to—such dull books."

"As what?" he asked mischievously, but he put his arm round her as he spoke, and placed the book in her hands.

"You find us very much *unter uns*, you see, Brentwood," he said. "It is good of you to take pity on our solitude."

"Your solitude does not seem to stand much in need of pity, sir," Brentwood answered with an admiring glance; "but it is very kind of you to let me share it for a day or two."

And so the three settled down to one of those charming intimacies that never can be reckoned on beforehand.

The evening was warm, and after supper they sat on the terrace till long after sunset. Wilhelmina spoke little, but she was so obviously happy and contented as she lay at ease on the *chaise longue* in which her father had installed her, that her presence made itself very pleasantly felt.

"What about that beauty sleep?" said Mr. Galbraith at last.

"Father," remonstrated Wilhelmina, "*is* that the way to speak to the mistress of the house? And before strangers too?"

"Ah, don't call me a stranger, Miss Galbraith!" entreated Brentwood. "If it is true, you have made me forget it so delightfully."

"The mistress of the house is the person who rises up a great while before day, if I remember rightly," said Mr. Galbraith.

Wilhelmina drew herself up and sighed. "Now-a-days the mistress has to adapt herself to the household. She can't give meat till somebody is awake to eat it. Good-night, Mr. Brentwood. Good-night, father dear. Take a good long rest in the morning."

For a few minutes after she had gone, the two men smoked in silence.

"I am sure it is very pleasant to see you here, Brentwood," Mr. Galbraith said at last. "I hope you don't mean to hurry away?"

"Thank you very much, sir. I have promised to go to a friend—a professor in Edinburgh. There is a paper in the Biological section that I am anxious to hear. This is Tuesday. If you will keep me till Friday morning, I shall be only too glad."

"Ah, I hoped you would stay till Saturday at any rate. I have a box at the Lyceum for the *matinée*.

Miss Evelyn is playing Pauline in The Lady of Lyons. Don't tell my little girl. It is to be a surprise."

"Miss Evelyn? Pauline? That *is* an inducement —if one were needed. Unfortunately my friend has asked some people to dinner on Friday evening——"

"Then come in on Saturday afternoon all the same."

"Thank you very much. I will."

When Wilhelmina awoke next morning she wondered why she was so happy. For a time she lay in drowsy content, and then she stretched herself with a yawn.

"So sunny!" she said, glancing out of the window. "Is it going to be another long delicious day like yesterday?"

After a late breakfast they spent the morning on the water. Brentwood did most of the rowing—Mr. Galbraith relieving him from time to time. Both were good oarsmen.

"Let me have a turn," said Wilhelmina at last. "I am so tired of doing nothing."

"You can't row, little one," said her father.

"Can't I! I often paddle about when you are away."

Brentwood gave her the oars, and her father watched her with quiet critical amusement.

"Your rowing is scarcely on a level with your sense of literary fitness, Vilma," he said. "'Paddle about' is just the expression."

Her face fell. She had become acclimatized so quickly to an atmosphere of admiration.

"Of course I can't row properly with you looking on," she said.

"Nay, when you say that, you show that you never did row properly—never even knew what rowing means."

His tone was kind, but she did not know him in this mood, and it seemed to her that he was humiliating her unnecessarily in the presence of a "stranger."

"But the boat *goes*," she said, flushing with a touch of resentment.

"True; and so would a mangle or a hurdy-gurdy or anything under the same treatment."

She raised the oars out of the water and allowed the boat to drift. She was evidently having a struggle with herself; but her moral thews and sinews were in good fighting form.

"Teach me then, Father," she said.

His face lighted up with real appreciation. "Ah, come! Now you are an oarswoman or anything else you choose. Brentwood, your work is cut for you."

Nothing loth, Brentwood applied himself to the task. At first shyness made her stupid, but when that was overcome, she learned with extraordinary rapidity. He had often heard of the quickness of women, but Honor's many remarkable gifts had prepared him for nothing like this. Once Wilhelmina had made up her mind to learn, her docility was perfect, and she would own to no fatigue. Before half an hour was over she was rowing, not strongly, of course, but rhythmically, feathering daintily, carrying back the oars with a fine level sweep, and dropping them with a clean cut into the water.

"Well, you have grit," Harley said admiringly, as he helped her out of the boat.

Her father did not echo the statement, but spoken praise from him was unnecessary. She was preternaturally sensitive to his approbation.

When they reached the house, she found a letter awaiting her—a letter from the quakeress. As though it were something to be ashamed of, she hastily put it in her pocket—and a week later she found it there.

In the afternoon Mr. Galbraith carried Wilhelmina off to do some copying for him, and kept her busy till it was nearly time for afternoon tea. Then she ran to the garden to gather fruit. Before she had reached the strawberry bed Brentwood overtook her. "I thought I caught a glimpse of flying petals," he said. "Let me carry your basket."

Together they stooped to gather the fragrant coral-pink fruit; "though I ought not to let you do it," Wilhelmina said shyly.

"You wouldn't be so selfish, I am sure. I think it is delightful work gathering fruit with a friend, don't you?"

She straightened herself with a long sigh of content. "Everything is delightful to-day."

"It makes a great difference to you to have your father here?"

"*Oh!*" Her voice was low but emphatic. "Isn't he perfectly splendid?"

"Perfectly splendid. You are much to be envied."

"Am I not? He has been working so hard this afternoon. We must make haste back. I will bring the tray out to the terrace."

After tea Brentwood declared his intention of going for a walk. "I am afraid you are too tired to go with me?" he said to Wilhelmina.

"I? I am as fresh as a lark. Where shall we go, Father? We might strike across the hayfield, and then along the coast to the right. It is lovely that way."

Mr. Galbraith nodded. "Very well," he said. "Don't be late."

So Wilhelmina and Brentwood set out together demurely. At first they conversed pleasantly, as young men and women do, striving to be amiable and to say something clever when they got a chance to bring it in. Presently they became boy and girl, chatting away at random; and before they had gone very far they were children again, unselfconscious and happy.

"What a nice flat stone!" Wilhelmina said, stooping to pick one up. "When I was little I used to love to send these things skimming over the sea."

"Oh, that is a recreation that never palls. Fire away!"

The game was amusing, but Wilhelmina was beaten so completely that it soon ceased to be exciting, and they strolled on till they came to a tiny limpid stream flowing across the beach to the sea. A pile of wood chips had been thrown down hard by.

"We'll have a boat race!" said Harley. "Choose your craft."

She laughed gaily. This reminded her of the games of her childhood. Was it possible that clever men were so easily amused?

"I hope you don't want to be Cambridge?" he said.

She drew herself up. "I wouldn't be Cambridge for the world," she answered severely. "Oxford is my father's university."

"That's all right. Have you got a boat?"

After considerable deliberation each of them decided on a seaworthy chip.

"How are we to know them apart?"

"What a pity!" she said regretfully. "I might so easily have brought some bits of blue wool from my work-basket!"

"No matter. One never foresees the great emergencies of life. I have got a blue pencil. I will block in an O for you, and hatch in a C for myself. That will give us the dark and light blue."

After several false starts the boats drifted off. The excitement of the race depended mainly on the shallowness of the stream here and there. In some places a jutting miniature sandbank, or a mere pebble, was sufficient to check the course of the tiny crafts. Now Oxford went ahead, now Cambridge, amidst wild excitement on the banks. As they neared the sea and the stream deepened, the two chips became entangled, and drifted out together.

"Oh!" said Wilhelmina disappointed. "Never mind. That is best. We have both won—or lost! Look, they are parting company again!"

"It is a tie," he said regretfully. "It doesn't matter what happens now they have passed the goal. But Oxford should not have fouled Cambridge."

"No. I am sorry."

Then they both laughed and turned homewards.

They did not talk much now. As they passed a straggling briar bush, Harley gathered a half-blown rose and held it out to his companion without a word.

"Let us rest a few minutes," he said when they reached the hayfield. "This half-demolished rick is more than I can resist. Let me give you a hand."

Her impulse was to decline; she was so unused to helping hands. Then she suddenly became conscious that it would be pleasant to have his help, and she took it.

He disposed himself comfortably on the roomy

couch. "I think there is nothing so delicious as to lie on one's back on the hay, and shut one's eyes to the sunny blue sky overhead."

"Why, do it then," she said smiling. "I will look out for robbers."

"For robbers?"

She laughed. "Such an old memory! I was in this very field years and years ago, with Hugh and Gavin. It was a hay crop that season too, and the rick was our castle."

"Then it is I who ought to be watching."

"No, no. Even the knight must sleep sometimes. Dear little Gavin—I wish he was here to run away with me again!"

"Do you?"

"Yes, I—I think so."

"*Do you?*"

"No."

"Content with things as they are?"

She did not reply at once. If she had been less content, she would not have hesitated to say so; but it was only after a curious inward struggle that she answered gravely, "Yes."

Then she rose. "Father will be expecting us," she said, and she slid down the sloping side of the rick.

"Stop a moment," he cried as he followed her. "You have got some clover in your hair. You must not go home looking like Ophelia in the mad scene."

She put up her hand to remove it. "It doesn't matter. If you hadn't been here, I shouldn't have known about it."

"Ah—but it does just happen, you see, that I am here."

A sudden impulse seized her to rush like a hare across the fields to her father; but while she hesitated, it was too late. His touch was on her head, and then —she felt very glad that her hair was so pretty.

Mr. Galbraith met the young people as they walked sedately home. Their silence was not lost on him—nor was the rose in Wilhelmina's belt.

"When the missis has decided what she means to wear this evening," he said, "we'll go to the garden and choose a posy for her."

Wilhelmina hurried upstairs, and in a quarter of an hour came down in the blue muslin frock.

"Ah," he said, "you meant to set me a puzzle, did you? Haven't you a pink gown? Wear that to-morrow night."

They strolled into the garden together. "If lily of the valley were in season," he said, "we would try that; but white is a cowardly way out of the difficulty. Ivy would be pretty, but too mature. Ah, I didn't know we had forget-me-nots. They are not decorative, but they are very dainty."

He arranged a graceful spray, and fastened it at her throat.

After supper Wilhelmina went to make the coffee, as she always did when her father was at home, and then the three spent another long peaceful evening on the terrace.

When the young girl went to her room, she read her chapter many times before her mind would take a grip of the familiar verses; and then she knelt down to pray.

"Oh, God, I am so happy! I am so happy!" Those were the words that forced themselves to her lips. She tried to remember what a sinner she was, but the remembrance brought no remorse. She did not ask herself why she was happy. When love first breathes a flying whisper in the ear of an innocent girl, he does not make her introspective or self-conscious. He draws her back to the bosom of Mother Nature and makes her at one with all the dear wild things in forest and meadow and stream.

CHAPTER XXXIII.

" LOVE AND LIFE."

NEXT morning at breakfast Mr. Galbraith received a telegram calling him in to Edinburgh on business. Wilhelmina and Brentwood accompanied him to the gate.

"I shall come back by the four o'clock train," he said. "Take care of yourselves and of each other; and if you have another rowing lesson,' be very cautious."

"Trust me, sir," said Brentwood.

Mr. Galbraith turned to him. "I do trust you," he said gravely.

As soon as he was gone Harley and Wilhelmina looked at each other, and then looked away again in sudden shyness.

"Well," he said, "shall we have another lesson?"

She hesitated. She had resolved the night before that she would put duty rigidly before pleasure, and she did not find it easy now to stick to her resolution.

"I have various little duties in the house in the morning," she said. "If you go on, I will join you in an hour."

"Oh, no; I will wait for you."

Shyness soon wore away in the healthy excitement of rowing, but Mr. Galbraith's parting words had exercised a sobering influence on Brentwood, and when they began to talk, he chose the safe subject of books.

"You are a great reader, I think," he said, mindful of Sartor Resartus.

"I am afraid not." For the first time she felt a pang of regret that her reading had been so limited in range of late; but such regrets, she felt sure, were a temptation of the evil one.

"Life is so short," she said sententiously.

He smiled. "True, oh, Queen!"

"And I think one ought to be careful to read the best books."

"Granted again. But how are we who are young and ignorant to know what is best? Don't you think

that in books as in wines we must have our fling? It is
only when the shadows begin to gather that we are entitled to say, ' That book, that wine, may be very good;
but these are the brands for me? ' "

"And yet," she said, "we surely know that books
which pertain entirely to this world must be a—waste
of time."

"And among such books you include Shakespeare?"

"Oh, no," she said, but her voice lacked the ring of
sincerity.

"Honour bright, Miss Galbraith! Carry your conviction loyally through."

"Yes," she said. "I am afraid I should include
Shakespeare."

"And Browning?"

"I don't know anything about Browning."

He wondered whether it was worth while to pursue
the subject, but he was young and it tempted him.

"In the books you find helpful," he said at last,
"don't you think the writers are apt to take a religious
idea, and then shape their incidents and characters to suit
it? The result may be very pretty and pathetic; but, if
your father read such a book, he would say, ' This is not
life.' *N'est ce pas?* "

She nodded gravely.

"On the other hand, let your father or any other
able man of the world read a work like Shakespeare's
Julius Cæsar, or Browning's Ring and the Book, and he
would say, ' This is life—real actual human life. These
are the men and passions I have known.' "

He paused, while Wilhelmina strove to recall her
vague impressions of Julius Cæsar.

Presently he went on—" In neither work do things
turn out pleasantly; nay, in both they seem to be going
very far wrong; and yet, as one reads, one says ' Yes,
here is life—real actual throbbing life; but life so represented that I see God in it.' "

It was some time before Wilhelmina spoke. When
she did, it was to say humbly—

"I think, Mr. Brentwood, you have a keener eye for
—for God than I have."

He blushed for very shame.

"Well, Miss Galbraith," he said; "that certainly is delivered straight out from the shoulder."

Wilhelmina raised her eyes. "I don't understand you," she said simply.

"And I won't try to explain myself any more. Forget all I have said; and let us both be thankful that the vision of God at least is reserved for the pure in heart."

He did not know whether to be glad or sorry for the turn the conversation had taken. Certainly it had removed Wilhelmina to a great distance from him again. She seemed to be in deep thought, and only half aware of his presence.

She was brought abruptly down to earth, however, by the discovery that the dinner hour was past.

"Oh, Mr. Brentwood," she said in laughing dismay, "Ann will be so angry!"

With a strong feeling of fellowship in misfortune they secured the boat and raced breathless up the hill.

Ann received them as if they had been naughty children. "It's weel seen that the maister's awa," she ejaculated.

"I do feel bad," Brentwood said when she left the room. "Can we do anything to propitiate her?"

"Oh, no!"

"Will it last long?"

"Not very long, I think. She is not due one of her really bad times." An unmistakable odour reached the room while Wilhelmina spoke. "I am afraid she is wreaking her vengeance on the pudding."

The suspicion ripened into certainty when the pudding appeared.

"I don't think we can eat that," Wilhelmina said timidly. "It is burnt."

Ann swept it from the table again. "An' I wonner who's to blame for that!" she said. Then, remembering that a visitor was a visitor—"There's a hantle rasps ootbye that wants eating."

If she expected Wilhelmina to go and gather some, she was disappointed. The young girl smiled across at her guest. "I am so sorry," she said. "Shall we adjourn to the garden for dessert?"

"That is putting a premium on our misdemeanour," he said, and they strolled off together.

The old garden was in its happiest mood—still and drowsy, breathing out fragrance. The hedge of sweet peas was in its glory; the river below lay dreaming in golden haze. The constant quiet buzz of insect life suggested a joy that scarcely left room for desire.

The raspberry bed was so overgrown that only an expert could find entrance. Wilhelmina led the way, and her companion felt a great thrill of pleasure when the thorny branches sprang back and shut them in. The fruit grew in royal abundance on a level with their lips.

"See," Harley said. "I have found a giant. You must have that."

Wilhelmina opened her mouth obediently, showing the gleam of her beautiful teeth.

"That *is* good," she said. "Now I must find one for you, or it won't be fair."

They grew weary of gathering at last, and made their way to the summer-house. Brentwood leaned back on the sloping seat, and gave himself up to the dreamy lassitude of the summer afternoon.

How pretty Wilhelmina was!—how sweet, how childlike! What a picture she made as she sat there at ease with her hat pushed back, and her hair brushed into wisps of curls by the unruly raspberry sprays! Involuntarily he moved a little nearer.

She was tired, too, he saw—pleasantly tired. Did she feel the summer day course in her veins as he did? Might he venture to take her hand?

While he hesitated she rose.

"I quite forgot," she said shyly, "I always go to read to an old woman on Thursday afternoon. She would be so disappointed if I didn't come."

Brentwood set his teeth hard. He felt as if she had thrown a douche of cold water over him.

"I have no doubt she would," he said frigidly.

"You will amuse yourself, won't you? My father

has lots of books in the smoking-room. You won't care for them all; but I know he has Browning—and Shakespeare."

"Damn Browning—and Shakespeare!" Brentwood could scarcely believe that he had not uttered the words. Was she really cold-blooded, this little girl? with her red lips and her entrancing curves? Was it possible that after all she did not care for him one bit? Brentwood was not exceptionally vain, but other women—clever cultured women—had let him feel his power, and who was this untaught child that she should defy him so calmly? Did she mean to mock him with her Browning—*and* Shakespeare?

Suddenly he became aware that she was looking at him with startled eyes, and he was forced to pull himself together.

"Thank you; I won't read," he said. "I will walk in to Queensmains by and bye, and meet your father."

Her face beamed. "Oh, that is a happy idea! He will be so pleased."

She hastened away, leaving him to walk up and down before the house like a sentinel till she reappeared. She had exchanged her pretty cotton frock for one of sober grey, and she carried under her arm two impressive-looking tomes.

"It is time you were away," she said brightly. "*Au revoir!*"

In silence he walked with her to the gate, and followed her with his eye as she took her way down the road. She was out of sight before he moved.

Wilhelmina lost no time after the hour's reading. Her father would be tired, and she must be ready to make tea the moment she heard the wheels of the hired dog-cart. Moreover it would never do for him to find her in the grey frock. She had not forgotten his flattering demand for the pink muslin.

Her toilet was speedily made, and she stood before the glass to judge of the effect. Ah, yes; it would be easy to find a flower that would go with this frock! She always kept a bowl of roses on her dressing-table, and she now chose two beautiful jacqueminots and pinned them on her breast. In a moment as if by magic the brilliant colour was reflected on her cheeks. Of course she would remove the flowers before she went downstairs, but just for a few minutes she might let them remain.

She moved about gaily, putting the room in order, when the sound of wheels caught her ear, and, forgetting everything but the expected arrival, she sprang downstairs.

The dog-cart was driving up to the door, but Mr. Galbraith was not in it. Harley Brentwood was alone.

His face brightened when he saw Wilhelmina.

"Your father has been detained in town," he said with a scarcely perceptible shake in his voice. "He sent a message by the lawyer's clerk. He will come as soon as he can."

Wilhelmina did not answer. She had become suddenly, bewilderingly, conscious of the roses at her breast.

She did not speak till she had regained her self-possession.

"I suppose we had better have tea," she said slowly.

He saw her hand shake as she raised the tea-pot, and felt sure that her whole nature was vibrating with some emotion. Was she merely disappointed at her father's non-appearance—or was she apprehensive, virginally apprehensive of another *solitude à deux?*

For an hour or two she contrived to keep him in doubt. She talked gaily, excitedly, impersonally—making him feel there was an armed neutrality between them—making him hope there was a traitor in her camp.

Supper time came, and still no Mr. Galbraith. It was one of his rules that they were never to wait for him, but neither Wilhelmina nor Brentwood ate with much appetite.

When Ann had removed the things, she produced a large family Bible and laid it on the table with the air of one who will tolerate no compromise.

Wilhelmina looked startled and uncertain, but the maid had seated herself doggedly on a chair by the door, and she was forced to speak.

16

"Ann and I always have prayers when we are alone," she said. "Will you—will you——?"

"I will read a chapter gladly," he said. "I am sorry I have no gift for—for prayer."

He read the thirteenth chapter of the First Epistle to the Corinthians, and then Ann knelt down. Slowly the others followed her example.

There was a long pause.

Wilhelmina was trying to think of a prayer that was in some way suited to a clever man. When an inspiration came, it was a happy one.

"'Oh, God, who art the Truth, make us one with Thee in everlasting love.

"'We are often weary of reading and hearing many things; in Thee is all that we wish or desire.

"'Let all teachers hold their peace; let all created things keep silence in Thy sight: speak Thou to us alone!'"

She pronounced the words sweetly and steadily, and then the others joined her in the Lord's Prayer.

Brentwood was amazed at the beauty of the words she had chosen. He knew they were not her own, but could not remember at the moment where she had found them. When they all rose from their knees, and he saw the young girl's face, he felt as if she were slipping away from him again.

He drew her to the window. "Come out on the terrace," he said huskily; "it is a lovely night."

She hesitated. "I wish father would come," she answered rather breathlessly; but she yielded to his wish, and they stretched themselves as usual on the *chaises longues*.

For a long time neither spoke. There was a drowsy languor in the summer night. The scent of the honeysuckle hung about them, enchained by the stillness of the air. Away down below the tidal river breathed like a live thing asleep.

"It *is* a beautiful evening," Wilhelmina said conventionally at last.

He turned to look at her. Surely, surely she was acting now!

A fair girlish arm lay on the rose-tinted gown. He
stretched out his hand and caressed it gently.

Ah! There was no mistaking that live thrill of response. A moment's hesitation, and then the other hand
came like a timid fluttering dove, and rested on his.

In another moment he had her in his arms.

"Vilma!" he cried, "I love you! Don't you love
me?"

When Mr. Galbraith came home he found Ann awaiting him on the doorstep.

"*Weel, sir!*" she said severely.

He looked down at her pleasantly.

"Well, Ann," he said.

"If yon young man has a mither, it's a peety but
what he had invited her as weel."

"Where are they? On the terrace?" He motioned
to her to follow him into the dining-room. "And you
think they want a chaperon? It is all right, Ann. He
is an honest fellow."

"He'd need be, I'm sure, sir."

"And you must know that the sooner Wilhelmina
marries, the better for herself. My life is too wandering, too uncertain to be shared by a young girl."

"Deed ay, sir."

"And Mr. Brentwood can support a wife."

Ann snorted. "If ye'd been content to wait, she'd
ha' mairriet the minister himsel'!"

"Mr. Carmichael? Well he *is* an honest man, without doubt. But you wouldn't marry a daughter of mine
to a country minister, would you, Ann? You know
the Galbraith blood better. Remember she is but a lassie yet."

"Will I bring you some supper, sir?"

"Thank you, I have—supped. You look tired, Ann.
I will get the whisky and soda for myself."

But he watched her movements absently as she placed
the spirit-stand and siphon on the table.

"No, no," he murmured to himself; "not life in a
paddock! Give her some sort of horizon, some sense of
beyond!"

CHAPTER XXXIV.

REACTION.

EDINBURGH in August is considered by those who are out of it to be a desert, but this year it was the scene of an important scientific gathering, and for a few days brilliant people from all parts of the world were assembled there.

A very solar system was the grey metropolis for those few days. The white-haired man of monumental attainment, who delivered the presidential address, ably represented the centre of the system: those who read the papers on such varying subjects were the planets: the daring theorist with his extensive following dashed across the field as usual with the erratic course of a comet: and satellites of every kind were grouped around, from the ardent student and the kindly hostess to the gay young things whose brain had been hard at work—not constructing a paper, but devising toilettes for reception and garden party.

So it came about that talent and beauty were well represented at the professional dinner on Friday evening, and a singularly attractive woman fell to Brentwood's share. She was some years older than himself, but he did not suspect the fact; he was struck only by the perfect ease and smoothness of her manner. She did not at first give him by any means her undivided attention, but by degrees she became more interested in his conversation, until at length she yielded herself up to it with a whole-heartedness that was very flattering. Not strictly clever herself, she had always lived with cultured people, and she saw life in a perspective that harmonized pleasantly with Brentwood's own point of view. Both were conscious of a feeling of regret when the hostess rose.

A former acquaintance of Brentwood's took the vacant place beside him.

"Well, old fellow," he said, "you have been a stranger of late."

"Yes, I have been abroad a good deal."

"We all thought you would have had a professorship before now."

Brentwood did not say that he might have had one in the colonies, if his mother's health had allowed him to leave her.

"I hope you are settling down here now?"

"My sister and I——" A great wave of feeling took Brentwood by surprise as he pronounced the familiar words. For the first time he realized the change that had come over his life. "——my sister and I mean to spend the greater part of the year in London; but we have a cottage near Silverton—quite within reach of Edinburgh."

"Are you staying there now?"

"More or less. I was in Kent a week ago. I come to-day from Windyhaugh."

"Windyhaugh!" An odd flash of intelligence came over the speaker's face. "That is Mr. Galbraith's place, isn't it?"

"It is."

"I was hearing about him the other day. An interesting man, I am told."

"Extraordinarily able and interesting."

"But it takes a long spoon to sup with him, eh?"

Brentwood's manner froze. "I don't know what you mean," he said coldly. "I find him a delightful companion."

The conversation went on for some time, but Brentwood could not afterwards remember a word of it save that odious little remark—"It takes a long spoon to sup with him, eh?"

He succeeded in banishing the subject from his mind for the evening, however, although he had no opportunity of resuming the conversation which had interested him during the dinner. When the gentlemen went to the drawing-room, his charming companion at once became the queen of a little court. She scarcely spoke to Brentwood individually, but now and then when she had made a somewhat audacious remark she allowed him to catch her eye as if she expected that he at least would understand.

"Well," said the hostess to Brentwood, when her husband was conducting the last of the guests to their carriage, "did I treat you handsomely?"

"You did indeed—very handsomely. What a fascinating creature Mrs. Le Mesurier is!"

"Fascinating? She is just irresistible."

Harley went to his room about midnight.

The smile with which he had bade Good-night to his hostess was still on his lips when he suddenly *became aware* of the remark, "It takes a long spoon to sup with him, eh?"

The words did not "occur" to him, nor did they sound in his ear as if they had just been spoken: they sprang at his throat like a bloodhound. It was no use trying to shake them off, no use—no use.

Ah, yes. The glamour was gone now. He could look at the whole situation sanely—from the outside. Three days before he had had no more idea of marrying than he had of standing in Parliament, and now—he was to all intents and purposes an engaged man. *Three days!* Was it possible that three days could revolutionize the whole life, not only of a fool, but of a sensible man? How incredible that three days should outweigh thirty long years! How absurd that one should not be able to take one little step back, just to cancel those three little days!

Like an echo from he knew not where the words came back—"Think well, thou too wilt find there is no Space and no Time." Were they only three days, or had he really been engaged to Wilhelmina from all eternity?

With a groan Harley returned to the facts of the case. Not a word of marriage had been spoken by any one. Was he really, irrevocably bound?

Ah me! for dear pity's sake—for pity of him, for pity of Wilhelmina—let us refrain from following his reflections! A young man is scarcely responsible for the last of his thoughts. There is no emotional reaction so tragic as that which follows on the heels of successful unpremeditated wooing. "Sour grapes," said the fox when he could not reach them; but we know what his thoughts were. We can guess what his thoughts would have been, had the fruit fallen into his mouth before he had quite realized that it was a thing to be desired. "The grapes are sweet! The grapes are sweet!" Harley cried to himself over and over again through the watches of the night. He lashed himself with the memory of Wilhelmina's sweetness, and charm, and reserve; but, for the moment at least, it was labour thrown away. The glamour was gone.

Of course he was not in love with his new friend, the lady who sat by his side at dinner; or rather he was in love with her in so far as she represented to him freedom, possibility, choice, the womankind that lets itself be sought, the womankind to which he was not bound—womanhood apart from Wilhelmina! He felt as if he had given the whole female sex in exchange for one little girl.

Acting under an irresistible impulse, Brentwood opened his desk and wrote—

"SORELLA MIA: I must write and tell you at once that I believe I am engaged to be married. It will seem odd to you—you being what you are—that I should not be sure, but so it is. To-morrow I shall know.

"Don't think I meant to take you by surprise, old girl. God knows I would not do that. The Fates—you remember the trite saying that character is destiny: should it not rather be that our emotions are our destiny?—the Fates have taken me by surprise, and here I am?

"Is this all Greek to you, my beautiful Honor? I suppose it is; but don't despise me altogether. Remember I never professed to be anything but a man.

"You will guess, of course, that it is Miss Galbraith. Circumstances threw us together a great deal. She is a charming girl—a world too good for me, and yet——!

"I should be a cur to write like this if you had not been my mother confessor always; but I may as well prepare you for what you would read in my face before we had been ten minutes together. Of course I may find to-morrow that I am taking an exaggerated view of what passed between us, so I won't post this until I have seen her.

"If there is any blame in the matter—beyond that which is due to 'the Power that made us girl and boy' —it is entirely mine, and I don't want to shirk an ounce of my due responsibility. I told her I loved her—this again you won't understand; I drew from her the confession that she loved me. It was I who led her on: she had never been there before. I would swear with my dying breath that she had never so much as *effleurée* by any man till now.

"Write me a line, dear, by return, in Heaven's name!

"What jolly times we have had together!

"Yours incoherently,

"HAL."

CHAPTER XXXV.

THE LADY OF LYONS.

DID ever the sun shine as it shone on Windyhaugh the next morning? The old place was a very fairy-land. The tall white lilies seemed to chime like bells, and every rose in the garden had lifted up its heart.

Wilhelmina was half dazed with delight. Her father was taking her to town for the day; he was in his happiest mood; he called Ann to admire the effect of the new hat above the white silk gown, and laughed to see an unwilling smile of surprise and admiration break up the dour lines of the disapproving face.

All this might well have been happiness enough; but, stretching far above and beyond it, like the golden haze around the landscape it irradiates and transcends, was the new, mystic, wonderful, half-apprehended joy.

One can do a good deal in two short summer nights and one long summer day. In that time Wilhelmina had succeeded in investing Harley Brentwood with all the virtues and graces of her ideal. The miracle had happened. The fairy prince had ridden out of the everywhere, out of the everywhere for her. How could she do enough to show her passionate appreciation? To think that she had judged life so harshly, so cruelly! Poor life! Generous life, that now was filling her cup with full measure, pressed down, shaken together and running over!

Wilhelmina lunched with her father at a big hotel in Princes Street, and then they set out on foot. Of course she asked no questions, and they were in the vestibule of the theatre before she realized what was taking place. Then a dozen conflicting thoughts and intentions ran through her mind. Of course she ought to turn back at once. She was perfectly sure about that. On the other hand, it was so pleasant to be at one with her father again! She did so want to be lovable and childlike! Moreover she could not refuse to go in without sacrificing his afternoon's amusement too, for of course he would not leave her alone in the street. While she hesitated, they reached their box, the curtain rose, Miss Evelyn flashed up a quiet glance of recognition, and it was too late to draw back.

Oh, that good, genial, sentimental old play, The Lady of Lyons! What a contrast to the flimsy webs of mood and epigram that fill—or empty—our theatres in these degenerate days! What a story to make a young girl's pulses leap with generous sympathy! One wants to see The Lady of Lyons at Wilhelmina's age—shall I add, in Wilhelmina's mood?—in order to know just all that a play ought to be.

At the end of the first act Brentwood joined them. His face was very pale, but in the uncertain light Wilhelmina scarcely noticed that. Of course the first rush of reaction was over for him; he felt almost calm now; but, if he still entertained any hope that he had not irrevocably committed himself, Wilhelmina's first upward glance dispelled it for ever. She could not speak, but her " soul stood up in her eyes," and claimed him for its own. Beyond all possibility of doubt, he was the one man in the world for her.

And all this had happened in three days—three days!

Well! She was pretty, and sweet—and young. At least he could mould her to his will. He could not conceive a more reasonable, more docile, wife than she would make: he could not imagine her really opposing him in any way. And, just as he was congratulating himself on this, he realized for the first time with a prophetic flash that the moment a man has moulded a woman to his will, her special charm for him is gone. He realized that in some way or another, spiritually, mentally or physically, a woman must constantly elude a man, if she is to retain her hold on him; and herein, he thought bitterly, lies a fine and inspiring, if also a humbling, truth, for may she not elude him by her very greatness?

Brentwood did not for one moment fail to see the situation from Wilhelmina's point of view; he was almost morbidly anxious that she should not find him cold; but on this score he need not have been uneasy. She looked for no demonstration in public, and indeed the reserve of his manner now, in contrast with the fervour of that wondrous night on the terrace, thrilled her with a sense of his power. His presence hemmed her in so completely that she scarcely noticed the fact of which he was overwhelmingly aware, that Mr. Galbraith had gone out, and left them alone in the box.

He returned, however, at the beginning of the second act, and now Wilhelmina gave herself up unreservedly once more to the play. She rejoiced when Pauline began to show a human heart beneath her worldliness and vanity, and when Miss Evelyn's fine voice uttered the lines—

> " Even then
> Methinks thou would'st be only made more dear
> By the sweet thought that I could prove how deep
> Is woman's love! We are like the insects, caught
> By the glittering of a garish flame ;
> But, oh, the wings once scorched, the brightest star
> Lures us no more ; and by the fatal light
> We cling till death !——"

Ah, when Miss Evelyn said that—it is well Wilhelmina did not know how the words affected Harley Brentwood!

So the story ran on to the three thrilling scenes of the renunciation, the rescue, the final explanation. Wilhelmina had a hard battle with her tears during the latter half of the play, and they got the better of her altogether when poor pale Pauline said in that low heart-broken voice—

> " Tell him, for years I never nursed a thought
> That was not his ;—that on his wandering way,
> Daily and nightly, poured a mourner's prayers.
> Tell him ev'n now that I would rather share
> His lowliest lot—walk by his side, an outcast,—
> Work for him, beg with him,—live upon the light
> Of one kind smile from him,—than wear the crown
> The Bourbon lost ! "

Wilhelmina felt that the thought of her heart had been expressed at last!

The sudden raising of the lights in the theatre disconcerted her sorely, and she kept her head down for a few moments after the curtain fell. Then she turned to Brentwood.

" And people say the theatre is *wrong!* " she said.

Mr. Galbraith smiled. " Miss Evelyn wants you to go and dine with her at her hotel, Pussy," he said. " She is not acting to-night. I will take you to her room now, and call for you in time for the train. Do you care to pay your respects to Pauline, Brentwood? All right. Come along. Perhaps you can arrange to walk a little way in my direction afterwards. I should like to have a word with you."

A visit behind the scenes is scarcely to be recommended to any young person who does not wish to be disillusioned. Unconsciously to herself, Wilhelmina half expected to find Pauline still in the surroundings in which she had left her; and the narrow dusky passages, the shabby professional loungers, the bare room with its litter of garments and cosmetics, struck chill to her heart. Miss Evelyn did not detain her long, however, and when they were seated in the great oriel window of the hotel, looking out on the sunny green gardens, the young girl forgot all about her brief reaction.

"Well, little one," said Miss Evelyn kindly, "how did you like it?"

Wilhelmina's eyes were shining.

"I feel," she said fervently, "as if I had listened to a dozen sermons."

"Oh, heavens, Vilma! I hope not."

"I do indeed. Do you know I am almost frightened. I think things are wrong, and then when I come to experience them, they are so different somehow! It is so difficult to see where the harm lies. I *must* be a better woman after to-day! Oh, Miss Evelyn, it was just—*uplifting!*"

The actress smiled. "Pauline is out of date," she said, "but there is no doubt she is very fetching."

"She is splendid! And what a hero Melnotte is! And even old Damas! I didn't care for him at first, but he rings so true. What a lot of good you must do! You made me feel as if I must go right away and give my very life for somebody."

Miss Evelyn looked mischievous. "Somebody in particular?"

The flush that rose to Wilhelmina's cheeks seemed to make her eyes shine more brightly than ever. "I didn't mean anybody in particular."

Her friend laughed. "Oh, Vilma, Vilma, don't try to deceive me. I have no doubt some old stagers in the house to-day thought The Lady of Lyons a very poor affair compared with the little drama that was going on in one of the boxes."

Wilhelmina did not speak. She was gazing out over the gardens.

"Happy, *petite?*"

"Yes." The commonplace little word shook under the weight of meaning it contained.

Miss Evelyn sighed, and glanced at the magnificent diamond on her own finger.

Wilhelmina was the one to break the silence after all.

"Isn't it wonderful?" she said.

"What? I don't know. One has heard of the same sort of thing happening before."

"But not like this. Oh, Miss Evelyn, isn't it wonderful that he should think of me?"

There was another silence.

"My dear child," said the actress at last, "you will think me a brute if I tell you a few home truths, and yet —there is no one else to do it. It is dangerous work to fall in love at Windyhaugh. Your life there is so quiet, so sentimental, so romantic, that you can't see this affair in its true proportion. I don't want you not to give yourself up to it, because of course it is the greatest happiness you will ever know. But don't squander it. If Brentwood was a god, it would be safe enough; but men are not built to stand this sort of thing. Try to keep just one little corner of your being *sane*. Worship him with all the rest if you like; but in that one little corner realize that he is only an ordinary young man— rather pedantic, a bit of a prig—though that, of course, is not a bad fault at his age."

Wilhelmina raised yearning pathetic eyes. Teachable though she was, it did not even cross her mind that there was truth and reason in her friend's words.

"Miss Evelyn," she pleaded shyly, "*don't* stop being Pauline!"

CHAPTER XXXVI.

THE CHAINS ARE RIVETTED.

"It takes a long spoon to sup with him, eh?"

The words had rung in Brentwood's ears all morning, but they were silenced and forgotten the moment he entered the box at the Lyceum. Mr. Galbraith looked so quiet, so scholarly, so completely master of himself and of the situation, that before long Brentwood began to wonder whether he had not been guilty of unpardonable audacity in making love to the daughter of such a man. Why in the world should Mr. Galbraith wish to have

him for a son-in-law? Was he not born to have his own
way? Even in the simple matter of the visit to Miss
Evelyn his manner was so distinctive of himself, so unlike that of ordinary green-room *habitués*, that—if Wilhelmina's eyes had only been less eloquent—she might
have had Brentwood at her feet once more.

The two men walked down towards Princes Street in
silence. Brentwood was wondering desperately what he
ought to say, or whether, indeed, it was absolutely necessary to say anything.

But his companion soon dissipated all doubt on that
score.

"Well, Brentwood," he said not unkindly, "you and
my little girl have stolen a march on me."

Brentwood's face burned. "I am sure I am very
sorry, sir," he stammered, all unconscious of the unfortunate *double entendre*. "Of course I ought to have
spoken to you first. I need not say—I need not say——"

Mr. Galbraith's smile was a sad one. "You wonder
how I know?" he said quietly. "Wild horses would not
have drawn the secret from the child—in words; but I
know her face so well. Ah, Pygmalion, Pygmalion! Of
course one has seen the miracle happen before, but you
can't guess what it means when it comes to one's own
little girl. It makes a man feel very old—and horribly,
unreasonably jealous. One does not want her to be an
old maid, yet no man on earth is good enough for—
one's own little girl!" The ring of sincerity in his voice
was unmistakable.

"That I can well believe," said Brentwood warmly.

"One never realizes till it comes so near how great
the change is. One day a child, heartwhole and happy,
thinking of nothing but her religion and her frocks—I
had almost said, her dolls!—and her poor old dad. The
next, a woman—born again—a woman with the love-light
in her eyes."

"I need not tell you, sir, that I am well aware how
much I am presuming."

Mr. Galbraith nodded. "I confess that at one time
I did look higher. You probably know that Wilhelmina
and I are the unlucky branch of the family. She was

to have come out next season under the auspices of her mother's sister, but the child had some odd religious scruple that I did not like to override. I have always tried, as far as I could, to leave her a free hand. She is a good girl, Brentwood, good as gold, and under your influence she will broaden and mellow. After all, she can do no better than marry a good and able man—who has won her heart."

"I am well aware that she is a world too good for me."

"Nay, you must not think that I cannot see the question as a man of the world. I gather from what you told me one evening that you are in a position to support a wife, not in affluence, but in reasonable comfort. We are not rich, and my life is in every way an uncertain one. Wilhelmina has her scant pin-money. At my death she will have Windyhaugh, and—whatever I leave behind; but I fear it will not be much. I am well aware, Brentwood, that the child will be more fortunate in her husband than she has ever been in her father."

"I would not hear your enemy say so, sir."

Mr. Galbraith laid his hand on the young man's shoulder. "I believe you would not, Brentwood," he said with real feeling. "God knows I quite realize what a loyal fellow you are!".

They walked on in silence for a little way. "I wish I could ask you to dine with me," Mr. Galbraith said at last, "but I am engaged to dinner with a friend at his club here. Good-night. I suppose we shall see you at Windyhaugh early in the week?"

An hour or two later he called for Wilhelmina.

"You had better be putting your hat on," he said kindly; "but don't hurry. We have plenty of time."

This at least was a hint that she was abundantly capable of taking. But he did not speak when she left the room.

"Well," Miss Evelyn said at last, "so it is settled?"

He nodded.

"And you are satisfied?"

He shrugged his shoulders. "Is it likely? I am

only human. I never imagined that I should be satisfied —when it was settled; but, to tell the truth, I had not realized how the child has made her way—has made her way—into my—my life."

"I think she is a darling."

"Still, it was the best thing to do under the circumstances. She overturned my own little plans for her welfare. I may be away for years, and it is not right that she should be alone at Windyhaugh."

"Is your American millionaire so irresistible?"

"He is something better than that: he is precisely what I choose to make him. The boy has taken a curious fancy to venerate me, and he does not get on my nerves. The combination is more than at my time of life I had any right to expect."

"True." She smiled cynically. "Especially in a millionaire."

"Especially in a millionaire."

"When do you start?"

"In September sometime."

"And where?"

"I don't know. Wherever the fancy moves me. Brentwood is a thoroughly reliable fellow?"

"Oh, yes, no doubt. 'A young lady decorously brought up should only have two considerations in her choice of a husband—first, is his birth honourable?— secondly, will his death be advantageous?'"

"His birth is well enough. His money is in the funds. Macintyre saw to that."

"I hope he is sufficiently in love?"

A cloud passed over Mr. Galbraith's face. "Wilhelmina will develop," he said tersely.

"I have been giving her a hint not to spoil the young man."

"That's right. I should have been afraid of overdoing it."

"Not much fear of that. She has taken the complaint in its full force."

"I suppose so. It is a family weakness."

"Indeed. I never observed the weakness in—the family, till now. She was so *exaltée* that I could not bring myself to tell her of my prosaic, *fade*, middle-aged marriage. Break it to her, will you?"

He smiled. "Poor Ronald!"

"Oh, Ronald is all right. He abundantly makes up for any shortcomings on my part. It is time you were starting. Good-night, George. We have been excellent comrades, have we not?"

"*Excellent comrades!*"

"Take care! I hear Wilhelmina."

Brentwood was weary with conflicting emotions when he went to his room that night. He knew in a vague way that his chains were rivetted now—"God knows I quite realize what a loyal fellow you are!"—and for the moment he did not greatly care. The one thing to which he definitely looked forward was his sister's letter; he longed to hear that she did not despise him, that she was not too cruelly surprised; but he had almost ceased to hope that she could throw any fresh light on the situation.

Her letter arrived without loss of a post. Honor had not knelt for hours in prayer before writing it, as Wilhelmina in her circumstances would have done. Of course it was not written without a struggle, and yet in a sense it was the spontaneous expression of her mind.

"MY DEAR HAL: I must begin by telling you that my first feeling on reading your letter was one of profound thankfulness that you should have written to me just like that. 'You being what you are,' it is a letter of which a sister may well be proud; but we have not been an ordinary brother and sister, have we, Hal?

"Well, dear, of course I was surprised, and, of course —in a way, as you say, I don't understand it; but if a good man's nature takes him by surprise—I dislike your word, *emotions*—if a good man's nature is his destiny, I must cling to the belief that in spite of appearances the destiny is a good, or at least a fine one. At worst I would rather you became engaged like this than that you set out in cold blood, as some men do, to look for a suitable wife.

17

"I say 'in spite of appearances,' because of course, for love of my sex as well as for love of Hal, I should have wished you to marry a woman to whom you would look up as much as she looked up to you. But your 'little *dévote*' is young: she may develop.

"Am I a brute, Hal—a cold-hearted brute, to write as I do? Some women, perhaps, would urge you to break this thing off, to treat it as a mere entanglement. I confess for one moment I did think of that; but of course you would not listen to me if I proposed it. I gather that circumstances were hard upon you, but after all you were a free moral agent; and if you drew from the lips of an innocent girl the confession that she loved you—you have to all intents and purposes married her.

"Do you remember the passage we liked so much in John Inglesant?—'It may be that in some other place God would have found for you other work; you have failed in attaining that place; serve Him where you are. If you fall still lower, or imagine you fall lower, still serve Him in the lowest room of all.' What more can you want, Hal, dear? There are your marching orders. We may live to bless the day when your nature took you by surprise, and you married the little *dévote*.

　　　　　　　　　　"Yours as always,
　　　　　　　　　　　　　"HONOR.

"*P. S.*—I open my letter in haste to tell you that Aunt Marian is seriously ill. They want me to go to her, so I am starting for Rothesay at once. Dear old boy, it goes to my heart to think I shall not be at The Pines to welcome you back, but I will write every day, and hurry home the first minute I can be spared. God bless you!"

CHAPTER XXXVII.

LOVE'S YOUNG DREAM.

IT was Brentwood who expressed the wish that the wedding should take place as soon as possible. Of course in doing so he was guided mainly by impulse, though he believed himself to be acting on mature consideration. In the course of the week following the *matinée*, he found that Wilhelmina had by no means altogether lost her charm for him. The tide had turned of course. Well, let him seize it before its lowest ebb! He anticipated great things from his first real love, and the feelings he experienced now fell very far short of his expectations. He had dreamed of a love altogether convincing, and he was bitterly ashamed of his own weakness and uncertainty and vacillation. He still believed himself to be capable of a great passion, and he dreaded lest he should meet the woman who would call it forth. Better burn his boats at once and be done with it! At least he could say now that there was no woman whom he cared for more than he cared for Wilhelmina. A year hence she and he would have settled down, and it would matter little whether love's young dream had been everything that he had longed for. After all, love was very disturbing: there were a thousand interests in life besides love!

For many reasons the suggestion seemed a desirable one. Mr. Galbraith was going abroad. Wilhelmina was eighteen—too old to return to school; not too young to be married.

Her heart beat fast when the idea of a speedy marriage was first mooted, but she raised no coquettish objection. She trusted Brentwood profoundly; she was never weary of his society; when his arm was round her she was perfectly happy. What more did she want to feel, to know?

Mr. Galbraith was greatly preoccupied with his own affairs for the next few weeks. Much of his time was spent in Edinburgh and London; but, when he came to

Windyhaugh, his manner was more than kind, it was tender; and he seldom came empty-handed. Sometimes his gift was a mere trifle; at other times it was of real intrinsic value; and of course it was he who chose the girlish white Liberty gown, so unlike the conventional wedding-dress of those days.

"Now I must not interfere any more," he said playfully one day. "She has excellent taste of her own;" and, sitting down to his writing-table, he wrote a cheque.

"Fifty pounds!" exclaimed Wilhelmina. "I can never spend all that!"

A look of real pain crossed his face, and there was a note of pathetic appeal in his voice that she had never heard there before.

"*Don't*, little one!" he said hastily. "No one knows better than the old dad that it is not what it ought to be. But as you are going to spend your honeymoon quietly at The Pines, you won't need much, and even in London I don't suppose you will be very gay just at first. It doesn't matter if you have few things, so long as they are good, and you know your boots and gloves must be specially good."

She nodded, blushing. It seemed to her extraordinary condescension that he should stoop to such details as these.

He drew her down on his knee in his quiet masterful fashion.

"She is a little bit fond of the old man?"

The tears started to her eyes.

"Oh, Father," she said, "I love you so that it *hurts!* It seems like a fairy tale that you should be so good to me."

"But she is quite happy to leave him?" he said with a playfulness that strove to belie the cloud on his brow.

"Never happy to leave him; but very very happy!"

"That's right! And yet the Fates might have been kinder to you and me, little one. Do you know I can't face a night in the old place without its missis? I will take the night train to London, and cross the Channel next day. We should have enjoyed a little more of each other's society, should we not?"

She kissed his hand, afraid to say one word more than she truthfully could. Indeed she would have been abundantly satisfied with his society for years; but, now that Harley Brentwood had crossed her path, her imagination failed to picture life without him.

"Have you heard again from Miss Brentwood?"

"Not since that beautiful letter I showed you. She is still in Rothesay."

Mr. Galbraith's lip curled almost imperceptibly. The letter in question had struck him as being somewhat oppressively beautiful, but there was no use in telling Wilhelmina that. He realized—what so few of us realize!—the absurdity of arming people with weapons they cannot wield. "Wilhelmina must win her way," he said to himself. "She will win her way."

With all his wisdom, however, Mr. Galbraith was at fault when he spoke of Wilhelmina's taste in dress. He had often seen her simply and becomingly attired, and had naturally assumed that the credit was due to her. As it happened, she had given extremely little thought to the subject until the last few weeks, and she had spent so small a portion of her life with well-dressed women that she had many false steps to make before she could be expected to find her feet.

When it came to the all-important choice of a "going-away gown," she mentally ran her eye over Miss Evelyn's many costumes in search of a fitting inspiration. One there was that specially appealed to her fancy—a dove-grey cashmere and little plumed bonnet with a spray of apple-blossom under the brim. Surely no conception could have been safer, but Wilhelmina had yet to learn that it is one thing to conceive, another to realize.

Miss Evelyn's gown had been bought in the Montagne de la Cour: it would have seemed to Wilhelmina unpardonable extravagance to have hers made by anyone more pretentious than the new dressmaker at Queensmains. This lady considered herself immeasurably superior to her predecessor—the creator of the roomy frocks that helped to darken Wilhelmina's childhood—her laudable ambition was to have "something fresh"

about every gown she turned out, and she made up her
mind that the one thing essential to Wilhelmina's quak-
erlike grey was an elaborate trimming of steel that she
had in stock. All Wilhelmina's instincts were against
that steel; but she was young, timid, uncertain; the
dressmaker was mature, loquacious, resolved; so of
course Wilhelmina gave way.

The hat was a source of trouble too. " That really is
the same dye," the shopman assured her; " of course it
doesn't turn out exactly the same in straw as it does in
wool; but, if you think of it, it is an excellent match."
So it was—an excellent match, and Wilhelmina scarcely
allowed herself to reflect that no one would have thought
it necessary to make that remark about Miss Evelyn's
bonnet. Then there was something wrong about the
apple-blossom. It didn't seem quite at home somehow;
but the poor little bride came to the conclusion that she
was hypercritical, and she resolved to banish from her
mind a subject which had already caused her a great
deal more anxiety than it was worth.

" What does it matter, after all ? " she said to herself.
" Whatever I wear, I am still Wilhelmina Galbraith."
And herein lay a great mistake, for of course there was
only one gown among hundreds in which she was quite
Wilhelmina Galbraith.

She was woman enough, however, to extract a great
deal of pleasure out of her simple trousseau. One article after another took its place in a golden dream. In
this she would pour out the tea after the sunny *tête-à-
tête* breakfast; in that she would await her husband's
home-coming in the lamp-lit evening; in a third she
would kneel by his side in church. With reckless extravagance she heaped the colours on her palette when
she painted her vision of the future. All that was noble
and chivalrous in man she heaped on Harley. With all
that was good and simple she endowed their common
life. How could she fail, in such surroundings, to be
an ideal woman ? She often kept a book of poetry open
by her side while she stitched her pretty white garments,
and her heart now thrilled in sympathy with the heroines
of romance, now poured itself forth in aspiration that

she might be worthy of them—worthy of Harley Brentwood. For the first time she read a letter from the leading girl with whole-hearted sympathy. " How surprised they will be," thought Wilhelmina, " when they hear that I am the first! "

The weather was very wet through the early part of September, and Brentwood was hard at work, so he did not often come to see her; but his letters and his presence alike harmonized with the tone of her dream. Once or twice in their intercourse she was conscious of a feeling of chill, like the easterly haar that stole up so often from the sea; but, almost before she had time to ask herself what it meant, his manner became tender as before, and she blamed herself for expecting too much. No real cloud of misunderstanding rose between them; Wilhelmina wondered what people meant who talked of lovers' quarrels.

She was not one of those women " who would like to stop everything at April "; but " her heart was still at the early spring " nevertheless; and, although it was Harley's rush of passion that had carried her off her feet, she liked him best in this quiet, self-restrained mood. The other almost frightened her. Of course she would have been sorry to think that the furnace had burned itself out, but was there not every now and then a ruddy gleam to convince her that this was not so? What experience had she to make her fear that the gleam rose from dying embers?

So the days ran on, and Wilhelmina dreamed her dream.

CHAPTER XXXVIII.

WEDDING GIFTS.

" *Mon brave!* " Enid's voice was very tender and pitiful. " Don't fret, Hugh. We'll get it put right yet. I believe half the men who do pass have no notion how to sit a horse. The British Army will soon be like those queer creatures we saw at Drury Lane—huge heads with little spindling legs underneath!"

"You're awfully good, *Mater*. I should have gone and hanged myself if it hadn't been for you."

"Hush, child! You make me shudder. Suppose you go and see Ronald. He'll cheer you up."

"Oh, Ronald's no good since he got engaged."

"And where's Gavin?"

Hugh smiled whimsically. "Gavin's writing poetry in his own room."

Enid laughed. "It is really too ridiculous—a girl he has not even seen!"

"What *gits* me is that he should be so frank about it. But of course he is scarcely more than a kid. You know, *Mater*, his poetry is awfully good. Just you listen—

"'Though only by thy name thou'rt known,
  Yet to my fancy's eye,
A form, a face, to match that name
  Seem ever passing by.

"'A form of matchless symmetry,
  A face divinely fair;
Such grace, such sweet simplicity
  Seem ever blending there.'"

Enid laughed again. "If the girl receives that effusion, she will be afraid to show herself. Any more?"

"Oh, he is hammering away at the third verse now. You see he can't stop *there*, and the question is—what to say next? I can't think how he does it. It seems to me quite as good as the stuff you read in books."

The conversation was checked by the appearance of the poet, a fair-haired lad, almost painfully tall, and certainly "much too pretty to be a boy." He put his arm round his mother's neck and kissed her—evidently for the sheer pleasure of doing it. Hugh had been right in saying that his brother trailed no clouds of glory, but in many respects Gavin was still the simple affectionate child he had been long years before at Windyhaugh.

"I have been reading such a delightful article in this month's Cartwright," Enid said—"'In the Hop

Country.' Have you seen it, Hugh? The pictures are charming."

Hugh took the magazine listlessly. "Who is it by? *Harley Brentwood!* Oh, *Mater*, what a duffer I am! I quite forgot I had a piece of news for you. Wilhelmina's engaged."

"Wilhelmina Galbraith?—and to whom?"

"This fellow—Brentwood. Don't you remember I told you Uncle George had saved his life? They are to be married almost immediately."

"Who told you? Are you sure it is true?"

"Brentwood told me. He ought to know. He had run up to see his publishers. The wedding is to be quite private."

It was a minute before Enid spoke. "Does he seem elated?"

"Oh, with a fellow like that you never can tell. I haven't the key to his blessed old clockwork. His face was like a mask. I felt inclined to suggest that he should go back to Geneva to be repaired."

"But didn't you try to draw him?"

"I did. I said if Wilhelmina wasn't quite so good, I should be infernally jealous. I said all she wanted was a dash of the devil."

"But he failed to rise?"

"Rather. He froze. He is an awfully clever fellow, but a beast of a prig."

"Then I should think they are well-mated—not that Wilhelmina is clever. Well! I am sure it is the best thing that could have happened. We must run up to town, Hugh, and see what Arrowsmith has in the way of tea-services. The child won't have many presents, and I should like to give her something really nice. Who did you say this Brentwood was?"

Wilhelmina's presents were certainly a pathetic sight. Enid's beautiful tea-service was followed by a pearl necklet from Ronald. Miss Evelyn sent a really suitable dressing-bag; Fergus Dalrymple a cheque for fifty pounds. Even Hugh and Gavin added their offerings, and Wilhelmina received from her father a remnant of her mother's jewels. The other gifts were chiefly provincial, or even home-made, articles from local acquaintances.

Mr. Galbraith expressed his contempt for the whole vulgar system of wedding-presents, but Wilhelmina was all innocence. She was amazed at the multitude of her possessions, and she apologized to Brentwood, not for the tea-cosies and antimacassars, but for the massive silver and pearls.

But what took them all by surprise was the showy expensive gilt clock which Mr. Darsie had chosen with such care.

"What is he driving at?" said Mr. Galbraith in bewilderment. "What does he want?"

"Father!" said Wilhelmina reproachfully, "he is the oldest friend I have. I can't tell you how good to me he was when I was a child."

"Your grandmother didn't see much of him surely?"

"No—nothing at all scarcely. But *I* did—a great deal."

"Well, you are an odd little puss!"

On the whole Mr. Darsie had been not a little pleased to hear of Wilhelmina's engagement to a "college man," and he could not understand why Mr. Carmichael refused to share his enthusiasm.

"What ails ye at the young man?" he asked in surprise. "Did ye hear he had a Double First at Cambridge?"

"Oh, nothing! In the first place Wilhelmina is too young to be married at all; in the second she is far too good for him; in the third—I am sorry she should marry a man who studied for the ministry, and threw it up because—because he discovered that his creed was all moonshine."

Mr. Darsie's face beamed with sympathetic interest.

"Did he *though?* My word, but I'd like to ha'e a crack wi' him!"

CHAPTER XXXIX.

AT THE PINES.

THROUGH the wet weeks of early September Honor Brentwood was kept in close attendance on her aunt. Harley spent much of his time alone at The Pines, struggling to work, steadily falling a prey to an overwhelming nervous reaction. Few educated, highly-strung men can hope altogether to escape such an experience in these days of nerve wear and tear, but the Fates are cruel indeed when they deal the blow on the eve of a man's wedding.

Poor Harley! Everything was against him just then. Although The Pines had been in the possession of the family for some years, Mrs. Brentwood's long illness had prevented their making it their home until recently, and Harley had not realized how much his enjoyment of the place was dependent on Honor's strong and restful personality. He missed her constantly, and the house seemed as lonely as the grave. He had loved the quiet of his "tame pine-wood," but now it was full of weird noises, and the cooing of the pigeons was becoming almost more than he could bear. He had revelled in the varying effects of the sunlight through the boughs, but now all was gloom; a raindrop hung from every twig, and the measured drip, drip, on the carpet of pine needles seemed to count the idle moments as they hurried him on. Oh, that endless drip! It caught the rhythm of Poe's grains of sand at last, and cried in Brentwood's ears—

> "How few! yet how they creep
> Through my fingers to the deep
> While I weep—while I weep!"

He ought to have worked? Of course he ought to have worked. But the work he had on hand might well have given him pause in his happiest hours. In a moment of sanguine self-confidence, mindful of his brilliant place in the Natural Science Tripos, he had suggested to

his publisher a book on plant life, "somewhat on the
lines of Ruskin's Ethics of the Dust." Ruskin's conception had suggested a few parallel instances from
plant life, and the publisher—whose faith in Brentwood's
future was enough to humble any man—had accepted
the idea with effusion. Could the book be ready for
Christmas?

"Yes, certainly," Brentwood had answered gaily, but
hitherto the scheme had not progressed very far, and,
now that he felt bound to tackle it in all seriousness,
the fount of his inspiration was dried up. The first
pages ran on happily enough; the more recent limped
and crawled. "I won't send you the last chapter," he
wrote to his sister. "It reads like a moral poem by
Dr. Watts. Picture to yourself The Busy Bee, shorn
of its pleasing jingle of rhyme, and you have formed an
adequate idea of the literary value of my work."

Honor wrote by return to remind him once more that
the bread was given, and the water sure; but this was
small consolation. As a boy he had resolved to do a
man's work in the world, and yet to be unlike other men:
now that his physical health had received a shake, his
great ambition was *to be like other men*—to earn a man's
wage.

And herein, perhaps, lies a paradox, for I do not mean
to imply that his early ideal was dimmed.

Am I fighting shy of the cause of all this depression?
Perhaps so; for I cannot quite lose sight of Wilhelmina,
as she sits, all unconscious of the rain, in the lonely
house on the other side of the firth, stitching a heartful
of loving dreams into that poor little trousseau of hers.
But Harley was making a gallant fight, and man can
do no more.

Windyhaugh was not far from The Pines as the crow
flies, but Brentwood knew enough now of the river's
moods to refrain in this stormy weather from crossing
the estuary in an open boat. He was obliged to go a
long way round when he visited Wilhelmina, and as both
houses stood at some distance from a railway station, it
was all he could do to lunch with her, and return before
nightfall. So his visits were rare, and she valued them

accordingly. They constituted the brightest hours of her joyous life, and, strangely enough, they were also the least dreary part of his gloomy existence. Her sunny presence cheered him at the time, but the depression always settled down again as soon· as he started on the homeward journey. Wilhelmina was sweet, loving, *prévenante*, but in his warmest moments he did not in the least want to marry her. He did not want to marry any woman for long years to come. All he asked was to settle down again to his restful *solitude à deux* with Honor.

He did not again take his sister into his confidence. Indeed he was half ashamed of having done so once, and, in his letters he carefully avoided any reference to his sleepless nights, and weary anxious days. Honor read between the lines that he was not very happy, but she had not the smallest idea of the extent of his suffering.

About the middle of September an Indian summer set in. Harley had attributed much of his depression to the weather, and he was startled to find that the sunshine made no difference. On the day of his last visit to Windyhaugh before the wedding, the glare positively annoyed him, and he almost wished the clouds would return. As usual on the homeward journey, he bought an evening paper to while away the time. He opened it idly, and instantly his eye fell on a paragraph headed, " DROWNED ON HIS WEDDING DAY." Brentwood shivered. He felt certain before he read the paragraph that the catastrophe was not an accident, and he was right. The bridegroom had taken a house, invited the guests, made all preparations, and then at the eleventh hour, had gone and drowned himself. The newspaper related the facts in the baldest way, without comment, without reference to the man's motives, or to the feelings of the bride; but Brentwood needed no one to fill in the details. He understood it all.

Presently he shivered again. He was not in the remotest degree tempted to follow the wretched man's example, his grip of life was as firm as ever, but it struck him as singularly ominous that he should have seen that paragraph just then.

As the raindrops had taken up the echo of Poe's lines, so now the booming of the train droned on through the gruesome words—"Drowned on his wedding day. Drowned on his wedding day."

CHAPTER XL.

THE LIGHT THAT FAILED.

THE quiet little wedding was over.

Apart from the splendour of the weather it had been a rather dreary affair. Owing to a sudden relapse on the part of her patient, Miss Brentwood had not been able to come. The bridegroom was looking ill, Mr. Carmichael was gloomy and unlike himself; and, for the first time since his boyhood, Ann had heard her master's voice break into a queer discordant sob when he least intended it. Ann could have found it in her heart to burst into tears herself, when she saw her bairn looking like an angel in her white robes, but, for very decency's sake, some one must put a bright face on things. So the poor woman smiled spasmodically in season and out of season, and threw half-a-dozen old shoes after the retreating carriage.

The day had become intensely warm about noon, and Brentwood's head ached acutely. Wilhelmina had little experience in headaches, and her timid overtures, her efforts to cheer him, only made matters worse. He longed to tell her to leave him alone, but the consciousness that the spirit was wanting made him cling the more closely to the form. His heart was full of the pity that is farthest removed from love. He would not run the smallest risk of hurting her feelings. So he smiled and endured till the pain became almost intolerable.

In spite of all his efforts, in spite of the dazzling sunshine, Wilhelmina began to feel that raw easterly haar stealing up—more definitely, more persistently, than ever before. Surely it was not only a headache that made him like this! A vague sense of terror took possession of her, and she began to lose her nerve. She asked no questions, but her manner was full of appeal; her very act and look seemed to say—"My lord, you once did love me!" How could she know that this was not the way to win her husband's heart?

By degrees Harley began to see, what he had felt all along, that her dress was singularly unfortunate. The steel trimmings flashed and burned in the sun, the flowers were tawdry, the whole effect cheap and commonplace. And this was his wife. This was her deliberate self. Glamour—glamour and chance had painted the seductive creature on the terrace at sundown with her pale pink draperies and the roses on her breast.

"I had another lovely letter from—from your sister this morning," she said at last. "Do you care to see it?"

He took it with evident interest, and spent a long time in the perusal of its few pages. While he read, black clouds surged up in the west, and an ominous roll of thunder was heard above the rattle of the train.

"That accounts for my headache," he said with a pitiful attempt at cheerfulness.

Ten minutes later the storm was raging in earnest. Flash followed flash in constant succession; the thunder kept up an almost continuous roar. Great thongs of rain lashed the window-panes, and the air grew suddenly cold. Wilhelmina begged Harley to put on his overcoat, and, although the movement irked him, he let her have her way. One effort of endurance more or less mattered little now.

The platform was almost flooded, but the stationmaster came forward gaily, and saw them into the hired barouche with a word of congratulation and a feeble jest that he deemed appropriate to the situation. "I think it is over now," he said, "but we haven't had a storm like this for years."

And so they started on the long silent drive to The Pines.

The quiet little house was full of welcome and comfort, and a bright-faced maid stood in the doorway to receive them. She was startled to see how ill her master looked.

"There is a letter for you on the sideboard, sir," she said.

Brentwood took Wilhelmina into the pleasant lamp-lit dining-room, where the table was laid, and opened the letter. "With your permission, dear," he said; and he read—

"MY DEAR HAL: I don't think I ever felt so apologetic in my life as I do just now. The Pines have taken me prisoner till to-morrow, and there is no escape.

"It always was in my mind to come to your wedding if I possibly could, but for several days things have been so serious that Dr. Smith was afraid he would have to wire for a surgeon. Yesterday, however, there was a slight improvement, and to-day he encouraged me to come. I knew I could only manage it if the steamer was in a happy frame of mind, and trains were favourable; but I missed my connection at Glasgow, and the chance was gone.

"I did not want to go back absolutely empty-handed, so—as trains just happened to suit—I hurried on here to see that everything was in readiness for you and your bride. Major Burnley gave me a lift in his dog-cart from the station, and I ordered a trap at the inn to take me back; but—owing, I suppose, to the storm—it has not come, and here I am fairly entrapped. I might go in your carriage, but that would mean sleeping in a strange hotel, and I suppose you would not approve.

"Of course I need not have told you I was in the house, but you might be vexed if I didn't. I need not say how grieved I should be if you felt bound to see me. Of course you won't tell your wife I am here.

"All good be with you!   HONOR."

Brentwood ignored the request contained in the letter. He glanced over it a second time, and then handed it to Wilhelmina.

"I am so glad!" she said. "I have so wanted to meet your sister."

"Come up, then, and get your things off. I will. bring her to you."

A few minutes later Honor knocked at Wilhelmina's door and the two women met for the first time. Honor was very pale. Her thick white woollen gown fell in heavy folds to the floor; her dark hair was coiled round and round the back of her head. Her personality would have appealed to almost anyone that night. It made its way straight as a die to Wilhelmina's susceptible heart. A thousand old dreams of noble womanhood seemed sprung into life. Here in actual human form was the ideal she had scarcely ventured to picture—the ideal she herself, with her storm-tost emotional nature, could never hope to realize.

Honor's first glimpse was of a drooping travel-worn figure in an ill-cut tasteless gown: her second was of a pitiful human soul that looked at her eye to eye. Assuredly this was not the wife she had pictured for her brother: still less was it the alluring "little *dévote*" she had seen in her mind's eye. Was it possible that even from the bride's point of view the marriage was a great mistake?

The fear made Honor's manner very gracious, almost motherly. She removed Wilhelmina's hat with her own hands, and drew her down on the sofa by her side.

In other circumstances the young girl would have blushed for her tear-stained face, her disordered hair, for the dress that formed so pathetic a foil to Honor's simple draperies; but one has no such feelings as that with one's guardian angel.

"You must be quite worn out," Honor said kindly. "The storm was terrible, and my brother's headache must have been just the last straw. Of course I have been used to these headaches for years. They quite prostrate him. The only thing to do is to leave him alone till it is over. He never has a word to say while it lasts."

Wilhelmina looked uneasy. "I am afraid I must have worried him," she said. "He does not look fit to be going about. Do persuade him to go to bed at once.

18

Perhaps he will be all right in the morning. Do you
think it is just one of his ordinary headaches?"

"Oh, I quite hope so. I have seen him look nearly
as ill as this before. He is greatly disgusted with himself for annoying you."

"*Me?* Oh, how absurd! As if that mattered! And
indeed I am quite happy now that you are here."

The pathos of this went to Honor's heart, and she
was kinder even than she had hoped or intended to be.

"When your aunt is better you will come back here,
won't you?" said Wilhelmina at last.

"Thank you very much, dear. My heart is heavy
about leaving her to-night, but there is no use fretting
over things one can't help. I sent a telegram by your
driver, and I shall get a reply early to-morrow. She
won't be able to do without me for some time to come.
When she can "—Honor smiled—" there is a lot of work
in the world waiting to be done, is there not? I have
been very happy here with my brother, but, when I hear
of all that women are doing, I feel like the old war horse
in the London cab when he hears the battle music."

This was partly said, of course, to convince Wilhelmina that Harley's sister was not jealous; but it impressed the listener profoundly. This was the first she
had heard on a subject—of which some of us have heard
enough.

Honor poured the warm water into a basin. "I will
leave you now," she said. "Come down as soon as you
can; dinner will be ready directly."

A bright fire burned on the dining-room hearth, and
the *tête-à-tête* meal was very cheering, but Wilhelmina
was disappointed to find that the depression and anxiety
returned when she went to her room. "There is no use
in thinking about it now," she said to herself wearily.
"When he is better, and I see him again, I shall
know."

It was not easy to banish the subject, however, and,
mindful of the maxim of some old divine that "if you
fill a sack full of beans you can defy Satan to fill it full of
peas," she resolved to think only of Honor, to forget all

else in the memory of her new sister's grace and kindness and beauty. She bethought herself that she would like to read Honor's letters again in the light shed on them by a glimpse of the writer's personality. The first letter was in her writing-case; the second she had seen Harley put absent-mindedly into the pocket of his overcoat when the storm came on. A moment later Wilhelmina's eye fell on the coat in question; her husband had thrown it down when he went in search of his sister. Without stopping to think, she plunged her hand into the breast pocket. Ah, yes, here was the dear letter! There was no mistaking the feel of Miss Brentwood's fine thick writing-paper.

Returning to the fireside, she sat down to read in comfort.

The letter was in Honor's handwriting, but, instead of " My dear Wilhelmina," she read " My dear Hal."

With a scarlet blush Wilhelmina folded it up, but, as she did so, her eye fell on the words, " You married your little *dévote*." Involuntarily she glanced at the date. It was written three days after *that night*. It must be, yes, it must be, a letter of congratulation. If she read this letter, her doubts would be at rest for ever. She would know how Honor and Harley really felt.

A few weeks before, so sordid a temptation could not have found an inch of foothold in her mind, but her love for Harley had dwarfed all the rest of her inward life, and in the warped mood of the moment she felt that if he had ceased to care for her, it was no use to be good, no use to be honourable. Her ideals were lost in the mists of her depression: she even forgot how that relentless conscience of hers would exact a ransom of pain—ay, and of confession—for every divergence from its teaching.

The first sentence threw no light on her difficulty, but the reading of it made her feel that the sin was committed now, that she might as well go on to the end. She tried to pray, and yet she was unwilling to pray, *for she wanted to read that letter!* She was struggling still when she suddenly stumbled on the signature.

The reader knows what she read—

"My dear Hal: I must begin by telling you that my first feeling on reading your letter was one of profound thankfulness that you should have written to me just like that. 'You being what you are,' it is a letter of which a sister may well be proud; but we have not been an ordinary brother and sister, have we, Hal?

"Well, dear, of course I was surprised, and, of course —in a way, as you say, I don't understand it; but if a good man's nature takes him by surprise—I dislike your word, *emotions*—if a good man's nature is his destiny, I must cling to the belief that in spite of appearances the destiny is a good, or at least a fine one. At worst I would rather you became engaged like this than that you set out in cold blood, as some men do, to look for a suitable wife.

"I say 'in spite of appearances,' because of course, for love of my sex as well as for love of Hal, I should have wished you to marry a woman to whom you would look up as much as she looked up to you. But your 'little *dévote*' is young: she may develop.

"Am I a brute, Hal—a cold-hearted brute, to write as I do? Some women, perhaps, would urge you to break this thing off, to treat it as a mere entanglement. I confess for one moment I did think of that; but of course you would not listen to me if I proposed it. I gather that circumstances were hard upon you, but after all you were a free moral agent; and if you drew from the lips of an innocent girl the confession that she loved you—you have to all intents and purposes married her.

"Do you remember the passage we liked so much in John Inglesant?—'It may be that in some other place God would have found for you other work; you have failed in attaining that place; serve Him where you are. If you fall still lower, or imagine you fall lower, still serve Him in the lowest room of all.' What more can you want, Hal, dear? There are your marching orders. We may live to bless the day when your nature took you by surprise, and your married the little *dévote*.

"Yours as always,   Honor."

Wilhelmina bent low over the fire, shivering with cold. She was not dazed, nor confused; her mind seemed preternaturally clear, and thoughts and memories marched through in battalions.

First—strangely enough—came the long-forgotten recollection of a library book she had read in her Bayswater days. It told of a man who was strongly moved by a passing fancy—of a woman who gave herself for less than the asking. Why had she never thought of that woman in connection with herself? Why had no one ever told her that—*even when she loves*—a woman must hold herself so dear, so dear, if a man is to value her enough for his own soul's good? She remembered how she had despised the girls at school who held themselves cheap. Why did the whole case seem so different when she was concerned?

She remembered how she had liked Harley from the first time she saw him—how she had *loved* him when he taught her to row—how she had never concealed her feelings for a moment. She remembered how she had allowed him to take the clover from her hair—to draw her out on the terrace at sundown. She remembered the roses on her breast.

Then with relentless accuracy memory recalled her father's words—" There are good and gracious and high-minded women whose very existence is a strength and an inspiration to the men who rule the world. Place you with such men, and what would they see in you? A little school-girl, ignorant, awkward, *gauche*." Why had she allowed subsequent events to banish the effect of those words? How true they were, how true! She saw it all now. Honor must be one of the women to whom her father referred: from Wilhelmina's point of view there was no serious difference between Harley Brentwood and the " men who rule the world ": and she, *gauche* little Wilhelmina, was his wife!

With a groan she stretched herself on the rug before the fire, and buried her face in her hands.

Next came the recollection of the vague suspicions that had crossed her mind after her engagement. Of course they seemed to her now far more definite than they had really been at the time, and she tingled with shame as she thought of the little thrill of pride with which she had reflected that, of all her schoolfellows, she "was the first."

Suddenly Miss Evelyn's words recurred to her with new force and meaning—"If Brentwood was a god, it would be safe enough, but men are not built to stand this sort of thing." "She was right," said Wilhelmina: "I put him in the place of God; and now—oh, it will be so long before I can find my own God again!"

With the memory of Miss Evelyn came the vision of Pauline, of Melnotte. How happy she had been that day! Was it really she, was it Wilhelmina Galbraith, who had been so happy?

Then at last came a rush of relief. What Melnotte had done for Pauline, surely she could do for Harley. She could leave him free!

CHAPTER XLI.

THE LIGHT THAT ENDURED.

THE housemaid was washing the doorstep when Wilhelmina came down next morning, dressed apparently for a stroll in the pine wood.

"It is a beautiful morning," she said timidly.

"It is that, ma'am, but I doubt ye'll find it very wet yet." The girl moved her pail aside to let her new mistress pass, and—laying a letter on the hall table as she went—Wilhelmina stepped out into the sweet fresh air.

An hour later Honor came down. She was anxious to see how her brother was, and then to return to Rothesay with the least possible delay.

"Mrs. Brentwood has gone for a walk," said the housemaid cheerfully.

Honor nodded, and picked up a letter that lay on the table. She did not at first recognize the unformed handwriting, but a moment later she stepped quickly into the drawing-room, and closed the door.

Wilhelmina had hesitated long before deciding how to address her correspondent, but this was the letter that Honor finally read—

" DEAR LADY: The letter you wrote to your brother has come into my hands, and I have read it. Of course I know that I have done a shameful thing, and I cannot ask you to care whether I have been in the habit of doing such things. All that matters is that I have read it.

" I suppose I shall be sorry some time for being so dishonourable. Just now I only say, Why, why, did I not see that letter twenty-four hours before? If I had met you—if I had just seen you as I saw you when you came into my room last night—I think I should have known that I never could be a wife to your brother.

" I have been thinking all night, and there seems to be *no right thing* to do now. It is my own fault. If I had been true to the light that was in me I never should have been swept off my feet by an earthly love.

" Of course I must go away. Dear lady, you will see that I must go away. Humiliation I have earned, but not the humiliation of meeting Mr. Brentwood again. I know it is an awful thing to be a wife who leaves her husband; yesterday morning I should as soon have expected to be a murdered, but if I go at once, Mr. Brentwood will have no difficulty in getting his divorce.* It makes my heart sick to think that I am bringing trouble and talk upon you and him. I would have wished to bring you only good!

" Of course I know Mr. Brentwood will be sorry for me; I know I cannot hide myself so that he would fail to find me if he wished; but he will be merciful and leave me alone. It would be terrible for both of us to meet. He might try to persuade me to come back; but that is surely the one thing that even God could not ask of me.

" Tell him your letter was just and true. It only

---

* A pathetic reminiscence of *The Lady of Lyons* here !

opened my eyes to what I must soon have seen for myself. Tell him I shall come to no harm. I have money enough to live upon, and I know sufficient of the evil of the world to keep out of its way. My old friend and servant, Ann, will come to me if she hears I want her.

"Don't think I am heartbroken, or in despair, or any of those things. Tell Mr. Brentwood I will pick up the pieces of my life and carry them back to God. I say this because then he will understand that no harm can come to me.

"If I had met you sooner—if I had met you differently—how much you would have taught me! As it is—by and bye perhaps you will forgive me.

"WILHELMINA GALBRAITH."

Honor allowed her brother to eat his frugal breakfast in peace before she gave him the letter. He was still looking haggard and hollow-eyed, though he declared himself quite well.

His face turned very grey, but he read to the end before he realized how much it meant. Here was a *contretemps* indeed; but nothing surely that a few caresses would not set right. His mind could make no room for the idea that Wilhelmina would cause him anxiety of this kind. It was the signature that roused all the hunter in him.

"*Good God!*" he cried, springing up in bed, "you don't mean to say she is gone!"

"Yes."

"When did you get this?"

"Half an hour ago. Wilhelmina had gone an hour before that."

"And what have you done?"

"Nothing. I did not wish to make an *esclandre* without consulting you."

He bit his lip, struggling to keep himself in hand.

"But why in Heaven's name," he said with laborious calmness, "didn't you bring the letter straight to me? Do you in the least realize how difficult it will be to find her now?"

Honor nodded. "Are you sure that it is desirable

to find her? You notice she suggests the novel idea of looking at the whole question from the standpoint of eternity."

"Desirable to find her! Great Powers, Honor, she can't leave me like *that!* She's *mine.* She is *my wife!* I will move heaven and earth to find her!" He drew his hand across his aching brow in utter bewilderment. "I can't even imagine what you are dreaming of. It is not like you to make such an infernal muddle of things. You have wasted *two precious hours*——"

Honor rose to her full height.

"You forget, Harley," she said quietly, "that Wilhelmina wrote to me. If she had written to you, the responsibility would be yours. Try to realize that I don't *wish* you to find her. I mean her to have her chance. She has put me to shame. My impression is that your Wilhelmina will be great."

PART III.

CHAPTER XLII.

PICKING UP THE PIECES.

In a quiet corner of the church Wilhelmina knelt unobserved.

I am afraid she was crying—for the music and pageantry, the massive columns and the white-robed figures, appealed to her profoundly after the severe simplicity of the kirk at Queensmains. The preacher, too, had that gift of sympathetic utterance—which may mean so much or so little!—and many of the congregation were conscious of a magnetic current that flowed from his personality to theirs.

But, although Wilhelmina was deeply moved, she felt as if she were looking on at the spiritual life through a grating. The preacher's manner made her think somehow of the loneliness, the humiliation, the trouble, she was struggling to keep at arm's-length, and she felt that she had not sufficient initiative of her own to start afresh on the uphill course. What it must be to have a friend like this in whom to confide, from whom to seek advice!

A printed paper before her gave the clergyman's name and address; and, as she read it, a sudden longing seized her to seek his spiritual guidance. Other people had found comfort in this way. Why should not she? Why should she not let herself go for once? Was it not a clergyman's business to be the friend of the friendless? Her heart leapt almost painfully at the daring thought, but she resolved to see him nevertheless. " To-morrow evening," she said, " to-morrow evening, I will go."

All through the next day she revelled in the luxury
of that prospective interview. She did not mean to tell
the clergyman much about her life, yet in imagination
she told him a great deal, and in imagination she saw
him listening with grave, pitying kindness. "You have
brought this darkness upon yourself," she fancied she
heard him say with the fine severity that so often proves
more inspiring than any sympathy—the severity that is
ably wielded only by the man who is severe with himself. "Accept it as the chastisement of God. Never
complain, never stand still, so long as you can see one
step ahead.

> "'The heights by great men reached and kept
> Were not attained by sudden flight;
> But they, while their companions slept,
> Were toiling upward *in the night*.'"

Her courage failed her when she actually stood in
front of the house, but she pulled herself together and
knocked. Then, of course, the reaction set in. All the
protestant spirit of old Windyhaugh rose in fierce re-
bellion against this extraordinary weakness. Why
should she lean on an arm of flesh? After all she had
come through, did she need a man, a stranger, to mediate
between her and her God? Was she not choosing at best
a lengthy luxurious way round instead of the straight
cut up the hill?

She had knocked, however, and she could not run
away. It would have been so easy to say, "I beg your
pardon. I have made a mistake"; but she was too
young, too honest, to think of that. She was speechless
with confusion, when an elderly woman opened the door.

"Did you call to see Mr. Ellis?"

"Ye-es."

"Was it about the nursery-governess' situation?"

There was a moment's pause. Like the hero of romantic adventure, Wilhelmina seized the door of escape,
regardless of the renewed perils that might lie on the
other side.

"Yes."

A minute later she found herself in a comfortable

lamp-lit study. "Mr. Ellis is just finishing dinner," said the maid. "He will be here directly." With that she left the room, shutting the door behind her.

And Wilhelmina had time to realize what she had done.

She had cherished many beautiful dreams of "work in the mission field," but that was all in the rosy light of the future. When she actually came to face the situation, she felt as unfit for the office of nursery-governess as for that of Grand Vizier. "I knew little enough at school," she said to herself, "and I have forgotten most of that. I don't believe I can remember the dates of the Kings of England—William I. 1066, William II. 1087——"

But what between the vast number of the dates she had learned, and the feverish anxiety of the moment, her fine memory was baffled, and she stuck fast somewhere in the Houses of York and Lancaster.

When she realized that she simply could not go on, she sprang to her feet and looked about for some means of escape; but at this moment the door opened, and the clergyman came in.

"I hope you will forgive me for disturbing you," she said in a trembling voice. "I have been thinking it over, and I see I am not fit to be a governess."

He adjusted the lamp, letting the light fall full on her face—so young, so honest, so sensitive, with the new wistful look in the eyes.

Then he smiled.

"Sit down," he said kindly, "and tell me about it."

"I am afraid there is nothing to tell," she faltered. "I had no right to think of it. I know so little."

"We none of us know very much, do we?"

This was a platitude with which she was familiar.

"Oh, but it is not in that sense I am ignorant."

Now that she was regaining her self-possession, her voice struck him as singularly pleasant—the voice of a girl who comes of cultured people.

"Don't distress yourself about your ignorance," he said, "and, above all, don't try to hide it. Let me be the judge."

His words were quite articulate to her moral sense, and she looked up with eyes full of simple trust.

"Thank you," she said.

He appreciated the reply. It seemed to him that not one girl in a hundred would have said "Thank you" just like that. Had he really chanced upon a pearl?

"What is your name?"

"Wilhelmina Galbraith."

"You have not taught before?"

"No."

"But you want to earn a little money?"

"Not exactly—— Yes, I ought to earn some money."

"Then you want to do a bit of good work in the world?"

Her eyes kindled. "Oh," she said, "if I were fit!"

"Are your parents alive?"

"My mother died a long time ago: my father is abroad."

"And where do you live?"

"In lodgings." She gave the address.

"Not alone?"

Wilhelmina smiled. "It is a very simple thing to *live* in lodgings," she said. "I used to *keep* them once long ago when my stepmother was ill."

"How old are you?"

"Eighteen."

"And does your father approve of your living alone?"

She blushed painfully. "He doesn't now. He thought he had—had—provided for me. I am afraid you must let me go. You are very kind, but I can't talk about that."

He drew down his brows in perplexity, and changed the line of attack. "Are you a Church member?"

"Yes—a member of the Church of Scotland."

"Ah!"

She did not miss the inflection of his voice. "But I like your Church quite as well," she hastened to add. "Better in fact."

His smile was very genuine. "You could get one or

two recommendations, I suppose—one from your clergyman?"

"Oh, yes," she said heartily. Then her brow clouded.
"That is—I don't know."

His manner became less friendly. "You are full of
mysteries, Miss Galbraith."

She rose to her feet. "I know I am," she said desperately. "It is not my fault. I hate mysteries. You
have been very kind. Forgive me for troubling you.
Good-evening."

"Stop a moment." He was authoritative now. "Sit
down, please. One question more I am entitled to ask.
What made you come?"

She did not answer.

"Did you see my advertisement?"

"No," she said resolutely. "I suppose I am bound
to answer you now. I heard you preach last night, and
I thought I would ask you to help me—in the Christian
life, I mean. After I had knocked, I saw quite clearly
that what I want is not more light, but grit enough to
live up to the light I have. Neither you nor anybody
else can give me that. So when the maid asked me if
I had called about the situation——"

He strove to suppress a smile. "I must give Mary a
hint not to ask leading questions."

"Oh, but indeed it wasn't her fault. It was because
I was too—too frightened to speak."

"We begin to understand each other, Miss Galbraith.
There is the door. You are at liberty either to go and
forget all about this little episode, or to apply deliberately for the situation—about which, by the way, you
know nothing."

"Then I apply for the situation," she said immediately.

"Notwithstanding your ignorance?"

"You were to be the judge of that."

He nodded gravely and took up his notebook.

"Your minister's name and address?" he said
quietly. "You see of course that I must write to
him."

She sighed. "I see that I have no right to object."

Then, as she gave the desired information, " Would there be any harm in my writing to him too? "

He smiled. " To quote your own words, Miss Galbraith, I see that I have no right to object. When I hear from Mr. Carmichael, I will ask you to call again."

On the threshold of the room she turned. " I quite forgot," she said shyly. " I have a good French accent."

CHAPTER XLIII.

A FRIEND IN NEED.

WILHELMINA knelt by the fire, making toast.

An English history lay in the old arm-chair by her side. A conspicuously new slate on the table was covered with sums. The comfortable little eyrie hung high above the noises of the street.

On leaving The Pines, Wilhelmina had walked to a different railway station from that at which she and her husband had arrived the day before, and, by a lucky chance, she had reached Edinburgh just in time for the day express to London. She gravitated to London as naturally as the apple falls to the ground. In Edinburgh she would have felt lonely and timid; London, in comparison, was like home. Her father and her husband would have been amazed had they known how thoroughly she was able to take care of herself. Indeed she knew so exactly what to do that she was scarcely conscious of making plans. Before hailing a hansom, she bought a handbag, and the few things that were absolutely essential for the night. This was not enough, she knew, to 'give her an air of respectability; she remembered well how she and her stepmother had been wont to regard the young woman who arrives at dusk without luggage; but she thought she could carry the situation through. A less experienced person, forced to such rigid economy, might have hunted long for a clean room in humble streets. Wilhelmina avoided that mis-

take. She drove straight to a respectable house in Bayswater—no other indeed than the lodging-house kept by
that Mrs. Brown who had "none of the little etceteras
that count for so much," but who "did the cooking herself." Wilhelmina knew that after the dining-room and
drawing-room floors in these houses were taken, there
often remained a room or two in the attics which the
landlady was glad to let for a small sum provided the
lodger did not ask for much attendance.

With her simplest, most businesslike manner Wilhelmina stated her requirements. "My luggage has not
arrived yet," she said; "but I shall be glad to pay for
a room in advance."

Her face was recommendation enough, and the landlady was satisfied. Wilhelmina paid the cabman his
legal fare, and, to her surprise, he thanked her. She
had not yet learned that in the matter of the woman
question, the London cabman has always been in advance of his sex. There is something quite beautiful in
his genial *camaraderie* with the young woman who
knocks about by herself, and has no sixpences to spare.

When she reached her little room, Wilhelmina's first
act was to walk to the window and look out at the house
over the way. "I am thankful I am not delivered over
to your tender mercies," she said contemptuously to her
old self. "The only wonder is that you got any lodgings at all."

Then her excitement gave way to a reaction of overwhelming depression, and she burst into tears.

The fire was a great glowing mass, and Wilhelmina
sighed to think that there was no one but herself to eat
such beautiful toast. As if in answer to her thought,
there was a knock at the door.

"A gentleman to see you, miss," said the maid, and
a moment later Mr. Carmichael was ushered in.

Wilhelmina relinquished her toasting-fork, and
blushed till she could blush no more.

"Tea?" he said with that ready tact of his. "That
is a friendly sight. I am so tired."

Somehow that fiery blush had brought the tears to

her eyes, and she was glad to wait on him in silence. He chatted on for some time without looking for an answer; but as soon as the meal was over he made her draw up her chair to the fire in the gathering dark.

"And now," he said cheerfully, "about that testimonial?"

"You don't mean to say," she said in an awestruck voice, "that you have come up to London about *that?*"

"Does it surprise you? Don't you think I was only too glad to know where to come? Do you so little realize the value your friends set upon you that you have tortured them like this? Do you think we shall soon find another Wilhelmina Galbraith?"

Hitherto, in his intercourse with her, he had carefully abstained from all appearance of flattery; but now —now that from his own point of view it was too late— he guessed enough of her intense self-depreciation to know how much she stood in need of a little loving praise.

She strangled a sob. In truth her self-estimate had sunk so low that this view of the matter was almost more than she could bear.

"Have you seen Mr. Ellis?" she said as soon as her voice could be trusted at all.

"Of course not. I am all in the dark. But I have come prepared to say whatever you wish me to say; so take time to think."

She took so long that his heart ached for her.

"There is very little that you need to tell me," he went on. "Of course Mr. Brentwood went to Windyhaugh the day you left; you must have known that he would, and——"

"But he was ill!"

"He did look far from well—and, failing to find you, he came on to me. I think I know enough to understand. He was in great distress. He—blames himself very much."

Wilhelmina had abundant command of her voice now. It was absolutely steady and expressionless as she said coldly, "It wasn't his fault in the least."

"And about Mr. Ellis—you like him?"

19

"Yes. He was very kind to me."

"Of course he assumes that you are unmarried. If you wish me to assume the same, I will do so; but he is sure to find out the truth sooner or later, and—and in his place I should resent the deception."

She sighed. "Then I must give up all idea of the situation. I knew it would come to that. He would have found me too ignorant in any case. Of course I can't tell him the truth."

Mr. Carmichael hesitated. "You don't trust me enough to leave the matter in my hands?"

"Oh, Mr. Carmichael, there is nothing in all the world I wouldn't trust you with. Do you mean to say you would?"

He bit his lip. "You would leave me an absolutely free hand to say as much or as little as I thought fit when the moment came?"

She laughed, but he saw her tears glisten in the firelight. "What an ungrateful wretch I am! Do you know, I have always taken your goodness as much for granted as the fresh air and the sunshine? It never occurred to me till now to think *how much* I trust you."

It was he who had difficulty in speaking this time.

"Very well," he said quietly at last. "I will come and see you again to-morrow. Of course I can't tell in the least what the result may be. I don't know what manner of man your—pastor—is."

"I hope he may be my employer some day. *You* are my pastor."

A few minutes later Mr. Carmichael rose to go. Wilhelmina rose too, but she did not take the hand he held out.

"Mr. Carmichael," she said desperately, "if you cared enough to come all this way, you must have more to say. Go on. You are my pastor, you know."

He leaned against the mantelpiece, and looked rather gloomily into the fire. "I promised Mr. Brentwood that I would let him know if I heard of you," he said. "I need not say that he is very anxious to have you back."

Her eyes dilated with terror. "You don't—don't think *that* is my duty?"

He hesitated again. "As far as I am in a position to judge, I think you are right to wait a while—if you get some work to do, and have will power enough to do it cheerfully." He had a dreary selfish certainty that there would be a reconciliation before long. "I will tell Mr. Brentwood that I told you so, but it won't be easy to convince him of the wisdom of it. I suppose you know that he is entitled to insist on your going back?"

Her smile was a sad one. "I have far too much respect for Mr. Brentwood to be afraid of his doing that."

The minister looked at her admiringly. "I think when you are a little calmer—a little more self-reliant, you should have it out with him. He will never quite believe you till you do."

"Oh, not now! You won't think it necessary to give him my address?"

He turned on her sharply. "Of course not until you wish it." Then his manner changed. "And what will Mr. Galbraith say to it all?" he asked almost shyly. He did not in the least realize how much tether she was giving him.

She sighed. "Poor father! He was so pleased to leave me so happy. You know—he is ever so good to me when we are together, but he hates writing letters, and doesn't expect many. I wrote to him—that first night at The Pines; just told him what a pretty place it was, and how much I liked Miss Brentwood, and so forth. It wasn't very honest, I am afraid, but the false step lay farther back. By-and-bye I will write again. I think I can manage not to distress him too much."

Mr. Carmichael had an uneasy suspicion that this was more than probable.

"I am afraid Mr. Darsie——" She could not go on.

"You may trust Mr. Darsie always to be very loyal to you. He is puzzled and grieved of course."

She thought of the talk that must be going on in the little shop, and shuddered. "If I could only explain to people that there has been no quarrel! Things would be so much easier than if there had been! Mr. Brentwood is all I ever thought he was—more in some ways."

"If I were you, I would not attempt to explain my-self, Miss Galbraith. Leave your life to explain you. It comes to that in the long-run with all of us." He smiled. "Have you been to Westminster Abbey yet?"

She shook her head absently, but a moment later her face lighted up. "Oh," she cried, "you offered to take me years and years ago. Will you give me the chance again?"

Yes, life gives us some very good half-hours when we have ceased to demand the impossible. Wilhelmina for-got her troubles next day to an almost incredible extent. Mr. Carmichael called for her before noon. He had al-ready had an interview with Mr. Ellis.

"I think you will be fortunate if you get the situ-ation," he said. "There are a great many applicants."

"I suppose so," she answered rather ruefully, "and many of them must know so much more than I do."

"Oh, no doubt! But Mr. Ellis seemed to think you the most human of those he had seen."

"Human?" said Wilhelmina puzzled. "Am I *hu-man?*"

This was the only question she asked with reference to the interview, though Mr. Carmichael volunteered no information. Her notion of trusting people was a very whole-hearted one.

They enjoyed their day in London as only country cousins can. Westminster Abbey in the morning, fol-lowed by dinner in an old-fashioned eating-house that Mr. Carmichael's father had patronized before him; the Park in the afternoon, and—oh, daring dissipation!—Hamlet in the evening!

Mr. Carmichael had not read the play for some time, and he was a little uneasy as to what Ophelia might say or do, but Wilhelmina was soon so absorbed in the cen-tral character that she had no sympathy left for Ophelia. Of course she fairly quivered at first under the recol-lection of the last time she had been in a theatre; her face tingled when Laertes and Polonius overwhelmed the love-struck heroine with advice that cut like a sur-geon's knife; but the moment that painful scene was

over, Wilhelmina turned to her companion with a quiet
frosty little smile. It was not an unqualified artistic
success that smile; she was new to the rôle of woman
of the world, and she did not even impose upon an honest Scotsman; but the very attempt was a promise of
better things.

On the way home she broke into a low laugh of real
amusement. "We used to recite 'To be or not to be'
at school," she said. "How *could* they let us do it?"

"It was a bit of a revelation, wasn't it?"

"It reminded me of a sermon of yours—'The letter
killeth, the spirit giveth life.' I never realized before
that it takes two people to make a book—the man who
writes it, and the man who reads it."

"It is the old story, isn't it—'He that hath ears to
hear, let him hear.' Well, Miss Galbraith, I have to
thank you for a very refreshing day."

"Oh, if you talk of thanks!" she said. "You have
simply given me a fresh start."

"That is right. Keep up your courage, and don't
look back. I will look in to-morrow on my way to the
station, and see if you have heard from Mr. Ellis."

"Thank you. May I come with you to the station?
I think my boxes should have arrived. I told Ann to
send them to the cloak-room at King's Cross. Dear old
Ann! When you see her—you will comfort her a bit?
You see, I am taking your kindness for granted again."

"I hope you always will—such as it is."

"Such as it is"—she sighed—"it is the thing that
makes a weary world worth while."

He found her in tears next morning, yet her face was
as bright as an April day.

"Oh," she said, "do you know it is *settled?* I
thought he would ask me a hundred questions first; but
he wants me to go at once—to live in the house. He is
responsible for my ignorance, isn't he?"

"Assuredly."

She threw back her head in playful pride. "Can you
believe it, Mr. Carmichael? I am a breadwinner—I am
a breadwinner! I'm a *made man!*"

CHAPTER XLIV.

NEW FRIENDS AND OLD.

" THE master would like to see you in the study, miss."

Wilhelmina turned pale. Of course she had expected the summons, and yet it filled her with apprehension. She had not the least idea how much Mr. Ellis knew of her history, and, in addition to her uneasiness on this score, she dreaded some exposure of her shameful ignorance.

But the clergyman's manner was very reassuring. " Well," he said kindly, " I hope they have made you comfortable."

" Very comfortable, thank you."

" And you have made the acquaintance of your pupils. Sit down, please. They are not very formidable, are they ? "

Wilhelmina smiled. " They are quite formidable enough," she said. " They have been telling me stories. I am afraid they know more about some things than I do."

He laughed. " Oh, I tell them all sorts of things when they come down here before dinner. Children are like the rest of us—they often learn most when they don't realize that they are learning at all."

She looked perplexed.

" But of course I want you to set them definite tasks. It is quite time. You won't find their three R's on a level with their general information, I assure you."

He proceeded to explain his wishes, and she listened intently. The amount of fresh air and games in his programme startled her.

" Well," he said, smiling at her earnestness, " do you approve ? "

" I understand now," she said, " how it is they look so happy. It seems to me you give them no chance to sin."

Sin. The uncompromising word carried with it a breath of old Windyhaugh.

Perhaps Mr. Carmichael had referred to Wilhelmina's early days, for the clergyman's voice was very gentle as he said—" I think those of us who have known the sorrows of childhood ourselves must be the more anxious to deliver the little ones from the evil."

Wilhelmina's face shone. " That's true! I often think people don't realize how good for us happiness is. After all, it is happiness that makes us humble."

Mr. Ellis smiled. " Some of us," he said quietly. " Well, good-night, Miss Galbraith. You must always let me know if you are in difficulty, or if there is anything you want. I don't suppose you have many books with you. Do you care to take one?"

" Thank you very much," she said. " Might I have Hamlet?"

" Certainly." He turned to his poets' corner. " Have you read it before?"

" I read it at school. Mr. Carmichael took me to see it the other night."

" Oh? Sit down and tell me about it."

This made her nervous. " I thought it splendid," she said feebly. " When Hamlet came in front of the curtain, I was so glad to see that he was still alive. The one thing that disappointed me was the ghost."

He smiled. This was a youthful criticism. " I suppose he did look a bit stagey."

" I don't mean that. I mean—I was disappointed in his views of things. If that is all a month of eternity does for a good man——"

Mr. Ellis did not answer immediately. Again he felt that sough in the waves and trees he had never seen. " I am afraid," he said, " if Shakespeare had set out to tell us what a month of eternity does for a good man— we should never have had the story of Hamlet, Prince of Denmark."

" *Of course not!* " Wilhelmina's eyes flashed admiration.

("*Du lieber Gott, was so ein Mann*
Nicht alles, alles denken kann!")

"So I suppose he gave us just very much what the people expected in the way of a ghost, or rather perhaps"—Mr. Ellis was paying his listener the compliment of thinking aloud—"he gave us what Hamlet expected."

She looked very grave. "Do you mean that there wasn't really any ghost?"

He smiled. "Who shall say when there is and when there isn't a ghost? In any case we see it through the medium of Hamlet's personality. However genuinely a man may reveal the supernatural—the eternal, the spiritual, call it what you will—it remains true in a sense that he is only revealing himself." Mr. Ellis had taken flight to a higher plane of thought. He was surprised to find from Wilhelmina's next words that she had followed him.

"You mean—he is God's window."

The clergyman looked at her. "That is a beautiful way of putting it, Miss Galbraith. Yes—God help him! —he is God's window." He paused. "And the moral is——"

Wilhelmina laughed softly. "Not to shut the shutters?"

He nodded gravely. "Nor to stain the glass. No; that won't do. It is precisely in his own involuntary colouring of the light that his self-revelation—that the artistic quality of his message—comes in. But at least he is bound to keep the glass clear and bright."

"Ah!" She sighed. "And that is not easy."

"No. It is just there that the whole genius of living lies."

She looked fixedly into the fire. The allegory fascinated her. "You know," she said shyly at last, "how some glasses distort things?"

He smiled. "It seems to me, Miss Galbraith, that we are making considerable headway with one of my future sermons."

Mr. Ellis was very glad that he had taken Mr. Carmichael's advice, but, as a matter of fact, he did not see much of Wilhelmina for some time after this. He had a thousand interests in life, and that dangerously sympathetic manner of his brought many people to ask his help and advice. He wished sometimes that he had an indefinite number of vacancies for nursery-governesses! He always meant to see more of the young girl, but when evening chanced to find him at leisure, it was apt to find him tired with the day's work, and more inclined to drowse in his arm-chair over a favourite book than to balance himself on the pedestal with which he was well aware his nursery-governess had furnished him. Enthusiastic youth is apt to be so merciless! One evening, however, when his head was tired, he sent for her to read to him, and the experiment was so successful that he repeated it once and again. The charm of her voice appealed to him strongly, and of course the reading proved an education for her. He was always interested too to hear her *naïve* criticisms of the books he lent her. He encouraged her to read romances and poetry as well as more solid works, but, after a few attempts, she refused. The " sentiment " was more than she could bear. Her one chance at this time was to divide her life into water-tight compartments.

What saved and steadied her more even than the work she had undertaken was the profound conviction that that work was too high for her. She never doubted that, even if she threw her whole self into it, she would still be found wanting—though not, perhaps, in her employer's eyes.

She made the most too of her occasional free afternoons. Those water-tight compartments were not so reliable that she could afford to indulge in leisure and reverie. In a profoundly conscientious spirit she visited the Tower, St. Paul's, the British Museum, South Kensington—thus learning to know her London, and gradually, without self-assertion, assuming her rights as a unit in that mighty aggregate of units.

One day, as was her wont, she had stopped at a bookstall, and was dipping into this and that, when she was struck by something familiar in the attitude of a shabbily-dressed young woman by her side. A moment later their eyes met.

" Wilhelmina! "

" Joan Burnet! "

They grasped each other's hands, and stood for some seconds without speaking. Miss Burnet's eyes slowly filled with tears. " You never wrote again," she said, rather incoherently.

" No. Are you free? Can you come for a walk? "

And they set off together through the streets of London.

Oh, wonderful, wise, all-knowing streets of London! What have you not heard and seen and felt! Is there a sorrow, a joy, that has been hid from your eyes? Have you not been in the confidence of all?—the enthusiast, the pleasure-seeker, the wondering country girl, the ardent lover, the desperate woman, the thief at night, the babbling child? The dross has been spread and flaunted before your eyes, yet, in its depths, you have caught the rare gleam of gold. Do you laugh?—do you weep?— or have you long ceased to look and listen? If we could open up your books at the great day, what should we read?—a chronicle?—a philosophy?—or merely an epigram? Are you poet, moralist, or cynic? You have seen it all—all; and there you stand impassive as the Sphinx—silent as God himself.

So, as the many thousands had done before them, the two girls carried their poor little confidences through the London streets.

Wilhelmina was the first to speak. " I didn't know you were in town," she said.

" I just came up for a week—for an examination. Oh, I do hope and pray that I may have passed! "

" But what are you doing it for? I thought you were going to be a missionary? "

" So did I; but—well, I suppose I was not worthy. We have been in sad trouble at home. We have lost almost all our money, and if the children are to have any proper education at all, we older ones must find the means. Mrs. Summers has been so kind. She strongly advised me to spend a year or two in study. She says the first few women who take their London degrees will get excellent salaries."

"And that is what you are doing now?"

"I am up for my Matriculation. If I pass I shall
come to London and work at the Napier Institute. The
classes there are good and very cheap."

"You had such a good education, hadn't you?" Wilhelmina said enviously. "And you always worked so
hard."

"Oh, I felt as if I knew nothing when I began this."
For the second time the quakeress pressed her fingers
firmly above her left eyebrow.

"There is a tea-shop close by here," said Wilhelmina.
"Come."

A headache was a thing full of significance for her
now, and she carefully refrained from speaking again
till they were seated at the little marble table and the
quakeress had renewed the conversation.

"Yesterday was the worst," she said. "I really had
crammed the subjects for yesterday."

"What were the subjects?"

"All of them? Latin, French, German, English Al-
gebra, Geometry, Arithmetic, Natural Philosophy, and
Chemistry."

She felt some pride in the enumeration, as a girl well
might in those days, but she strove not to show it. That
was the crushing part of the announcement. She ran
over the dire list as glibly as if she had been saying,
"Butter, eggs, milk, cheese," or "Ribbons, ruches,
gauzes, flowers," or anything else that was simple and
frivolous.

Wilhelmina's face fell. "Nothing else?" she asked
whimsically.

"Do you care to see the papers?"

"Very much."

They were sipping their tea in comfort, and the quakeress produced the formidable sheaf which now-a-days
the London Geisha girl must know so well.

Wilhelmina glanced over the grey-white slips, and
then looked hard at her friend. "What I can't make
out," she said, "is how it is that you look so much the
same as before. I suppose your head is bigger, but even
that is not noticeable."

Miss Burnet smiled. "*You* have changed," she said frankly.

"Grown old and ugly?"

"No. Yes, you do look older. I can't express it. You look so much more mistress of yourself."

Wilhelmina flushed—partly with pleasure. "One had need be," she said tersely.

"Your letters did help me so, Wilhelmina. They were just beautiful." There was no reply, so she went on, "And how do you come to be in London?"

"Oh, I have been in trouble too, and have to work for myself." She was thankful to find that the quakeress knew nothing of her marriage. "But I am only a very inferior little nursery-governess."

"In a family?"

"In a clergyman's family."

"That must be a great privilege."

"It is indeed—very great. He lends me books, and his sermons are so helpful. Shall you be in town to-morrow? Would you like to hear him?"

Miss Burnet hesitated. "There are so many wonderful preachers in London," she said, "but I should like to hear your clergyman. Of course I am going to the Tabernacle in the morning. In the evening I could go."

So they arranged a meeting and parted.

Wilhelmina met Mr. Ellis on the staircase when she went home.

"Well," he said pleasantly, "have you had a good time?"

Her face brightened as it always did when she spoke to him. "Very good, thank you. I met an old school friend."

"That's right. Suppose you come down and pay me a visit this evening?"

"May I? Thank you so much."

He wondered when she came that he did not ask her oftener. She was so earnest, so sympathetic, so ready and eager to talk of his children. "And what book do you want now?" he asked when she rose to go.

. She hesitated. "I wish you would put me in the

way of getting a little education," she said shamefacedly.

"Education? Don't Shakespeare and Ruskin and
Fitch mean education?"

"Oh, yes. I suppose I mean instruction. I have no
foundations. There are constant references that I don't
understand."

He looked amused. He judged—rightly—that her
intellect was not her strongest point. "Well," he said,
"choose. I believe in a man's reading the book he
wants to read."

She coloured painfully. "Might I have a Latin
grammar?"

Mr. Ellis laughed. "I didn't know you had learned
any Latin."

"I haven't."

"Then I am afraid you won't make much of it by
yourself; but there is no reason why you shouldn't try."

If his aim had been to spur her on, he could have
chosen no better means of doing it. Appreciation made
her diffident: to doubt her powers was to double them.
But in truth her hour had come. She needed no spur-
ring now.

She took the shabby old volume as a starving man
takes bread. Her whole intellect hungered for it. Her
eyes caressed those little columns of nouns and verbs.
What joy to seize and devour them one by one! How
had she been content to forego for so long the exquisite
joy of sheer learning? The soil had lain unused for
years, and now it gathered rich and warm round the dry
little seeds. It glowed and thrilled like the bosom of a
mother at the touch of her first born. Alas for the girls
who learn so much at school that they never can bring
to a subject the richness of fallow ground! The woman
of twenty—forty—years ago cried out for learning because she was anhungered, athirst! but now she had
taken good care that her daughters shall hunger no
more. It is all very wise and right and profitable no
doubt—but it is just so much less joy in the world.

CHAPTER XLV.

BY THEIR FRUITS.

On Sunday evening the two girls went to church together. Mr. Ellis was in his most sympathetic mood,
and Wilhelmina rejoiced that her friend should hear
him at his best; but the quakeress was slow to express an
opinion when they came out.

"Well," Wilhelmina was forced to say at last, "how
did you like it?"

"I noticed that he fought very shy of the word
convert."

Wilhelmina stopped to think. She kept her doctrines in a back cupboard, but she kept them as cherished
heirlooms, and she felt sure that they were all intact.
"The people there were not all unconverted."

"But think of those that were! If there had even
been a few words at the end to point them in the right
direction! If one of those unconverted people dies to-
night, I should not like to see Mr. Ellis."

Wilhelmina did not answer. She was striving to
think of any occasion on which the clergyman had
preached conversion. She had derived so much help
from his teaching, that she had never been struck till
now by the absence of doctrinal substance in it.

From that day she began to listen to him in the spirit
of an old inquisitor. She longed to acquit him of the
charge the quakeress had brought; she made the most
of many a little reference and quotation; but—looked
at from the point of view of "the man who must die
to-night"—there was no doubt that Mr. Ellis's sermons
left much to be desired. In her search for what was not
there, Wilhelmina grew blind and deaf to the good and
true thoughts that were there. In this particular she
had certainly contrived to hit upon the least profitable
way of looking at life.

One evening in February Mr. Ellis bethought him of
his nursery-governess, and her Latin grammar. Smil-

ing, he laid his hand on the bell. "Ask Miss Galbraith
to speak to me," he said, "and to bring me the book
I lent her some weeks ago."

Wilhelmina lost no time in obeying the summons,
but she felt less at ease with him than she had done for
long.

"Come and have a chat," he said genially, pointing
to the arm-chair at the other side of the fire. "Well, I
think the congregation behaved very well last night,
don't you?"

She looked perplexed.

"When there was that little alarm of fire?"

Perhaps—we are all human—he wanted her to say
that he had managed the congregation extremely well;
but for once Wilhelmina looked blank.

"Was there an alarm of fire?" she said, "I wasn't at
church."

"Tired?"

"No. I went to the Tabernacle."

His eyes grew round. "That was enterprising of
you."

"I have been there repeatedly of late. Perhaps I
ought to have told you before."

"I don't know why you should have told me," he
said rather doubtfully. "Remarkable man, isn't he?"

"Very. He preached *conversion*. If any unconverted person there died last night, the preacher would
have nothing—*nothing* to reproach himself with."

"*Ah!*" The least suspicion of a smile played about
the clergyman's mouth, but Wilhelmina was gazing fixedly into the fire. Her face was very red. Her breath
came fast. "You don't agree with me then, Miss Galbraith, that the best preparation for a good death is a
good life."

"Why—yes," she said, drawn this way and that by
instinct and belief, "a good life built on the right foundation."

He seemed uncertain whether to reply, and finally he
changed the subject.

"And how goes the Latin grammar?" he said.

"Not so well as I should like." This was honest.

Wilhelmina had no ordinary student companions by whom to reckon her progress.

He held out his hand for the book. "Is this your marker?"

"Yes."

It is difficult for the public-school man to realize what it means to bring a fairly mature mind to the study of Latin. Mr. Ellis had expected Wilhelmina to travel at the rate of a boy in the preparatory school; but he succeeded in showing no surprise.

"Then we will put you through your paces," he said quietly.

He read the terror in her face—the longing for an evening in which to " revise "; he was quite aware that it took all her pluck and common-sense and ingrained humility to make her hold her ground. That was what gave the situation its piquancy—from his point of view.

He was a good examiner. His first questions were so easy that she almost took them for a joke; when the time came really to exercise her mind, she was in full possession of it. He laughed a good deal, for of course the mistakes she made were precisely those which a schoolboy would not have made, but it did not take her long to find out that she was surprising him, and then his amusement ceased to hurt. Before ten minutes were over, she was seated in a low chair by his side, her face all aglow with unselfconscious enthusiasm. The night was late when they bethought them of looking at the clock.

"Well," he said, "there was nothing to be so much alarmed about, was there?"

She drew a long breath. Any ordinary word of thanks seemed ridiculously inadequate. "I haven't been so happy for—*a hundred years*," she said.

He laid his hand on her shoulder very kindly. "I thought you looked more at home when you were learning from me than when you were sitting in judgment on my doctrine."

She blushed, but it did not occur to her to deny that she had been sitting in judgment on his doctrine.

"Indescribably," she said, naïvely.

"That's right! Then I would try to remember for my comfort, if I were you, that 'we are none of us infallible—not even the youngest.'"

Her head was resting on her hand. She did not speak, but the curves of her face ran into the expression of receptivity that is so rare in the young.

"About this word 'conversion,' for instance; and all the other words of the kind—don't you think one may deliberately elect to avoid them because they have become mere counters, so to speak—so familiar to us that we have come to take the word for the thing?"

She drew a deep breath.

"And about the 'foundations'—are you quite sure that they are any business of yours? 'By their fruits ye shall know them. Do men gather grapes of thorns or figs of thistles?'"

Her face grew firm and dogged, as if she were addressing, not him, but some imaginary opponent. "Why should not one simply take one's stand on that, and refuse to pry and probe?"

"Why indeed?—especially if one is young and very—very ignorant?"

She smiled. It was comforting that he should take that ignorance of hers for granted.

"Our whole chance of education lies in looking to things—books, pictures, sermons, people—for what they have, and not for what they have not."

She looked puzzled. "But whenever I get to know *anything* or *anybody*, I seem to see good in them."

"Then thank God you are not blind to the good."

"But that is such an easy way of looking at life!"

"Then thank God that it is easy."

Wilhelmina rose to her feet. "It seems ridiculous now," she said, "but it is quite true that I have been sitting in judgment on your doctrine, and it has just felt *horrid!*" She drew a long breath. "It is so much pleasanter to be content with the fact that there is more wisdom in your little finger than in the whole of me—twice told!"

"We must have another Latin lesson," he said. "Let

20

me see—Tuesday, Wednesday—Friday I shall be at home."

Friday evening settled the matter.

Wilhelmina had worked hard all along. In the days that intervened before her second lesson, she poured into her Latin exercises a wealth of penitence and gratitude that could not fail to bear abundant fruit.

At the end of ten minutes Mr. Ellis laid down the book.

"You had not done any Latin before?" he said.

"No."

"Not at school?"

"No."

"Nor with your father."

"No."

"And you have not dabbled in it by yourself?"

The tears rose to her eyes. "Oh, Mr. Ellis," she said, "I am not very honest, but at least I have suffered too much to lie about a thing like that!"

He was too preoccupied to pay any attention to her natural resentment. He rose from his arm-chair, and, going over to his writing-table, dipped his pen in the ink.

"Now," he said simply, "tell me how much money you have apart from the pittance you get from me— what your father gives you, I mean."

"Forty pounds a year." She did not think it necessary to specify that her father did not give it to her.

"And what did it cost you to live in lodgings before you came here?"

"Fifteen shillings a week."

"Forty pounds. Dress?"

"Oh, nothing—for years to come. Besides—I have saved a little here. I have fully fifty pounds in hand."

He laid down his quill, and returned to his arm-chair. "In that case," he said, "my next duty is to look out for a new governess."

Her face fell. "You are not going to send me away?"

"I think so. I think so unquestionably. I have no great enthusiasm for the higher education of women, as they call it; but you certainly have a turn for—for

scholarship, and I should like to see what you will make
of it."

"But can't I teach and study too?"

He hesitated. "I think not. No, I think not. How
old are you? Nineteen? From the point of view of
sheer scholarship, you have wasted some of the best
years of your life already. The question is—where are
you to get your classes?"

"At the Napier Institute," she responded glibly.

"But won't you meet some very rough people there?"

"Shall I? Oh, I don't mind that. Besides, I have
a friend who has to be very economical, and who is
going to work there."

"And could you arrange to live with her?"

"I think so."

"Well, we might make a trial of the Napier," he
said slowly. He spoke with quiet matter-of-course interest, as if he were arranging for a daughter of his own.
In truth he had meant to help her out with her fees, but
if she could pay her own way in the first instance—so
much the better.

Wilhelmina's face was like a landscape on an April
day. "I do hope I shan't disappoint you," she said. "I
have such a *way* of disappointing people!"

He looked at her seriously. "I am not at all sure
that you won't disappoint me," he said. "You have
begun well, but it may turn out that you have no stay-
ing-power. Both you and I must lay our account for
that. Then perhaps you will work too hard, and turn
out a mere blue-stocking. That would be a much greater
disappointment. You must come often and have a romp
with my girls and keep yourself human. I want to introduce you, too, to a Shakespeare Reading Club. You
have a real gift for dramatic reading. And finally—
people are so ready to flatter a woman! They will soon
begin to tell you that you are clever and learned, and I
am afraid you will believe them. That would be the
greatest disappointment of all. I should not call you
clever, Miss Galbraith; and you are very ignorant—
shockingly ignorant. It may be years before you know
as much as an ordinary schoolboy."

She nodded, smiling brightly through the tears that
shone in her eyes, but did not fall. " I shall be con-
ceited indeed," she said, " if the thought of your kindness does not keep me humble. After all, what am I
to you ? "

She rose to go as she spoke, and he held out his
hand. " My friend, I hope," he said.

" Oh ! " Her eyes looked eager question. " Thank
you. That is the best of all."

Mr. Ellis closed the door behind her, and stirred the
fire. " Poor fellow ! " he said to himself. " Poor Carmichael ! "

Wilhelmina did not sleep much that night. Her
brain was in a whirl. She never would have had sufficient faith in her powers to take this step on her own
responsibility; but now that Mr. Ellis had suggested
and fostered the idea, her heart was full of exultation.
Her mental thews and sinews were just getting into
form, and she rejoiced literally like a strong man to run
a race. Some day, please God, she would be an educated woman, and—and—would Harley Brentwood ever
know ? "

CHAPTER XLVI.

HARLEY BRENTWOOD.

It was a Sunday afternoon in March, and great
flabby flakes of snow were melting feebly into blackness
on the London streets.

In Miss Evelyn's room the fire burned brightly, and
as usual the fragrance of hothouse flowers mingled with
the faint aroma of the soothing weed.

" I expect Mr. Brentwood this afternoon, Rose. Just
give me that roll of paper on the secretaire. Bring
coffee by-and-bye. I am not at home to anyone else."

Punctual at the appointed hour Brentwood arrived,
looking intensely calm and self-possessed.

"Nervous," was Miss Evelyn's mental criticism as
she regarded him placidly.

"Very pleased to see you," she said. "Sit down.
Wretched weather, isn't it?"

"Most depressing."

They exchanged a few more platitudes, and then she
took up the roll of manuscript. "Well, I have read
your play."

He smiled. I need not say that I have been amazed
at my own audacity in troubling you with it. I am
immensely obliged to you."

"You had better postpone all that till you hear how
crushing I can be." She paused. "It is extraordinarily
clever."

He drew a long breath of relief, though of course
there had been moments when he had thought so himself.

"At least it seems so to me. But I am not at all
clever in a literary way, and therefore perhaps I am
better able than you to foretell its effect on the British
public."

"I should think you were!"

She seemed to be reflecting. "There is singularly
little *action* in it."

"Don't you think we have had rather too much action of late?"

"Perhaps. But on the other hand we are not quite
ripe for a play which demands an arm-chair, strong
coffee, a cigarette—and an encyclopædia at one's elbow."

Brentwood laughed.

"I don't possess an encyclopædia," she confessed;
"but I did have recourse several times to the dictionary.
On the other hand your play certainly is quite unique.
It bristles with good things—as the reviewers say of the
books one never reads; and a clever woman might make
some splendid points. I wonder how far you meant
them? I should like to know where you yourself would
lay special stress. A play like that should be underlined
in red ink here and there for the guidance of uncul-
tured actors; or you might insert 'sensation' at intervals, as they do in a *cause célèbre*."

Brentwood laughed again rather more noisily than was his wont.

She held out the manuscript. "Just read me some of your favourite passages, will you?"

He flushed with anticipation. This was better than underlining in red ink.

She criticised his rendering repeatedly, and they had a warm combat over several passages. Some of her suggestions, of course, struck him at once as admirable, but she was anxious to put in a few high lights and deep shadows that from his point of view would have spoilt the chiaroscuro of the whole picture. He was flattered, however, to find that she had such strong views. Whatever she might say, his heroine obviously did appeal to her.

"It certainly is interesting," she said at last. "I think the chances are that no manager would produce it, but if anyone did—it might just catch on. I am trying to be quite candid."

He smiled. "I hope you have been fairly successful. I am sure I don't know how to thank you," he added as he rose to go.

She looked up calmly. "I know very well how you are going to thank me. Sit down, please. I have given you of my best, such as it is. Now it is your turn. I want news of Wilhelmina."

"Not in love perhaps," was her mental comment a moment later, "but certainly not indifferent."

His self-control was perfect, however, as he replied, "I am afraid you have come to the wrong quarter for that."

"Not really?"

"Really."

"Well, in case of need it is useful to know that one can conceal oneself so easily."

"When a woman strongly states her wish to be left alone for a time, concealment is excessively easy—unless she chances to be dealing with a brute!"

"Short of being a brute one might wish to know how she fared."

"Oh—I am told she fares well."

" You know, Mr. Brentwood, I am very fond of Wilhelmina."

" That is a feeling with which I cannot fail to sympathize."

" Pretty hard hit," she reflected, and she continued aloud—" Of course I have no conventional views on the subject of the marriage relation. I don't see why a man and woman should be doomed, as so many are, to go on perpetually—consuming each other's souls."

" It does seem an unprofitable form of spiritual repast."

" Will you give me Wilhelmina's address ? "

" I don't know it."

" Good heavens! Do you know what she is doing ? "

" Teaching, I believe."

" *Teaching!* And is that your idea of faring well ? "

" Pardon me. It is a question of her idea, not mine."

" Has she anything to teach ? "

For the first time the shadow of a smile flickered over his face. " Not too much, I fancy."

Miss Evelyn was seized with a brilliant inspiration. " I do wish I could meet her. If she really means to live her own life—and you have no objection to her doing so—why doesn't she go on the stage? She would make a fascinating *ingénue,* and, if she inherits any reasonable share of her father's gifts——"

Ah! She had drawn blood that time. Harley bit his lip hard. It was almost a minute before he could bring himself to say coldly—" I should have thought that was the last thing for which she was qualified."

" I prefer a man's judgment to a woman's any day —except on the subject of the qualifications of his womankind."

Brentwood bowed.

" A woman judges her male relatives in the light of the great world and its interests: the male relative judges her in the light of his dinners and shirt-buttons."

Brentwood had heard something of this kind before.

" That is more or less true, and not altogether unnatural, but I fail to see its relevance to the present case."

Miss Evelyn's temper was rising. "You mean you have not had much opportunity of judging Wilhelmina from the dinner and shirt-button point of view?"

Brentwood flinched. Then he smiled. "I admit my indebtedness to the full," he said; "but don't you think you have had your pound of flesh?"

"It is flesh, is it?"

"That I can't undertake to say."

Miss Evelyn changed the line of attack. "She was very much in love with you."

Curiously enough he resented this on Wilhelmina's account, though he did not see fit to question it. "You choose your tense with discrimination."

"I should not fancy her fickle."

"No? Yet she can't help being her father's daughter."

Miss Evelyn raised her head defiantly. "And why should she help it? My hope is that she will show herself her father's daughter. That reminds me—Mr. Galbraith said Macintyre of Queensmains was the family man of business. He will put me in communication with Wilhelmina. I will write to him at once."

Brentwood lost control of himself for a moment. "I beg you will do nothing of the kind!"

Miss Evelyn laughed. "Issue your orders to Wilhelmina, if you please. I don't acknowledge the jurisdiction."

He held out his hand. "Good-bye," he said cheerfully, with a change of tone that suggested histrionic possibilities to her professional mind. "Many thanks for your kind help."

She relented when she saw the pain in his face. "If you only knew it, I should be glad to help you in another way. I think this—misunderstanding is awfully hard upon you."

There was a dangerously sympathetic cadence in her voice, and for a moment he was really tempted. Here was a woman who knew the world as it is—a kindly tolerant critic before whom it was quite unnecessary to pose.

Brentwood drew a long breath, but, with the reflec-

tion that Miss Evelyn had not many ideals to lose, came
the vague echo of a rumour that she was engaged to
Ronald Dalrymple.

"You are very kind," he said cordially; "but do we
stand in need of help? It is absurd for you and me to
assume that the marriage relation is a uniformly happy
and desirable one. Wilhelmina and I have muddled
things, of course; but at least we have no cause to envy
the spiritual cannibals to whom you referred so graphic-
ally. We are not occupied in consuming each other's
souls."

"You prefer that she should eat her own heart
out?"

His lip curled. "Not much fear of that. I am told
she is well and happy."

"I don't believe a word of it. Why, Mr. Brentwood——"

A knock at the door. "If you please, ma'am, that
is Mr. Ronald Dalrymple."

Miss Evelyn frowned. "All right. He can wait."
She turned to Brentwood with a friendly smile. "Con-
found Mr. Ronald Dalrymple!" she said frankly.

But the mention of the name was enough. "I fear
I have outstayed my welcome," said the young man hurriedly. "Thank you a thousand times."

A minute later Ronald was ushered in.

"What the dickens brings that fellow here?" he
asked.

Miss Evelyn glanced up with languid eyes. "What
the dickens brings *this* fellow here?"

"Oh, come, I say, Gertrude, if you knew how I have
been worrying about you, you wouldn't be down on a
fellow like that!"

She arched her fine eyebrows. "No?"

"I came up to see my lawyer. Do you know, if I
died to-morrow all my money would go to Fergus and
his boys—most of it to Hugh?"

She laughed light-heartedly. "I am quite prepared
to take the chance of your dying, Ronald. You don't
look at all like it."

"Oh, I am not so sure. I have been riding a brute with a devil of a temper."

"Why will you be so silly?" she said fretfully. "I thought you had more sense." If he had not rasped her, she would have begged him not to ride the brute in question, but she was in the mood in which we see the foibles of our friends through the cold blue glass of the intellect, and not in the rosy light of the affections.

"And how is Brentwood?" he said.

She yawned. "Who shall find a virtuous man, for his dulness is beyond conception. I forgot—one ought not to be profane with you, Ronald. You will lay the flattering unction to your soul that I am in earnest."

"Is Brentwood virtuous?"

"How should I know? He is dull enough, and priggish enough."

"Has Wilhelmina gone back to him?"

"I imagine not, but as you broke in on our interview, you can't expect me to give you much information."

"Did I really? I told her not to announce me." His voice softened. "Do you mean to say you really sent him away for me?"

She was not dishonest enough to insist on the point. "Mr. Brentwood is never expansive," she said.

"I thought you would draw him if anyone could."

"So I did in a sense. Oh, I know the whole story as well as if he had told me, and, as he gave me no confidence, I have none to keep. Wilhelmina was the one who kissed: he bent his cheek." Miss Evelyn had no wish to touch on George Galbraith's part in the programme. "I never quite believed that the marriage would come off, but apparently she found him out too late."

"Found out what?—that there was another girl?"

She sighed. "How crude you are, Ronald! Mr. Brentwood thinks my intellectual retina is not sensitive to subtle lights and shades. I wonder what he would think of yours?"

"Well, all I can say is—if there wasn't another girl —it is confoundedly awkward for him."

" It is rather."

" I can't make it out. She never struck me as that
sort of girl. Enid is racy on the subject. Thanks the
guiding hand that warned her to leave the child alone.
Always felt in her bones that the filly would come to no
good. Says it's the Galbraith blood."

Miss Evelyn bent over the fire. " She is right, of
course. It is the Galbraith blood, though not in the
sense she means. It was a stroke of genius on Wilhelmina's part to leave him. She forced him to recognize
her once for all as a personality."

Ronald stared. " And was Brentwood never in love
at all ? "

" Oh, dear, yes. You know what a man's love is
worth. He is a little bit in love still."

" Then why the mischief doesn't he just trot her
back ? "

Miss Evelyn turned on him sharply. " Because he
doesn't happen to be either a fool or a brute ! When
you talk like that, you make me feel that God made a
few men and left the devil to produce the rest."

" Good Lord, Gertrude ! what have I said now ? "

She laughed. " Poor boy ! What a life I do lead
him ! Brentwood doesn't ' trot her back,' as you poetic-
ally phrase it, for two reasons. First, because she has
asked to be let alone, and he is a chivalrous fool."
There was a little inconsistency here, of which Ronald
was dimly conscious. " Secondly—well, I haven't seen
Wilhelmina yet, so I don't know how much it would
take to make her go back, but I fancy it would take a
good deal. She is still in love, of course, but she has
been taken in by the guinea stamp once, and she will
need the genuine article next time. In other words,
Brentwood will have to ' weep, to fight, to fast, to tear
himself.' He would like to have her back, if he could
have her without much fuss, but he is not prepared to
' drink up eisel, eat a crocodile.' See ? "

Ronald nodded doubtfully, and changed the subject.
" Hugh pointed out Miss Brentwood to me the other
night. What a stunning girl she is !—reminds one of
Helen of Troy, and all that kind of thing."

" Yes, as her brother says, she is the kind of woman who has never gone out of fashion. That type has no limitations of space and time. One cannot imagine her out of place anywhere—except perhaps at the court of Louis XV. She links the ages, so to speak."

" If Brentwood often talks about his sister like that, I don't wonder Wilhelmina left him."

Miss Evelyn laughed merrily. " Well done, Ronald! In point of fact I believe Vilma adores Miss Brentwood. Do you go down to-morrow? "

" Yes, I have told Aitchison what I want. He is to whip the thing into shape, and bring it down for me to sign. Fergus is abroad just now, but he likes Aitchison to have a day with the hounds now and then. Oh, by the way, Enid wants *you* to come down for a week before the hunting is over. She will write to you herself."

The last vestige of a cloud vanished from Miss Evelyn's face. " Come, it was good of you to engineer that, and it can't have been easy."

" Oh, well, you see she is a capital sort, but she is a bit conservative and conventional."

Miss Evelyn nodded. " I quite understand. You have got me the invitation. It is my look-out now. Have a cigarette? "

When Brentwood went home that evening, he felt that he had behaved like a churl to a delightful woman, and he wrote a pretty note to thank Miss Evelyn again for all her kindness. He congratulated her, too, on her engagement. " I have no doubt Mr. Dalrymple quite appreciates his good fortune, and will realize that it is too late for any one man to monopolize the resources of the woman whose art has been an education and a joy to so many."

He was quite honest—even selfishly honest—in saying this. Miss Evelyn's acting appealed to him strongly, and he had half hoped that she might be tempted to take the part of his heroine. His interest in that play of his was almost crucial. It was the first bit of live work that he had done for six months, and it had sprung into life and form so quickly, so spontaneously, that in his heart of hearts he took no credit for it at all. But the writing of it had given him a fresh lease of vitality, and if it should prove a success, he felt as if there might be a chance for him still. Of course, in his letter he did not refer again to his own private affairs. Was he not thankful to have escaped the day before by the skin of his teeth?

And after all, how little he had to tell! The news of Wilhelmina's flight had filled him for the moment with the hope that he really was in love, but swift upon this came Mr. Carmichael's intelligence that she was independent and happy (I am afraid the old Adam in Mr. Carmichael made the most of that happiness and independence), and then Harley realized that his docile little Wilhelmina had made him ridiculous in the eyes of his fellow-men. This is an injury difficult to forgive under any circumstances, and forgiveness is not rendered easier by the fact that a woman has contrived to inflict the injury without so much as soiling her own white robes in the process. The only atonement Wilhelmina could have made was to starve, or break her heart, and apparently she showed no inclination to do either.

Worse, too, than making him ridiculous in the eyes of others, she had made him ridiculous in his own; for, viewed in the light of subsequent events, how feeble and melodramatic seemed the anguish he had undergone during the weeks that preceded his wedding! Brentwood had always been advanced and chivalrous in his views of women; in his future relations with them he had justly pictured himself as acting with fine moral virility: but now he was painfully conscious of the sheer brute desire to conquer a woman by force. He was too angry to think of gentler wooing.

And indeed one is forced to reflect how impossible it is to reckon on any woman! If Brentwood had been false to his troth, what surety had he that Wilhelmina would not pine away and die? But, *because he had been true*, she had thrust him into a position in which no ordinary moral compass was of any avail. In her impulsive woman fashion, she had acted with a dash of the heroic, and he was quite disposed to pay her back in her own coin; but she had acted so that no heroic revenge on his side was possible.

It seemed to him that his life had been a mistake and a failure from the day he saw her springing like a kitten at her father's book; and yet he would have been the first to admit that she had done nothing wrong. That was the maddening part of it. His sister, Mr. Carmichael, and Miss Evelyn were perfectly right when they said she was too good for him, and yet no unbiassed observer could deny that she and the fates between them had treated him most cruelly.

Miss Evelyn was pleased and disappointed when she read the letter. She did want to play Providence to Brentwood and Wilhelmina.

"That delightful moody heroine of yours—Hagar, I mean, not Wilhelmina—has taken an extraordinary grip of me," she wrote. "I was actually thinking in the watches of the night how much might be made of her. Why did you not create her a year ago? I am bidding farewell for the present to the scene of my labours, and I assure you it is no small sacrifice. If the nostalgia becomes unendurable, I shall take a leaf from Wilhelmina's book. I trust Ronald may be induced to take one from somebody else's."

Honor, sitting opposite to her brother at the breakfast table, did not fail to note the lights and shadows that drifted across his face as he read the letter in what Mr. Galbraith had once happily termed the "bold bad black handwriting"; but she asked no questions. That confidence between brother and sister was less perfect than formerly. Harley laid down the letter and took up his Standard without a word. "How can she marry a man like that?" he thought,

"'Finished and finite clod, untroubled by a spark.'"

It seemed an odd coincidence that at that moment his eye, sweeping over the columns, caught the name Dalrymple. It was a common enough name, of course, and yet something prompted Harley to return and look for it. Ah, here it was! " Mr. Ronald Dalrymple," too. " Death in the hunting field."

" Good God, Honor! " he cried. He felt almost as if he had committed a murder.

CHAPTER XLVII.

WILHELMINA'S DREAM.

THERE was a pleasant buzz of activity in the chemical laboratory.

The students had worked steadily during term, but now the excitement of examinations and holidays was in the air, and an undercurrent of conversation accompanied the work. Many a time in the winter evenings that warm bright room had been a haven of comfort and peace: now the level rays of the sun threw its shabbiness and grime into strong relief, and reminded one that, far away, fields were green and flowers were blowing, and cool waves breaking on the sandy beach.

There was the usual succession of minor incidents to break the monotony of the proceedings. From time to time a test-tube cracked, and a stream of mordant liquid contributed its share to the mellowing of those stained, charred, whittled tables; or the fumes of bromine called forth an indignant protest from those who were not responsible for their production; or " strong sulphuric and heat," added to some unknown factor in the test-tube, caused an explosion that sent the rash experimenter in haste and perturbation to the water-tap.

Socially, the class was a curious mixture—more so, perhaps, than any other in the place. The rising mechanic, for whose benefit the institute had been primarily founded, was there of course; the lad whose school curriculum was wanting in just those subjects for which he had a natural aptitude; the struggling teacher who burned to add the magic letters B. A. or B. Sc. to his name; and the medical student who had failed in Chemistry, and who was glad to rub up his ignorance at the cost of a few shillings.

Wilhelmina was working in a quiet corner, working neatly and economically as some girls do. She was so much at home in the laboratory now that it was difficult even to recall the evening when she had first crept up the dreary stair with beating heart, fearing she knew not what. She had found to her dismay that she was the only woman in the class, and had suffered agonies, not so much of shyness, as of dread lest the men should resent her presence there. She had not ventured to look at them, and so was happily unconscious of the extent to which they looked at her. When a handsome lad offered to wash her test-tubes, the rush of surprise actually made the tears start—poor Wilhelmina!—and she accepted the offer just for once—the water-tap did seem so very far away! Then a young mechanic from Glasgow laid an honest grimy paw on her note-book. "What did you pay for that?" he asked simply. "Fourpence-halfpenny," she had replied with beaming face; and the barrier thus broken down, she was soon on terms of potential *camaraderie* with every man in the class. It was a fine initiation into practical socialism. The consciousness that she was not in the marriage market gave her manner an ease and repose that was very unusual in so young a girl. She never again allowed anyone to wash her test-tubes for her; by degrees she took her place, assumed her rights as a student, with a simplicity that went as far as anything could to make the men forget the difference of her sex.

Many happy hours she had spent in that dusty laboratory; but to-night the summer had got into her blood, and for the first time in months she was seized with a great longing for Windyhaugh. How cool the shade of the limes must be!—how fresh the breezes!—how fragrant the hay-ricks! Heigho!"

"May I walk home with you, Miss Galbraith?" said a deformed intellectual-looking lad as she ran downstairs.

"Not to-night, thank you, Mr. Dunn. I am going on the top of the 'bus to Kensington Church."

"That's right! I wish I could come too." He hesitated; but his examination was imminent, and a fourpenny 'bus-ride *was* extravagant!

Wilhelmina walked to Gower Street station and took her place in the front seat of the omnibus with a long sigh of anticipation. This was not Windyhaugh, but it was something. The city was sultry and airless, and among her fellow-passengers were a number of bleached weary workers—dressmakers, clerks, shop-hands, and the like. A royal boon to the over-wrought is that ride to Kensington Church! It lifts them just a little way above the dust and the hubbub, the sameness of their daily life; gives them a glimpse of trees and shrubs and restful greensward; and as they leave the densest traffic behind, they meet the gay procession bowling cityward, they catch a glimpse of the pinnacles and minarets of the great social edifice, they coast with eager eyes along the margin of another world.

On the homeward journey a young man took the vacant place beside Wilhelmina. As he seated himself, he glanced pointedly under the brim of her hat, and she proceeded to turn on him the languid, icy, unseeing glance which had proved her best weapon in such circumstances. But a moment later she held out her hand. "Good-evening, Hugh," she said.

He was greatly surprised, and seemed more confused than the occasion warranted. "Vilma!" he exclaimed.

Neither found it very easy to proceed.

"I am awfully glad to meet you," he said at last.

This was more than she could honestly reciprocate. His jaded young face was not attractive.

"We can't talk here," he continued. "Do you mind coming in a hansom instead?"

"I think I would rather not have a hansom; but if you care to walk home with me——"

He nodded, and helped her down from the 'bus with the exaggerated courtesy that appeals so strongly to women. "You have no idea how often I wanted to meet you."

"I wonder why."

21

" Oh, so many things have happened since we met. You know "—he became almost shy as they approached the delicate subject—" I backed you up all along the line."

She smiled a little bitterly. The friends who are eager to tell us of their championship forget sometimes that, unless we value their judgment very highly, our appreciation may not be sufficient to compensate for the reminder that we stood in need of such aid.

" I am afraid you found your work cut out for you," she said.

" Oh, well, you know what the *Mater* is. I told her I wished I had had the sense and gumption to marry you myself."

Wilhelmina broke into a pleasant laugh. " Oh, no, Hugh," she cried, mindful of the *Autocrat*, and thankful to relax the tension of the situation. " Think of all the nice girls who would have drowned themselves if you had ! "

" That's just it." He laughed with the uneasy feeling of a man who feels himself overweighted by the woman he is talking to. " Oh, of course I know you wouldn't have had a word to say to me, but at least I am not a prig."

" It seems to me," said Wilhelmina thoughtfully, " that I like prigs."

" Then I should have thought——"

But she could not allow this. " How warm it has been to-day ! " she said.

" Yes. One begins to think of the moors. Where are you staying, Vilma ? "

" I am in a flat with a friend."

" Doing London ? "

" No." She blushed as if she were owning to a crime. " I am studying—attending classes."

He looked at her almost incredulously. " I suppose you enjoy that kind of thing ? "

" Immensely. It seems too good to be true that I am free to study, and learn as much as ever I can. I was— am—so frightfully ignorant, Hugh."

" It seems to me," he said thoughtfully, reflecting her

manner of a minute before, "that I like ignorant women."

She laughed. "I know. Yes, I quite see that point of view. One half of me hates the thought of trying to be a learned woman, but the other half does so want to grow!"

"And what does Uncle George say to it all?"

She hesitated. "He was distressed and uneasy at first, but he can't help seeing that I have got the thing I want."

"Poor little Vilma! You have seen so little of life. You didn't know what love meant."

"And then of course he can't worry when he knows I have good friends."

"Have you good friends?"

Her face glowed. "Oh, one or two splendid friends."

He wondered what would happen when she fell in love really. He longed to ask next what Brentwood said to it all, but he did not dare.

"And now," she said, "I am hungering to hear about you. I saw Aunt Enid in the Park one day, looking lovely. Are you all well?"

"Oh, I think so. Of course Ronald's death was an awful shock to us all."

"*Ronald's death!*"

"Do you mean to say you hadn't heard of it?"

"Not a word. Oh, Hugh, how terrible!"

"It was so frightfully sudden, too. There was a horse in the stables that the governor wouldn't let anyone ride except himself. But the governor went over to Germany for a few days, and then Ronald would ride him, and he was thrown." Hugh's lips quivered. "It was just *ghastly*, Vilma—the whole thing from first to last! And father being away, I was nearest male relative. You've no notion what it means to be nearest male relative at such times."

"Was he—conscious?"

"Not properly—no. The *Mater* would send for a clergyman: women are like that: and she flatters herself—— But I don't believe he heard a word the fellow said." Hugh gulped down a sob.

"How terrible!" said Wilhelmina again.

"It is an awful shock to Gertrude too."

"Miss Evelyn?—Yes, I suppose so."

"Of course I don't mean to say that she was just gone on him, but he was awfully good to her. He was making a will in her favour, but it is just so much waste paper. However, I'll take care that she doesn't lose it all."

"Yes, do, Hugh. That is good of you."

"I suppose she will go back to the stage after a bit. By the way, she is very anxious to see you."

"Is she? She has always been very kind to me. I will go before I leave town. Poor Miss Evelyn!"

Hugh's thoughts were evidently wandering. "If there's any life at all beyond the grave," he broke forth impulsively at last, "I suppose you think it is a poor look-out for him. You know, Vilma, he was awfully kind. Lots of pious people aren't half so kind as he was."

She did not answer immediately. She was touched to see this precocious man of the world show so much genuine feeling. "Surely, surely," she said at last, "God will give him another chance!"

Hugh's face brightened. "Do you really think so, Vilma? You wouldn't have said that once. You were awfully religious."

"Indeed, Hugh, I don't mean to be less religious now, but I have come to see things differently."

"What made you do that?" he asked eagerly. He had taken a genuine, if fitful, interest in religion since his uncle's death.

"I think the beginning of it was that in books and in life I saw people living good lives without believing the doctrines I had thought to be the foundation of a good life. I tried at first to persuade myself that they were not really good, but that was barren work, as Mr. Carmichael would say. My heart was at rest when I gave up that attempt, but my mind wasn't content to stop there. 'Is the doctrine essential then?' it asked; and then, 'Is the doctrine true?'

"So by degrees I began to look at the different doc-

trines as I had never done before, and a thousand things
I had read in Carlyle came back to my mind. I thought,
too, of a poem Mr. Carmichael is very fond of—

> " ' Who fathoms the eternal thought?
> Who talks of scheme and plan?
> The Lord is God! He needeth not
> The poor device of man.'

I read a great deal, and especially I read the Bible——"

" Why, Vilma, you knew it by heart when you were
a baby."

" Many of the finest passages were terribly familiar. ·
I had to read them over and over again before I could
look at them with any freshness at all."

" I am afraid all the reading in the world wouldn't
get rid of the fire and brimstone? "

She did not answer, and presently she stopped in
front of a block of respectable workmen's houses. " This
is where I live."

Hugh tried to conceal his surprise. " May I come
up with you? " he said. " It is so awfully nice to meet
you again." As a rule he was ill at ease with virtuous
women, but Wilhelmina's somewhat anomalous position
appealed to him.

She nodded, and led the way to a room on the third
floor. It was freshly papered and painted, and very
bright with hardy plants and flowers.

" Well, you do keep it nice! " he exclaimed.

She smiled. " I'm so glad you think so. I am
dreadfully lazy about such things; so I keep reminding
myself that my father may drop in any day. He likes
pretty things, and at Covent Garden the plants and cut-
tings cost almost nothing. Ann sent me the rugs from
Windyhaugh, and I stained the floor myself."

" What a lot of books you have got! I suppose you
want to be at them. I shan't stay long. I want to hear
what you found in the Bible."

She was silent for a few moments, struck by his
recurrence to the subject. It was an extraordinarily
novel experience to meet Hugh Dalrymple, so to speak,
on a spiritual plane. Like one who encounters a home

friend in a far country, Wilhelmina was moved to treat
him with all the hospitality her soul could provide.

"You are quite right, Hugh. There was no getting
rid of the fire." She drew a long breath and her face
grew pale. "I wonder if I could tell you a dream I
had when I was a child. I have never told anyone before. You know I used to suffer terribly with thoughts
of hell. Do you remember the picture in Peep of Day
of the lake of fire? Well, one night I dreamt I was out
walking with my grandmother, feeling very unhappy,
and away in front of us we saw a mass of flame rising
from the ground. 'Is that hell?' I asked. 'No,' she
said, 'but those who go to heaven must first pass through
the fire.' In a moment I had left her side and was running towards the glare as if I had wings to my feet. I
found the flames rose from a great square space built
into the ground. They did not fill the space. There
was a wide, clear passage round about, the outer half
of which was divided by partitions like a stable with
its stalls. In most of these stalls a man or woman was
sitting, and I took my place in a vacant one without a
word. I was wondering—wondering—what was going
to happen. Presently"—her voice shook and she lost
her self-control for a moment—"Christ came round. I
suppose He was just the Jesus of my picture-books, but
His face and form have grown with my growth, till now
I see Him as the Man of Sorrows, the Light of the
World. He held in His hand an unlighted torch, and,
when He came to me, He lighted it at the great fire,
and held out His other hand for mine. Of course I
gave it in a moment—I never could 'believe' in my
waking hours, but how I trusted Him then!—and, taking it in His, He passed the torch slowly across the
palm. 'Is that all?' I cried, and the rush of surprise
was so great that I awoke."

"Oh, I say, Vilma, did you really dream that?"

She nodded, striving to blink away the tears.

"Then I suppose you didn't suffer any more?"

"I wish I could say so. It did calm me a bit, but
the teaching of my childhood was too deeply ingrained
for that. The dream impressed me so much that I tried

and tried to make it fit the creed I had been taught, but I couldn't. Oh, Hugh, if you think of it—how could a child appreciate a dream like that? Of course it was only a dream. All the queer little jumbled atoms just chanced to make a picture for once. But it was the one dream of my life. I have never had another that I would place beside it for a moment." She laughed apologetically. " I keep it in a chapel by itself."

Hugh did not answer. The room was growing dark, and he felt the atmosphere of the story intensely, but he wished Wilhelmina would be a little more explicit. When he spoke his words were disappointing.

" Well, all I can say is that if hell *isn't* in the Bible —the real genuine article, I mean—the priests have a deal to answer for."

" I felt that too. For a time I felt dreadfully bitter —I sometimes feel bitter yet; but we had to make mistakes, Hugh, and God was over all."

He glanced round the room. " You do a deal of thinking here, Vilma."

She nodded.

" Don't overdo it. You don't grow fat on it."

" I am going to Bournemouth for two months. I shall grow fat there."

" Who is taking you? "

" I am taking two little girls—former pupils of mine. Their father is going to Switzerland."

" May I look in again soon? "

" Do."

" I'll bring Gavin some evening."

" Oh, I should like to see Gavin again, but—would Aunt Enid like it? "

Hugh shouted. " If he goes to no worse place that his mother doesn't approve, he'll do! But he is a vast improvement on me, Gavin is. You see, he fell in love young, and sticks to it, though the girl doesn't care a straw for him so far, and her father wants her to marry money. It's an awful curse to be in love with the whole sex, as I am. Good-night, little coz! "

He stopped to speak to a pretty girl on the stair, and after strolling about the streets for a time, ended the evening in a music-hall. Wilhelmina would have been sadly disappointed, had she known, but the reader will be more tolerant, recognizing how rarefied the air can be in a block of workmen's houses!

"How *could* I tell him my dream?" Wilhelmina was saying to herself reproachfully. That dream had become the symbol of her whole spiritual life, and she thought in her simplicity that others must see as much in it as she did.

The quakeress broke in on her musings. "Are you never coming to supper?" she asked in a resigned weary voice. She had been working at quadratic equations instead of driving to Kensington Church on the top of the 'bus.

"I quite forgot. Why did you wait for me?"

"How could I tell that your visitor would stay so long? Was it Mr. Dunn again?" she continued coldly.

"Oh, dear, no. It was one of my cousins."

Mr. Dunn was the deformed student at the Institute with whom Wilhelmina had struck up a Platonic friendship. He was a bit of a free-thinker, and it was partly in the effort to drag him in to shore that she had felt the sand yielding beneath her own feet. They lent each other books and had great discussions over them, much to the distress of the quakeress. At first she had pleaded with Wilhelmina in a spirit of sweet reasonableness; but hot summer days in London—days crammed to the brim with intellectual work and competition—are apt to knock a little of the bloom off the most consistent Christian. Wilhelmina, on the other hand, was just at the stage when intelligent youth is most intolerable to those who disagree with its opinions. She talked more about logic than her limited stock of the commodity strictly justified, and when the quakeress assured her that logic would never save her, she either referred darkly to the comparative unimportance of her own salvation, or replied, "That's very true," with a far-away look in her eyes that was trying even to sanctified flesh and blood. Instead of "doubting" things, she was tempted to "regard them as more than controvertible," and she had latterly shown a tendency to "leave her sister when she prayed, her early heaven, her happy views "—that was positively insulting.

The two girls were warmly attached, but at this time each certainly drew out the least amiable side of the other.

"Don't let us argue, dear," Wilhelmina said at last, "we only become strengthened in our own opinions." She thought with a little glow of self-satisfaction how powerless Miss Burnet's creed would have been to affect a man of the world like Hugh.

"Your new views have certainly strengthened me in my ' old old ' ones."

The quotation-marks were too obvious. "And, if you only knew it, your *vis a tergo* has moved me far more than Mr. Dunn's *vis a fronte.*"

The quakeress helped herself to more salad. "Your Latin flourishes, but I am interested to know whether you call that logic."

This was a home-thrust. "I think there is logic in it," Wilhelmina answered, "but I don't mind owning to human nature."

"And pride of intellect?"

"*Pleasure* of intellect, rather. One cannot help enjoying the healthy exercise of a function."

"Yet I think you must admit that greater intellects even than yours have been content to accept the old-fashioned gospel?"

Wilhelmina rose. In her present mood a platitude was more than she could bear. "Good-night," she said. "We must try to remember that we are both honestly seeking the truth."

The quakeress laid her hand affectionately on her worn old Bible. "God has given us the truth."

"Truly—for those who have ears to hear."

I am afraid the reader will think that Wilhelmina too might almost as well have ended the evening in a music-hall!

The window of her room stood wide open, and, after the heat of the day, the night air seemed cool and fresh. Not a star was visible, but the darkness brought its own message of peace. The young girl was amazed at the

wave of petty irritation that had swept over her. "Make
my motives thrice pure!" she prayed. "Deliver me
from pride of intellect!"

And on the other side of the wall Miss Burnet was
praying too. "Make my motives pure! Let no jealousy mingle with my anxiety for her. She is so much
prettier and cleverer than I am! but I do love her
dearly!"

Innocent hearts! When our friends are ungracious
to us, how often might we console ourselves with the
thought that their souls are very white in the eyes of
their Maker!

CHAPTER XLVIII.

SEEKING.

Not for many years of our threescore and ten is it
given to poor human nature to live with such intensity
as Wilhelmina did now. Her very rest was greater activity. Everything about her was surcharged with
meaning. Nature, art, literature, daily life—it was as
if some great magician had touched them all with his
wand and converted them into gold. The world was
burning with divine fire, yet was it not consumed. The
ideal was no longer in the clouds; it was here, around
her, everywhere. How beautiful life was, how sad, how
earnest! Yet in the midst of it Wilhelmina was constantly *seeking;* her heart thrilled with the divine un-
rest of youth. Her whole being seemed to keep step
with the battle-music of the prophets. "*Awake, awake!
put on thy strength, O Zion; put on thy beautiful garments, O Jerusalem, the holy city.*" Or again—"*I too
could now say to myself: Be no longer a chaos, but a
world or even a world-kin. Produce, Produce! Were it
but the pitifullest infinitesimal fraction of a Product,
produce it in God's name. 'Tis the utmost thou hast
in thee; out with it then. Up, Up! Whatsoever thy
hand findeth to do, do it with thy whole might. Work*

*while it is called to-day; the night cometh when no man
can work."*

Yes, the night was coming, and the fields were ripe
unto the harvest. Oh that she were ready to go forth,
and put the sickle in! With that reflection she would
lay aside the prophet, fold the wings of her imagination,
and take up her Euclid or her Virgil.

She was in the happy stage in which one has discarded the doctrines that pain and irk, while retaining
those that are inspiring and beautiful. Some people
contrive to spend all their lives in this stage—often with
excellent result so far as those lives are concerned—
and Wilhelmina never doubted that she would do the
same; but the process of intellectual gravitation had
begun.

Mr. Ellis had exacted a promise that she would not
study much during her holiday, so that she had plenty of
time for thought. All morning she romped with the
little girls, or built sand castles, about which she helped
them to spin the most wonderful romances; but after
dinner the children slept, and then walked with the
maid, while Wilhelmina wandered on the cliffs or in
the pine-woods, sometimes reading, more often meditating, or just drinking in "the open secret" that lay all
around.

It was during this time that she began to wonder
whether the path on which she had entered might not
lead farther than she wished to go. The thought caught
her breath with a vague terror, but she would not on
that account draw back. Indeed, after the first few
days, her fear was not so much that she might wander
far, as that her emotional nature might compound with
something short of "the Truth." Poor little minnow
in the creek! Her great prayer was that she might not
be "led away by sophistry and feeling." "Let me not
find a creed only to lose it again! Let me not drift
into tacit unreasoning belief that will brighten all my
life with a light that must in a few years die out with
me! Give me strength to bear the dark till *Thou* dost
send me a gleam of light!"

One evening she sat looking through a fringe of

trees on the sea at sundown. The day had been very
still, and there was not a breath in the leaves and
branches. Pondering over many problems, she watched
the sun sink below the horizon. "After all, *God is*,"
she said with a sigh. "What else matters?"

For a moment the stillness around her was greater
than before, and then all at once a long shuddering sigh
seemed to shake the trees to their very foundations.
It was unearthly. "*What if there be no God?*" it
seemed to say. For the first time, as by a lightning-
flash, Wilhelmina's mind entertained the conception of
a world without God.

It was a mere unreasoning conception, nothing more;
but for a moment it seemed to blot the life out of the
landscape; the very throbbing heart within her was as
if turned to stone, and the skin rippled on her body like
the surface of glassy water in a breath of wind.

"*What if there be no God?*"

Indignantly Wilhelmina turned to her intellect.
"Do you hear?" she said. "They doubt the existence
of a God. You have never doubted it all these years.
Prove it. Make haste!"

But intellect did not rise to the task with the alacrity
that might have been anticipated. Calling memory to
its aid, intellect began slowly to talk of the argument
from design, the existence of a moral law within us, the
notion of perfection, the end of an infinite cause—
and its words sounded cold and misty and very far
away.

"Manifestations" Wilhelmina had known, but intellect did not seem to make much of them. She was
forced to fall back upon the manifestations vouchsafed
to other men. And, now that one came to think of it,
in what did these consist? How had God revealed Himself in olden times? Not audibly: nor visibly: then
how?

Alas, poor intellect! Alas, poor Wilhelmina!

Of course her mind did not travel so far that day.
As night came on she grew weary of thinking, and the
old beliefs settled down again like homing birds. But
not to stay. Day by day their flights grew longer, more

sustained, and Wilhelmina stood at the window of the ark looking out over troubled waters.

For some time she had kept a conscientious list of "books to be read," and now she duly inscribed therein certain works by Paley and Butler—also a primer of Logic by one Jevons. It is an awful moment in the history of a believing soul when it cries out for Paley and Butler!

A curious memory, too, came back to her of that sunny morning with the racers in the field, when Brentwood was first announced. "Chucked the Church," Hugh had said. "Honest doubt business."

If she and Brentwood could have been friends—only friends, nothing more—how she would have loved a long, long talk with him! It gave her a sense of comfort to think that he had been over this ground before her; and that yet he could talk of "throwing oneself like an unattached sea-weed into the ocean of God"!

Sometimes she dreamed of having a long talk with Mr. Ellis, but that idea she resolutely put from her. That he would be kind and sympathetic she knew only too well, but his influence over her was so great, she wanted so much to please him, that she could not trust herself. This question must be decided fairly, or left open for ever.

At times her depression was so great that it was more than she could do to be bright and cheerful with those about her. Yet she redoubled her efforts to be faithful in life.

> "Having missed this year some personal hope
> I must beware the rather that I miss
> No reasonable duty,"

she said to herself; and, with her eyes strained in the direction where she believed the east window to be, with a thousand ghostly shapes hovering in the arches above her, she still prayed that she might have courage not to light the candles on the altar with her own hand. For of course she had her hours of reaction—hours when she was haunted once more by the spirit—or the letter —of old Windyhaugh, when she almost pictured a jeal-

ous God writing down in wrath the passionate outpour-
ings of her heart and mind: and more frequent far
than these were the hours of childlike longing for the
creed that her fancy pictured, the God that her soul loved.

When she went back to town, she summoned all her
courage to aid her in telling Mr. Ellis that she would
rather work at Natural Science than at Classics. His
obvious disappointment cut her to the quick.

"Your Latin is getting on so well too," he said regretfully. "I thought it really interested you."

"So it does, immensely, and if you strongly advise
it, I will give up my idea; but it is more than my mind,
it is my *soul* that is thirsty for a little science. I will
keep up my Latin and come back to it later; but surely
Biology is the all-important subject just now. I don't
see that anyone has a right to teach, who has not grappled with its problems at first hand. It has simply come
to this, that I can't get on with my life till I know more
about it."

Mr. Ellis smiled. Grappled with its problems!
Here indeed was a child of the age! "Well!" he said,
"have your own way; but don't miss your Matriculation in your enthusiasm. And you must not go to the
Napier for this. I will make enquiries as to the best
place."

So, with trembling feet, as one crosses the threshold
of a darkened room to submit to some mysterious initiation, Wilhelmina entered on the serious study of Biology. She had long since read the famous lay sermon
on The Physical Basis of Life; now she was going to
probe the great mystery for herself. She was surprised
to find the laboratories so cheerful, the demonstrators so
fresh and breezy. The teaching of Biology was just
entering on its heyday: Nature, perhaps, was depicted
as a little gratuitously "red in tooth and claw," and
some painful half-truths were unpleasantly emphasized;
but, fortunately, only a small number of the students had
come, like Wilhelmina, in search of food for their souls.
Sometimes the sheer delight of work carried her on with
a sense of exhilaration that blinded her to every ulterior

consideration: on other days, with lens and scalpel and forceps she strove to find out God.

Her diary at this time was pathetic.

"A sad, sad afternoon at the Zoological Gardens—sad, because of the endless problems that suggest themselves. Can we not have protoplasm and soul *too?* In evolution we must believe, but does it necessarily follow that all species have sprung from a common origin? Yet if a penguin is a link between a bird and a reptile —what next? Surely there is a break between 'animal' and man. Yet the more I think of it, the more incredible it seems that there is such an infinite difference between a man and a dog. The latter as well as the former has thoughts, feelings—love, trust, sorrow. From dogs to lower animals—from those to plants—I might shake hands with a nettle (!) and call him a man and a brother."

Such a common experience it was!—so common that I write of it only as one paints the flowers by the wayside. And yet it was an interesting phase through which the earnest youth of those days passed. It reminds one almost of the crusades, of the search for the Holy Grail—this strange determined resolution to go out in pursuit of the Truth. Solitary souls—groups of two or three—have gone forth in all ages; but here was a whole army with its enthusiasts, its raw recruits, its mercenaries, its troop of mere camp-followers. Well that the army had leaders so noble—leaders to remind them that "obedience is the organ of spiritual knowledge," that "America is here or nowhere." Nay, was not a great seer faithfully reiterating the forgotten words of Pascal—"*Je sais que Dieu a voulu que les vérités divines entrent du cœur dans l'esprit, et non pas de l'esprit dans le cœur. Et de là vient qu'au lieu qu'en parlant des chose humaines, on dit qu'il faut les connaître avant que de les aimer; les Saints, au contraire disent, en parlant des choses divines, qu'il faut les aimer pour les connaître, et qu'on n'entre dans la vérité que par la charité?*"

I shall be told—the charge has been brought against

greater folk than Wilhelmina—that her mind travelled
fast in outgrowing the creed of her childhood. But she
was not one of those people who, at occasional intervals,
take a doctrine up between finger and thumb and regard
it with critical eyes. Her creed seemed to be a matter
of life and death; she fancied that it involved her whole
spiritual existence; it was the one burning question—
the one thing that must not rest. So she slept with it,
woke with it, lived with it, prayed with it; and her mind
travelled—not fast, but constantly.

What cheered her through all was the hope that she
was travelling in a spiral—that a chastening hand was
leading her round the hill. Perhaps in time it would
bring her back to a point of vantage on the side from
which she had started—a point from which she would
see sun and moon in the same position as before, while
her view over land and sea would be infinitely widened
and glorified.

But the chastening hand will not be hurried nor
guided, and he who gives himself up to it must be content to wait and to obey.

CHAPTER XLIX.

AN ORDINATION.

" Does Miss Galbraith live here? "

" Yes." The quakeress stared—civilly. She was
ceasing to be surprised at Wilhelmina's visitors, but here
again was a new type. " She is engaged just now, but
I think she will be at liberty in a few minutes. Will you
come in? "

Miss Evelyn was ushered into what was really the
kitchen of the tiny flat, though the girls made it their
dining-room as well. " What charming quarters you
have! and how spick and span! There is nothing like a
bonâ fide kitchen fire on a really cold evening." Miss
Evelyn loosened her furs and ensconced herself comfortably.

"I hope Miss Galbraith is well?"

"Yes, thank you. She has a bad cold."

A rippling laugh heralded the response. "Oh! I thought it was only we poor stage-folk who called *that* being well."

Stage-folk! The quakeress turned pale. And this was a friend of Wilhelmina's!

Fortunately at this moment Wilhelmina herself entered the room. It seemed to Miss Evelyn that she looked very far from well. Her face was thin, her eyes unnaturally bright, and there was a vivid red spot on each cheek.

"How kind of you to find me out!" she said. "Come into my room."

"You have not been to see me since Christmas. It is quite time somebody found you out," said the actress cordially. "My dear girl, you are knocking yourself up."

"Oh, no, I am not. I did work very hard just before my Matriculation, but that is over now, and I have scraped through."

"Well done! Why, Vilma, I know lots of *men* who can't get through their Matric."

Wilhelmina smiled. "It is a comfort," she said.

"Yet you don't look exuberant."

"I am worried to-night. Talk to me. Tell me something nice."

"That is possible—oddly enough. I have news of your father. A mutual friend met him and his companion in Egypt. That is partly what brought me here to-night. I know he it not a first-rate correspondent, and in any case it is always interesting to hear an outsider's opinion."

"Yes?" Wilhelmina's eyes were all impatience.

"You don't hear from him too often, I suppose?"

"No. He sent me fifty pounds the other day." She tried to say this in an easy incidental fashion. "Egypt! They will never get round the world at this rate."

"I don't think they will. But they are prospering famously. My—correspondent says your father looks well, and seems very bright and self-confident."

22

" I am so glad."

Miss Evelyn read a few extracts from a foreign letter.
" I would not try to hurry him home if I were you.
This sort of thing is so good for him."

Wilhelmina laughed softly. Was she at all likely to
hurry him home?

" You are very fond of him, *petite?* "

" Who wouldn't be? "

Miss Evelyn had a gift for frank brutality, but she
paused before the next question. " Were you so fond of
him in the Bayswater days? "

Wilhelmina flushed hotly. "*It was not his fault,*"
she said after a pause, with the air of a counsel for the
defence. " He did help us a great deal at first, but the
case was hopeless. My stepmother was more than good
to me, but—she always thought our misfortunes were an
accident. She took the house at Bayswater while my
father was abroad. It was not his fault. The case was
hopeless."

Miss Evelyn fell a-musing. " I like to hear you
stand up for him," she said, " but now that you are a
woman, it won't do for you to go on spoiling him. My
belief is that most of his inconsistencies are due to the
fact that Provvy meant him for a good man—a deliri-
ously, melodramatically good man—and that everybody
insisted on spoiling him. He is my very dear friend,
Vilma, but he is selfish, you know. His own people
always asked too much of him, and, when he turned to
the circle of his choice, they asked too little. It was
demoralizing. Do you see what I mean? "

Wilhelmina did not answer. She saw only too well,
but to say so would have seemed disloyal to the absent
father.

Miss Evelyn went on, musing. " In other words, he
is like a man who has plenty of silver in his pockets.
His friends keep asking him for gold, and, after worrying because he hasn't got it to give, he suddenly dis-
covers that there are lots of pleasant people who will
be abundantly satisfied with copper. Then he had a
great misfortune in his youth. That nearly wrecked his
life."

Wilhelmina seemed to have heard a rumour to this effect. " I wish you would tell me about that," she said, " if you think he wouldn't object."

" I can't. I never knew the details, and now they are buried for ever. Even Ronald refused to say much about it. But it made me sorry for your father always. How hot your hands are, child! Tell me what it is that is worrying you."

It was some moments before the young girl replied.

" Such a horrible thing has happened!" she said, impetuously, at last. " The friend who was with me just now—a woman who lives in the flat below—is in such trouble! She had a daughter—such a bonny kitten-like thing——"

Only the old old story—of sin and shame! Yet a story which, when first understood, forms an epoch in the life of a generous girl.

Miss Evelyn was disappointed. She did not understand impersonal grief. " So," she said calmly, " you have just got to that particular stage."

Wilhelmina raised reproachful eyes.

" Oh, I know you think me a cynical brute. Ten or fifteen years hence some sweet young girl will come to you—her eyes just open to the wrongs of her sex. Think of me then, Vilma! "

Wilhelmina's eyes blazed. " How *damnably* selfish we good women are! "

" I admit the first impeachment, not the second. What have I done that you should call me good? Is all this a revelation to you, little one? "

" I have known about this particular case for a fortnight, if that is what you mean. The mother came to consult me to-night. She has just found out that the man is—a *gentleman!* "

" That seems satisfactory so far." Miss Evelyn reflected. " I thought you were initiated early. I remember seeing a bonny bairn in a cottage near Windyhaugh, whom your parlour-maid introduced to me as—well—' *une petite indiscrétion de sa jeunesse* '! "

" That was different. Jane was old—or seemed so to me. Molly is a child—seventeen! "

Miss Evelyn shrugged her shoulders. "She is not the first."

"I know. That is my point. Oh, Pauline, what can we *do?*"

"Lend a helping hand here and there in an individual case. It will probably be rejected with scorn. The evil is eternal."

"*Then there is no God!*"

The actress shrugged her shoulders. "That's as may be. I have no reliable information. I am sorry to disturb your illusions, Vilma; but I decline to spout rosewater sentiment for the benefit of a married woman!"

There was silence.

"What on earth did the mother come and harrow *you* for, I wonder?" said Miss Evelyn sharply at last.

Wilhelmina looked up indignantly. "Because she is my *friend*. Because I *care*."

"I suppose it is as much as my place is worth to suggest that the girl may have been partially to blame?"

"To blame?" Wilhelmina rested a crimson face on her two hands, and looked doggedly across at her friend. "Where are we to draw the line of blame? A perilous path is the path of love!"

"Oh, I know that! Crossing Niagara on a tightrope isn't in it!"

"But the man had one sure guide. *He knew quite well what it must mean for her.* God do so to me and more also if I ever forget my sisterhood with women like that!"

She rose to pace up and down the room, pausing at last before a reproduction of Guido's Cenci on the wall. "I keep that there," she said slowly, "to remind me of —what women have suffered! When life runs smoothly, and men are chivalrous, and everyone is kind—one is apt to forget——!"

"I will give you a Bacchante to hang opposite. We can't have you grow one-sided. How did you come by that?"

"Hugh gave it to me. He knew I admired it."

"*Hugh?*" Miss Evelyn looked startled. "Does *he* come here?"

" Sometimes."

" He is a good generous boy; but I fear he is going the pace." Miss Evelyn's eyes returned to the picture. " Do you know the story ? "

Wilhelmina sighed. For the moment all the fathom-less woe of Guido's conception was in her eyes. " Is there any sorrow like unto thy sorrow ? " she said. " Poor child! Poor child! "

" Have you read Shelley ? "

The young girl shuddered. " Yes, I thought I should never sleep again; but the last part is magnificent— soul-stirring! " She drew herself into an attitude of simple unselfconscious dignity, glancing over her shoulder with a chilly courteous smile that only seemed to accentuate the depth of woe beneath it.

> " ' Give yourself no unnecessary pain,
> My dear Lord Cardinal. Here, mother, tie
> My girdle for me, and bind up this hair
> In any simple knot ; ay, that does well,
> And yours I see is coming down. How often
> Have we done this for one another ! now
> We shall not do it any more. My Lord,
> We are quite ready. Well, 'tis very well.' "

" *Vilma!* Have you ever acted before ? "

" Occasionally. I belong to a Shakespeare Reading Club. Was I acting now? I beg your pardon. What an inhospitable wretch I am! " She laughed and held out both hands to her friend. " Do you remember the princely feast you gave me one night when I was starving ? May I retaliate with—with—let me see—! Bread and cheese, a glass of draught ale from the public-house, and—oh, I would make you such a lovely omelette! "

Miss Evelyn looked serious. " The omelette carries it," she said—" especially if I may come into the kitchen and see you make it."

" Why, of course! Eggs are becoming possible again even in London. If only I had Windyhaugh air to beat into them! "

The omelette was a great success, but it did not tempt Wilhelmina's appetite. She talked gaily, how-ever, all through the meal, bridging over, for the moment, even the gulf between Miss Evelyn and the quakeress.

"Now I am going to see you safe into your room," said Miss Evelyn firmly. "You are *fey* to-night, as your old Ann would say. You must promise to go to bed at once."

Wilhelmina led the way. "Yes, I shall be glad to go, my head aches. It was good of you to come—and bring me news of my father."

"You know, Vilma, I was half disappointed when I heard of your engagement. You had an influence over your father that no one else ever had."

"Miss Evelyn! *I?*"

"You, little one. You were making him human— drawing out the father in him." Miss Evelyn thought of all the child must have suffered in the Bayswater days. "He must have been surprised to find his daughter so generous."

Wilhelmina bent low over the fire. It was in moments of praise and appreciation like this that her heart *insisted* on a God. In her humility she felt that she must get down at the feet of someone!

"Miss Evelyn," she said, as her friend was leaving the room, "I ought not—even in the heat of the moment —to have said what I did."

Miss Evelyn drew down her brows in perplexity. "You have made so many memorable remarks in the course of the evening——"

"I said if the evil was eternal there was no God. Even if it were true, it is too awful a thing to say."

"Oh! All right. I am not susceptible, you know. And besides—pardon me, dear—the remark was not original!"

Wilhelmina laughed feebly. "I own the softness of the impeachment," she said. "Good-night."

Before leaving the house Miss Evelyn paused at the kitchen door. "I hope you will persuade your friend to stay in bed to-morrow," she said. "She seems feverish. I will call in the morning to see how she is."

Miss Burnet's manner froze. If Wilhelmina was

going to be sick, it was most undesirable that she should have "stage-folk" about her. She was destined to be sorely tried, poor girl, for next day the patient was so unlike herself that Miss Evelyn bundled her up in rugs, and announced an intention of carrying her off to her own rooms in a cab.

In vain the quakeress protested. "I may at least call to enquire for her?" she said almost defiantly at last.

"Oh, certainly." Miss Evelyn took a card from her exquisite filigree case. "I can't promise that you will see her."

"Then let me have one minute alone with her now." Miss Evelyn frowned and left the room.

"Wilhelmina, dear," said the girl in a trembling voice, "if you are not better in a day or two, do let me send my minister to see you! I know he would come; he is very kind, and he would explain away your difficulties. I am afraid I have been horribly unsympathetic. You say I drove you farther from the truth; but he is wiser than I am, and he would help you. Indeed, indeed he would!" Her affection, her earnestness, were unmistakable.

Wilhelmina's head ached acutely. A wretched sensation of *malaise* permeated her whole being. The thought of discussing any subject on earth was intolerable, and a discussion with Miss Burnet's minister——!

"Dear," she said, "I may have said anything in a moment of irritation. You have been kind and good to me always; but I shall be all right soon. We——" Her head swam. She wondered whether Mr. Brentwood had felt like this when she had worried him with her shy caresses on that memorable railway journey.

"Time's up," said Miss Evelyn's pleasant voice. "Now, little one!"

"You will keep an eye on Molly," Wilhelmina said feebly. "Ask her to tea some day. Would you mind calling her to say Good-bye to me now?"

An hour later Wilhelmina was at rest in a bed that enlarged for ever her views of comfort and luxury. Miss Evelyn's own hands had administered a cup of beef-tea, and had laid a cold compress on her aching head. The fire burned cheerily; the window admitted a glimpse of crisp March sunshine.

Wilhelmina was able to think a little now. She certainly felt very ill. Did the quakeress suppose she was going to die? If so, where was she going?—or was she going anywhere at all? Years before, she had faced death calmly with her head gently pillowed on a creed that rendered her all-secure. What if the old doctrines were all true, and the experiences of the last few months had been a temptation of the devil? She felt her nerve slipping away from her.

The arrival of the doctor interrupted her train of thought. Of course he said little, wisely declining to commit himself at this stage.

"I don't think it is anything infectious," he said to Miss Evelyn afterwards; "but you have run an extraordinary risk in bringing her here."

"I know." Miss Evelyn nodded. "It is one of the comforts of a life of leisure that one can afford to run extraordinary risks."

Wilhelmina dozed a good deal during the afternoon. Towards night she felt worse, and a panic of apprehension came upon her. As a man in a burning house is prompted to lay his unnerved hands on the most nondescript possessions, so was she tempted to lay hold of any creed that might avail her now. For hours she lay perfectly still in a ferment of inward strife. Then she made her choice.

"I must have faith enough not to try to believe," she said wearily. "If Mr. Ellis—if a clergyman—could help me, God can help me much more. Oh, if there be a God——!

"'Into His hand I commit my spirit.'"

Ah, that sharp, threatening illness of adolescence— what an ordination it is! How many bright spirits have passed through it! Just when the world is all aglow with ideals that have not been realized—the curtain falls. Sometimes—as in Wilhelmina's case—it drops to rise again; but alas, alas for the beautiful lives on which it falls for ever!

What happens behind the dread curtain that is proof against all our longings? Do they put out the lights, set aside the stage fittings, and send the players home? Or does fresh music arise on a new scene—a new act—that far transcends the things that have gone before?

God knows! God knows!

CHAPTER L.

RETURNING LIFE.

"What I want to be at," said Miss Evelyn, "is—the end of all this?"

They were sitting on the sea-front at Hastings some weeks after the onset of Wilhelmina's illness.

"Well, of course I hope to take my degree."

"And then?"

"Then I suppose I should have no difficulty in getting a situation as science mistress in a girls' school."

Miss Evelyn drew designs with the end of her umbrella. "I know several schoolmistresses," she said. "What a life it is! Grind, grind, grind!"

A flash of the old enthusiasm lighted the young girl's face. "If they make you feel that, they have no right to be teachers."

"You will just be ill again. The doctor said the touch of congestion of the lungs was not nearly enough to account for your weakness and prostration. You must have been working far too hard."

"It wasn't that. It was life. The current was too strong for me. But I shall never again have to go through all I have gone through in the last year."

Miss Evelyn looked surprised. "I should have thought the year before that was worse."

"Oh, no!"

"Wouldn't things be easier for yourself, Vilma, if you trusted me a little more? Do you think I can't

see that you are breaking your heart for Mr. Brentwood?"

Wilhelmina raised large eyes of innocent surprise.
" It wasn't that," she said simply.

" Then all I can say is, that you are a cold-hearted
little brute. Do you know what men are made of,
child? It must be more than a year and a half since
your wedding."

" Two and a half years more," thought Wilhelmina.
She had long since learned that even in Scotland a divorce is not to be had for the asking. " Mr. Brentwood
is only thirty-two," she said. " Lots of men don't marry
before thirty-five. Even that is not so very old."

Miss Evelyn did not guess the idea in her mind.
" So Brentwood is to wait till your ladyship takes her
degree, is he?"

Wilhelmina smiled sadly. " When one has made a
big mistake that can't be put right," she said, " the only
thing is to begin afresh on a new track."

" Big fiddlestick! It was no more a big mistake than
ninety-nine marriages out of a hundred. My dear baby,
you must stop crying for the moon. Any woman can
make any man fall in love with her. Your business is
to make Brentwood fall in love with you. He is as
much in love with you now as most husbands are with
their wives, but you ' ask to be let alone,' start a crowd
of fresh interests, and deliberately elect to drift apart.
What do you think is going to happen?—a special inter-
vention of Providence?"

Wilhelmina did not answer. She had a very definite
idea what was going to happen. At the end of the four
years Brentwood would get his divorce unless—unless—— But the alternative was so unlikely that she
would not allow herself to dream of it.

Villette lay open on her knee. She had been reading novels again since her illness, partly because her
mind was equal to nothing else, partly because she was
afraid of growing " cold and hard " if she closed her
eyes too completely to the romantic side of life. She
. was glad Miss Evelyn could not see a passage she had
read and re-read till she knew it by heart.

"I kept a place for him, too—a place of which I never took the measure, either by rule or compass. I think it was like the tent of Peri-Banou. All my life long I carried it folded in the hollow of my hand—yet, released from that hold and restriction, I know not but its innate capacity for expanse might have magnified it into a tabernacle for a host."

"Brentwood called to enquire for you repeatedly while you were ill," said Miss Evelyn calmly.

The colour leapt into Wilhelmina's face, and all the muscular power of which she was capable tugged at the sinews of her hand. Would the tent expand in spite of her?

"I wanted him to see you the last time, but he said, if you would allow him, he would call when you returned to town."

The colour died away, and the tense hand relaxed. Of course Miss Evelyn had manœuvred the whole thing. Oh, if people would only leave her and Brentwood alone! Surely circumstances brought enough pressure to bear on him without this well-meant interference.

"Vilma"—Miss Evelyn's voice was low and vibrating. "You will find it takes so little—so little—to bring him back."

Wilhelmina looked up coldly. The tent was thoroughly manageable now, neatly packed in her tense young hand. "I am afraid the little thing will be wanting," she said.

But it never was easy for her to play an ungracious part. "Forgive me, dear," she said. "Indeed I don't forget how much I owe you. I hope some day you will give me a chance to prove it."

Day by day the colour returned to Wilhelmina's cheeks, and with it came the old delight in life. The return of spring brought her a joy that was almost ecstasy. She could have kissed the budding trees and radiant yellow flowers. The subtle scent of the fruit-blossom tingled along her nerves. How blind she had been every year till now! Behold the great miracle! For the moment she had ceased to worry over the problems of life.

How good the world was! How sweet just to be alive!

"I haven't felt so well for years," she said. "I want to do something outrageous. I feel as if I could sing in the Albert Hall, or jump through hoops in the circus. But for you I should be a haggard wreck, clammily toiling to and from my classes."

"I am glad I was at leisure to come down here. But I have a bit of work that will take me back to town in a day or two. I have promised to organise some amateur theatricals for Mrs. Cavendish."

"What fun! Oh, Miss Evelyn, do you think you could smuggle me in to see them? I am hungering— simply hungering for a frolic."

"Of course you shall come. By the way, you told me you had acted yourself occasionally. I want to hear about it. What was your first rôle? Lady Macbeth?"

"Your Highness is pleased to jest. It was a horrid little soubrette part that I hated."

"Did you do it well?"

"They said so. I know I enjoyed it when the time came. They spoiled me so that that evening was a turning-point in my life. I began to see that I could be—well, as nice as other girls, and I let myself go— took off my bearing-rein, so to speak."

Miss Evelyn looked at her critically. "You were born with a good voice production," she said. "Mrs. Dalrymple has it too, and your father speaks well. Suppose we read a bit now? I have two copies of The Cenci here. We will read the last act. There is nothing too dreadful in that. I thought you did the closing lines admirably the other evening. I will take all the other parts. You will find your hands full with Beatrice."

"Overflowing I fancy."

So she thought when Miss Evelyn began. Giacomo's opening words created an atmosphere of tragedy that affected Wilhelmina profoundly, and the atmosphere grew denser with every line. To the very marrow of her bones she felt the gloom that—like the contracting chamber of the Inquisition—was hemming in, crushing, choking that vivid young life. The sorrows of her sex had touched Wilhelmina very nearly of late; and now her youth and her womanhood alike stretched out their arms across the ages to Beatrice—supreme type of the suffering of both—" God's angel ministered upon by fiends." To the tips of her fingers she felt the shrinking of the fair young flesh from the torture of the rack, the human horror of untimely death, of the " cold, rotting, wormy ground." Her heart thrilled with sympathy in the awful uncertainty as to what might lie beyond " the only world we know," in the inability to accept conventional consolations. How peaceful a death would her own have been in comparison!—a death made easy by every luxury and kindness—yet how she had shrunk even from that! Strong men might well have been unmanned by Beatrice's fate, yet how sublimely, how simply, she rose to it in the end! In Beatrice, Wilhelmina found expression for the storm and stress, the scepticism, the paganism, the passionate seeking, the forced renunciation and potential heroism of her own adolescence.

She spoilt the fine climax by feeling it too much, but that was a fault that Miss Evelyn could forgive. From a professional point of view, Wilhelmina's rendering was crude and sorely wanting in technique, but it was all alive. She really was expressing a personality. There was not another girl in London who would have acted Beatrice Cenci just like that.

There was a long silence when they had finished. " Well," said the actress at last, " you will do that for me a month hence? "

" *Beatrice?* At amateur theatricals? "

Miss Evelyn was in no hurry to respond. Mrs. Cavendish had received her more cordially than had any of Ronald's other friends; and, when Ronald died, Mrs. Cavendish was one of those who had not gracefully dropped her. Miss Evelyn meant this entertainment to be a success. Mrs. Cavendish herself made an admirable Lady Teazle, and one of her friends a more than passable Juliet; but the circle for whom she had to cater was advanced in its views, and was more or less inured to the histrionic triumphs of Mrs. Cavendish and

her friend. A new and charming amateur as Beatrice
Cenci would be worth many Juliets and Lady Teazles.

Moreover Miss Evelyn did not consider that she was
sacrificing her protégée. Wilhelmina's interpretation
of the part would, she felt sure, disarm hostile criticism:
it was pure and strong in Shelley's conception. Her
name would not be given; her relatives had no right to
resent anything she did, and if Brentwood was angry
and indignant—so much the better! He wanted something to rouse him. This would rouse him like a thun-
derclap. Wilhelmina would awake to find herself famous, and her husband at her feet. Nothing but passionate wooing would win her now, and passionate
wooing she should have.

But not a word of all this did Miss Evelyn say. She
knew her audience better.

"They are not ordinary theatricals," she said at last.
"Mrs. Cavendish is a very cultured woman, and Ibsen
is a household word in their circle. I think it is a mistake to suppose that anything we *do well* is too good to
give to the world."

"I thought I did it abominably."

"So you did, in one sense. You need a deal of
coaching; but you have hit the soul of the thing."

"And in public——"

"I am not asking you to do it in the Albert Hall, or
even in a circus. It is only a charity performance in
a private drawing-room."

"But the story is too horrible."

"There is nothing too horrible in the fifth act. You
needn't tell me you don't think it a noble conception."

"But it was so mean of Beatrice to let those men be
executed."

"Oh, my dear child, we hadn't all the advantage of
being brought up by a pious grandmother at Windyhaugh!" Miss Evelyn paused. "Did you ever think
of the self-sacrifice involved in an actor's life? He
often has to be a dark shadow that someone else may be
a high light. I remember your father consoling me with
that reflection when I was so young—so young!"

Wilhelmina's face kindled.

"Think of Beatrice's training. You can't expect her to possess all your virtues."

"Oh, indeed, I have done lots of nasty mean things myself in my time. This would be a just expiation. I should feel like poor Hester standing in the market-place with an A on her breast."

And so it came about that Wilhelmina yielded. She knew nothing of the world and its prejudices. She had no social circle to reflect her actions like a mirror. The charity appealed to her; she wanted to please Miss Evelyn; but above all, the youth and force and spring-time in her veins hungered to find expression, to take some tangible form. She scarcely realized the awful keynote of the drama: for her it was mainly the tragedy of blighted ideals, of unfulfilled youth.

CHAPTER LI.

BEATRICE CENCI.

MRS. CAVENDISH'S beautiful house in Mayfair was a brilliant spectacle on the night of the entertainment. The great drawing-rooms were decorated with bold floral designs, and, from the outset, the buzz of excitement among the audience foretold that the evening would be a success.

"Don't look at the people," Miss Evelyn said. "Imagine you are still at the rehearsal." She was almost more nervous than Wilhelmina herself. In proportion to the audacity of the subject would the failure be— if The Cenci failed.

Wilhelmina felt as if she had stepped through the portal into another world. She had never been in society before; a schoolgirls' tea-party was her standard of gaiety; and the flash of diamonds, the fragrance of the flowers, the appealing note of the music, the radiance of the whole spectacle as she peeped from behind the scenes—intoxicated her. She forgot the existence of good and evil, and was conscious only of beauty. This was not the world she knew, nor was she Wilhelmina. The ordinary conditions of time and space were suspended. Surely in a world like this one could do anything.

A great hush of expectation preceded the rising of the curtain on the last act of The Cenci. The first two scenes went off more or less conventionally. Wilhelmina had been well coached, but she did not know the Beatrice who confronted Marzio with the spirit that defied all ordinary moral canons, and her acting wanted the ring of reality. Perhaps the idea of Hester in the market-place still lurked in the background of her mind, and few things could have been less compatible with Shelley's conception.

She looked very charming, however. Miss Evelyn had thought more of beauty than of rigid historical accuracy in designing the soft white silk robe that responded to every movement of the rounded limbs; and Wilhelmina was just at the age when the human countenance answers like a perfect instrument to the life behind, when the moon face of youth is gone, and dominant thoughts and moods and aspirations have not yet had time to carve relentless lines.

It was in the third scene that she first got her chance. She looked very pathetic in her sleep of exhaustion, and when she woke unwillingly—all forgetful of her grim surroundings—she was for the moment the very type of innocent childhood. Nothing could surpass the simplicity with which she smiled on her brother and said—

> " ' I was just dreaming
> That we were all in Paradise.' "

And then the tragedy closed in.

The young actress rose to it well. She was indignant, defiant, hopeful, terrified, suppliant, tender, all, as it were, in a flash; and when, in that atmosphere of imminent doom, she took her feeble, shrinking mother in .her arms, and, with the look of wistful yearning that was never quite absent from Wilhelmina's face, crooned the "dull old" song—there were moist eyes among the lookers-on.

> " ' Have I forgot the words?
> Faith! they are sadder than I thought they were.' "

The last scene was the most difficult, but it was the one for which Wilhelmina had undertaken the part. It was in this that she found real self-expression.

She began with fine dignity—

> " ' I hardly dare to fear
> That thou bringst other news than a just pardon.' "

Then in a moment, came the reaction into sheer pagan girlish terror.

> " ' O
> My God! Can it be possible I have
> To die so suddenly? So young to go
> Under th' obscure, cold, rotting, wormy ground;
> To be nailed down into a narrow place;
> To see no more sweet sunshine; hear no more
> Blithe voice of living thing; muse not again
> Upon familiar thoughts, sad, yet thus lost—
> How fearful! To be nothing! or to be—
> What? Oh, where am I? Let me not go mad!
> Sweet Heaven, forgive weak thoughts! If there should be
> No God, no Heaven, no Earth, in the void world;
> The wide, grey, lampless, deep, unpeopled world!' "

Lucretia's timid conventional words force her daughter to pull herself together, and Wilhelmina did full justice to that rise into self-possession, that quiet acceptance—pagan still—of inevitable doom, that fine refusal to gloss it over with words that for the young victim meant nothing.

> " ' 'Tis past!
> Whatever comes, my heart shall sink no more;
> And yet, I know not why, your words strike chill;
> How tedious, false and cold seem all things.
>
> .   .   .   .
>
> I am cut off from the only world I know,
> From light and life and love in youth's sweet prime,
> You do well telling me to trust in God:
> I hope I do trust in Him. In whom else
> Can any trust? and yet my heart is cold.' "

23

The restrained tenderness of Beatrice's farewell to her young brother brought tears to many eyes, and then came the fine, simple, exquisite climax that had so deeply impressed Miss Evelyn two months before.

When the curtain fell, some of the audience were appreciative enough to check the applause of the merely enthusiastic. Miss Evelyn's great *coup* had been a success.

It was an amateur study, of course, and yet it possessed points that a finished professional performance might have lacked. Wilhelmina acted the part with intense feeling, with instinctive purity, and with an intellectual breadth that was more surprising than either. Of course there were those who said, " *C'est magnifique, mais ce n'est pas la Cenci*": one man of extraordinarily fine perceptions was heard even to expresss a doubt as to whether the attractive young actress knew what the play was all about, but no one doubted that she was a fine representative of the—

> "fair sister . . . in whom
> Men wondered how such loveliness and wisdom
> Did not destroy each other "—

a finer representative still of the youth that "could be bounded in a nutshell, and count itself a king of infinite space"—did not cruel fate inflict "bad dreams."

The days were just beginning when a young woman was expected to "do something" if she would justify her existence. Wilhelmina had done something with a vengeance.

Miss Evelyn had invited Hugh to the last rehearsal, and he had been so much impressed that he had persuaded his mother to go to the performance. He felt sure that she would not recognize her niece, and he reflected that, when the act was over, he could use his own discretion about telling her.

When the great drawing-rooms blazed into light again, he was relieved to see the tears in her eyes.

"Poor little soul!" she said. "What a pathetic face!"

" Do you know who it is, Mother? It is Wilhelmina."

Her voice sank to an almost inaudible whisper.
" Wilhelmina Galbraith? "

He nodded.

" *Well!* " Enid fell into a vortex of thought, in
which all her vague and discordant notions of her niece
whirled about her. Then her cynicism came upper-
most. " So this is what she calls ' walking in the
twilight! ' Or has the Lord changed His mind concerning her? "

Of course Hugh had read that historic document.
" Don't be down on her, *Mater*," he said. " This was all
Miss Evelyn's doing. She is awfully humble, really."

Enid did not answer immediately. The buzz of appreciation all around was quite unmistakable. " Is she
coming here? "

" No. Nothing would induce her to. She is strictly
incog. She is going home."

" Then you had better take her home. Tell her to
come and see me. Stop a minute. It really is very
awkward. What a pity she married that young man!
And then this play—it is rather dreadful isn't it? Tell
her I will write."

Hugh was off like a flash.

He found Wilhelmina on the threshold of the dress-
ing-room, surrounded by a group of fellow actors. Their
frankly-expressed admiration was opening her eyes for
the first time to the magnitude of the thing she had
attempted, and her startled eyes fell on her cousin with
evident relief.

" May I take you home, Vilma? " he asked. " That
is, if you are sure you won't stay to supper."

" Thank you very much. I will be ready in five
minutes."

Of course Miss Evelyn had taken care that Brentwood should be at the performance. He needed no urg-
ing when he heard that the last act of The Cenci was
to form part of the programme. " It will be a fiasco,"
he said; but he went. He was not the only man who

paid a fancy price for the sake of seeing a young gentlewoman who was willing to act the part of Beatrice.

Wilhelmina had never looked so beautiful in her life
as when she came on the stage. Miss Evelyn had taken
care of that. Brentwood did not recognize her, but he
saw the resemblance in a moment—and, with a sudden
sense of shock, every drop of blood seemed driven back
to the core of him. Was this an older Miss Galbraith
of whom he had never heard? In that remarkable family no mystery would be incredible.

The second scene was over before he was fully conscious of all that he saw and heard. Trying to recall
it afterwards, he told himself that it was a " very effective " performance; but the awakening in the prison cell
went straight to his heart. *Could* this be Wilhelmina?
He remembered how Miss Evelyn had threatened to urge
her to go on the stage.

From that moment the young actress held him spell-
bound; her sudden heartbreaking—

"O
My God ! Can it be possible—?"

sent a thrill through his very vitals. Obviously this girl
had a gift of throwing her own personality into the
part. It was Wilhelmina—how she had grown!—how
she had felt the burden of the mystery! But who in
the world was responsible for her acting the part of
Beatrice Cenci?

All through the last scene he thought her acting
wonderful; the *paganism* of it seemed to him a master-
piece; and when the curtain fell on that childlike figure,
standing so proudly knee-deep in the river of death, he
thought of how Wilhelmina had stood years before with
the waves tumbling idly beneath her feet. " ' For I am
persuaded——' " Ah me !

Brentwood gulped down a sob. If this was his wife
—it was infamous—infamous—that she should have
been allowed to act such a part. If she was not his wife
—this " fine piece of nature "—*how he could have loved
her!*

" Quite an amateur," he heard Miss Evelyn saying.

"In fact she is a science student. Oh, no, she would never forgive me if I revealed her name. She is very shy and retiring—one of the people who only find their own personality by losing it. Such a sweet girl!"

The cheap truth of this maddened Brentwood; but at that moment Miss Evelyn advanced to him. "Pity we hadn't a pair of gloves on it," she said in a low voice. "What do you think of it?"

It was a second or two before he could reply. The lines of his face were as hard as those of an old doge. "Is she coming back to this place?"

"No, she is going home."

Without another word he turned on his heel, leaving Miss Evelyn just a little alarmed by his manner.

Wilhelmina had made ready as speedily as might be, and, with a pleasant sense of protection, had taken her cousin's arm. In his other hand Hugh carried a glorious bunch of *Bride* and *Niphetos* roses.

Brentwood was sick with fury. "Pardon me," he said, "I am going to take this lady home."

Hugh turned on him with a defiant scowl.

Wilhelmina's heart stood still, and then throbbed as if it would burst. Fortunately the tension of the evening had not yet relaxed. "I asked my cousin to take me home," she said quietly; but, womanlike, she trembled for very loyalty to her husband. "I shall be at home to-morrow evening if you care to call." She gave him the address, and turned away on the arm of the "he-minx."

"It was stunning, Vilma, simply stunning. Do you know the *Mater* was in tears?"

He had to repeat the remark before she heard it, and then her face burned. "Was Aunt Enid there? How —horrified she must have been!"

"Not a bit of it. She wants you to come and see her; but she is going to write."

Wilhelmina shook her head ruefully. "I am afraid she will think better of it before to-morrow."

"Nonsense!"

He did not speak again till they were up in her sitting-room, and then his mood had quite changed. He sat gloomily for a time with his head buried in his hands. "So you do care for him all the time, Vilma," he said.

"For whom?"

"Oh, come now! I clearly see there will be a reconciliation to-morrow evening, and then—good-bye to our pleasant friendship!"

She drew herself up. "How can there be a reconciliation when there has been no quarrel? We made a mistake; that is all. Is it because you are a man that you are so unable to understand? Do you think a woman capable of no emotion save one? Is it likely, after all that has come and gone, that I should meet Mr. Brentwood quite as an ordinary acquaintance? Of course I haven't had time to forget, but—but all that doesn't mean *love*."

Hugh did not answer. He would have given a good deal to know how much had "come and gone."

"Any news of Uncle George?" he said at last.

"He was sailing for India from Suez when he last wrote. He seemed in capital spirits."

"Did he really? Yes, I always feel that he has got hold of some secret, if one could only get at it."

"What kind of secret?"

"Well, there must be something that makes it worth his while to *go on*. Here am I not half his age—and I have just about squeezed the orange."

"Nonsense, Hugh!"

"It is true. Some fellows fall back on religion or a woman; but neither religion nor woman seems to pan out with me. You know, Vilma, at the time of Ronald's death I was awfully low—made up my mind to reform and all that kind of thing. I really did pray for strength to—to resist temptation, as the pious folk say, but the strength never came—nary a bit! You've no notion what a bad lot I am."

His lips quivered. Did he wish to make her his mother confessor?

If so, Wilhelmina missed the opportunity. She smiled sadly. When one thought of all the great souls who had agonized in vain, it seemed ridiculous to hope that Hugh's casual little prayers should meet with any answer. And yet, if they met with none, how could he gain strength to " go on ? "

" You did not pray hard enough, Hugh."

She was in no mood for such talk to-night. She wanted to think of her success, to wonder how it had affected her husband. Hugh might have said with Beatrice—

"And yet, I know not why, your words strike chill;
How tedious, false and cold seem all things !"

" Uncle George doesn't look as if he prayed—much. Religion hasn't done the trick for him, nor has any one woman. Yet he goes on, and you say he still enjoys it."

" He has a great many interests in life."

Hugh rose to his feet with a whimsical smile. " So you recommend a course of lectures at the Royal Institution ? No, no, Vilma, it won't do. Good-night. You are no end of a genius, dear. It was simply first-rate. *Good-bye.*"

Well ! The leaf was turned. This was his last visit to Cousin Vilma. Again he saw Brentwood's white furious face, and felt Wilhelmina's trembling hand on his arm. Of course they would kiss and be friends, and in their joint life no place would be found for a sinner like him. He hated Brentwood, and Brentwood did not consider him fit to tie a decent woman's shoe-lace. Wilhelmina had changed too. That momentary meeting had been sufficient to remove her a hundred miles from him and his poor little strivings.

Well, thank God that all women were not clever and high-minded and—in love with other men ! Thank God for a soft rosy kitten-like thing who asked no questions, and looked up with worshipping eyes !

CHAPTER LII.

THE INTERVIEW.

" THERE is absolutely no use in trying to forecast an interview of this kind," Harley said to himself. " The only thing one can be sure of is that it will be entirely different from anything one anticipated."

He resolved to banish the whole subject from his mind, with the natural result that he thought of little else till he found himself at Wilhelmina's door. He was ten minutes before his time, and she had not returned from a class, but the quakeress ushered him at once into the pretty room.

It chanced to be looking unusually pretty, for Miss Evelyn had driven over in the afternoon with a quantity of flowers and of congratulatory notes that had been left at her house for Wilhelmina. " Quite worthy of a lady in the variety line," Brentwood reflected bitterly. He even thought for a moment that he could say this to Wilhelmina. Many a pointed remark and repartee has been lost to the world because it came to life in the brain of a gentleman—God bless him! Wilhelmina seemed fated now to rouse Brentwood's primal instincts. He was actually tempted to throw her laurels out of the window. How dared they send flowers—these accursed men, who would never have dreamed of allowing their own womankind to act the part of Beatrice Cenci! Brentwood did not want Wilhelmina himself, but he was in the mood in which he could have killed any other man who wanted her.

He turned from the flowers, however, to take stock of the more permanent furniture of the room—the books, the microscope, the instruments—all the stepping-stones that had led from the " little *dévote* " he had known to the vivid pagan of the night before.

And yet she was obviously not a pagan at heart. The books, the pictures—with the exception of an exquisite Bacchante—were the natural expression of a mind that was rooted deep in the soil of old Windy-haugh.

. Ah, those books!—how they poured from the press in the strenuous days!—books literary, books scientific, books philosophical, touching hands round the mighty problems with which men's hearts were full. The selection here was small, but a whole library might well have expressed less. Battle-music, battle-music!

When Wilhelmina entered the room, she was pale and a little out of breath—perhaps with climbing the long stair. It was hard upon her that Brentwood should have got there first.

She took off her hat as a schoolboy might have done. The room swam round her a little, and to steady herself she caught at Hugh's words of the night before—" I clearly foresee there will be a reconciliation to-morrow." Her lip curled with a touch of self-contempt, and she met Brentwood's eye frankly. "I am afraid you have had to wait," she said.

(What a fine keen face hers was!)

(How much older he had grown!)

He smiled. "It could scarcely be called waiting. Your room had plenty to say for itself—and for you."

Startled, she glanced at the books and pictures from a new point of view. "I hope it treated my faults with discretion."

Involuntarily his eyes fell on the flowers, and she appreciated to the full the sudden hardening of his face. Here at least was a note of disapproval in the chorus of adulation. But his glance returned in a moment to the books.

"Well," he said almost genially, "have you evolved a complete philosophy of life yet?"

"Shall I ever? I seem to be just drinking in the mystery."

"You seem on the whole to find it exhilarating."

She pondered. "That is the curious thing.' One day it sits on one's heart like lead; the next it goes to one's head like wine."

"Yet on the whole you are happy."

She gave her head a pretty little toss of something

like defiance. " I don't know that ' happy ' is the word.
I am *alive*, and life is intensely interesting."

" And are you still ' persuaded that neither death, nor
life, nor angels, nor principalities, nor powers, nor things
present, nor things to come, nor height, nor depth, nor
any other creature, shall be able to separate us from the
love of God, which is in Christ Jesus our Lord ' ? "   He
spoke in a low emphatic voice.

What a pity she could not respond—" And are *you*
still persuaded that ' a fool waits for an answer ' ? "

But her eyes were full of yearning when she raised
them to his.   She dwelt so constantly among such
thoughts—she had so often longed to talk to him about
these things—that the turn the conversation had taken
seemed most natural. " Mr. Brentwood," she said, " I
wanted to ask you—does one *ever* come back to that ? "

He paused before replying. " It was you who quoted
the words—not I."

" Surely, surely, the time is ripe for another revelation!   We are all in a muddle, the blind leading the
blind.   Just look at all the people who are praying for
light.

" ' And yet God has not said a word.' "

" Hasn't He ? "

" *Has He* ? "

" I don't know.   There are those who say that the
kingdom of God cometh not with observation."

She sighed. " But one does so long for something
definite.   If there be a God, He must know how thankful we should be to be good if we only knew He was
there."

" And would that be walking by faith ? "

" Wouldn't it ? "

" Would it ?   I don't know.   It seems to me that if
we had a new revelation to-morrow, we should be squab-
bling over its unimportant details within a week.   Sometimes I think it is not a question of *knowing* at all, but
of *seeing*."

" But I don't *see*."

" Perhaps you do see, but don't realize that that is

what you are looking for. I don't profess to be a religious man, but as a mere matter of common-sense it seems more suitable that we should adapt ourselves to God than that He should adapt Himself to us."

"But He is so big—so big!"

"If you could build Him to your liking now, would you not have outgrown Him within a year?"

Her face lighted up, as it always did when a fresh truth came home to her.

"And how about preaching to the masses?" she asked at last thoughtfully.

"I did not mention preaching, did I? Have I ever denied the *usefulness* of dogma?"

She looked up quickly, then smiled half sadly at the audacity of her own words.

"*But I want to save mankind!*"

He nodded. "I am less ambitious. All I ask for in my wildest moments is the grace—or should I say the decency?—to keep my own corner clean."

Suddenly he awoke to self-consciousness. Assuredly there was no use in trying to forecast an interview of this kind. Who could have dreamed that it would take a turn like this? All the time of their separation he had pictured Wilhelmina as cherishing a Christian and womanly contempt for him: it was pleasant to find that this had not been the case. The primal instincts began to sink into their true place.

"I want to hear all about your life," he said kindly. "I don't need to say, do I, that you can tell me nothing too small to interest me?"

She seemed so bright and successful as she sat there, that he felt the distinction conferred on him by his own failure. He was no longer conscious of any bitterness —only of a warm wave of generous feeling that raised him pleasantly in his own esteem. With a sudden sensation of rest he realized that his way was now perfectly clear. Of course no man worthy of the name would ask this brilliant young thing to forego a life full of eager interest in order to share his moody and morbid existence. What he would like now would be to share his income with her, and leave her free. His very figure filled out as he realized that under the circumstances this was the virile—and modern—thing to do. But thank Heaven he was no longer bound to dangle round on the outskirts of her success! He need only accept the hint of his old chief in Edinburgh, and apply for that temporary appointment abroad.

She blushed painfully at the sudden personal kindness of his tone, and then she began her tale. After the first few moments she told it well, with a keen eye for her own mistakes. As her nervousness wore off, he felt her dramatic gift almost as much as he had done the night before. Between the lines he read the record of her pluck and enthusiasm, and the story called forth his respect, admiration, amazement—everything, indeed, except his love.

Of Mr. Ellis she spoke in the warmest terms.

For once Brentwood's curiosity overcame him. "And what did he say to—last night?"

Wilhelmina looked unhappy. "To tell the truth, he didn't know," she said. "I put off and put off, and when at last I called, he had gone away for his holiday." She smiled, but not without apprehension. "So I have got that on my mind to tell him when he comes back!"

There was a knock at the door.

"May I come in?" cried Miss Evelyn's voice. "More offerings for the fair unknown."

She stopped short in overwhelming annoyance when she saw what she had done.

"Come in," said Wilhelmina without effusion.

Brentwood rose. "I was just going in any case," he said.

He was gratified to see the remorse in Miss Evelyn's eyes. His was not a forgiving nature, and he felt that his turn had come.

"Oh, don't go!" she cried. "My cab is waiting. I must run."

"Thank you very much. But Wilhelmina will tell you we have already scoured the universe in our talk. Good-bye," he said, holding out his hand to his wife, "I think Honor would greatly like to come and see you. You would find her a kindred spirit in many ways."

Wilhelmina was fighting fiercely with the threatening tears. "It is one of the dreams of my life that she should be my friend."

"She has been that—and your very warm admirer—from the day she saw you."

A moment later he was gone.

There was a great silence in the room. Wilhelmina had walked over to the window.

"Vilma, dear," said Miss Evelyn at last, "I am inexpressibly sorry."

Wilhelmina tapped the ground impatiently with her foot. "*Don't*," she said. "What is the use of talking? But pray take those flowers to somebody else—I am sick, sick, *sick*, of the whole thing!"

Miss Evelyn was startled. Such an outburst as that from most of her friends would have meant—just nothing at all; but most of her friends had not been brought up at puritan Windyhaugh.

And indeed Wilhelmina awoke next morning, feeling as though she had come to the end of all things. What did life contain that made it worth while to get up and dress and go on living? No doubt much of this feeling was sheer physical reaction after the excitement of the play. The wonder is that it had not set in the day before; but the flowers, the adulation, the prospect of the meeting with her husband, had kept up her spirits till now.

Of course she went to her classes as usual, though for days her perceptions were as if wrapped in a thick dank fog.

But youth is youth, and for Wilhelmina life at the worst was always life. On the third day the fog began to clear, and a sudden sharp storm dispelled it wholly. Molly—pretty peccant Molly—disappeared. For weeks —until the play began to absorb all her energies—Wilhelmina had been treating the girl like a sister, and now the disappointment was great. Older women—women inured to good works—treat cases like this on a regular system. Wilhelmina's system was still to make. We never fall into such grave mistakes as when in the ardour of youth we treat each case as though it were the first that had occurred in the history of man; but do we ever again do such good work?

"Do you suppose she has gone to marry him?" she asked of the mother.

The woman took her apron from her eyes, and laughed with the harsh practical cynicism of the working woman. "Bless your innocent soul, miss. I doubt he's got her cheaper than that."

Wilhelmina's eyes blazed. "If we could only find out who the man is——"

The woman hesitated, and moved uneasily from one foot to the other. "My husband dared me to tell you," she said, "but I think myself it is only fair to you. We're afraid it is—the gentleman—the gentleman that was with you on Friday evening."

Wilhelmina sprang to her feet, her youthful bloom gone to ashes in a moment.

"*No!*" she gasped.

"I doubt it's only too true, miss. You see he's been about the place a good deal for a year past, and he's noticed Molly from the first."

Wilhelmina sank into her chair, faint with relief. "Oh," she said, "you mean *Thursday* evening." Then she awoke to a recognition of her own selfishness. "Forgive me," she said. "What does it matter to you which evening it was? God knows it is bad enough in any case, but if it had been the other, I could not have borne it. I will write to—to my cousin to-night."

There was not much compromise about the letter.

"MY DEAR HUGH: I hope they are maligning you here. They say it is you who have taken away our pretty Molly. Please write me an emphatic denial by return. The mother is my friend, and, if I had been the means of bringing this curse upon her, my heart would break.   Your affectionate cousin,

"WILHELMINA GALBRAITH."

She posted the letter with her own hands, and again she might well have quoted Harley's poem—"A fool waits for an answer."

But as soon as the letter was posted, she began to ask herself how far she had been responsible for what had taken place. During the week that had preceded the play she had been far too preoccupied to pay much attention to Molly. Perhaps the child had looked for an opening to confide in her—had " found no place for repentance though she sought it with tears." And Hugh himself—how had she received his pathetic attempt to lift the conversation on to a higher plane that very Thursday night? " You didn't pray hard enough, Hugh "—as who should say, " I am too preoccupied with my own affairs to take any interest in your salvation." Brute, brute, that she was!—selfish, cold-hearted brute!

So it came about that Miss Evelyn, choosing, as she thought, an· admirable moment for the suggestion that Wilhelmina should seriously adopt the stage as her profession, was met by an incomprehensible rebuff.

" All the world's a stage! " sighed Wilhelmina.

" Really, Vilma, the originality of your remarks is most striking, but the *apropos*——? "

" It is only too clear to me. We may act on the toy stage or not as we choose, but we have got to act on the real one whether we will or no. You seem extraordinarily successful in combining the two. I don't say that you lose no opportunity of doing a kind action, because in truth you go out of your way to do them; but I—I am so taken up with my trumpery lime-light effects that I miss the most obvious duty next to hand. No, dear, thank you very much, but I will never act again."

That very evening brought a letter from Brentwood —an ordinary commonplace inland letter from the postman's point of view, delivered with as much haste and indifference as if it had come from—anybody else in the wide world! It was a long time before the envelope had delivered the whole of its message, but at last Wilhelmina opened it.

" MY DEAR WILHELMINA: I fear my awkward lips refused to tell you the other night how much I respect and

admire you for the way in which you have taken life by
the horns. Your success is not an accident; you have
deserved every inch of it; and, now that you have begun
to succeed, I feel sure you will go on. You are one of
those women who are strong enough to stand alone, and
you will only grow the stronger for all the poor souls
who will cling to you for comfort as life goes on. 'How
does one preach to the masses?' By being such a woman as Wilhelmina is becoming.

"As for me—I have given up trying to be clever.
I have had a good piece of hard work offered me at the
University of Sydney, and I mean to accept it. One
thing I should like to ask you before I go. After all,
we are not quite strangers to one another. I want you
to accept—say a hundred pounds a-year out of my income. I would gladly make it twice or thrice the
amount, but I only ask for a hundred. Don't you think
it is your duty to give yourself every advantage for the
sake of those whom you wish to benefit?—I am,

"Yours always most truly,
"HARLEY BRENTWOOD."

"On second thoughts I have sent £100 to Macintyre
now. It will do you no harm to have it in his keeping,
and if you should want it—it will be there. If by any
chance you should ever want *me*, I would come from
the ends of the earth."

Verily Harley Brentwood's turn had come. Wilhelmina had no wish to start for Sydney before she had
taken her degree; she was too much interested in her
work for that; but, with true feminine inconsistency,
she cried over the letter till the fount of her tears was
dry. Then the night was dark, and she carried her aching head down to the quiet coolness of the deserted
street.

Heavy rain had come on at nightfall. It soothed her
a little to hear it swish on the dust and grime. As she
stood, gazing into the lamplit darkness, an elderly gentleman passed with his wife on his arm. She clung to
him so closely that one umbrella served abundantly for

both. His stalwart figure was the type of protection, just as hers was the embodiment of trust.

Wilhelmina turned, and dragged her weary steps upstairs. "Strong enough to stand alone." Oh God, oh God!

If she could only have seen Harley again, just for ten minutes—just to tell him how miserably she had failed in this little bit of work that had been placed before her—how she would have thanked God for all the rest of her life!

But she had not forgotten that fateful night on the terrace; she would not make the same mistake a second time. "My father sends me plenty of money, thank you"—a poor little white lie, this; but the recording angel has not shed the last of his tears—"God bless you, and good-bye."

CHAPTER LIII.

L'HOMME PROPOSE.

WILHELMINA was justified in fearing that on second thoughts Mrs. Dalrymple would regret her friendly overture. Enid would fain have taken up so sweet and interesting a girl, but there really were too many odd things about Wilhelmina; it would be better for the present to leave things as they were.

Gavin had called at the flat before going to Woolwich. He was taller than his brother and extraordinarily attractive for a lad of his age. He kissed Wilhelmina as if she had been his sister, and talked to her with a simplicity and lack of reserve that went straight to her heart. He had brought a photograph of his fair lady, and he proceeded to fill in colour and expression with eager ready lips.

"Her father won't hear of it yet," he said. "You see I am so awfully poor; and there is that lucky dog, Hugh, scattering his money as if it were waste paper.

24

If he had a nice woman to show for it, one wouldn't mind, but—ugh!"

" How is Hugh?"

" Oh, well enough. We scarcely see him now-a-days. He and the governor are not on speaking terms."

Wilhelmina returned to the photograph. It was sweet and sonsy—nothing more; only through Gavin's eyes could she see the wonder of it. On the margin, in a round schoolgirl hand, was written the name, "Daisy Lauderdale." "Daisy, Daisy," Wilhelmina was thinking, "what is there in you to keep a man's heart when I have so utterly failed?"

" If the girl herself cares," she said, " and you get on well, the father will give in."

Gavin smiled. " She has never *owned* that she cared," he said: " she keeps me at arm's length, but that just makes me all the keener."

Ah!

For two hours they talked of nothing but Daisy: her simplest words and acts were full of meaning and mystery to Gavin, and yet she was only one girl among so many!

After this visit, Wilhelmina dropped quite out of touch with her cousins again. She regretted this because the simple poverty of her own life made her appreciate keenly the atmosphere of elegance and luxury that the Dalrymples carried about with them.

What distressed her much more than this, however, was the fact that Mr. Ellis was genuinely shocked to hear of the part she had taken in Mrs. Cavendish's theatricals. He was unable to reconcile it with his conception of her, and, after a feeble effort to explain why she had done it, Wilhelmina gave up the attempt in despair. If he had *seen* her act, he might still have sought an excuse, but never an explanation. " Come and see me again," he said kindly enough, when she took her leave, but his voice had not the old ring, and she did not go. She might have put matters right by telling him how deeply she repented that episode in her life, but the very fact that she felt his disappointment so acutely— the fact that the emotional part of her was tempted to bow to the priest in him—sealed her lips. She was too much on guard against her own nature.

Honor Brentwood told her of Harley's arrival in Sydney, and of his professorship there. Honor herself was with her aunt in Scotland a great deal, but between her and Wilhelmina there existed that deep understanding of friendship which has to be our compensation in life for all the lost opportunities of intercourse. From Miss Evelyn, Wilhelmina had drifted apart, as people do drift apart in life, for no very adequate reason.

And was she left desolate? Oh, no. A bright young woman with real force and charm of character never needs to be desolate, even if she be poor. Wilhelmina was very popular with her teachers and fellow-students. All through the year that followed the Cenci performance, hospitable doors stood open, and on the whole she enjoyed life keenly.

One pretty episode the year contained. Discovering the open secret of her poverty, one of her professors procured for her a holiday engagement to coach a junior student. The work was light and well-paid, the conditions of life all that could be desired, and Wilhelmina returned to town towards the end of September with a balance of health and energy.

She found a letter awaiting her from Mr. Carmichael. He was coming up to town for a week, and hoped to see as much of her as possible. Seized with a sudden inspiration, Wilhelmina wrote to ask if he could not bring Mr. Darsie. She could get him a room in the flat below her own, and for the moment she was free to take him about as much as ever he liked. She had some thoughts of offering to pay his fare, but decided that, with his simple ways, he must have a little money laid by.

" Of course he won't come," she said when the letter was posted; but he did come. He accepted with effusion. He packed his best broadcloth, and ordered a new suit of light tweeds! He grew younger every day at the prospect before him, and even the journey did not knock him up too much.

What a week that was! It was to contain two Sundays, so they began by scouring the columns of the

newspapers to find out how many distinguished preachers they could possibly fit into the time. What with a
few week-day services in addition, I am really afraid to
say how many celebrities they " sat under." " Sheer
spiritual debauch," Mr. Carmichael said, laughing, and
he and Wilhelmina cautioned the old man in vain. Mr.
Darsie knew exactly whom he most wanted to hear, and
what to expect from each; and he listened to the various discourses with an unswerving attention that was
beyond all praise. The mental effort would have overcome any man save an old-world provincial Scotch
elder. I am afraid Mr. Darsie showed a partiality for
" heretics," but his catholic taste included the saints
and the seers.

Then, in the evening, what talks they had about all
they had heard and seen! With what respect Mr. Darsie
dipped into Wilhelmina's books! With what genial
courage he laid aside his Scotch reserve to tell her how
much he admired her!

When at last Wilhelmina saw her two friends off at
the station, she felt as if she never wished to hear a
sermon again for the rest of her natural life.

A few days after Mr. Darsie's return to Queensmains,
he had a sudden, unexpected heart attack, brief but
alarming. He would not allow Mr. Carmichael to tell
Wilhelmina, and a week later he seemed as well as ever,
but he felt that he had received a' shake. No matter.
The week in town was worth much more than that. A
human life is not best measured by its years.

It was a lovely evening in June, and Wilhelmina's
examination was drawing near. Teachers and fellow-
students alike assured her that she " could not miss it ";
and, although she knew how unlucky it is to be confi-
dent, she could not help feeling very hopeful. From
the point of view of sheer success in her work, she was
fortunate in having no home claims to distract her attention.

She was very happy that June evening, happy—as
one is sometimes—in a sense of the appreciation of her
friends. It chanced that one and another had expressed

this appreciation very warmly of late, and, as Wilhelmina recalled the kindly words, a pleasant unaccustomed conviction grew upon her of her own moral worth. Judged by any ordinary standard, she was a good woman—kind and helpful—was there any reason why, just for the moment, she should not admit the fact to herself? Yet the admission made her uneasy, she could not have told why. "Woe unto you when all men speak well of you!" Was life turning out too easy after all? Its mystery was still unsolved, but for the moment she was content to let that rest. Were her moral thews and sinews growing flaccid? She certainly had no grave temptations. As Alexander longed for fresh worlds to conquer, so did puritan Wilhelmina almost long for a besetting sin on which to prove her strength.

It was at this moment, at this precise point in her train of thought, that the door opened and her father walked in.

Wilhelmina sprang to meet him, her face bright with welcome. She had learned to look at him very sanely during his long absence, and yet—what a wonderful creature he was!

He seemed almost boisterously glad to see her, lifting her right from the floor in his embrace. She had never known him like this, and his impulsiveness half frightened her; but a moment later she laughed at her own folly. Was he not her father? How glad, how glad she was to see him! She would not allow herself even to formulate the wish that he had come a month later when her examination troubles were over, and she could give herself up to the luxury of having him.

His hair was much whiter than when she had seen him last, and at first she thought him handsomer than ever. He was so light-hearted, so ready to be pleased with everything. "What a pretty room! and what a bonny lass it is!"

As soon as she had time to collect her thoughts at all, she wondered what he would say on the subject of her relations with her husband, but he did not refer to Brentwood in any way. He seemed only too glad to have his daughter to himself. He expressed himself abundantly satisfied with the frugal supper she set before him, and, instead of asking her questions, he talked eagerly about his own adventures. Wilhelmina was profoundly interested in all he said, but every now and then she was conscious of a vague sense of disappointment. He had always been a good narrator, but in former days he had left his own pluck and *aplomb* to be inferred. Did he doubt her intelligence that he should now find it necessary to be so explicit? In another man such frankness might have been mere lovable *naïveté*, but George Galbraith had never been *naïf*.

It was late when he rose to go, and she was almost glad that he did not appoint another meeting. His personality was so absorbing, and she had so many ends to tie up for the all-important examination. Judging by her experience of him in the past, she might not see him again for weeks.

She had been in the habit of sleeping sweetly and sanely, but that night she could not sleep at all. There was a change in her father. *What was it?* His dress was less scrupulously perfect than of old, but after a journey that was to be expected. If it had only been his dress! But his face, his manner, his very ways of eating and drinking, were all of them less scrupulously perfect. The impression left on her mind, compared with the impression of three years before, was as that of a man who has moved imperceptibly while being photographed. His whole personality was just a trifle *blurred*.

There! No doubt he had arrived in London tired, and had drunk an extra glass of champagne. In the old days at Windyhaugh she had often known him to drink enough to make him gay and tender, but she had never seen him quite like this. Still, if it rejoiced his heart to see his little girl again—how glad she ought to be!

She was just starting for the biological laboratory next morning when, to her great surprise, she met him at the door.

"Oh, nonsense!" he cried gaily, overruling her feeble little protest, "the old man doesn't come home from foreign parts every day. I have such a lot to say to you. Come in and sit down."

After all, one day's work would not make much difference. Wilhelmina was ashamed of her own reluctance, and, slipping her arm within his, she went back with him to her room.

He threw down his hat, and walked over to the window. "The fact is, Vilma, I can't stand London. I must get out of it. It is so cursedly provincial."

She started at the word, but he did not seem aware that he had said anything unusual.

"Why, Father, you have only just come back."

"The more fool I. I tell you what, little one, we'll start off on our travels together. How soon can you be ready? To-morrow?"

She laughed to conceal her uneasiness at the suggestion. "And where is the money to come from?"

"Money? Do you really think we need to consider money? You dear little girl!"

So he had been gambling again. Alas, alas!

"Well?" he said kindly. "You want some new frocks, do you? Is that it?"

"No; it is not that," she said, taking her courage in both hands. "I should love to travel with you, but I am just going up for an examination. I must get that over first."

He looked perplexed. "And what is that for?"

"Well, I want to be a teacher, and support myself by-and-bye."

As it chanced, this was the worst thing she could have said. He broke into a genial laugh. "Support yourself?—you! Why, you little innocent, have you the least idea how much money we've got?"

She was really frightened now. "But I have worked so hard for this examination. It would be a dreadful disappointment not to go in for it."

A sudden angry light flashed into his eyes. "And my disappointment is nothing? I am to kick my heels for a month in this infernal hole while you pass your examination? I never heard such a confounded piece of nonsense. There, there, dear, I know you didn't mean it. Put on your hat, and we'll go and see about those frocks."

She put on her hat obediently, feeling as though the earth was yawning under her feet. She had not the least intention of giving up her examination, but there was no use arguing now. He certainly had been drinking, or he would not talk like that. To-morrow he would see things in another light. No doubt she too had been to blame. The freedom and independence of her comings and goings had made her chafe unduly at the necessary restrictions of family life.

But every step they took when their hansom reached Bond Street seemed to rivet her chains. Nothing could exceed her father's generosity. In vain she protested against the extravagance of the things he bought. The shopwomen looked at Mr. Galbraith with admiring eyes, and evidently considered his daughter a most inappreciative young woman.

While they were lunching together at his hotel, she noticed for the first time a curious *fluttering* about his mouth. Was it possible that his excess was a matter of habit? And if so, what about the future that lay before him—and her? He was drinking freely now, but not more than she had often seen him drink at Windyhaugh. She had no idea how much wine a man of the world was supposed to drink. She looked hard at the waiters to see whether they considered that he was taking too much; not the least glance of silent comment would have escaped her keen young eyes; but, except that they treated Mr. Galbraith with exaggerated courtesy, there was nothing to see, and their civility was abundantly accounted for by the amount of money he was spending. It was clear that waiters and shopkeepers thought her father a very perfect gentleman indeed.

"And so he is," she said to herself indignantly when she was back in her little room. "He is three years older, he has knocked about the world, and he is tired. I am three years older too, three years more observant, and no longer able to idealize him as I once could. I had seen so few people in those old Windyhaugh days." But she sighed. Whether the old air of hothouse bloom had existed in her imagination or in reality, it had been a very beautiful thing to see.

"To-morrow," she said, "he will be rested. I will talk over this question of my examination with him then. It is only that he does not understand."

When he was away, she imagined herself talking to him quietly, clearly and at length, convincing him of the justice of her views; but when the moment came, she felt as if she were shouting to him through a brick wall. It was impossible to get into any kind of touch with him. Still she would not face the idea that she might have to give up her examination. That would be too dreadful. If only one of her professors could meet Mr. Galbraith, and talk to him on the subject!

If she had been on the old terms of intimacy with Mr. Ellis, she would have asked his advice, but as it was —she did not. Miss Evelyn was away yachting, and there was no one else to whom she could confide her father's weakness.

On the fourth day after his arrival, he came up to her room in excellent spirits as usual. "Ah, I see your things have come," he said, glancing at the parcels. "We will go down to Dover to-morrow morning. Normandy or Brittany will be pleasant while this hot weather lasts, and then my little girl shall see Paris. When it begins to grow cold, we'll go down south."

With sinking heart she made one last effort to explain her position, but before she realized that he was taking her seriously, he burst into a sudden tempest of wrath. She had never seen any one in a passion before, and it seemed to her almost indecent that she should be the witness of so painful a moral collapse. She sat motionless, her face as white as death.

But at that moment a knock at the door announced the arrival of another parcel—a new hat, as it chanced; and, with a sudden change of manner, more suggestive of pantomime than of sober daily life, he insisted that she should try it on. Ah, well, it was not the first smart hat that has been tried on with an aching heart!

He threw his arm around her affectionately. "To think she has never been prettily dressed in her life before!" he said with a rush of tears. "My bonny bairn! For the future she shall have all that money can buy."

Wilhelmina had never realized before *how little* money can buy.

"To-morrow morning, then," he said. "I will call for you at eight. *Sans adieu*, little one."

She was thankful to be left alone that she might review the situation in peace. Looking at the matter superficially, one thing was clear. Either she must go with her father next day, or quarrel with him. Looking at the matter more deeply, something else was equally clear. For some reason, her father was not to be judged at the present moment quite as a rational human being. It is impossible to describe the wave of depression with which she admitted this to herself. We become more or less used to the experience as we go on in life, but it is a tragic moment when youth first realizes that the old relations are reversed—that it must make allowance for the weakness of the being it has looked upon as something more than human.

And now the application—what was her duty? She no longer hungered for renunciation in the abstract. She wanted to make the very most of her own powers. She could not bear to disappoint her teachers. And yet, and yet—she knew that she would have to go. That old relentless memory of hers brought back Miss Evelyn's words. "You had an influence over your father that no one else ever had: . . . you were making him human —drawing out the father in him. He must have been surprised to find his daughter so generous."

Wilhelmina sat down to write to one of her teachers; she tried to compose a quiet little note; but when she read it over she seemed to hear the ring of anguish through all its lines—so she tossed it into the fire, and the tears streamed down her face like autumn rain.

It did not even cross her mind to suggest that her father should consult a doctor. Had she done so, he would have assured her that he had never been so well in his life; but in after years it was strange to reflect that on that very evening men and women all over the world had been seeking medical advice for the merest fancies and finger-aches.

CHAPTER LIV.

THE SKELETON IN THE CUPBOARD.

" WELL, *chérie*, does this amuse you ? "

" Immensely. How quiet they are ! It is like watching an ant-heap."

Wilhelmina and her father were sitting in roomy fauteuils on the first floor of the Hotel Terminus in Paris, looking down on the ever-varying scene in the great hall below.

An imposing array of newspapers was drawn up on the centre tables, and people of all nationalities were poring over their columns. Business men and gay tourists shared the comfortable writing-tables in the corners, family groups here and there discussed their plans in a whisper, an actress in gorgeous plumage strolled up and down on the arm of a stout young man, and other men, lounging in quiet corners, lazily took in her points from under drooping lids.

Every minute the great doors swung open as people passed in and out, or the groom of the chambers came forward to arrange the disordered journals. But there was no bustle, no noise. The whole scene was like an ant-heap, as Wilhelmina had said.

" Well, let us go and have some lunch. What do you say to a partridge, and a bottle of Chateau Lafite ? "

Wilhelmina rose, and rustled softly downstairs in her Bond Street gown. She had come to the cynical conclusion that those gowns did more for her than any number of letters after her name. She had and her father had travelled together now for months, and she had acquired the easy air of the people who are used to be waited on. Yet her face was a little worn with anxiety. From the moment they left London, her father's manner had be-

come more stable, and she had felt rewarded for the
sacrifice she had made; but every now and then a curious fit of excitement or talkativeness raised her fears
afresh, and her manner began to attain the gracious
dignity and aloofness of the woman who knows well
the effect of her pretty gowns, but who feels all the
time underneath the sting of the thorn in the flesh.

Wilhelmina was tall, and father and daughter formed
a striking couple. The head-waiter received them with
much ceremony, and, as he pushed in Wilhelmina's chair,
and placed a footstool under her feet, she became aware
of a pair of hungry envious eyes directed towards her
from an adjoining table. They were those of a poor
little elderly Frenchwoman who seemed to be filling the
rôle of maid and courier to two exacting English ladies.

"I must speak to her by-and-bye," thought Wilhelmina. She was acquiring an unerring instinct for suffering in others, and she had a strong feeling that it is
the duty of the people whose skeleton is considerate
enough to remain in its cupboard, to be helpful to those
whose skeleton frankly takes its place by the fireside.

Her opportunity came in the afternoon, when the
English ladies were resting in their rooms.

"I think you will find this a good pen." How naturally the remark came! How the little woman's face
lighted up when she heard it! It seemed to Wilhelmina
strangely pathetic that any one should be flattered by a
little notice from her—poor Vilma Galbraith!

But when the little woman's face lighted up, it looked
ten years younger, and, when the owner of the face began
to speak, Wilhelmina had a strong conviction that all
this had happened before.

"I do believe," she said at last, "that you are my
very own Mademoiselle. Do you remember Windyhaugh
and Wilhelmina Galbraith?"

What it is to be French! If Mademoiselle had met
her dearest friend, she could scarcely have experienced
a more lively emotion. She laughed and cried, and em-
braced her old pupil with effusion.

"Who would have thought that you would turn out
like this?" she said with admiring eyes. "And that was

your father—Monsieur Galbraith?" She sighed deeply. "*Enfin!* At last! How I have longed to meet Monsieur Galbraith! I have remarked him at lunch, and wondered who was this handsome man." She sighed again. The contrast between Wilhelmina's lot and her own was too painful. "How happy you must be!"

"My father is smoking just now. I will introduce him presently."

At that moment the swing door opened, and two young Englishmen entered, laughing. Of course there were thousands of trivial causes for their mirth, but Mr. Galbraith had been unlike himself at lunch, and a sudden fear crossed Wilhelmina's mind that he might have been giving himself away in the billiard-room. Once or twice before, she had seen men nudge each other as he passed, and indeed she had sometimes heard him talk of his own doings to complete strangers in a way that a gentleman does not do. These were the moments that graved the lines in her face.

She was relieved to see her father come in just then. It was a comfort at least to have him in her sight. She hoped he would be cordial to shabby old Mademoiselle, but soon found that she need have had no anxiety on that score. He was overwhelmingly cordial—congratulated the little woman on Wilhelmina's accent, discussed Paris, and finally proposed that they should all three go for a stroll.

With infinite regret Mademoiselle declined, and he took Wilhelmina. She proposed a drive in the *Bois*, but he insisted that she must have a peep at the shops. Remembering Bond Street, she trembled, for she could not help fearing that he was not nearly so rich as he said. He seemed to be under the impression that his purse was bottomless.

They went first into a jeweller's. Wilhelmina had learned that it was useless to argue with him—that the only chance of changing his purpose was to turn the conversation, and for ten minutes she worked hard. After refusing all sorts of things, she allowed him to give her a great purple daisy, very simple, very choice, just the sort of trinket that appealed to the tastes of both.

"Now," he said, "we must get something for Mademoiselle."

"Why, Father, that is kind of you. I should never have thought of it."

It struck her as an extremely graceful idea on his part, but when he chose a brooch that cost three hundred francs, she could not help thinking him unnecessarily lavish.

"Now, let us go and look at some pictures," she said.

"All right. Have you noticed these little gold pencils? I think I will take one to—what's his name?—that young fellow at the hotel."

"But why *should* you? He will be very much surprised."

Mr. Galbraith laughed, and put the pencil with the other things.

"*Don't*, Father!"

His eyes flashed. "Good God, Vilma! Is it your affair or mine?" he shouted.

She blushed deeply, and the shopman turned away his head, but the pencil was bought.

Mademoiselle was overjoyed with her brooch, and it was by no means the only present that came to her during the days that she and the Galbraiths were in Paris together. She salved her feelings by assuring Mr. Galbraith that no pupil had ever been so much to her as his daughter was, and perhaps the statement was not so outrageously false as Wilhelmina supposed.

In any case the poor girl would have forgiven much to anyone who so frankly admired Mr. Galbraith. She could never be grateful enough to Mademoiselle for *seeing nothing wrong* with her father.

The weather continued fine for the time of year, and Paris was full of tourists returning to England. One morning a local letter was slipped under Wilhelmina's door, addressed in a handwriting that she knew well, though she had seen it seldom. A crowd of old recollections brought the colour to her face as she read—

. "MY DEAR VILMA: I have just heard that you are in Paris. I am only stopping a day or two, and am very

busy with my dressmaker. Could you come and see me?
I shall be at home to-morrow afternoon, and I want to
see you *alone*. I am in great trouble about Hugh.

"Yours affectionately,

"ENID DALRYMPLE."

"I think that should prevent her bringing her father," Enid had reflected as she sealed the letter. "I
have no wish to be sponged upon as the pepsin man was."
For, although the young millionaire had been loyal on
the whole, Enid had heard some strange stories concerning the latter part of that tour.

But she need not have been afraid. Wilhelmina had
no wish to take her father. After reading the letter, she
coiled her beautiful hair rather more elaborately than
she had intended, and reflected for the first time with
satisfaction on the exquisite French gown her father had
insisted on giving her. All her meetings with Enid
hitherto had been full of humiliation for herself: now at
last she could meet her aunt on something like equal
terms.

"I wonder what form the chameleon will take this
time," Enid said to Gavin with languid curiosity. Her
brain was confused among pictures of the shabby long-
legged girl, the writer of pious letters, and the beautiful
Cenci; but no one of the three prepared her in any
way for the figure that entered the room.

Enid would not have called her niece *smart*, any
more than Mr. Ellis had been able to call her clever, but
her whole appearance was that of a high-bred English
girl. She was not beautiful, but those wistful eyes were
far more pathetic in an elegant woman than they had
been in a shabby child, and when they met her aunt's
look with a grave thoughtful directness, Enid became
suddenly conscious of the necessity of changing her
whole mental focus.

"Well, dear, it was good of you to come. I do so
want a long talk with you," she said, as if they had been
excellent friends all their lives. "I *was* surprised to
hear you were in Paris. How do you like that great
caravanserai?"

"It interests me immensely."

"Most unlike your father to go there. I hope he is well?"

"Fairly well, thank you." Wilhelmina smiled. What good points the child had—teeth, complexion, hair. Of course any woman could wear coils like that, but the thick straight growth above the ears was delicious.

"And what are your plans now?"

"I believe my father means to work leisurely down to the Riviera, stopping at Lyon and Avignon."

"The Lauderdales are going to the Riviera. I wonder whether you will meet them. Daisy Lauderdale is Gavin's divinity, you know. I wish you could come and meet them at dinner here to-night."

"I think I could. My father is engaged, as it chances."

"That is right. Mr. Lauderdale has a great admiration for learned women, and Hugh tells me you are tremendously learned."

A little flicker of pain passed over Wilhelmina's face.

"I will do you the justice to say you don't show it. I am very proud of you, Vilma."

"Thank you. I feel better for having your *cachet*. You certainly gave me the chance to develop, Aunt Enid. It is my own fault if I refused it."

There was a new ring in Enid's voice. "I wish you had come to me, dear."

"So do I. I should have been saved a lot of mistakes. And yet what folly it is to regret anything in life. The design is so big—so big! Of course I was an unutterable prig, but it was all very real to me at the time."

"You made me feel very wicked and frivolous, I know. But you lost nothing by refusing to come to me. It is better not to be quite like other girls, and you have got that touch of—melancholy is it?—that was so attractive in your father."

"It is a liberal education to live with my father. But you were going to tell me about Hugh."

Enid's face grew old. "Oh, poor Hugh—yes. You have no idea what an anxiety that boy has been to me.

I really don't know how to tell you, but of course you are not a girl?"

"No."

"I never had any great objection to a young man sowing his wild oats, but poor dear Ronald made Hugh his companion, and I am afraid they were very wild."

Wilhelmina nodded gravely.

"Hugh behaved most nobly about Ronald's money —insisted on sharing it with Miss Evelyn, though of course she had no claim on him whatever. Now he has run through many thousands in a year or two. Even that we would have overlooked if he would have married a nice girl and settled down; but some time ago he took up with a quite common——"

"I know."

"Everybody knows now, no doubt. They went together down to some watering-place—I really don't know how to tell you the rest of the story. There was a man preaching on the beach, and this pretty pair of fools stopped to listen. Can you believe, Vilma, Hugh wrote to me a few days later to say that he had been *converted!*"

Wilhelmina did not say so, but she certainly had great difficulty in believing it. Hugh, the man of the world, the sceptic, the boy who four years before had asked her whether she was "particularly gone on the doctrine of eternal punishment"! Wilhelmina was young, and this was a blow straight between the eyes. She had hoped some day to impress Hugh with her own fine view of life. If one may use the parlance she had left behind, Wilhelmina had looked upon Hugh as her own special sheaf, and behold a mere evangelical preacher had carried him home!

Her face encouraged Enid to go on. "If it had been a Churchman, I should have been so thankful. If it had been a Romanist—or even a Buddhist—I should have felt it less—so many people are becoming Buddhists just now—but a common ranting Methodist!

"After listening to the preacher for several evenings —on the beach, remember, with a mob of trippers— Hugh stayed behind to speak to the man—who is not

25

even in orders, though Hugh declares he is a gentleman.· He seems to have confessed with a most unnecessary amount of detail, and the result is that the
preacher has convinced him it is his duty to marry the
girl!"

Wilhelmina's face broke into a great dawn of emotion. "Oh, Aunt Enid," she said, "*you have made me
feel so small!*"

Enid's disappointment nearly brought the tears to
her eyes. "I thought you would have helped me," she
said pitifully. "Nobody has the influence over him that
you have. You should hear how he used to talk of
you! If things had been different——"

Wilhelmina winced as if an insect had stung her.

And then Enid rose to an act of real generosity. It
was all very well to scoff at the idea of a husband whose
main recommendations might perhaps be his money and
position; but who did Wilhelmina suppose was paying
for that Parisian gown?

· It would have been easy to instil the poison-
ous thought with a mere needle-prick, but Enid refrained.

"Nobody has the influence over him that you have,"
she repeated.

Wilhelmina's eyes were very bright. "Forgive me,"
she said. "I am abominably unsympathetic. Of course
Hugh is your heir. This must be a great disappointment in many ways. I do feel that. I feel it so strongly that, if Hugh had asked me, I could not have advised
him to marry M——the young girl. But "—she clapped
her hands softly as if she were looking on at some feat
of strength or skill—"Hugh has taken the lead. My
business is to follow *him.*"

This untried enthusiasm of youth is very galling to
those who know life; but the case was so nearly desperate that Enid was glad to hear consolation of any
kind.

"Of course," she went on more composedly, "I am
quite aware that this world is not everything. Dear
Ronald's death brought that home to us terribly, though
I can't help trusting all was well with him at the last.

But you must see, Vilma, that this is the world we have got to live in *just now*."

"I know. For you who are beautiful and sought after, the reconciling of the two worlds must be the great problem of life."

"It is very difficult. I sometimes think the great comfort of Heaven will be that there will be only one standard to reckon with. Perhaps even a marriage like this is better than living in sin, and fortunately the property is not entailed. Fergus has stood a great deal, but if Hugh marries this creature, of course his father will cut him off with a shilling. It will make a great difference in Gavin's prospects. I doubt if Mr. Lauderdale would ever have given his daughter to a younger son in Gavin's position."

"Gavin was born—not so much to succeed as to be successful. Poor Hugh! Does he know this?"

"Oh, dear, yes! It does not weigh with him in the least. He declares he has squeezed the orange, has tasted all the pleasures this world has to offer, and has found them apples of Sodom." Enid actually laughed. "There is a strong fruity flavour about his letter. He means to invest his few remaining hundreds in land in the Argentine, and take to farming."

Soon after, Wilhelmina took her leave. Of course at her age she could not but feel much older and wiser than her aunt, but it warmed her heart like a cordial to be on such friendly terms. She longed to say that she would be a sister to Molly—would try to do for the child what Honor had done for her; but the time for saying so had not come. When she reached the hotel, she sat down in the great hall to write.

" MY DEAR BRAVE OLD HUGH: I have been finding life rather hard and barren of late—though you would not think so if you saw me!—and have been greatly cheered and comforted by the news of your moral pluck. Will you forgive my obnoxious conceit? Surely I shall never dare to judge people again. Even when they commit a sin that seems to me impossible, I will remember that a year hence they may make that very sin a stepping-stone to a greatness I may never attain.

"And this I owe to you.

"Your grateful and affectionate cousin,

"WILHELMINA GALBRAITH."

Wilhelmina was much admired at the little dinner-party that night. Daisy Lauderdale, who had been quite prepared to dislike the "learned woman," fell in love with her promptly, and Gavin was amazed to see how demonstrative his divinity could be. From that evening he looked at his cousin with different eyes. "Mr. Lauderdale only wishes I had half as much in me as she has," he told Miss Evelyn, with that instinctive frank-ness of his, when he met her in London a few days later.

So it came about that in the course of time Brent-wood received a letter informing him that his wife was in Paris with her father, "having a good time, and prov-ing a great social success."

Brentwood was working very hard just then, and the news made him feel very lonely. He had been thinking a good deal of Wilhelmina of late—but not of a Wil-helmina like this.

CHAPTER LV.

THE SKELETON BY THE FIRESIDE.

NIGHT had come at last, thank God, dear Mother Night!

Wilhelmina had seen her father into his room; now she opened the window in her own, and stretched her arms on the great wide sill.

The March air cut sharply, but the moonlight fell in a silver flood, irradiating the bold outline of the Maria della Salute, and falling in an almost unbroken expanse on the grassy surface of the Grand Canal. Away in the distance voices were singing in chorus.

Beautiful Venice! You have seen so much. What care you for one breaking heart the more?

There was no keeping the skeleton concealed any longer. It was flaunting itself in the light of day, and yet—and yet its outline was strangely indistinct. *What was it?* It is a comfort to classify even our woes, but Wilhelmina's sorrow escaped all the bounds of her previous experience, and even of her previous imaginings. Now it bore the bearable aspect of tragedy; again it became a nightmare pantomime or farce. All the ordinary laws of existence seemed to be suspended. Had she been suddenly transported to another planet, she could not have felt more obsolutely uncertain as to what might happen next.

To-night her father's boastfulness had made them both more ridiculous than usual downstairs, but only a few new arrivals had laughed. Most of the guests had looked disconcerted and sorry—sorry for her, Wilhelmina! They seemed to see through her constant pitiful effort to control him—to keep him at his best. The waiters were obsequious as ever, but she was always trying now *not* to see the meaning glances that so often passed between them.

Yet she had almost given up the idea that her father drank. He *did* drink, of course, abundantly, but not enough for this. She thought he must be taking some mysterious drug—or was his moral nature simply used up? Could he, in the old days of his fine reserve, have seen himself as he was now—seen how he ate and drank and walked—*ah!* Wilhelmina shuddered. To the tips of her fingers she realized what his sufferings would have been. To a man of his sensitive refinement, the vision would have meant—just hell. How dared she think of her own humiliation in comparison? If he ever woke up and *felt*—and yet, oh, if he only would wake up and feel!

Drawing the window-curtains, she undressed and went to bed. If only they were not so far from home! It was terrible to be among strangers at a time like this. But, for her father, strangers had ceased to exist. He had offered that evening to buy the watch of a gen-

tleman he had never seen before; and, ignoring a quiet
snub, had raised his bid three times! Wilhelmina buried
her face in the pillows and groaned. To think of that
whipper-snapper daring to snub George Galbraith!

Her dread was that the manager would speak to her
on the subject, and so deprive her of all power to persuade herself that her sensitiveness was exaggerating an
insignificant eccentricity; but her father was running
up a lordly bill, and the manager knew him of old.

It was only since they came to Venice that things
had been so bad. They had lived very quietly on the
Riviera, and Wilhelmina's chief anxiety had been her father's occasional trips to Monte Carlo, where his luck
seemed phenomenal.

It was the irony of the situation that affected her
most. If ever a man had seemed equal to any and every
occasion, that man was her father, and now——! On
the landing-stage that day she had called to him, and he
had seemed almost unable to turn. In an effort to come
to her, he had made a great shaky circuit, and the gon-
doliers had laughed! Sometimes when he was almost
his old self, talking quite sensibly, though always with
that queer thick utterance, he would forget a word, and
his distress at the lapse was indescribably painful.

"Oh, my Father!" sobbed Wilhelmina, "my great
strong beautiful Father! God help you, God help you!
God help us all!"

"*If you should ever want me I would come from the
ends of the earth.*"

Wilhelmina was sometimes tempted to take her husband at his word; but he could not travel, like Uriel, on
a shaft of light, and she felt that a crisis was at hand.
Things simply could not go on as they were going now.

When she went down to breakfast next morning she
was startled and distressed to see Mr. Lauderdale in the
room. She caught his eye for a moment, and glanced
away again, hoping that he would not recognise her.
In truth, he might well have failed to do so, for she
looked older by years than when he had met her in
Paris, some six months before; but he had noticed their

name in the Visitors' Book the night before, and the manager had told him how strangely Mr. Galbraith was behaving. " I am sorry for the young lady, sir."

Mr. Lauderdale was one of the few people who had always succeeded in maintaining a contempt for George Galbraith; he had no wish to be thrown with him under any circumstances, and he might have followed Wilhelmina's lead if her face had been less pitiful. He would not have liked his Daisy to look like that.

So he was quite merciless, shaking hands with her gravely, and asking leave to share her table, " as you and I are the only members of our respective parties energetic enough to come down to breakfast. How is your father ? "

Her face turned so white that he regretted introducing the subject before she had drunk her coffee. " He is not very well."

This was the first time she had admitted even so much.

" Perhaps the climate doesn't suit him. Why not go home ? "

" If he only would ! "

" Shall I go and have a talk with him ? "

" I think not, thank you."

He did not reply, and she looked up to see if he was offended. Mr. Lauderdale was a mere man of the world, but—how good a mere man of the world can be! Wilhelmina suddenly resolved to make the plunge. " You are very kind," she said nervously. " I ought not to let you share my burden, but—it has come to that. I wish you would have a talk with him, and—and advise me."

Mr. Lauderdale's face was very grave when he joined her after the interview.

" Has your father been drinking ? " he said quietly.

How she blessed him for asking the question straight out like that, without any " tactful " beating about the bush !

Yet her breath came very quick as she answered. " He does drink a good deal, but not enough to account for—for that. I have seen lots of men drink more. At least," she added with characteristic honesty, "I have seen one or two men drink more. I sometimes think he takes some drug."

"Perhaps. I am quite sure he ought to be at home, but he seems very unwilling to go."

"Yes."

"And apparently he has plenty of money?"

"I don't know how he came by it," she panted. "We have always been poor."

"Do you know when he last paid his bill?"

"I don't think he has paid it at all since we came here. The manager has known him a long time. I hope my father realizes how large the bill will be."

"Shall I suggest to the manager that he should ask him to pay? It seems to me your father wants something to rouse him."

Wilhelmina assented, and that afternoon the manager very civilly suggested that, if it would not inconvenience Mr. Galbraith——

But it did inconvenience Mr. Galbraith very much. He burst into one of his storms of rage, and for one awful moment Wilhelmina was afraid that he would knock the manager down. He had never heard such a confounded piece of impertinence. He could buy up the blessed hotel a dozen times over; but it did not suit him to pay just now. He had hundreds—thousands—coming in any day. Send up a bottle of that *Veuve Clicquot!* He was going out.

Wilhelmina went with him, trembling. The afternoon was cold, but he would not put on his overcoat, and, as they drifted along in their gondola, she shivered with nervousness and chill.

All night she heard him coughing on the other side of the wall, and, when she went into his room next morning, an extraordinary change had come over him.

"We are beggars, Wilhelmina," he said, "simply beggars! I don't know what is to become of us."

If it had been heartrending to see him self-confident, it was worse to see him so abject. With all a mother's tenderness, she gathered him in her arms, assuring him that, if he would only come home, all would yet be well;

but it was useless to contend with his overwhelming depression. How were they to get home? he asked. He declared now that he had only a few francs in the world.

Wilhelmina resolved to avail herself of Brentwood's hundred pounds: her scruples seemed very small in the stress of present events: and—after wiring to Fergus Dalrymple for instructions—Mr. Lauderdale became surety for the remainder.

It was a week before George Galbraith was strong enough to travel. Then he emerged from the blackest depth of his depression, but—mercifully perhaps—he never quite regained the old self-confidence. He allowed Wilhelmina to make all arrangements for the journey, and he accepted them with a patient apathy that touched her profoundly. Mr. Lauderdale was differently affected by his attitude.

"Good-bye, Miss Galbraith," he said, when he had seen to the luggage, and had helped her father into the high carriage. "You must not regret that you were forced to take me a little bit into your confidence. If my girl is ever in trouble and her dad is gone, I should like to think some old man felt for her as I have felt for you."

Wilhelmina could not speak. Her eyes were full of tears.

They slept at Milan that night, and next morning her father insisted that she should go to see the picture and the cathedral. She was in no mood for sight-seeing, but to humour him she went.

Weary and preoccupied, she entered the sacred room and for ten minutes sat looking at the picture with unseeing eyes. Its general outlines had been familiar from her babyhood, and at first she saw nothing more in the original than in the smug copies round about.

Then, all at once, the battered fresco began to live. Its blemishes disappeared. It stood out quick with interest, while she and her sorrows shrank almost into nothingness. The old story was real—the realest thing in the world.

Why had no one told her of the landscape seen

through the window—the wondrous suggestion of the peaceful days gone by? What a world of expression in those two hands, the left so full of resignation, the right of instinctive recoil! "Father, if it be possible——!" But it was not possible. The tragedy had to be faced. The hour of doom was just as much in the order of things as the sunlit mornings on the Galilean hills. And we don't know why, we don't know why. We can only live on and trust.

The first sight of the cathedral jarred on her mood. It was like a scene out of the Arabian Nights. But as soon as she entered the door, her feeling changed. As if disdaining the exquisite filigree of the spires and buttresses outside, these great columns rose up—up—up— in a way that satisfied her inmost soul. "God!" they seemed to say. "God! Nothing but God!"

Slowly and reverently Wilhelmina walked up the nave. The level rays of the March sun struck through the yellow windows on the great brass crucifix. A burst of music soared up among the arches. Her heart swelled with triumph. In that one morning she had seen the wheel of time spin round through centuries. *Vicisti Galilæe!*

And there He hung on the Cross.

Oh, Man of Sorrows! Oh, Light of the World! What wonder that men have fallen in adoration at Thy feet? "Oh, Lamb of God that takest away the sins of the world—

"*Grant us Thy peace!*"

Wilhelmina was very weary with the struggle. It was time a great wave of emotion should lift her towards the shore.

CHAPTER LVI.

THE VALLEY OF THE SHADOW.

"YOUR father will sleep now," said the great man quietly. "Sit down."

He looked straight across at her, reading her face, her attitude, her involuntary movements, like a book.

" You must have had a trying time."

Wilhelmina did not answer.

" Your father is very ill. I don't mean to say there is any question of imminent danger; but he is very ill, and the illness must have been coming on for many months. I want you to realize that a thousand little things, which may have struck you as moral failings, were really symptoms of which you may talk to me as frankly as of a cough or a headache."

He was pleased to see the gratitude in her eyes.

" And now I want you to tell me all about it."

Thus encouraged, she told him more of the story than she had ever expected to tell in this world. What a relief the telling was!—and what a comfort to see the matter-of-fact way in which he took it!

" Will he get better? " she ventured pitifully at last.

" Under favourable conditions, he may improve very much, but the truth is, his is not a suitable case for home nursing. Don't you think you had better trust him to me? "

" Oh, no! I will take such care of him."

" And what about yourself? "

" Oh, that's all right."

" So young people always say when a breakdown threatens: when the breakdown actually comes, I don't notice that they look upon it with the same philosophy."

She smiled. " It has been the travelling—the publicity—that has knocked me up. Now that we are home —Windyhaugh seems like a haven of rest in comparison; and we have a wise old servant there who has known my father from his boyhood. She worships him."

The great man reflected that it would take all the old servant's worship to carry her through. " But you have told me of fits of violence. They may not return —this convulsion must have left him weaker—but I can't guarantee that they won't."

" I have thought about that. At worst I could get our old gardener's son to help."

" You could have a trained attendant."

She hesitated. " I am afraid we can't afford it. We are very poor, absolutely, literally poor. That is partly why I can't send him to you."

She did not say that she could not bear to have strangers see her father in his present state—strangers who had never known him in his prime! Her great hope, too, was that his moral nature would wake up again. And if it did, she must be there to tell him how she loved him, to comfort him in his remorse, to help him to rise above the selfishness that had blighted his beautiful life.

The great man was watching her face. There were good strong lines in it, but were they strong enough for this? The fiat had gone forth. George Galbraith must drink the cup of dissolution to the dregs. He would not suffer much. He would drink the cup by proxy; and his proxy was this fair young girl.

The doctor tried to break to her something of what she might expect, but all he said only added fuel to the flame of her love and loyalty. How our little grievances and humiliations melt away in the presence of that great word, Death!

The doctor was essentially a sane man; his view of life was eminently physiological; but, as he looked at Wilhelmina, his mind fell back on the words of another physician—" Ah, long illness is the real vampirism; think of living a year or two after one is dead, by sucking the life-blood out of a frail young creature at one's bedside! Well, souls grow white, as well as cheeks, in these holy duties: one that goes in a nurse, may come out an angel. God bless all good women! "

" You see, doctor," Wilhelmina said gravely, " I have no other claims upon me. I can't help looking on this as the thing I have got to do."

" Very well," he said abruptly, " try it." He rose from his chair. " Who is your local doctor, down at Queensmains? "

Wilhelmina mentioned the name.

" Ah," he said with the air that only a very great man can assume. " I don't seem to have heard of him somehow. However, I will write to him. And now I have something to say to you. We are all students, you know, we doctors, and this illness of your father's is one that interests us very much. It will be a real favour to me if you will write occasionally, and tell me how he gets on." He smiled. "And you can just throw in a sentence, you know, to say how you are yourself." Then he paused to reflect. "It is quite possible, even probable, that you may have no more acute anxiety; and, for the rest—you must not let yourself suffer too much. Just bear in mind that your father is growing old— not slowly and imperceptibly as some men do; but, as it were, in a fiery chariot. I expect he has lived intensely, and the end will just be in keeping with all the rest. I don't know that he is to be pitied. We can't enjoy our pennyworth and keep our penny."

Wilhelmina saw a blurred image of the great man's figure as he drove away. His news had been bad, bad —and yet how he had lightened the burden! There are those who, passing through the valley of Baca, make it a well.

So, step by step, Wilhelmina went down with her father into the valley of the shadow. There is no education in life to compare with such a journey; but what comfort is there in that for the suffering of the one who must go?

She tried to prepare Ann by letter for the change in her beloved master, but the shock of the meeting was very great. For days the old woman was almost speechless with resentment against fate. Then she bent her back to the burden, and bore it nobly.

In the finest sense of the words, she had always been "one of the family," and there was comfort in the way she accepted this, not as Wilhelmina's sorrow, but as her own sorrow. "Dinna tell me," she said, when her young mistress spoke of hope. "He'll never be himsel' again i' this warld. What do we want wi' yon callant aboot the place? Tell him we'll send for him gin we want him. Do ye think he's fit to haud his tongue when a'body's speirin'?"

So the young doctor was not encouraged to pay un-

necessary visits. Wilhelmina learned from him how to
administer morphia hypodermically, and this proved
sufficient to control the patient's diminishing attacks of
excitement. How wonderfully it soothed him! Almost
every day the two faithful attendants helped him out on
the terrace, and at first they hoped that his native air
was doing him good. He grew stouter, and his physical
health improved. But it soon became evident that his
mind was growing feebler, and his efforts to speak were
a painful thing to see. No need to talk of all those
women went through. God save all we love from such
an end as this!

Mr. Carmichael was the only visitor who was allowed
to see him. Had not Mr. Carmichael admired him too?
To her friends, Wilhelmina wrote that her father was an
invalid, and that she was nursing him with Ann's help.
There was little in the words to suggest what they were
actually enduring.

And yet how acclimatized one becomes to an atmosphere of sorrow! Wilhelmina's cheerfulness was a constant source of amazement to Mr. Carmichael. She
began to read Latin again, and when she felt herself
growing too despondent, she invented gymnastic exercises, and raced round the garden in the gloaming. Anything to make the blood circulate, and drive away the
morbid humours.

She made an early opportunity of having a long talk
with Mr. Macintyre about their affairs. He told her
Mr. Brentwood had placed another hundred pounds at
her disposal, and that it was quite impossible for her to
live even at Windyhaugh without accepting it. She
formed and rejected a dozen plans for earning money,
and then quietly swallowed the bitter draught. "My
father is very ill," she wrote, "and I am compelled to
accept your kind loan—or gift, if it must be so. It is
something to be free at least from money anxiety, and
it is much to be able to devote myself entirely to him in
his great need.

Brentwood wrote by return, offering to come home,
but although she had been compelled to accept his charity herself, she would not throw her father on his mercy,

and her speedy reply dissuaded him even more decidedly than she had intended.

She wrote once to the great specialist; but her letter was so brief and to the point that it failed to recall to a busy man the charm of her personality, and it required no definite reply.

At midsummer Miss Evelyn proposed a visit. Wilhelmina all but declined to have her, but in due course she arrived, bringing with her some pretty toilettes, a guitar, a budget of news, and a breezy whiff from the world outside.

" Poor Miss Evelyn ! " Wilhelmina said when she met her at the station. " You little know the desert island to which you are coming."

Miss Evelyn stroked the pale face. " You want me to cheer you up a bit, don't you? I am not such a fool as I look in a sick-room. Perhaps I may be able to cheer your father too."

Alas, alas!

She put on her prettiest gown, and her brightest smile, but George Galbraith did not know his old friend. And she—would she ever have known him? He seemed to her a ghastly caricature of a helpless infant. " Pretty, pretty," he gurgled, pointing to the rose on her breast, and, smiling, she put it in his hand, but a moment later he had forgotten and dropped it. When she had left the room—smiling still—she burst into such a tempest of tears as Wilhelmina had never seen. If only she too could cry like that!

" What a mockery ! " cried Miss Evelyn at last. " He of all men ! "

" Yes."

" That, Vilma, is the one man in the world for whom I have ever cared—two straws ! "

Wilhelmina nodded gravely. She had never formulated the idea, but of course that was why she had allowed Miss Evelyn to see her father.

" Has he ever—realized it all ? "

" I think not. I kept hoping that he would, but I fear he never will now. Don't cry, dear. One has just got to bear it."

"Have you morphia in the house?"

"Yes; but he doesn't often need it now."

"And you are never tempted to overdo it?"

Wilhelmina shook her head resolutely. "If we knew what it all meant, I might be tempted. Sometimes I think he and I are just the plaything of fate. And yet, who knows? God may be behind it all. The off-chance is worth a deal of endurance."

There was a long silence.

"And now," Miss Evelyn said slowly, "we shall never know whether he did it or not."

No need to ask what she meant.

"Never," said Wilhelmina quietly. "You would like to leave to-morrow, wouldn't you? Shall I order the trap?"

It was in late autumn, when the cooing murmur of wind and wave was transformed into a constant moan, that her nerve began to give way. At first she was merely depressed, but after a time sleep forsook her, and the wakeful hours were filled with a nameless terror. The old anguish of her childhood had returned, but it was not hell that she was afraid of now. What was it? She could not have told, and yet the fear was there. Could one go on enduring this and keep sane?

One night, in sheer desperation, she took the little syringe and injected into her arm half the dose she had been in the habit of giving her father. For a moment she waited, then her heart rushed off in a frantic chase; but a minute later it settled down, and a blissful calm came over all her faculties. Her mind could no more grapple with worries and terrors than her hand could grasp the tiny instrument by her side.

"How heavenly!" thought Wilhelmina. "I must never do this again." Then she floated off on a tide of boundless well-being.

But Mr. Galbraith lived on for many months after that.

CHAPTER LVII.

WRESTLING.

"Miss Galbraith has taken to morphia," said the doctor with the self-satisfied air of one who has made a neat diagnosis.

Mr. Carmichael started. "Miss Galbraith? *Nonsense!*"

"Fact."

"Is she sleeping badly?"

"I don't know. She dislikes me—never lets me approach the subject of her health. If she takes it in moderation, it will do her no harm."

But to Mr. Carmichael—as to Wilhelmina herself—it seemed that to take morphia at all for mental or nervous suffering was a sin. "Does she know you suspect it?"

"No."

"And I am quite sure that nobody else will." Mr. Carmichael flashed on the young man the full light of his honest eyes. "God knows it is no wonder!"

"Oh, no! Her father ought to have been in an asylum for the last year. And it has been such wasted labour. A trained nurse would have done it without all the nerve wear and tear."

"True. To what purpose is this waste? And yet I sometimes think it is the perfume of the wasted labour that keeps the whole world sweet."

Mr. Carmichael was on his way to Edinburgh, having promised to lunch with a friend; but he sent a telegram instead, and walked out to Windyhaugh. Perhaps his views on the subject of opium-eating were provincial, but he could not rest. If George Galbraith would only die! It was awful to see a woman make so brave a fight and fall at last—and when that woman was Wilhelmina——!

He found her out of doors, vigorously playing a tennis ball against the high wall of the fruit-garden. She

26

laughed half shamefacedly when she saw him. "Now you know what a baby I am," she said.

"You are extremely sensible; but I would rather see you playing with a fellow-baby. For the sake of your friends you must not bring too great a strain to bear on yourself. Are you still determined not to let your father go?"

She raised sad eyes. "I must not fail in *all* the relations of life."

"And won't you go away yourself for a week or so?"

"Think if he woke up and missed me!"

"Then why not ask someone to come and stay with you?"

"There is no one—who could come—who would not worry rather than rest me. Besides, we are too poor to entertain even very modestly. Some day you may find me scouring the doorstep."

"Making 'that and the action fine'?"

"The action, I hope. Ann would say she 'had her doots o' the doorstep'! Indeed I am much better than I was a month ago."

She met his eyes so brightly and honestly that he went away reassured. "The doctor is at fault this time," he said.

But the doctor was not at fault. Wilhelmina was having a hard battle with the enemy. At present the advantage lay with her, and she felt all the exhilaration of victory. She would invite no one to share her burden; she did not wish to have the conditions of the battle made easier; she must beat the enemy on his own ground. A woman is much slower than a man to learn the full value of the prayer—Lead us not into temptation. "You wanted a sin to conquer," Wilhelmina said to herself defiantly. "You found life too easy! Here is your chance to grow strong!"

If only the flesh had proved a better ally! She did all in her power to reinforce it, and the crisp frosty weather aided her efforts mightily; but the poor flesh had been heavily overtaxed, and was sorely unequal to the combat. From many a cruel struggle Wilhelmina

came forth victor, but, sooner or later, there always came
a day when she yielded. "It was worth it," she would
say, as the delicious languor stole over the jarring nerves;
but when full consciousness returned, and her moral
nature once more took the reins, she would cry in sore
humiliation, "It was not worth it! It was not worth
it!" To redeem that failure she must meet the enemy
in his full force again.

She smiled bitterly to think how she had looked upon
the fear of hell as a motive force beneath the contempt
of a full-grown soul. If only the fear of hell would restrain her now! Were not the shattered nerves of the
opium-eater a hell upon earth? Already she felt her
will-power growing weaker. What if the day came when
it would fail her altogether? Could she even now re-
trace her steps?

Long since she had experienced the communion of
saints. She was tasting now the communion of sinners.
"You didn't pray hard enough, Hugh." How little she
had known of temptation then! She seemed now to feel
the great struggle going on all around her—the whole
creation groaning and travailing. If she did not conquer here and now, who should conquer anywhere? Were
sins never conquered, then? The thought was too terrible. Obviously the victory over this temptation was
the contribution she was called upon to make towards
the salvation of the world. Her mighty dreams of saving mankind were narrowed down to this. How much
easier to preach Christ on the housetops than to live
Christ in the inmost recesses of one's soul! But if
she failed now—the spiritual world was a chimera,
God a myth. Where should God be if not in her soul?
Verily His Kingdom cometh not without observation.

"How does one preach to the masses? By being such
a woman as Wilhelmina is becoming."

What were all great schemes compared to this? It
was only by *being good*, by ringing true, by rooting out
the besetting sin that lurked beneath the fair flower of
one's virtues, that one could be sure of helping others.
They would never hear of the struggle, and yet it must

affect their lives more than all one's fair words.* "For the sake of those whom you wish to benefit." . . . "For their sakes I sanctify—I consecrate myself." . . . "We are God's windows"—shall we shut out the light?

A great motive this. One of the few motives worth naming in the fight with imminent temptation. Yet even this did not always avail. With the awful realism of her father's protracted death-in-life constantly before her, it was hard to keep her eyes fixed on the ideal. " There are worse links than a sin between the soul and God," Mr. Carmichael said in his sermon one day, " and what link can compare with a conquered sin? No doubt there is joy in heaven over a successful Exeter Hall meeting, but one cannot help feeling that the joy is greater when only one poor human soul on earth is at all aware that anything has happened."

One night the old homestead was vibrating to the storm like a lyre in the hands of a musician. Wilhelmina had been sleeping better of late, but to-night she could not sleep. She was struggling to read, struggling not to think of the little instrument of peace on the shelf above her; but her whole being tingled with longing. " Even if I conquer to-night," she thought, " I shall fail to-morrow—what is the use of striving?"

The sound of wheels on the carriage drive startled her. A vehicle was stopping at the door. It was past midnight, and a curious superstitious awe came over her shaken nerves. But she pulled herself together and opened the window. " Who is there?" she asked firmly.

"It is I. Mr. Carmichael. Mr. Darsie is very ill. Can you come?"

Wilhelmina glanced at her father's sleeping, expressionless face: she had ceased to hope for any change in that. Then she said a word to Ann, wrapped herself in a cloak, and joined the minister. He gave her a few details as they drove along, but the noise of the storm was so great she could scarcely hear. Mr. Darsie had been ailing for some weeks, and now the doctor thought the end had come.

---

* This idea is beautifully and forcibly expressed in Dean Paget's address on self-consecration in *The Hallowing of Work*.

The old man lay supported by pillows in his great four-post bed. He looked ill and anxious, but his face was still his own. What a contrast to the face she had left behind!

"He is beginning to wander," said the doctor softly. "He has been talking of his visit to London."

"Mr. Darsie," said the minister, "this is Wilhelmina. . . . You know Wilhelmina?"

"Williamina—Williamina——" The old man's hand groped feebly towards her, as he struggled to express his thoughts. Did the effort recall the day long ago when he had striven in vain to reach her across the gulf of the years?

The anxiety passed from his face, and the tense muscles relaxed. "It's getting late," he said feebly. "We'd best be on the road."

The storm had lessened when they drove home.

"Well," said Mr. Carmichael at last, "we could scarcely have wished our friend a better passing than that."

Wilhelmina brushed away the tears. "It was a beautiful death. I am so glad you fetched me. And yet" —a hard little sob broke through her voice—"how cruel it seems!"

"You poor brave girl! Courage, dear! The end is near; and, when it comes, your father will be to you again all that he was in his prime. A day scarcely passes without my seeing him as he was that evening in the sunset, saving a young man's life on the beach at Windyhaugh."

Again that unwilling sob broke out. "If it were pain he were enduring," she said, "I could bear it; and he did suffer at first, but even then—I don't know how to say it—he had not moral nature enough to turn it to any account. What hurts me, too, is that I never got a chance to tell him what—what an education he was to me always. When he asked me to leave my work and go away with him—how niggardly I was!—how I grudged the sacrifice!"

"Yet you went. You have borne your burden nobly."

She winced. "Don't! You don't know me."

"Then suppose you enlighten me."

For a moment she was tempted to confide in him; but she still felt the aura of the death-chamber, and it seemed as if she never could yield to temptation again. "Let the dead past bury its dead!"

Next day Mr. Carmichael did what he had often felt it his duty to do before—wrote a long account to Brentwood of what Wilhelmina was enduring. "She wishes her friends to think she is merely nursing her father through an ordinary illness," he said, "and it is with implicit confidence in your tact that I tell you all these details. The strain is telling on her sorely. I am afraid she even takes refuge in morphia sometimes, and God knows it is little wonder!"

Brentwood received the letter in due course, and by the same mail came one from Miss Evelyn, informing him that a London manager had accepted his play; but this news, for which at one time he would have given so much, scarcely affected him at all.

Wilhelmina—strenuous, puritan, buoyant Wilhelmina—was flagging by the way, and he was separated from her by the whole width of the world!

CHAPTER LVIII.

BRENTWOOD'S RETURN.

It was George Galbraith's funeral day.

Fergus Dalrymple and Gavin did not return to Windyhaugh after the ceremony was over. Men in the prime of health and strength might well be glad to escape from the dreary place; but father and son alike had been very kind to Wilhelmina. Gavin was shocked to see the change in her. "You must come and pay us a long visit now," Fergus had said. "Your Aunt Enid will write."

Wilhelmina smiled faintly. She had heard that remark before.

Brentwood had been at the funeral too. He had arrived in England just in time. Wilhelmina had not expected him, but she received him very simply, without any appearance of emotion.

And now it was all over.

She sat in the old summer-house at the foot of the garden, too weary to think or feel. The river was shrouded in mist to-day; everything seemed in keeping with the greyness of human life.

A step on the gravel roused her.

" May I come and sit with you ? "

She raised her eyes with a quiet sad smile. " Yes."

The roses had been dashed with the rain of the night before, and the breath of autumn was in the air. What a contrast to that glorious summer afternoon five years ago!

Brentwood turned to look at his companion.

She was sitting in the same attitude now as then, leaning back wearily, but her weariness then was the momentary lassitude of youth and life; now——

How pale she was, how worn, how sad! The merciless light fell full on her face, but she made no effort to ward it off. Was the womanhood dead within her? She had not ordered new mourning, and the shabby black gown fell full about her shoulders. What a contrast to the bluebell in her physical prime!—to the vivid young student with her wealth of heart and mind!

And then, as Harley looked, a strange thing happened. In spite of his instinctive jealousy, in spite of Miss Evelyn's kindly plans, the beautiful Cenci, with her chorus of admirers, had left him cold. As he looked at this weary solitary woman who sat by his side so trustfully, with all the pretty defences of her sex laid down, his heart leaped within him. Already he respected, admired her more than enough. Now glamour—glamour sprang up, and took his eyes by storm. Was she trampled in the dust? She was more to him than any queen on the throne. Plain—she was all-glorious. Solitary and unsought-for—she was the desire of his eyes, the joy of his heart, the one woman who lived on all God's earth.

The conviction went surging through his veins like some wonderful Eastern drug. It made his head swim, his heart turn faint. He trembled so that he dared not lift his hand, dared not trust his voice. And yet he must speak, for the waves of passion that shook him did not so much as ripple the hem of her garment.

" *Vilma!* " he said at last.

She opened her eyes, wondering.

His face was revelation enough. No woman on earth need have asked what he meant—least of all poor Wilhelmina with all the coquetry burnt out of her.

" *Harley!* " she said in a low thrilling voice. She glanced down at her shabby gown. " Oh, you are a good fellow! "

The tears rose to her eyes, but she spoke as though she were holding out her hand to him across the river of death.

He drew closer to her; she could feel him tremble now; and for a time they sat in silence.

" Thank you, dear," she said at last. " Of course it can never be now; and yet—you are very good. You have taken away such an old sting. If only I had kept myself worthy of your love! "

He flushed hotly. " Worthy—*you!* Don't mock me, Vilma."

But she nodded quietly. " I always meant to be a good woman, and I have been so weak and wicked. Look. Do you know what that means? " She unfastened her sleeve at the wrist and drew it up.

He stooped and kissed the white arm passionately, but there was no thrill of response as there had been that night on the terrace to the mere touch of his hand.

" Wicked? " he said. " Oh, white-souled Vilma, is that your notion of being wicked? Poor little girl, strained beyond even her endurance! " He laughed. " I have no doubt it was the best thing you could do," he said cheerfully. " You never could have stood it without something to oil the wheels of life a little bit."

But her face showed no comfort, only disappointment, and he saw that he was on the wrong tack. "Don't, Harley! It was a sin for me. I held it as one all along, yet often I yielded. Call it by its name —and help me!"

"But the temptation is gone now, isn't it?"

She shook her head quickly, emphatically.

"It will go, I am sure, when you are a little stronger. But I am sure, too, that you will be brave, and conquer before the reinforcements arrive."

She smiled now, though sadly, and put her hand in his, as his sister might have done. "I think the reinforcements have come," she said simply.

Again there was a long silence. "I might well be loath to make it a sin, dear," Harley said at last. "'If the righteous scarcely be saved, where shall the ungodly and the sinner appear?' Of course I never was your mate. It made me angry when Miss Evelyn and the others kept throwing that in my teeth; but now——! Give me a motive, Vilma! Saint Vilma! Let us share each other's burdens!"

Her voice broke into a low cry. "Oh, my dear, my dear, the might have been!"

"Nay," he said, "the shall be. We have wasted time enough."

"Too much!" she said. "Five years! It was all we had. I don't complain. I made my choice. I have had my pennyworth and—I have spent my penny! Do you know how long I have got to live?"

A great fear turned his lips white. Was there something more than strain and weariness behind that pale worn face?

An almost imperceptible dew rose to her forehead. "I thought I should never tell anyone," she said. "It is good of you to make it possible to tell you. I suppose I shall be dead in a couple of years, and of life—real life— I have only got a very few months."

"What is it?" He spoke peremptorily, but his voice shook.

"It is too awful. You see how thin I have grown. You see how my lips tremble when I speak. If you asked me to turn in that narrow walk, I couldn't do it. I

should have to make a big circuit. If you asked me to
say a long word, I should stumble over it. They are all
the symptoms that my father had."

Harley gave a great shout of relief. "Oh, Vilma,
my darling, my poor, poor little girl! What fools these
doctors are! Thank God you have told me. Why,
sweetheart, you might just as well have yellow fever
here at Windyhaugh; you might as well have the Black
Death, or—or delirium tremens—as the disease your father had! Why, my own silly darling, you are nervous
and worn out. You want me to take care of you—that
is all."

He took her in his arms as if she had been a child,
and bent over her, murmuring the childlike ridiculous
language of love. To think that the self-conscious Harley Brentwood should have come to this!

As he watched the look of relief steal over her face he
felt as if he had never known what happiness meant till
now. Then his wooing grew urgent, passionate, and she
drew herself out of his arms.

"You have taken such a load off my mind," she said.
"I *could not face* that living death—and yet he had to
face it! I thank God on my knees for what you have
told me. But even now—what have I to do with love?
I am a worn-out wreck—as old as the wandering Jew."

"You are so good, so clever, Vilma," he said, "that it
is very difficult for you not to be proud."

"Have I been proud with you to-day?"

"You are very proud now. We won't argue as to
what you are. Let it be, if you will, a worn-out wreck.
Then all I can say is that a worn-out wreck is the thing
I need to complete my life. Let us say you are nervous
—silly—over-strained—I want you all the more for that.
I want you to come to me as you are, to lay down your
pride and let yourself go. Can't you trust me enough
for that?"

There was a fine light of gratitude in her eyes.
"Nay, dear," she said, "only death—not love nor life—
has a right to woo like that. Marriage is not an end.
It is a great beginning. Of all others it is the burden
one should take up strongly and joyously. I am ill and

tired. Thank God it is not *that!* But I have suffered so long. Nobody can say whether I shall ever be strong and joyous again. We must wait. Even now when you have been so good—so good—when my heart is so full of thankfulness—I feel *so—cold!* Even when you "—she faltered, but went on steadily—" when you took me in your arms—my pulses did not leap as they did long ago when you just—touched—my hand."

Harley's sigh was almost a groan. " Then at least let me come and see you every day."

She shook her head. " Don't think me perverse, dear; but, if you came to see me every day, I should watch myself constantly for your sake as well as my own. You say well that I am nervous and silly, but you haven't the least conception *how* nervous and silly I am. I must try to get out of myself altogether."

" Then promise to go right away from here, to new surroundings that will give you a fresh start."

" I am afraid I can't."

He took her face in his hands, and turned it to him. " I am very longsuffering, Vilma, but is that perversity, or isn't it ? "

The imprisoned face flushed scarlet. " I have scarcely a penny in the house," she said with trembling lips; " and the bills——"

He drew a long breath of relief. " *At last* you throw a crumb to a starving wretch! Money is very plentiful with me just now, dear. Will you remember that, and use it as if it were your own? " He took a cheque-book from his pocket. " Promise to go right away to the country, and spend without scruple."

" Thank you."

" Promise! "

" I do promise," she said simply.

" Oh, Vilma, if you had only asked me before! "

" How could I, dear? " she said. " It was very bitter having to spend what you gave me. Things are different now."

" Yes, thank God! Things are very different now. He is a poor old fellow, Vilma. Love him a little."

It was late in the evening when Brentwood started for Queensmains. He was very unwilling to leave Wilhelmina; for he could see that, with the shadows of night, a great cloud of depression was settling down on her. "Leave me to fight it out by myself," she had pleaded; but, before he was a mile away from the house, he found himself regretting bitterly that he had yielded. The feeling became so strong that at last he turned, and ran back most of the way to Windyhaugh.

When he reached the lonely old homestead, it was dark. A light burned in what had been the sick-room, but the blinds were not drawn down, and, as he approached the window, he could see Wilhelmina pacing restlessly to and fro. At last she paused resolutely, and, taking a tiny phial and case from the shelf, she left the room. The front door was not locked, and, without even stopping to think, Harley followed her upstairs. The door of her room was ajar, and the light of a candle guided him to the threshold. His heart was too full of loving solicitude for him to realize that he was doing a dishonourable thing. He only knew that a sore struggle was going on, and that he had come in time to help. Had she not asked his help? How sweet to feel this new dependence of hers!

Wilhelmina's back was turned to him, but he saw her fill the syringe with trembling hands. He took a step forward and would have spoken, but at that moment she threw herself on her knees.

Then, seething, eddying, molten-hot, the words surged forth—

"Great God, who either art not at all, or who art in all things, even in me—*be in me with all my will!* Penetrate into the farthest fibre of my being, and, when Thou art there, by the heat of Thy righteousness *burn* —everything that is not Thee. I shall shrink and cry out and draw back, but do Thou keep hold until Thy work is done, and I am—*Thee!*"

There was a moment's silence, and then a little jet of fluid rose from the syringe into the air. The struggle was over.

Harley had never felt so guilty in his life. He crept downstairs like a thief, and ran as if for dear life. Wilhelmina was safe for that night.

CHAPTER LIX.

AFTER LONG GRIEF AND PAIN.

I THINK Wilhelmina's friends profited ever after by that tussle of hers with what she believed to be mortal sin, but she never could take any credit to herself for the victory. It seemed as if suddenly everything conspired to help her.

Two days after the funeral she received a long and cordial letter from Honor, begging her to come to a quiet little country inn many miles from the nearest station. Of course Wilhelmina knew that the proposal had originated with Harley, but she trusted both brother and sister too deeply to ask any questions. She accepted gladly. She had been idealizing Honor for five strenuous years. Now she would really learn to know her. Honor little guessed the heights to which she was expected to attain! Wilhelmina's letter of acceptance was scarcely written when Mr. Macintyre was announced. His shrewd business-like face beamed with gratification. "I am the bearer of good news at last," he said. "I find from Mr. Darsie's will that he has left you his sole heir. I thought it better to make full enquiries before speaking to you. His money is admirably invested. You cannot do better than leave it where it is. It will bring you an income of about two hundred and sixty pounds a year."

Wilhelmina thought she must be dreaming. "But he was poor," she said.

The lawyer rubbed his hands. "So he was to all practical purposes—and you are the gainer."

"If only I had done something for him!" she said regretfully.

"I think you did a good deal. He was never tired of

talking of that visit to you in London. You were a
never-failing subject of interest—and I think I may say
of joy—to the old man. Heigho! Queensmains won't
be the same place without him. You will realize later
on how much this means, Miss Galbraith. I hope you
won't think me ungallant when I say·that few things
make so much difference in a woman as the possession
of a cheque-book. I don't know when I have been so
pleased about anything in my life."

Of course Harley took a very different view of that
will, but Honor was genuinely delighted to hear that
Wilhelmina was not dependent on her brother's bounty.
She soon foresaw that a capitulation was inevitable, and
she wanted Wilhelmina to hold her own to the last.

I don't know which of those two women enjoyed that
meeting the more. Wilhelmina always looked upon
Honor as a being much wiser and better than herself;
but, after their first day of life in common, Honor certainly never thought so. "It gives me a lump in the
throat to look at her," she wrote to her brother. "However mistakenly, she has surely scaled the 'toppling
crags.' When the mists of physical depression clear
away, she must find herself on

> "'the shining table-lands,
> To which our God himself is moon and sun.'"

Honor could only allow herself a month's holiday—
she had almost as many interests in life as Mr. Ellis himself—but it was May of the next year when Wilhelmina
returned to town.

It was a strange experience to find herself in London
again, stranger still to be in London without worries,
without work, and with sufficient money to live in quiet
comfort. How little changed other people were! And
she—she felt as if she had been away for a hundred
years.

Four points of contact she had with the mighty city
—the quakeress, Miss Evelyn, Mr. Ellis, and Mrs. Dalrymple. By means of the four she pegged out a spiritual
tent sufficiently roomy for her own free life and expansion. Of course she had to a great extent dropped out

of their lives, but now that she really appeared among them in the flesh once more, she received a welcome that warmed her heart.

Miss Evelyn had returned to the stage some time before.

" I never was so thankful in my life," she said, " as when I heard it was all over. Now we have got our old ideal back again."

" Yes," said Wilhelmina dreamily; " or it will come. I can't trust myself yet to go to sleep without seeing him—as you saw him that day. You must come and pay Windyhaugh a long visit under happier auspices."

The quakeress was now a successful and enthusiastic schoolmistress in receipt of an excellent salary. She worked hard, lived sparely, dressed in the most uncompromising fashion, and educated two young brothers. The simple elegance of Wilhelmina's black gown was a barrier between them at first, but Miss Burnet soon forgot all about the dress. " I have often thought," she said, " of how you gave up everything to go away with your father. With your prospects, I could not have done it. I am sure God must have rewarded you."

Wilhelmina did not answer. The reward would have been less real if she had been aware of having received it.

" And now that you are free, you will do great things yet."

" Oh, no. Never now. I have learnt my own measure."

" Don't, dear! You have not forgotten your old ideals ? "

" No," Wilhelmina smiled. " I remember I wanted to save mankind, but the process has been reversed. It has always been other people who have taught me, helped me, saved me. All one can really do is to walk humbly and unselfishly, striving to see God in other men, to feel God in oneself."

There was a long silence. " Even that," the quakeress said at length, " is a good deal."

Mr. Ellis could scarcely believe that this full-grown

woman was his little Wilhelmina. She seemed to him quite five years older than her age. The "phantom of delight" had given place to

> "The Being breathing thoughtful breath,
> The traveller between life and death."

He led her on to tell him more about her life of the last few years than she had told anyone before. "When I was so weak and depressed," she said, "and thought it was all over with me, how I wished I could sit in this dear old library again, and just say, *Thank you!*"

He turned away his head. "You are very generous," he said, "to a narrow-minded old man. Can you stay and dine with us? I want you to be the friend of my little girls."

But it was Mrs. Dalrymple's reception that surprised Wilhelmina most.

"You shall simply take off your hat and *stay,*" Enid said emphatically. "Pearson shall go and pack your things. You will find us dreadfully frivolous, of course."

Wilhelmina laughed. "I cannot come just now," she said, "but I think I must accept your invitation by-and-bye if only to convince you that the censor in me is dead. Looking back on my life, I really don't know which have helped me the more—the saints or the sinners. How is Hugh?"

Enid smiled. "Is that *àpropos* of the saints or the sinners? I am sure I don't know. He tells me that after a long period of backsliding he has returned to the fold. I never expected this phase to last."

"It may last yet," Wilhelmina said, but she felt a little uneasy. Hugh's was not the nature that could safely indulge in a long period of backsliding.

Daily she looked out for some sign from her husband; but Harley—though of course he knew she was in London—did not come. His play was to be produced in a few days, and it seemed to him that, with the exception of Miss Evelyn, the actors did worse at every rehearsal. He had taken a cottage at Richmond, too, and was busy weeding out the furniture, and introducing lamps, pictures, arm-chairs, books—making of the place an ideal little home.

He first saw Wilhelmina at a concert in the Queen's Hall. It was a wonderful concert, and a smart social function. Everybody was there, and the whole place was *en fête*.

Everybody was there, and the music was entrancing; but Harley was only aware of the presence of one woman; the music scarcely reached his consciousness; it formed a soft harmonious background to his dreams. Wilhelmina did not see him, and of course he did not speak to her. Oh, no! He had waited for his happiness long enough. He approached it now in the spirit of an epicure; he played with it as a cat plays with a mouse. For this first evening it was quite enough just to look at her. And *how* he looked!—feasting his eyes on every curve, every gesture, every glance. And to think that she was his by right—his very own! He tried to imagine how she would impress him if he met her now for the first time—or how he would impress her—and he felt very glad of the tie that already linked them indissolubly —he felt very grateful to George Galbraith.

A week later they met at somebody's crush. This time she saw him, she even caught his eye, but, instead of bowing, she glanced away again with odd girlish shyness. A moment later she was ashamed of her *gaucherie*, but of course it enchanted him: it was so unlike the woman he had watched at the concert a week before. He saw her face turn white to the lips, and then—a knot of people drifted in between them. ʼ

Coming out of the music-room, she was separated for a moment from Mrs. Dalrymple, and she suddenly became aware that Harley was by her side. His sleeve was touching her arm. She could not speak, and it seemed at first as if he could not. How ridiculous it all was! Simply to relieve the tension of the situation, Wilhelmina made a little movement to overtake her aunt, and then Brentwood bent low.

" I am glad to see you looking so well," he said quietly, without preamble.

27

" Thank you. I am quite strong now." How calmly she had contrived to speak!

" *And joyous?* " The words were uttered in a tone scarcely above a whisper, but they brought a fiery wave to her white face and neck. How humiliating to blush! Young girls are the lawful prey of that dread enemy. By what bold miscalculation had it attacked a mature woman like herself?

At that moment Enid looked round, and Wilhelmina joined her.

Next morning Honor called.

" Well, dear," she said. " It is good to see the life in your face once more."

" I took a long rest, didn't I? "

" You did indeed. I began to think you had given all your old friends the slip. I have run up to see Harley's play. Have you seen that it is proving quite a success? "

" Yes."

" You haven't seen it? "

" Oh, no."

"It is not eternal, you know." Honor laughed. "But I can't help liking it very much. It is extraordinary how the public taste has changed. Of course the heroine is as much Miss Evelyn's creation as Harley's."

" Hagar? Yes, they all say she is very fine."

" Do you care to come with me to-night? I have a box."

" Thank you. I should like to come very much."

When evening came, Wilhelmina dressed with extraordinary care. She was very pale, but her eyes shone brilliantly. Honor was almost more nervous than she was.

Assuredly the play was not eternal, but it had taken the fancy of London for the time, the house was well-filled, and everything promised a long run. To Wilhelmina the drama seemed amazingly clever. This was her first experience of the problem play, and it appealed to her keenly. After the first act she was quite carried away, and, from behind the scenes, Harley watched her

eager face. She constituted the audience for him that
night; and she could not have looked more triumphant
if the play had been her own.

Towards the end of the last act she became aware that
he had entered the box, and was standing in the shadow
at the back. Honor nodded to him brightly, but Wilhelmina did not turn her head. She was very pale again
—almost as pale as Harley himself.

The curtain fell, and, as the actors came forward to
receive their meed of applause, Harley came up to her
side. She glanced quickly round. Honor had disappeared.

The house was full of noise, but these two were conscious only of an overwhelming silence. They heard
nothing save the beating of their own hearts.

During the day Harley had thought of many things
that it behoved him to say, but now he took her cloak
and held it up without a word. He had made no definite
plans, but, as their eyes met, they knew that they were
not going to part any more.

"It is a long drive," he said huskily. "Shall you be
warm enough?"

But she did not answer at all.

A tumult of applause filled the theatre. Miss Evelyn,
bowing in response to the ovation, looked up eagerly at
their box, but they did not turn their heads. They did
not know she was there.

Before she had made her last bow, they left the auditorium, and went downstairs.

A few minutes later Harley closed the door of the
hired carriage, and they rolled off into the night.

And then? Did they talk of the sorrows and mis-
understandings of the long years? Nay, verily. Mother
Nature took care of that. The time was past for vows
and explanations, even as it was past for marriage bells
and documents, for forms and ceremonies, for curious
eyes and jesting lips. The very time for words of love
was past. Here were two living thrilling human souls,
old yet young, bound yet free, alone on God's great earth.

CHAPTER LX.

THE CYCLE IS COMPLETE.

THE children lay stretched full length in the hay-field, like kittens momentarily exhausted with a romp.

"Let's pretend——" said Wilhelmina dreamily at last.

Has time's wheel run back?—or is the cycle complete?

Even so. The cycle is complete. Wilhelmina the Second is a fascinating witch, but she is not much concerned about her soul. I am afraid she is not even on bowing terms with the successful young grocer, though he has rebuilt the grimy old shop, and has fitted it up with " every modern improvement." What with rabbits to be fed, and plants to be watered, and a great family of dolls to be put to bed every night, life really is a very busy and responsible thing.

Wilhelmina's small brother, George the Second, is not a very interesting playmate at present. Uncle Gavin has just got his company, and George can play at nothing but soldiers. He has a thousand questions to ask Uncle Gavin when that wonderful being brings Aunt Daisy to Windyhaugh next month.

Fortunately Wilhelmina the Second is not shut up to George's company just now. Mr. Ellis' two tall girls are kindly willing to lay aside the dignity of their years, and join in many a frolic.

Mr. Ellis himself is seated some distance off with Harley and Wilhelmina the First. Mr. Carmichael has just joined the party, and Mr. Ellis is reading aloud from a book he has brought from London.

> " 'Yet Faith, ofttimes He taught,
> Was nowise bare believing ; since belief
> Comes hard or easy as minds go. . . .
> What Faith He asked of whoso entered in
> The slave may have in bondage, if he lifts
> Eyes of sad hope ; th' unlettered hind may have
> Who, at his toil, hungers for better bread

Than what toil buys; the little child may have
Content to love and trust; all souls shall have
Which, when the light shines, turn themselves to light
As field-flowers do; and, like the flowers of the field,
Are glad of the great sun for the sun's sake;
And, being evil, are for good; being weak,
Will give what thews they own for Righteousness,
Will lay what gifts they may at Love's fair feet,
And follow, with quick step or slow,—through faults,
Through failures, through discomfitures, through sins,—
The march of that majestic King whose flag,
Distant and dim, they hail, and with true hearts,
Though will be wilful, and though flesh be weak—
Burn to obey. These are Heaven's men-at-arms
In van or rear; informed or ignorant
Of whither battle rolls, and what shall prove
Its issue; and, for them, whether high spoils
Of Victory at last—the Leader's eye
Ware of their wounds—or some forgotten grave
Where they that gained Him glory sleep unnamed;
Always to orders loyal, standing fast
In what post be assigned; in life and death
Right-minded, but not blameless; loving God
With lowly heart, and earnest striving soul
Which trusted, seeing darkly; loving man
For brotherhood, and God that lives in man.
Such have the Faith, to such is much forgiven.'"

The reader paused, and looked round his audience.
Wilhelmina had turned away her head.

Mr. Carmichael was the first to find words.

"It seems to me," he said with contracted brows, "he
is defining a good deal besides faith."

Harley laughed. "It is a good thing you said that,
not I," he cried, glancing with loving eyes at his wife's
eager face. "Now that you have committed the Church,
I may remark that the definition—with all its beauty—
did strike me as resembling an old prescription, so full of
ingredients that it was bound to bring down something."

"Mr. Ellis takes my part," Wilhelmina said composedly, smiling across to her old friend. "Do you remember the night you taught me to look at a good thing for
what it is, and not for what it is not? Will Mr. Carmichael define faith?"

The minister shook his head. "I have been trying to define faith all my life."

" Fools rush in where angels fear to tread," Harley remarked quietly. "Is not faith the power of seeing life *sub specie æternitatis?*"

"Good!" said Mr. Ellis.

"Bad!" said Wilhelmina, looking at her husband with appreciative eyes. "What is the use of a definition that only great minds like our own can understand? Harley's version wouldn't go far towards making a poem."

They all laughed.

"Isn't that the Ryelands carriage?" asked Mr. Carmichael.

"It is. Come, Harley. Let us meet them at the door. Will the Church honour us?"

But the Church elected to remain *perdu.*

"Don't go, Muvvy!" piped two sweet little voices in unison.

Wilhelmina turned her beautiful mother-face to them. "Not for long," she said. "I will send Mademoiselle. You must be very gentle with her, you know."

Poor old Mademoiselle has come to spend a long holiday at Windyhaugh. She can scarcely believe the old homestead is the place she knew a quarter of a century ago. For Windyhaugh has entered on a third phase of existence. The old divines still retain their place, but the library has grown to such mighty proportions that these worthy ancestors have assumed something like their true perspective. The house seems full of sunshine and fresh air, of peace and goodwill. The one thing Mademoiselle has to fear is a chance meeting with a hedgehog or an escaped caterpillar on the stair. She is even beginning to take an interest in natural history—wants to know when caterpillars may reasonably be expected to assume that much-talked of chrysalis stage! Fortunately the children are prepared to give her any amount of information. They have long chats with their mother about animals and plants; and indeed it was after listening to one of these talks, that Harley finally committed to the flames his manuscript Ethics of

Lower Life. Times have changed; he can afford to burn a manuscript now.

The beautiful stables are rather thrown away on one good roadster and two shaggy ponies, but the billiard-room is in great demand. The river is an ocean once more; the grim old shrubbery a primeval forest, but its recesses are often enlivened by the shriek of Red Indians and the roar of wild bears. Wilhelmina the Second thinks Bunyan all very well for Sundays, but, for sheer literature, commend her to the author of The Dog Crusoe! She can scarcely be induced to bend her mighty mind to the pronunciation of *miouw,* but she loves to hear Mademoiselle tell of what a noble gentleman her grandfather was, and to see the lovely brooch he gave the old lady in Paris.

How Wilhelmina the First worships that child! How she dreams about her future! " She shall have ' wings where I had weary feet '! "

Mr. Ellis and Mr. Carmichael were watching Harley and Wilhelmina. It was pretty to see them stroll off together.

" I think their happiness was worth waiting for," Mr. Ellis said at last.

Mr. Carmichael did not answer immediately. " Perhaps. The question is, was Brentwood worth it all? "

" If Brentwood had been worth it all in the ordinary human sense of the words, we should never have had our Wilhelmina. I think she had chosen more wisely than women of her calibre usually do. Nature has an extraordinary love of bringing things back to the average. But Brentwood has real spiritual insight."

" He has an intellectual grasp of things spiritual, at least. I don't know that it is quite the same thing. There is nothing so easy as to convince a fine woman that her husband is her superior."

Mr. Ellis laughed. " I don't know that you and I are the people best qualified to pass an opinion on Brentwood! He leaves her a wonderfully free hand."

" Having no one to be jealous of—save God."

They both fell a-musing.

"It is interesting to see the Ryelands carriage here," Mr. Ellis continued at last. "Does Mrs. Berkeley know that Miss Evelyn was the last guest, and that Mrs. Hugh Dalrymple will be the next—not to mention that crooked little anarchist, Dunn?"

"It was a long time before the Ryelands carriage came here. Young Berkeley was shot accidentally by his brother two years ago, and Wilhelmina had to tell the mother." Mr. Carmichael bit his lip. "That was the kind of crucible to bring out the gold in both women. Wilhelmina is a real social link. She takes care that people who don't want to meet shall not meet under her roof. For the rest, *she can do as she likes.* When you come to think of it—that is the great tangible reward of goodness."

Mr. Ellis shook his head. "Goodness alone would never achieve that," he said. "It wants goodness *plus* a real strength and breadth of personality. Miss Brentwood was telling me the other day that Wilhelmina ought to have achieved more, that she had never taken the position to which her gifts entitled her. It seems to me——"

Mr. Carmichael nodded quickly and emphatically, as if afraid that Mr. Ellis would think it necessary to finish his sentence.

Perhaps the reader will agree with Honor Brentwood that Wilhelmina ought to have accomplished more.

It is true she achieved little as we reckon achievement in these days. She carved no statue, painted no picture, composed no oratorio; she did not even write a book, nor take a degree; but when all these things have been excluded, there remains that little art of living which has been open in all ages alike to the wise and to the simple.

THE END.

FÉLIX GRAS'S ROMANCES.

THE TERROR. A Romance of the French Revolution. By FÉLIX GRAS, author of " The Reds of the Midi." Uniform with " The Reds of the Midi." Translated by Mrs. Catharine A. Janvier. 16mo. Cloth, $1.50.

" If Félix Gras had never done any other work than this novel, it would at once give him a place in the front rank of the writers of to-day. . . . ' The Terror' is a story that deserves to be widely read, for, while it is of thrilling interest, holding the reader's attention closely, there is about it a literary quality that makes it worthy of something more than a careless perusal."—*Brooklyn Eagle.*

" Romantic conditions could hardly be better presented than in a book of this kind, and above all, in a book by Félix Gras. . . . The romance is replete with interest."—*New York Times.*

" There is genius in the book. The narrative throbs with a palpitation of virile force and nervous vigor. Read it as a mere story, and it is absorbing beyond description. Consider it as a historical picture, . . . and its extraordinary power and significance are apparent."—*Philadelphia Press.*

" The book may be recommended to those who like strong, artistic, and exciting romances."—*Boston Saturday Evening Gazette.*

" Many as have been the novels which have the Revolution as their scene, not one surpasses, if equals, in thrilling interest."—*Cleveland Plain Dealer.*

THE REDS OF THE MIDI. An Episode of the French Revolution. By FÉLIX GRAS. Translated from the Provençal by Mrs. Catharine A. Janvier. With an Introduction by Thomas A. Janvier. With Frontispiece. 16mo. Cloth, $1.50.

" I have read with great and sustained interest ' The Reds of the South,' which you were good enough to present to me. Though a work of fiction, it aims at painting the historical features, and such works if faithfully executed throw more light than many so called histories on the true roots and causes of the Revolution, which are so widely and so gravely misunderstood. As a novel it seems to me to be written with great skill."—*William E. Gladstone.*

" Patriotism, a profound and sympathetic insight into the history of a great epoch, and a poet's delicate sensitiveness to the beauties of form and expression have combined to make M. Félix Gras's ' The Reds of the Midi ' a work of real literary value. It is as far as possible removed from sensationalism ; it is, on the contrary, subdued, simple, unassuming, profoundly sincere. Such artifice as the author has found it necessary to employ has been carefully concealed, and if we feel its presence, it is only because experience has taught that the quality is indispensable to a work which affects the imagination so promptly and with such force as does this quiet narrative of the French Revolution."—*New York Tribune.*

" It is doubtful whether in the English language we have had a more powerful, impressive, artistic picture of the French Revolution, from the revolutionist's point of view, than that presented in Félix Gras's ' The Reds of the Midi.' . . . Adventures follow one another rapidly ; splendid, brilliant pictures are frequent, and the thread of a tender, beautiful love story winds in and out of its pages."—*New York Mail and Express.*

D. APPLETON AND COMPANY'S PUBLICATIONS.

STEPHEN CRANE'S BOOKS.

*T*HE THIRD VIOLET. 12mo. Cloth, $1.00.

"By this latest product of his genius our impression of Mr. Crane is confirmed that, for psychological insight, for dramatic intensity, and for the potency of phrase, he is already in the front rank of English and American writers of fiction, and that he possesses a certain separate quality which places him apart."—*London Academy.*

"The whole book, from beginning to end, fairly bristles with fun. . . . It is adapted for pure entertainment, yet it is not easily put down or forgotten."—*Boston Herald.*

*T*HE LITTLE REGIMENT, and Other Episodes of the American Civil War. 12mo. Cloth, $1.00.

"In 'The Little Regiment' we have again studies of the volunteers waiting impatiently to fight and fighting, and the impression of the contest as a private soldier hears, sees, and feels it, is really wonderful. The reader has no privileges. He must, it seems, take his place in the ranks, and stand in the mud, wade in the river, fight, yell, swear, and sweat with the men. He has some sort of feeling, when it is all over, that he has been doing just these things. This sort of writing needs no praise. It will make its way to the hearts of men without praise."—*New York Times.*

"Told with a *verve* that brings a whiff of burning powder to one's nostrils. . . . In some way he blazons the scene before our eyes, and makes us feel the very impetus of bloody war."—*Chicago Evening Post.*

*M*AGGIE: A GIRL OF THE STREETS. 12mo. Cloth, 75 cents.

"By writing 'Maggie' Mr. Crane has made for himself a permanent place in literature. . . . Zola himself scarcely has surpassed its tremendous portrayal of throbbing, breathing, moving life."—*New York Mail and Express.*

"Mr. Crane's story should be read for the fidelity with which it portrays a life that is potent on this island, along with the best of us. It is a powerful portrayal, and, if somber and repellent, none the less true, none the less freighted with appeal to those who are able to assist in righting wrongs."—*New York Times.*

*T*HE RED BADGE OF COURAGE. An Episode of the American Civil War. 12mo. Cloth, $1.00.

"Never before have we had the seamy side of glorious war so well depicted. . . . The action of the story throughout is splendid, and all aglow with color, movement, and vim. The style is as keen and bright as a sword-blade, and a Kipling has done nothing better in this line."—*Chicago Evening Post.*

"There is nothing in American fiction to compare with it. . . . Mr. Crane has added to American literature something that has never been done before, and that is, in its own peculiar way, inimitable."—*Boston Beacon.*

"A truer and completer picture of war than either Tolstoy or Zola "—*London New Review.*

NEW YORK: D. APPLETON AND COMPANY.